THE SHAPIRO DIAMOND

The Shapiro Diamond

Michael Legat

Heywood Books

© Rosmic Productions Ltd 1984

First published in Great Britain
by Souvenir Press Ltd in 1984

ISBN 1 85481 023 5

This edition published in 1989 by
Heywood Books Limited
55 Clissold Crescent
London N16 9AR

Printed in Great Britain by
Cox & Wyman Ltd, Reading

To Jonathan

I should like to thank Mrs Muriel Lacey and the staff at Kimberley Public Library, and Mrs Judy Hoare, Chairman of the Historical Society of Kimberley and the Northern Cape, for their kind assistance, and I acknowledge with much gratitude the debt I owe to Mr Brian Roberts, whose excellent book *Kimberley: Turbulent City* has been invaluable to me.

M.L.

1

'I know I can do it,' Jan said to himself. 'I'll show him I can.'
The only sounds in the cramped little workroom were
the squeak of the treadles and the whirring of the spinning iron
discs and the slight high keening sound as Jan's father and his
younger brother, Abram, polished the diamonds. Through
the open window came the clatter of a horse and cart trundling
over the cobblestones.

Jan wiped the perspiration from his forehead. It was hot in
Amsterdam on this late summer's day in 1871, and he was
about to cleave a diamond, the first that he had attempted
entirely on his own, without help or advice from his father. He
had studied the rough stone for hours, deciding exactly how
the grain lay and how best to cut it so that the few tiny flaws
would be lost in the polishing process.

He glanced across the room. His father was hunched over
his work, applying the stone to the polishing wheel with
precise care, totally absorbed. 'Concentration,' he would say,
'that's the secret, Jan. You just don't concentrate enough.' But
no matter how hard Jan concentrated, he had never developed
the skill of getting the angle and size of the facets exactly right.
It had to be done by sight alone, and his eyes just did not seem
to function that way. Abram had had the knack from his early
teens, and was his father's trusted assistant, while Jan had to be
content with running errands, keeping the machines in working order, cleaning up the workshop. He felt frustrated at
the lack of responsibility – after all, he was twenty-two –
especially since the Shapiros had been diamond cutters and
polishers for generations, and he had grown up expecting that
eventually he would succeed his father as head of the business.
Recently, he had been learning the art of cleaving, and had
shown some promise at it, so that now he had been trusted to

7

cut this valuable stone. He had to prove to his father that he could do it.

He caught Abram's eye, and grinned at him almost ruefully. Abram quickly averted his gaze. While they were both children, Abram had looked up to him in hero-worship, but in the last few years they had grown apart, as though Abram were embarrassed by his own skill and Jan's lack of it.

Jan wiped his forehead once more, and firmly gripping the small flat cleaving blade, placed it with great care in the groove in the stone that he had cut with another diamond. He raised the little cylindrical mallet and gave the cleaver a sharp blow, and at that very moment Abram sneezed. The world seemed to stop turning. Jan was aware of his father looking up from his work, of Abram's face hidden behind the flourishes of his handkerchief – and then the dreadful fact sank in that the diamond had shattered into a thousand worthless fragments.

He swore.

Jacob Shapiro looked at him in disapproval. 'There's no need for that sort of language, Jan.'

'It was my fault, Father,' Abram said. 'I sneezed at just the wrong moment. Sorry, Jan.' He giggled nervously.

'If he'd been concentrating properly, he wouldn't even have heard you sneeze,' Jacob said. 'I didn't.'

'Neither did I,' Jan lied. He waited for the storm to break.

'Clear up the mess,' Jacob said mildly. 'We can grind those fragments down for dust.' The faceting was done by coating the polishing discs with a mixture of diamond dust and olive oil.

The fact that his father unaccountably offered no other word of reproof or even disappointment left a tension in the air, and Jan suddenly felt a desperate need to escape. He stripped off his working coat and snatched his jacket from the hook on the wall.

'Where are you going?' Jacob cried, the anger he had previously suppressed now plain in his voice.

But Jan was already outside. As he passed the window he heard Abram saying, 'You can't pluck feathers from a frog, Father. You're either a diamond man or you're not. Jan isn't.'

'Smug little sod,' Jan muttered to himself as he strode away.

He walked for miles. There was no pattern to his wandering, and he turned into this narrow street and that, and crossed and re-crossed the canals, until eventually he found himself standing on one of the bridges over the Herengracht, gazing down into the still waters and seeing in them not the reflections of the tall houses with their variegated gables, but the scene in the workshop. How could he have made such a botch of the cleaving? It was not Abram's sneeze. A diamond cleaved against the grain is liable to shatter, and he must have chosen the wrong place for the groove that he had cut. Unless the stone was flawed. But after all the time he had spent with the loupe screwed into his eye, studying its every aspect, he was sure it was not that. It was simply, as Abram had said, that he was not a diamond man. Then what, he thought, more in fury than despair, could he do for the rest of his life? Stay in the family business as its general dogsbody? Perhaps he should ask his uncle for a job on his farm – he might be more use humping manure than trying to cleave diamonds. But that was absurd. Whatever Abram might say, he knew that his future must be something to do with diamonds.

He looked at his pocket watch. It was nearly eleven. Old Ernie would be open for business. He crossed over the Singel and walked quickly to the house with the narrow black door. The ground and first floors had been turned into a gymnasium, and at the back downstairs Ernie Blakestone held court – he who had been the toast of the English prizefighting enthusiasts, until forced into exile by the laws against the Fancy, unwilling in any case to stay and adopt the namby-pamby Queensberry rules of gloves and time-limited rounds. In Amsterdam he made a living by coaching promising young boxers. He had never learned Dutch; if his pupils did not understand his Cockney English, that was their look-out.

Of all the young men who came to the club, Jan was his favourite. From the moment he had first seen him, he had recognised a natural talent. Jan was slim but but broad-shouldered, and had speed and lightness of foot, and there was a surprising power in him, as of sprung steel. But what Ernie liked most about him was the way he enjoyed the sport, exulting in his ability and yet able both to laugh at himself when he made a mistake and to learn from it.

Occasionally he could tell that Jan had been upset in some way, because his punches would be more punishing than usual, and there would be anger in his eyes and an expression on his face which made Ernie think of a wild animal. It never lasted long, and Jan would end up laughing again, his dark eyes sparkling and the white teeth flashing. This was a day when Jan's fists sought their mark with extra force and fury.

'What's up with 'im?' Ernie asked himself silently. 'Something's got 'is dander up. Some tart, I s'pose. Bet 'e's got a dozen of 'em, all after 'im. Proper bobby-dazzler, 'e is.' He stepped back. 'Look out!' he said aloud. 'I'm yer bleedin' mate, remember! And keep yer guard up. If yer don't, and yer go slammin' into yer opponent like that, 'e might just take it into 'is 'ead to 'it yer back – like this!' And one-two, one-two, his fists shot out to tap Jan lightly on the face. 'Nah, keep yer guard up. That's it – then 'e can't get through, see? All right – take a breather.' He rubbed at his chest where two of Jan's angrier blows had landed.

'Sorry, Ernie,' Jan said. 'Didn't mean to hurt you.' His English was fluent, though heavily accented.

''Urt me? *'Urt* me? Yer'd 'ave to go 'arder than that to 'urt *me.*'

'Oh. Oh, well, that is good.' Jan's eyes were twinkling.

'Yer all right, mate.' Ernie grinned at him, his honour apparently fully restored. 'And one day, if yer do as I tells yer, yer might even make a boxer o' sorts.'

Jan felt better as he left the gym, but still not ready to go home. He would have to face his father's anger in due course, but first he would go and see Rebecca. As he cut through to the Dam, he realised how hungry the exercise had made him. No doubt Aunt Suzanna, who had kept house for them since his mother died, would have their midday meal already on the table. 'Too bad,' he thought. 'All the more for Father and Abram.' He stopped and bought himself a dish of raw herring at one of the fish-stalls. A street organ was playing nearby, and the merry tunes lifted away the remains of his depression.

The Kremers lived in Nieuwehoogstraat, just around the corner from the Shapiros. Their house was tall and narrow, hemmed in by other buildings, but its dark interior was lightened by the cheery welcome that Jan always received there, especially from Rebecca. They had been childhood friends, and though, as Ernie Blakestone had guessed, Jan could have had his pick of a dozen or more girls, and flirted from time to time with many of them, he always came back to

Rebecca. They would marry one day, just as soon as he was able to support a wife, though God only knew when that would be.

Rebecca opened the door to him. 'Jan!' Her rather plain but pleasant face lit up as she saw him. 'What are you doing here?'

'I've come to see you, of course.'

When she had shut the door he took her in his arms and kissed her. She pushed him away, blushing. 'Jan, you mustn't. Not here.'

That was the trouble with having a girl-friend who had been strictly brought up and who lived under the eyes of her parents. It was very difficult to be alone with her, and even more so to get her to allow him any liberties. An occasional kiss and a passionate holding of hands were the most he could hope for until they were married.

'Come in,' she said. 'We've had our lunch, but you're in time for coffee.'

She led the way into the dining-room, where her parents were. Mijnheer Kremer, a small dapper man, was an importer of diamonds, and Jan's father bought most of his rough stones from him. Mevrouw Kremer, who in bulk would have made three or four of her husband, nodded at Jan and, silent as ever, bustled out to get more coffee.

'Sit down, Jan,' Kremer said. 'Have you heard the news?'

'What news, sir?'

'From Africa. The whole city's buzzing with it. It's confirmed at last – a new source of diamonds richer than anything we've heard of before. It looks as though the Cape really will replace Brazil and India for our supplies. You tell your father when you go home.'

'I'm afraid he'll only scoff, sir. We've been hearing these rumours for months, and Father always says –'

'It's no rumour this time, young man. All the stories we've heard so far have been about the river diggings. The diamonds they've found there are alluvial – they've been washed there – so they're widely scattered and comparatively few and far between. But no one knew where they came from in the first place – until now. The main source is just a few miles away from the Vaal River, at a place called Colesberg Kopje, and the experts say there are enough diamonds there to supply our needs for generations. We shall never again have the bad times like – well, you're too young to remember, but we had a very difficult period about fifteen years ago, when the industry here in Amsterdam was near to collapse.'

'That was when my Mother died,' Jan said. 'Father always says she starved herself in order to keep the rest of us properly fed.'

'Yes,' said Mijnheer Kremer non-committally. 'Of course, she was never a strong woman, your mother.'

'Is the quality of the stones good, sir?'

'Excellent. Naturally there are variations in colour, but a good proportion of them are a fine white. You tell your father. It's something to celebrate.'

'I expect he'll want to drag us all off to give thanks in the synagogue.' The words slipped out of Jan's mouth before he could stop himself.

Mijnheer Kremer frowned. 'There's nothing wrong in that.'

'No, sir.'

'Anyway, you tell him to drink a toast to the diamond diggers of Colesberg Kopje.'

'Are there many of them?'

'Hundreds, thousands, young man. They're flocking there from all over the Cape, hoping to make their fortunes.' He took out his watch, and exclaimed in dismay as he looked at it. 'I must fly. It will be a busy afternoon, and a long one.' He kissed his wife and patted Rebecca on the shoulder, then held out his hand to Jan. 'Tell your father the news. What are you doing here anyway? Did you bring a message from him?'

'No, sir. I just came out for . . . for a breath of air . . . and I thought I might call in here.'

'Yes. Yes, of course,' Kremer said, his mind already on other matters. He left the room and a moment later the front door slammed.

Mevrouw Kremer sighed, put the coffee cups on a tray and carried it out.

'Why *did* you come, Jan?' Rebecca asked. 'Another row with your father?'

'Ten out of ten. Well, it wasn't really a row. Let's say eight out of ten.'

'What about?'

12

'Oh, nothing.' He was reluctant to talk about the shattered diamond.

She looked at him with a tinge of amusement. 'Nothing? In that case you'd better hurry back. Your father'll be wondering where you've got to.'

'I'd rather stay and talk to you.'

'Well, you can't. Mama will be back in a moment.'

'Then come for a walk.'

'Oh, Jan! There's so much to do. It's Sabbath tomorrow.'

'Sabbath!'

'Now, don't start on that again. That's not what the row with your father's about, is it?'

Rebecca had often enough listened to Jan's views on the Jewish religion as practised in their families. Early in his adolescence questions had arisen in his mind: why should they observe a string of dietary laws formulated for hygienic reasons in a Middle Eastern country, laws that made little sense in the nineteenth century in the temperate climate of Amsterdam? And why should they recite prayers in the synagogue and at home which had become so ritualistic as to be meaningless, and follow an artificial code of behaviour for the seventh day of the week? Why indeed worship a God who had allowed his Chosen People to be reviled and persecuted all over the world?

'Do you wish you hadn't been born a Jew?' Rebecca had asked him.

'No, it's not that. I think I'm even proud of being Jewish. We're survivors, aren't we? We've survived the worst that the rest of the world could do to us, and that's something to be proud of. No, it's not being Jewish that I resent – it's just all the irrelevant rules and the ritual.'

She had not argued, but had let him go on, enjoying the fire in his eyes, the curl of his lips, the harsh music of his voice. And then, as always, his sense of humour had taken over and he had ended up laughing at himself and mocking his own pomposity.

He had not, however, changed his views, and Rebecca always remembered the time when he had defied his father and refused to attend the Portuguese Synagogue with the rest of the family. There had been no laughter that day, but only her pleading that he should beg his father's forgiveness, and agree

13

to go to the synagogue again, even if it meant nothing to him. But he told her he could not do that – it would be dishonest. It was several months before the Shapiro and Kremer families accepted the situation and gave up their attempts to get his unorthodox views out of his head. Every now and then the argument would flare up again, and Rebecca had come to dread those occasions, for when he told her about it Jan always sounded so bitter against his father, and she hated that, even though she recognised that the bitterness was really directed against himself and the guilt he felt.

She was relieved when this time he grinned at her and said, 'No. I just made a bit of a fool of myself in the workroom, and walked out. I suppose I'd better go back and make my apologies.'

He left, calling out a goodbye to Mevrouw Kremer and managing to steal another brief kiss from Rebecca. But he did not go straight home.

*   *   *

It was late when Jan got back to the house in Onkelboeren-steeg, but it was still light, and he looked at it with eyes made perceptive by the decisions he had made. It really was a strange, squat little building, dwarfed by its high-gabled neighbours, and especially by the elaborate spire of the Zuiderkerk less than a hundred yards away. His great-grandfather had bought the house, which was old even then, and the Shapiros had lived and worked there ever since, using the ground floor for their workshop and storage space, and living in the two storeys above, always cramped in the tiny rooms. But of course Jacob Shapiro would not even consider moving to more capacious accommodation, any more than he would question a single item in the religious code he lived by.

Dinner was already on the table. Jacob said nothing, but glowered as Jan muttered an apology and slid into his place. Aunt Suzanna, clucking to herself about good food being spoilt, filled a plate and put it in front of him. The meal was eaten in silence. No one ever spoke at family meal-times unless Jacob began the conversation. When they had finished, Aunt Suzanna cleared the dishes away and retreated to the kitchen, and at a sign from his father, Abram scuttled from the room.

'I'm sorry about today, Father – about everything,' Jan said. 'Father, have you heard the news?'

Jacob looked at him. 'Do you call that an apology? You shatter a valuable diamond, you rush out without a word, you stay out all day, and you think you can just say a couple of words and it'll all be forgotten.'

'I'm sorry, Father,' Jan said with heavy patience. 'I'm sorry about the stone, and I'm sorry I went out without your permission, and that I stayed out and came home late, and that I've upset you. I'm sorry about everything – truly I am.'

'I don't like your tone, Jan. You will not speak to me like that.'

'Father, *have you heard the news?*'

'What news?'

'About the diamond discoveries in the Cape.' He told him all he had learned, not only from Mijnheer Kremer but from others he had talked to during the afternoon.

Jacob, forgetting his anger, listened, sceptical at first, asking questions, gradually allowing himself to be convinced.

When he had finished his story, Jan took a deep breath. 'I made a decision this afternoon, Father. I'm going to Africa, to the Cape.'

'What?'

'I'm going to go and dig for diamonds. It suddenly came to me when Mijnheer Kremer was telling me about it. I can send all the diamonds I find back here, and cut out the middle men. You'll be able to buy diamonds direct from me for much less than you'd pay an importer.'

'Wait a minute, Jan, wait a minute. Let me get this straight. You're going out to Africa to dig for diamonds, and this is to be a kind of branch of our business – is that it?'

'Yes, Father.'

Jacob raised his eyebrows. 'Oh, Jan, Jan . . . It sounds all right in theory, but –'

'I'm serious, Father.'

'You may be. But I'm not sure that I can take you seriously. Have you any idea what this would cost? By the time I've paid for your journey –'

'No, Father, I've –'

'– and all your other expenses, and –'

'Please listen to me. I've been to the shipping office to find out the cost of the voyage, and I can afford it easily out of my savings and still have enough over to get to Colesberg Kopje and buy a claim there. The next boat leaves Rotterdam on Tuesday, and I've booked a passage on her.'

'What? Without a word to me?'

'I had to, Father. I knew if I didn't book straight away I'd never do it, and then I'd never get away from here.'

'You want to leave your family? Your home?'

'I'm no good at polishing, or at cleaving, am I? I want to do something with my life, but I can't do anything here. I heard what Abram said this morning – "You're either a diamond man or you're not, and Jan isn't". Well, perhaps I'm not his sort of diamond man, but if I go to the Cape I can be another sort.'

Jacob looked at the eager face of the firstborn son whom he loved so much. The boy had always been difficult – impulsive and stubborn. He tried to contain his impatience. 'But, Jan, you know nothing about digging for diamonds.'

'I can learn.'

'And there are so many other matters to consider. I can see the attractions of this kind of venture for you, but it's not something to plunge into without a moment's thought.'

'I've thought about it all afternoon, Father.'

Jacob bit back an irritable response. Somehow the boy had to be stopped. If he went off to the Cape, he might never return. He could be killed, or die of some tropical disease, and even if he survived his likelihood of making any kind of living was remote. But he had to appear reasonable. 'Look, Jan,' he said. 'Let's be sensible about this. Let's take a little time to find out more about conditions in the Cape, what is needed, what the chances of success are. This news has only just come through, and it may turn out to be a flash in the pan. If after a few weeks it's been confirmed, and we've found out a lot more about it, then I'll consider –'

'But don't you see?' Jan said. 'It'll be too late then. Men are flocking to the diggings already. I've got to go now. And I'm sorry, Father, but my mind's made up. Please don't try to stop me.' He slipped to his knees in front of Jacob, and bowed his head. 'I want to go with your blessing, Father. Please tell me I have it.'

Jacob peered at him, and mistook what he saw for hypocrisy. His patience snapped, and he was seized by an unreasoning anger which he could not contain, as though Jan's words had been a match to gunpowder. 'My blessing! I should give you my blessing – you who despise our religion, who won't even go to the synagogue for Yom Kippur?' He began to shake with rage. 'God is not mocked, and neither am I mocked. I should give my blessing to someone who's ashamed to be a Jew.'

'That's not true!'

'Oh, yes, it is. Deny it as much as you like, you're ashamed of being a Shapiro, ashamed of being Jewish, ashamed of the Lord our God!'

It was so unjust that Jan could hardly speak. 'Father, please listen,' he whispered. 'That's not true, I swear it. None of it is true.'

But Jacob was not to be stopped. 'My blessing? No, you shall not have my blessing. I forbid you to go, do you hear? I absolutely forbid it!'

2

The voyage was at first a purgatory for Jan. The steerage quarters were unpleasantly crowded and the food barely adequate, and though it was high summer there were gales in the Bay of Biscay and along the Portuguese coast, so he kept to his narrow bunk, his queasiness increased by the sight and sound and smell of the other seasick passengers.

As the ship sailed into calmer waters, he began to find his sea legs, and went on deck and watched the blue waters go by, and the flying fish and dolphins and sea-birds which followed in their wake.

A young man came up to him. 'I say, do you speak English?'

'A little.'

'Thank God for that! I thought I was going to have to spend the whole journey with no one to talk to. My Dutch is of the extremely shaky variety.' He put his head on one side, and smiled. He was plump and not very tall, with a round pink face and sandy hair.

'Most Dutch people speak some English.'

'Yes, I know, and it's awfully good of them, but they're all so old, the ones on this boat. There's hardly anyone under thirty, except you and me. My name's Templeton, by the way, Harry Templeton.'

He held out his hand, and Jan shook it, looking into the friendly blue eyes. 'Johannes Shapiro,' he said. 'But they call me Jan. And I'm twenty-two.'

Harry laughed. 'Oh, you're an old man. I'm not twenty-one yet.' He noticed Jan's puzzled look. 'A joke,' he said. 'I'm glad it's a bit calmer now. I've been feeling like a dying duck in a thunderstorm.'

'Please?'

'A dying duck in a thunderstorm. It means feeling awful.'

'A dying duck in a thunderstorm,' Jan repeated slowly. 'I do not understand.'

'Look, you know what a duck is, don't you?' Harry began to waddle about, flapping his arms like wings, and saying, 'Quack! Quack!' His legs gradually bent and the quacks became weaker, and slowly he sank to the deck and rolled on to his side, his free arm still flapping feebly. 'Quack!' he whispered.

Jan watched in amazement, and started to laugh. Soon a crowd of other passengers had gathered around.

Suddenly Harry sprang up, and described violent zigzags in the air with his hands and summoned up from the depths of his chest the most extraordinarily resonant growling sounds. It was not much like thunder, but there was no mistaking his meaning. He began to flutter his fingers downwards and to make a gentle hissing sound. 'Rain,' said someone in the crowd, and Harry nodded happily. He dropped back to the deck, becoming the duck again, and put up an imaginary umbrella. But his hand seemed to let it fall, and the quackings grew fainter and stopped, and finally he lay completely still.

The crowd applauded, and Harry jumped to his feet and bowed. 'Thank you, thank you, ladies and gentlemen. The next performance –' He sprang to one side, and in a deeper, gruffer voice said, 'The next performance will not take place owing to the fact that the performer is non compos mentis.' He moved back to his original position, put a hand behind his neck as though it belonged to someone else and jerked himself upright by tugging at his jacket collar, and still in this position moved awkwardly sideways, as if he were being dragged off stage by an angry theatre manager. Then he joined Jan at the rail. 'Do you understand now?'

'No,' Jan laughed.

'Ah, well, never mind. All great artists are misunderstood.' He turned and waved a languid dismissal at the crowd, which slowly dispersed. 'Where are you going?' he asked Jan.

'On this ship? To Port Elizabeth.'

Bound for the East Indies, the ship would call at Cape Town, Port Elizabeth and Durban, and Port Elizabeth was nearer to Colesberg Kopje than either of the others.

He had shown Rebecca where it was in her atlas. On the night of the bitter argument with his father, Jan had gone to the room he shared with Abram, and refusing to answer questions, had packed his few possessions. At the last moment, he had pushed into his bag his skull-cap and prayer-shawl and phylactery. It was all a lot of mumbo-jumbo, but somehow it would have seemed all wrong to leave without them. As he finished, he said to the open-mouthed Abram, 'It's all yours now, dear brother – the room and the business. And you're welcome to it!' Then he ran down the stairs and out of the house.

As the door shut behind him, he felt a moment's panic. What was he doing? Where was he to go? But he set off firmly for the Kremers' house.

Mijnheer Kremer was much disturbed. 'Go home, Jan, and have a good talk to your father. I'm sure he'll forgive and forget, and if you think about it, you'll see you have rather rushed into . . .' His voice trailed off as he saw Jan's expression. 'Oh, very well. Make the spare bed up, Mother. I don't know what your father will say to me, nor I to him. We've been friends since long before you were born. I shall have to make my peace with him somehow. Somehow.'

Jan had much to do in the four days, which included the Sabbath, before the ship was to sail from Rotterdam. Money had to be drawn from the bank for his ticket and the balance turned into a draft which he could cash in the Cape, purchases had to be made – writing paper, soap, a pair of stout boots, and for use on the boat, an enamel plate and mug and a knife, fork and spoon – and farewells said to old Ernie Blakestone and a few other friends. And he wanted to spend as much time as he could with Rebecca.

Mevrouw Kremer, who always had a soft spot for Jan, allowed them to be together on their own as much as was consistent with propriety. On the Monday afternoon they went to the Begijnhof, and strolled around the peaceful little square beneath the chestnut trees. Preoccupied, they hardly spoke, but after a while Rebecca said, 'Jan, I know you won't like my saying this, but won't you at least write your father a note? Not to apologise or anything like that, and just to say you're sorry that you and he can't agree, and that you'll send him your address in the Cape.' He was frowning, but she felt she had to go on. 'Papa was talking about your father before you came down to breakfast this morning. He says he's a very

20

stubborn man, and he'll never forgive you unless you make the first move.'

'Well, I'm stubborn too!' Jan said. 'I don't care whether he forgives me or not! I don't care if I never see him again!' He was almost shouting, and Rebecca put her hand on his arm. When he went on, his voice was softer, but just as vehement. 'I'm certainly not going to write to him now or at any other time, except when I send him the diamonds I find. Oh, yes, I'm going to do that. I'm going to prove to him that I'm still a Shapiro, and that I do care about the family business. But the only person I shall write to properly is you, and I don't want you to pass on anything of my letters to my father or Abram. Will you promise me that?'

She nodded unhappily.

'And you'll write to me, won't you?'

'I'll try,' she said. 'I'm never much good at letters, so you mustn't be disappointed if they aren't very long.'

'I'll be grateful for just a plain sheet of paper, if it comes from you.'

When they got back to the house, he stopped her in the dark passage. 'Rebecca,' he began, and took her hand. He felt her beginning to pull away. 'No, wait,' he said. 'Rebecca, you know I love you. I want to marry you, but I can't ask you that – not yet. But will you wait for me?'

She whispered, 'Yes!' so quietly that he knew what she said only from the expression on her face. He took her in his arms and kissed her. His tongue played against her lips, probing until they opened and he could taste the sweetness of her mouth, and as he held her he was conscious of the enchanting softness beneath the armour of her clothes. She responded, her tongue flickering against his, her arms twined around his neck.

'Children?' called her mother. 'Is that you? What are you up to out there?'

They had to go into the drawing-room and pretend they had been brushing mud from their shoes.

She and her mother had come to the station to see him off on the train to Rotterdam. Much as he longed to, he could not kiss Rebecca properly in front of Mevrouw Kremer. He had to content himself with kissing her hand, and that, in sheer politeness, meant doing the same for her mother.

21

'Such a nice boy,' Mevrouw Kremer cooed. 'Such good manners.'

He realised that while he had been day-dreaming Harry Templeton had asked a question. 'Please?'

'I asked where you are going from Port Elizabeth.'

'To Colesberg Kopje.'

'Digging for diamonds, eh? Me too. They're calling the place New Rush now, you know. You're crazy to go to Port Elizabeth. Cape Town's the place to disembark.'

'Port Elizabeth is much nearer.'

'Yes, but there's regular transport from Cape Town to the diggings. It takes weeks to get there from Port Elizabeth. A chap in Rotterdam who'd just got back from the Cape told me all about it. In fact, it was talking to him that made me decide to go there.'

'Do you know anything about diamonds?'

'No,' Harry said cheerfully. 'Except they're a good way of getting rich. And if I've got one ambition in life, that's it.'

*   *   *

They spent almost the whole of the voyage in each other's company. The other passengers grew accustomed to seeing them together – the tall, lithe young man with the dark hair and the sharp handsome features, and the other shorter and fair, with a pudgy face and little of the athlete in his appearance. They seemed very different, but the one thing they had in common, which was always in evidence, was their laughter.

They exchanged life stories. Harry was the son of a well-to-do London wine merchant. He had been at Oxford. 'And then in the first Christmas vacation I met this girl – a real little sweetheart! – the daughter of one of my father's clerks. Have you got a girl?'

'Yes. Her name's Rebecca.'

'I bet she's a smasher too. Well, I got this one in the family way. There was a devil of a row. No question of marriage, thank God. Her parents packed her off to some aunt in the country, and my revered Papa decided I should do a bit of a vanishing act. That's not why you've left Holland, is it? You haven't given your – what was her name? Rebecca? – a little stranger?'

'No,' Jan said, and unwilling to confess that there was no chance of it, then added, 'At least, I don't think so.'

'Ah, dirty dog!' Harry grinned, and dug him in the ribs. He went on to explain that his uncle, who ran a branch of the family business in Rotterdam, had found him a clerking job. He had hated it, and had hoarded every cent of his pay, planning to take himself off, once he had enough saved, to one of the British colonies – anywhere he could escape from his family. 'Then I met this chap back from the Transvaal, and he told me about the diamond diggings. I went to the shipping office, found that if I sold my watch and my cuff-links I'd just got enough with my savings for a passage to Cape Town, and here I am.'

'You mean you've got no other money?' Jan asked.

'Not a penny,' Harry replied blithely. 'Well, that's not quite true, but to all intents and purposes I'm broke.'

'But how are you going to get to New Rush?'

'No idea. Something will turn up. I'll find myself a job in Cape Town. Or maybe someone will employ me to drive a waggon up to the Vaal.'

Jan looked at him warily. At any minute he would be asking Jan to pay for him, or at least to lend him the money.

'Oh, don't worry, old man,' Harry said, as if he had read Jan's mind. 'I'm not going to sponge on you, though it might be an idea to work together. And travel together, if I can raise the wind.'

'The wind? You mean the money?' Jan's vocabulary was enlarging rapidly, but Harry's idioms were very confusing. 'But how can we travel together? You're getting off at Cape Town, and I'm going on to Port Elizabeth.'

'So you are. But you're a fool to do so. Get off with me at Cape Town.'

Jan shook his head, and turned his attention to the un-appetising salt pork and dried beans that were their midday meal.

When they were only three days' journey away from Cape Town, Harry raised the topic again. 'I've been to see the Purser,' he announced. 'I asked him if someone who was booked through to Port Elizabeth would get a refund if he got off at Cape Town. He grumbled about it, but in the end he said you'd get a few florins back. No, wait a minute,' he said, as Jan began to protest. 'I also asked him about the best way to get to New Rush. He says it'll take anyone who starts from Port Elizabeth weeks longer than from Cape Town. So I was thinking, first of all, why don't we go into partnership? Two of us to share the work and a tent and everything. And if you'd lend me what you'll save by getting off at Cape Town, that'll probably pay for me to get to New Rush. And I'd pay you back as soon as I could.'

'Harry, I'm going to need all the money I've got to buy a claim.'

'I'm only asking to borrow the refund on your ticket. And when you get your claim, I'll work on it with you for nothing. I wouldn't expect any share of the diamonds until you'd got enough money back to pay for everything you'd spent on me and for my share of the claim. And I'd save as hard as I could until I could buy a claim next to yours, and then we'd have double the opportunities. But,' he said in melodramatic tones, placing his hand over his heart, 'your friend would never forget the debt he owed you for staking him at the start, and he'd suggest a remarkably generous split of the ultimate profits – say, a magnificent sixty per cent to you and a miserable forty per cent to me.'

Harry made a joke of most things, but this time, despite the play-acting, there was no doubt of his seriousness. It was crazy, Jan thought. He would be taking all the risks, putting up all the capital for the partnership, and after all, much as he liked Harry, he knew very little about him. On the other hand, Harry was offering free labour and his pleasant companionship, and, if he was right about leaving the ship at Cape Town, good advice. And two people working together would probably achieve more than double the output of one man trying to do everything himself.

Harry's bright blue eyes were fixed on him, with a kind of amused confidence. 'I'll have to think about it,' Jan said.

'Of course. Take your time. I can't supply any references, but I do have an honest face. At least I think I have. It looked honest enough when I saw it in a mirror this morning.'

Jan laughed, but Harry's joking put a sudden thought in his mind. 'What would your parents say about you going into partnership with a Jew?'

Harry's eyes opened wide. 'What's that got to do with

anything? I don't choose my friends or my business partners according to their religion. My father'd probably tell me I was showing a bit of sense for once. What about you?'

Jan wished he had not raised the matter, though perhaps it was as well to have it out in the open. He tried to laugh. 'As you say, what's it matter? I think my father would be very pleased I've got a friend like you.' It was not true of course – his father would have disapproved of Harry even more than he disapproved of everything else.

He went to the Purser to check for himself what Harry had reported. The man confirmed it all. 'There's a train from Cape Town to Wellington, a hundred kilometers away, and a weekly waggon service runs from there to the diggings. There's no regular transport from Port Elizabeth, and what there is goes slowly and by a roundabout route. Durban's even worse.'

Jan went on deck again to think over his problems. Finally he made his mind up – he would tell Harry that he was taking his advice and leaving the ship at Cape Town, but once there they would shake hands and part. If by his own efforts Harry got to New Rush and bought a claim, they might be able to form some kind of partnership, but that was all he was prepared to offer.

After they had eaten their meagre breakfast the next morning, the two young men set out on their daily walk around the ship's deck, a routine which Jan insisted on for the sake of the exercise.

Eventually Harry said, 'Well, old man, are we partners?' He was smiling, and if there was a hint of anxiety in the blue eyes it was hard to discern.

'I don't know,' Jan said. 'I've got to have better terms, Harry. I'm not doing this just for myself, you see – I've got to think of the family business too.' It had suddenly occurred to him that the easiest way out of his difficulty would be to suggest so harsh a financial arrangement that Harry could not possibly accept it. 'Any profits we make the first year will be all mine, for the second year, they'll be split eighty per cent to me and twenty per cent to you; after that we'll work on a sixty-forty basis, but only if you invest a fair share of capital into the partnership.'

Harry considered for a moment. 'That's steep! Damned

steep!' Then he grinned. 'But it's better than no deal at all. As my mother would say, what's a few bawbees between friends – she's from Scotland of course.' He pumped Jan's hand. 'Partners! You won't regret it, Jan. Shapiro and Templeton, Diamond Diggers! Quack! Quack, quack, quack!' He threw his hat into the air and did a dance of exultation, regardless of the amused glances of the other passengers. Suddenly he ran to the ship's rail. The smart bowler with its curled brim was floating on the calm sea, being left rapidly behind. 'Hat overboard!' he cried. 'Dammit, I didn't mean to do that. Now you'll have to lend me the money to buy a new one, Jan!' And he roared with laughter and hugged his new partner.

*　　*　　*

On the following day, the twenty-seventh of October, 1871, Jan and Harry were up early and on deck, with most of the other passengers, straining for their first view of Cape Town. A strong south-easterly wind had sprung up and it was a relief when they turned into the shelter of Table Bay and could at last see the little town nestling in the hollow of the high rocky hills which surrounded it, dominated by the strange curving shape of Table Mountain.

Jan could scarcely contain his excitement. It was here that the adventure would really begin, the adventure that he believed would bring him success and fortune, and marriage to Rebecca, and his father's respect.

3

As soon as they got off the boat, Jan and Harry went to the station, and learned that the train for Wellington did not leave until the next morning.

'I'm not sorry,' Jan said. 'Gives us time to have a look at Cape Town.'

'And to find a couple of nice girls,' Harry added.

First Jan had to look for a bank where he could cash his draft, and a post office so that he could send off the letter to Rebecca which he had written in daily instalments during the voyage. Then they had to find somewhere to spend the night, and it took a while to make enquiries and discover a lodging-house where a reasonably clean room was to be had for a few coppers. By that time they were ravenously hungry. They picked out a cheap restaurant and gorged themselves on a thick stew called *bredie*.

They had both expected, as sophisticated Europeans, to look upon Cape Town with some condescension, and would have been prepared for it to have a primitive, shanty-town appearance. But as they strolled up Adderley Street after their meal, they were impressed by its breadth and the splendour of the modern buildings which lined it. And the people were indeed cosmopolitan: sailors and beggars, servants and farmers, road-sweepers and aristocrats, pedlars and clerks, with skins of every hue from the fair complexions of the Whites to the chocolate and ebony of the Africans and the dark yellow of the colourfully-turbanned Malays. There were girls in plenty, but those of European extraction seemed to be as closely chaperoned as they would have been in London or Amsterdam, and they felt reluctant, being unsure of local customs, to approach any of the coloured women.

They walked around the gardens at the head of Adderley

Street, and then wandered through a maze of side streets; from everywhere they went they could see the Lion's Head and Devil's Peak and the great curving mass of Table Mountain, towering over the city as though to demonstrate how puny Man's achievements were.

'I suppose,' Harry said, 'we could go back down to the harbour. There's sure to be women there – the kind who do it for money.'

'We can't afford that.'

'No, we can't, can we?' His regretful tone vanished as he said, 'Then let's go and eat again.'

They went back to the same restaurant and sampled its *sosaties*, and because being in Africa was something to celebrate, and because they had not wasted their money on whores, and because in any case it was so cheap, they had a couple of glasses each of the fiery, strong Cape brandy.

'You know what?' Harry said, with the careful deliberation of the slightly inebriated. 'You know what?'

'What?'

'We are going to find the largest diamond in the world.'

Jan frowned. 'We've got to find more than one,' he said ponderously.

'All right, we're going to find the *four* largest diamonds in the world.'

'Why only four?'

'Because that's enough. Two each. And when we've found the four largest diamonds in the world, we shan't need to look for any others.'

This statement seemed so funny that the proprietor came over and asked them to laugh less noisily. They ordered another brandy each.

'We shall be so rich that we'll live on nothing but caviar.'

'And *bredie* and *sosaties*,' said Jan.

'And *bredie* and *sosaties*. And champagne.'

'And Cape brandy.'

'Yes. But don't interrupt. And we shall have a dozen beautiful women each in constant attendance, to see to our every need. And when I say "our every need",' Harry continued solemnly, 'I mean our *every* need.'

They laughed as wildly as before, and when the proprietor again asked them to be quiet, took offence and left the restaurant, and immediately forgot their ill-humour, and made their way towards the lodging-house. The wind that had been blowing all day had increased and they had to battle against it. At least it seemed to clear the fumes of alcohol from their heads.

The part of the town that they were walking through was deserted and quiet. Just as they passed a narrow alley, they heard a muffled cry for help. It was repeated, and then came a grunt of pain. Jan stopped. Some distance away along the alley he could just make out in the dim light a small group of struggling men. The cry for help came again.

'Come on,' said Harry. 'It's no concern of ours.'

But Jan knew somehow, instinctively, that it *was* his concern. The last of his light-headedness vanished as he ran along the alley, with Harry slowly and reluctantly following behind. As he got nearer, Jan could see that there were three men. Two were big, brawny fellows, one of whom had pinned the third man's arms behind his back, while his companion aimed vicious blows at the captive. 'Sodding little Yid! Jewish bastard!'

The ruffian who was holding the victim suddenly became aware of Jan's approach, and yelled, 'Look out!'

He was too late. Jan seized the other man's arm as he drew it back for a further blow, and as he turned in surprise, put all his strength into a punch which landed on the side of the thug's jaw, knocking him to the ground. The other rough released his victim and sprang at Jan, reaching out massive hands to fasten round his throat. But Jan was too quick, and a hard blow to the heart, followed by a left to the chin, sent him to sprawl beside his companion.

The fight, if it could be called that, had lasted a few seconds only. Jan stood ready, waiting for the ruffians to attack again, but by now Harry had arrived, and as they scrambled to their feet, one of the men said, 'There's more of 'em. Run for it!' They disappeared into the darkness.

Their victim was leaning against the wall.

'Are you all right?' Jan asked.

'Yes, I think so. A bit winded.' He took a few deep breaths. 'That's better. I'm very grateful to you, sir. You came along at just the right time. And your assistance was very effective.'

'Smote them hip and thigh, didn't he?' said Harry.

'Indeed. A veritable Samson.'

'Shouldn't we send for the police?' Jan asked, rubbing his bruised knuckles.

'I suspect that would be a waste of everyone's time.' There was a sardonic amusement in his voice.

'Or a doctor?'

'That would undoubtedly be a waste of *his* time. Fortunately, I think there is more damage to my clothing than to me.' He hesitated briefly. 'However, I should be grateful if I could impose on you and ask you to be so kind as to escort me back to my hotel. It is not very far away. I think my legs are strong enough to get me there, but I cannot be sure. Unreliable things, legs, sometimes.'

'Of course,' said Jan. 'Take my arm, sir.'

'Besides, at the hotel I can thank you properly for your timely assistance.'

As they walked slowly along, Jan and Harry both supporting him, he told them that his name was Isaac Meier, and that he was a dealer in ostrich feathers, here from London on a business trip. That evening he had been to visit a friend, and was on his way back to his hotel when he was stopped by the two thugs, who demanded money. 'But I never carry cash or valuables with me at night,' he went on. 'Everything was securely locked away in my hotel room. Of course they didn't believe me, and they rifled my pockets. When they found I had nothing they could take, they began to hit me. Fortunately, you came along before they had done much damage.'

By this time they had reached Mr Meier's hotel. He insisted that they should come in. As they entered, they could see him clearly for the first time. He was short and plump, and older than Jan had thought – a man of at least his father's age. One eye was badly bruised, and there was a trickle of blood at the corner of his mouth, but he refused to admit that he was seriously hurt, and was far more distressed over his torn jacket. The hotel receptionist was horrified and wanted to send for a doctor, but Meier would not allow him to do so, asking only that a jug of hot water should be sent up to his room.

'You should go to bed and rest,' Jan said.

'No, please. I want you to wait here for me, you and your friend. I will be down again shortly.'

Fifteen minutes later he reappeared. 'A bruise or two and a

cut lip – that's all,' he reported with a smile. 'Of course, my coat is ruined and I have lost two shirt buttons, but it could have been much worse.' He was very pale, and there was tension in his voice despite his effort to sound relaxed. 'And now, sir,' he went on, 'I must thank you properly. You were brave and strong, and I thank God for your bravery and strength. No doubt you will be insulted if I offer you a pecuniary reward, but I have never known a young man of your age who is not in need of money, so I hope you will be prepared to swallow the insult, if you really consider it such – which it certainly is not – and do me the pleasure of accepting this small token of my gratitude.' He took out his wallet, and extracted two five pound notes. Jan noticed that his fingers were shaking. He protested, but Meier was so insistent that after a protracted argument he finally took the money. 'And let me buy you a brandy – none of that Cape rubbish – good French brandy.'

This time Jan was able to refuse. 'I have already had more than I am used to,' he said.

'It did not seem so when you set about those roughnecks. But I would never force a man to drink against his will.' Meier turned to Harry. 'How about you, young man?'

'I don't think I've earned it,' Harry said, 'but I won't say no.'

'Good. And I will have one too.' He ordered the drinks. 'Now, tell me about yourselves. Do you live in Cape Town?'

'No, we're just passing through. We arrived this morning, and we leave first thing tomorrow.'

'A pity. I was hoping that tomorrow you would have dinner with me. Where are you going?'

'To New Rush.'

'Ah, in search of diamonds, no doubt. Yes? I might have guessed. I have a friend in New Rush, a diamond dealer called Samuel Rosenberg. You must take any diamonds you find to him. Mention my name, and he will give you a good price. Well, he would do that anyway – he's an honest man.'

He asked more about them, and then in response to their questions told them how ostrich farms had been set up in the Cape to meet the world-wide demand for the fashionable plumes. 'Poor birds. When their plumage is at its best, they are plucked. They look very indignant – it must be most upsetting for them. But the ladies love those feathers, and I am happy to supply their needs.' He drained the last of his brandy. 'I come here every two or three years to see my suppliers, but, alas, this is my last trip. I find it difficult to leave my business, and I have a son who will make the journey for me in future. I shall have to warn him not to walk in the side streets alone at night.'

'Have you been attacked here before?' Jan asked.

Meier looked at him sharply. 'Physically, no. Abuse? Well, we are used to that, aren't we? You will find no more anti-semitism here than anywhere else, but it is never pleasant.' He seemed suddenly to shrink, as though the shock and pain of the attack had caught up with him in a single moment. 'I am sorry, my young friends, but I find that I am more tired than I thought, and I would like, if you will forgive me, to go to bed. Thank you again for rescuing me. If you ever come to London, please visit me, and we will dine together then. Ask for my shop in the Clerkenwell Road – everyone knows Isaac Meier. And don't forget, when you have diamonds to sell in New Rush, go to Samuel Rosenberg. He was a good friend when he lived in London.' He stood up, swaying with fatigue.

'Let me see you to your room,' Jan said.

Meier shook his head, and took a deep breath. 'No, I am all right, my friends. But go, please, before I demonstrate my weakness. One of the servants here will help me. Thank you again, and God bless you.'

Jan went quickly to the reception desk and summoned help for Meier. As a burly porter helped him towards the stairs, Meier waved goodbye.

'Poor little man,' Harry said, when they were out in the street. 'I hope he'll be all right.'

'Yes.'

Jan was clearly abstracted, and Harry continued, 'I suppose you're thinking of the anti-semitism. I shouldn't let it worry you. Most chaps don't mean it, you know – don't *really* mean it. It's just something they're brought up with.'

'Oh. I see. Well, thanks – I'll try to remember that.'

'That's the ticket!' said Harry, completely unaware of the bitter irony in Jan's voice, and believing he had helped his friend. He went on, enthusiastically, 'I say, I didn't know you could fight like that. It's just as well you could – I'm afraid I wouldn't have been much good. Fisticuffs is one thing the

Templetons are *not* famous for. You were marvellous – not to mention the fact that we've got ten pounds more towards our claim.'

★ ★ ★

In the morning the lodging-house keeper called them early as he had promised and gave them a small breakfast. On their way to catch the Wellington train they passed Meier's hotel, and called in to enquire after him.

'Mr Meier is still asleep,' they were told.

They left a message to say that they had called, and hurried to the station. Jan was quiet and answered Harry in monosyllables, but as the morning wore on regained his spirits. Soon they would be in New Rush . . .

The train was crammed for the three-hour journey to Wellington with men of many nationalities and ages, all bound for the diamond diggings and the chance of a fortune. Packed into the middle of the stifling carriage, Jan and Harry could see little of the country. Every so often the train would stop, and the men would pile out to relieve themselves and grumble at the engine-driver for his slowness.

Pulling into Wellington, which appeared to consist of no more than a small cluster of buildings, the new arrivals were greeted by a crowd of men, all shouting at once. 'Transport to New Rush! This way for the fastest waggon.' 'The best hotel in Wellington!' 'Get all your need here, gents – food, tents, picks and shovels!' Already warned not to be seduced by these touts, Jan and Harry pushed their way through to the offices of the Inland Transport Company.

'Yes?' said the harassed clerk.

'How much are tickets to New Rush?'

'Twelve pounds.'

'Twelve pounds each?'

'That's right. When do you want to go?'

'Straight away.'

'All seats booked until three weeks from today. Want to book for then?'

Jan looked despairingly at Harry, who told the clerk, 'We need to discuss it.'

Outside the building, Jan said, 'That's impossible. Twelve

pounds each! And we'd have to pay for somewhere to stay here while we waited.'

'Let's go back to the station,' Harry said. 'Maybe we can do better with one of those fellows there, whatever they say about them.'

Several of the touts were still at the station, and one of them came up to Jan and Harry. He was tall, broad-shouldered and powerful, and Jan thought he might be in his early thirties, though it was difficult to judge, for his unkempt hair and thick black beard left little of his face visible, except for the sharp eyes and a long bony nose. 'Looking for transport to New Rush, gents?'

'We might be.'

'Just the two of you?'

Jan nodded.

The man put out his hand. 'Watson's the name. Conrad Watson. They call me Black Conrad, on account of me beard. You've come to the right place, me hearties.' He grinned suddenly. It changed his whole appearance, and instead of having a faintly sinister air he looked friendly and almost handsome.

'How much?' Jan asked.

'Fifteen pounds a head.'

'Fifteen!'

'Sounds a lot, but you work it out. By Inland Transport it costs you twelve pounds, right? Plus you're going to wait here for three weeks before you get a seat on one of their waggons, and to stay in Wellington'll cost you another four or five pounds. Plus by the time you get to New Rush the price of claims will have gone up again. I hear a first-class claim costs fifty, sixty quid now. God knows what it'll be by the time Inland Transport gets you there. Fifteen quid's cheap to be there in half the time.'

Jan turned to Harry and shook his head. He had the ten pounds that Meier had given him, and his bank draft had produced a little over sixty pounds, some of which had already gone on their meals and lodging in Cape Town and the fares to Wellington. To pay out so much of what was left would certainly not leave them enough to buy a reasonable claim, though he did not believe they would be as expensive as Watson said.

34

'Please yourself, mate,' Watson told him. 'There's plenty others'll take the places if you don't want 'em.' He added quickly, 'Food's thrown in.'

Harry pulled Jan aside. 'You go with him. I'll stay here and earn some money somehow so I can buy a seat on the Inland Transport waggon.'

Jan was tempted, but he had pledged himself to Harry, and it was unthinkable to desert him now. He turned back to Watson. 'Twenty-five pounds for the two of us.'

Watson grinned in his likeable way, and shook his head. 'Thirty's the price.'

Jan hesitated, and then made up his mind. The vital thing was to get to New Rush as soon as possible. 'All right.'

'I'll take it now.' When he saw the look on Jan's face, he continued, 'You're right, me friend. Plenty of rogues around. But Black Conrad's word is good – you ask anyone. Pay me now, and as soon as I've stocked up we'll be on our way. Come with me to the store. I shan't be out of your sight till we're in New Rush.'

Jan took out his money, but Harry put his hand on his arm. 'It's daylight robbery.'

'We haven't got any choice,' Jan said.

Watson overheard him. 'Oh, yes, you have. Plenty. You can go to Sid Morris over there.' He pointed vaguely towards a group of other touts. 'If you're looking for a real bastard, that's him. He'll only charge you a tenner, but a day's journey out, in the middle of the Karoo, he'll steal your gear, turn you off and come back here – that's if he don't slit your throats first. Oh, you can stare, but it's true.'

Jan looked at Harry, shrugged, and handed over the thirty pounds.

'Come on, then,' said Watson, striding off towards Wellington's main street. 'You're in luck, me hearties,' he went on. 'Coming to me, I mean. For why? For two reasons. First, you need a young and healthy driver, like me, to take you across the Karoo, and second, he has to know the way.'

'That certainly sounds fairly important,' Harry said, laughing.

Watson apparently did not think it funny. He continued, quite seriously, 'I got the best route to New Rush, and that comes of knowing me navigation – I was in the Navy afore I

35

took to this business. Tried me hand at digging first, but had no luck. Mind you, they hadn't found Colesberg Kopje then, and it was just the river diggings, and all the best sites taken. So I decided I'd do better in the transport line, and looked for a job, and found one working for a gent name of Bell, Mr George Bell. One of the top men in New Rush. I'll introduce you when we get there. He'll probably be able to help you – his main business is buying and selling claims.'

By this time they had reached a small general store, where Watson bought various supplies, including a sack of mealies and a quantity of biltong.

'What are mealies and biltong?' Harry asked.

'Mealies is ground maize. Makes porridge. And biltong's dried meat.'

'You don't expect us to survive on that, do you? Sounds disgusting.'

'You won't enjoy it, but it keeps body and soul together. You two got water-bottles?'

'No.'

'How d'you expect to manage in the Karoo?'

'What is this Karoo you keep talking about?'

'Just about the worst place in the world, me lads. Desert. Mile upon mile of sod-all. If it don't kill you, it'll break your heart, like as not.' He laughed. 'Cheer up! You'll be all right with me to see you through it.'

'Why don't we buy two water-bottles each?' said Harry. 'Or three, or maybe four.'

When Watson was satisfied that they had all they needed, the three of them carried their purchases to a stretch of open ground just beyond the little town, where they first saw the waggon that was to take them to New Rush, a ricketty contraption which looked as though it would collapse at any minute. It was some twelve feet long, with small wheels in front and much larger ones at the back, and over the rear part was a torn and stained canvas canopy. There were two horses. They were thin and dull-coated, and their flanks were scarred, as though they had been unmercifully whipped.

Harry was horrified. 'We're travelling seven hundred miles in that?'

Watson laughed. 'What did you expect? Her Majesty's coach and four fat greys to pull it?'

36

'But it looks as though it'll fall to pieces.'

'It won't. If it does, we repair it.'

Harry persisted. 'Surely those horses can't take us all the way to New Rush?'

Watson laughed. 'Best little pair of horses on the veld, these are. Most waggons are pulled by oxen. They're slow. My little beauties will get us there much quicker, as long as we give 'em a good rest at night. Come on, let's get loaded.'

Trying to conceal their misgivings from each other, Jan and Harry began to pile the things on to the waggon. Jan in particular, in addition to worrying about the journey, felt uneasy about Watson. He could not put his finger on what it was – the man seemed friendly and open, and Jan did not suspect him of planning to murder them in the Karoo, as he had said some drivers might – but he did not altogether trust him.

When the tent and all the supplies and their bags had been loaded, there was little enough room left for them to sit. Jan and Harry clambered up, perching where they could, Watson cracked the whip, and the waggon, creaking and protesting, moved slowly off.

At first, spurred by an occasional flick of the whip, the horses clip-clopped at a leisurely trot, but this soon slowed to a walk. Wellington passed out of sight behind them, and they travelled through a dreary countryside in which the track they were following was the only sign that any other men had ever been there.

For a while Jan and Harry were silent, but then Harry asked, 'Is this the fastest we can go?'

'Yes,' said Watson cheerfully. 'Slow but steady. We'll get there.'

Soon they came to a hill, and Watson told them to get out and walk so as to lighten the load for the horses. As they plodded along, they discussed the situation, whispering so that Watson could not hear.

'It's going to take weeks at this rate,' Harry said.

'Yes. Still, I'd rather be on the way than waiting in Wellington.'

Harry seemed to consider the matter. 'I must say if I were on my own I'd be tempted to go back. But in fact I'll stay with you, friend of my bosom.' He grinned. 'After all, you've got the money. How much is left, by the way?'

Jan calculated. 'Just over thirty-seven pounds.'

'Well, this is costing a lot more than we expected, but we did have Mr Meier's ten pounds, and we weren't counting on that.'

'Yes. I wonder how he is.'

'Anyway, thirty-seven pounds will probably buy us a reasonable claim. Not the best, perhaps, but that just means it'll take us a little longer to find the four largest diamonds in the world.'

The day seemed endless. Every now and then they stopped for long periods to rest the horses, with only the meagre shade of the waggon to shield them from the scorching sun. At last they made camp for the night – 'outspanning', Watson called it. He brought out cold beef and cheese and rough bread and a small flask of Cape brandy. It tasted wonderful, and it did not even take the bloom off their pleasure when he told them, 'Don't count on this again. From now on it's mealies and biltong.'

The next day they entered the Karoo. 'Mile upon mile of sod-all,' Watson had said, and it was indeed a boundless stretch of sun-flayed waste, with not a single tree to break the monotony of its featureless aridity. Because the veld was so bare, and landmarks were scarce, their progress across it seemed interminably slow. The horses were labouring and Watson lashed them viciously.

'What's the use of doing that?' Jan asked. 'It doesn't make them go any faster.'

'Makes *me* feel better.' He raised the whip again, but Jan snatched it from his grasp and threw it into the back of the waggon. 'What the hell are you playing at?' Watson stared angrily at him. 'Bloody fool!' But he made no move to retrieve the whip.

The horses ambled slowly on for a few paces and then stopped. Jan jumped down from the waggon and began to lead them forward.

'Bloody fool!' Watson repeated, sullenly.

From then on Jan and Harry often took turns to lead the horses. Sometimes the animals would walk on by themselves, encouraged only by the reins slapping across their backs. But there were also times when Jan and Harry watched unprotesting as Watson plied the whip. The Karoo changed one's view of life.

The longer the journey across this desert lasted, the more their discomforts grew. Despite the intense heat, Watson insisted that they should wear their shirts at all times as protection against sunburn, but even so the backs of their hands and their faces were badly affected. Hatless, Harry wore a handkerchief knotted over his head. Although they walked often, their ankles became swollen, making every movement painful. Worst of all was the torment of thirst. The waggon was loaded with many cans of water, but this was reserved primarily for the horses, and during the day the men could allow themselves only tiny sips from their water-bottles. They prayed for the evening to come, when they would make camp and prepare the main meal of the day. The mealies made a sickly, tasteless mush and the biltong took an age to chew, like old leather in their mouths, but at least it satisfied their hunger, and there was the almost blissful accompaniment of a whole cup of coffee.

As soon as they had eaten, they dropped into an exhausted sleep, lying on the bare ground, a thin blanket over them, for the temperature dropped sharply at night, using their jackets as pillows and making a small hollow for their hip-bones. They were barely conscious of the discomfort, though perhaps that was why their sleep seemed to provide no real refreshment, and to complete their misery, they would find when they awoke that they had once again provided a feast for the insatiable mosquitoes.

'Oh, for a hill!' Harry said wearily one day. 'Or even one of those perishing thorn trees.'

Jan nodded. But what he missed most was the presence of other people. It was like being marooned, as though the three of them were totally alone on a limitless desert island. 'Do any people live here?' he asked Watson.

'In the Karoo?' He laughed. 'Only a few Bushmen – and they need their heads looking at, if you ask me.'

Once a well-equipped waggon with a team of twelve oxen passed them.

'I thought you said we could go faster than oxen,' Harry said. Their pace was unbelievably slow, for the horses were near to dropping, and needed longer and longer periods of rest. 'These horses seem to be going to a funeral. Only thing is I'm not sure whether it's theirs or mine.'

'You trying to be funny?' Watson said.

Harry sighed and plodded on. There was nothing else to do.

The journey was made worse by the fact that though the Karoo seemed flat and featureless, the terrain was broken here and there by creek and river beds. Those that held water were a welcome sight; the horses could have their fill, and the men could drink and wash and replenish cans and water-bottles. The trouble was, however, that all the creeks seemed to have steep banks, and the waggon had to be manhandled down one side, across the stream and up the other bank. It took all their efforts.

After struggling across the Karoo for over a week, they came to yet another dry river bed. They unloaded the waggon, carried their goods across, unharnessed the horses and led them to the other side, and came back for the waggon. Slowly, in a routine that had become familiar, they lowered it down the bank. Watson, his muscles swelling with the strain, had the strength of two men as he heaved and pushed at the dead weight, and then crawled underneath to life the waggon an inch or two on his back. As they were hauling it up the opposite bank, a loud crack echoed across the veld. The two rear wheels splayed outwards, and the back of the waggon settled on the ground.

Watson swore at length, and then sat in an attitude of dejection. 'The bloody back axle's gone!'

Jan and Harry looked at him in dismay, waiting for him to make some move, but he stayed where he was, muttering to himself.

'Isn't there anything we can do?' Harry cried. 'We're not stuck here for good, are we?'

'Of course we're not stuck here for good. Get the axe. We'll use that young stinkwood over there.'

Quite often along the banks of the creeks there would be a little vegetation and an odd tree or two. The stinkwood, Watson said – 'You'll have to put up with the smell!' – was hard enough to be just what they needed. The trunk was not very thick, and they chopped it down easily enough. Shaping it into an axle was much more difficult, especially as the only suitable tools that Watson had were a mallet and a blunt chisel.

'I think,' Jan said, 'I prefer trying to cleave diamonds.'

It took them almost all the daylight to complete the task, but at last they had a rough and ready axle which they were able to fix in place.

'Supposing it had broken where there wasn't a tree we could use?'

Watson grinned. 'Then you and your mate would have had to walk until you found one, and then you'd have to cut it down and drag it back to the waggon. But most of the breakages happen in these damned creeks, and there's usually something around to repair 'em with.'

Their crossing of the Karoo took ten days. Thereafter the territory became easier, and there was a low scrub, dotted with occasional thorn trees, some of which bore the strange hanging nests of weaver birds. But it seemed an inhospitable land in every way, and their weariness stretched the journey interminably. Deep lines of tiredness were etched into their faces, and neither Jan nor Harry found it easy to laugh. Even Watson was subdued. Jan thought it strange that anyone should be prepared, even with passengers at fifteen pounds each, to make such a trip regularly, but when he asked about it, Watson simply replied, 'It's a living,' and refused to be drawn further.

Once out of the Karoo, however, much of his cheeriness returned, and he enlivened the boredom of the journey with information about the plants and animals of the veld and reminiscences of his life as a sailor. Jan sometimes wondered whether either the information or the reminiscences were entirely accurate – Watson seemed too young to have done all he described – but kept his suspicions to himself.

Curiously, Watson seemed reluctant to talk in any detail about New Rush. Jan and Harry tried several times to get him to describe the place and the diggings, but he nearly always replied, 'You'll see soon enough.'

'Why won't he tell us about New Rush?' Harry asked Jan one day.

'I don't know. Perhaps there's something he doesn't want us to know.'

'Like what?'

'I don't know that either. Just be on your guard when we get there.'

'You think he may be up to something?'

'Probably not, but it's best to be prepared.'

Although Watson refused to give them information about the diggings, he was more forthcoming when Harry asked whether there were any women in New Rush. 'Oh, yes,' he said. 'Not many, and most of 'em are married and their husbands keep a very close eye on 'em. Then there are a few singers and dancers and such like, who entertain in the canteens, but don't get any fancy ideas about 'em, me hearty – they're mostly fully booked, you might say.' He wagged his finger. 'And that applies most of all to Kate Jessup. Any monkey business with her, and you'll have yours truly to reckon with. Mind you, you're welcome to come and hear her sing. Any night in the Ace of Diamonds.'

'Is that a whorehouse?' Harry asked.

'Bloody hell, no! It's a canteen, a bar.'

'Are there any whorehouses?'

'Of course. Very pricey, though. If you want to dip your wick, me hearty, your best bet is a bit of black stuff. Plenty of that around, and cheap too. You can even get one to live in with you – cook your meals, and so on. Specially the so on part. You could share her between the two of you.' He laughed uproariously at the thought. 'Have a word with me mate, George Bell. He'll be able to fix you up.'

On the twentieth morning after leaving Wellington, they were riding slowly along when Watson suddenly stopped whistling and pointed ahead. On the horizon was a small blue smudge. 'That's it! That's New Rush!'

Jan and Harry strained to see, their exhaustion dropping away. With maddening slowness, the blue smudge became a group of tents and shacks.

'There are no trees,' Jan remarked.

'All been cut down for fuel,' Watson explained.

Another mile or so and they began to appreciate the size of the community, much more of a town than Wellington had been. The tents seemed to stretch far into the distance, and beyond them they could just make out the shape of many low buildings. Then suddenly they were within the boundaries of New Rush, passing scores of tents, massed together in camps.

'These are where the men who can't afford a claim live,' Watson told them. 'They get the ground – the earth, that is – that the diggers have combed through and discarded, and they go through it once more, and sometimes they're lucky and find a small stone that's been missed.'

The camps gave way to rudimentary houses constructed of canvas, and then, as they approached Market Square, the centre of New Rush, they saw wooden houses and shops and hotels and bars, all single-storeyed, with roofs of corrugated iron. The streets of beaten earth, reddish in colour, were thronged with men, the Kaffirs all but naked, the white men often bare-chested. There was an air of purposeful activity everywhere. Jan and Harry pointed out the sights to each other, laughing and bubbling with excitement.

Apart from its unexpected size and bustle, two other things about New Rush were notable. One was the stench which hung over the whole community – a smell of excrement and rotting food. It seemed to come in waves, as the breeze carried it towards or away from the nostrils. 'There've never been any proper latrines,' Watson said. 'Just trenches. Everyone uses the same place – if they can stand the smell – and it stinks to high heaven. They heave all the rotten meat and vegetables there too, and any sort of rubbish. Proper midden it is.' The second thing was the flies. They were everywhere in armies, settling on your hands, your face, on any and every object they could find. 'Come from them latrines,' Watson said. 'Stands to reason. Places like that are bound to breed the little bastards.'

Jan did not care about the stench or the flies. No doubt there was much squalor in New Rush, and few amenities, and life there was rough and hard. But it seemed to him that his whole life had been directed towards this place, and now that he had reached it at last he knew it was where his destiny lay. He belonged here, he would prove himself here, and here he would make the name Shapiro famous.

4

Market Square, New Rush, was a wide open space crowded with waggons and carts and oxen and horses and mules and busy humanity. Watson drove slowly along, looking in vain for a space to pull up. He flicked his whip at the tired horses, driving them back to the main street. 'We'll try the London Hotel, me hearties. What do you say to a bath and a thumping great meal, with a bit of honest liquor to wash it down, and then a good night's sleep?'

'And even the ranks of Tuscany could scarce forbear to cheer!' Harry quoted. 'Macaulay,' he explained. '*The Lays of Ancient Rome*. Oh, never mind. The general idea, friend Watson, is that Mr Shapiro and I approve your plan.'

Jan and Harry had expected the London Hotel to be a grander establishment than the large, barn-like hut of corrugated iron to which Watson took them. However, after they had unloaded their gear and stabled the horses, it seemed like luxury to down a stiff brandy, to go out to the rear and wash the dirt away under the primitive shower of a water-bucket with a rope to tip it, and then to gulp down a meal of fried steak and bread which tasted better than anything they could remember.

Private rooms were not to be had, and they bedded down in a dormitory, the floor of which was covered with thin, straw-filled mattresses.

'Good night,' said Harry. But Jan was already asleep.

*　　*　　*

After breakfast, Watson took them to meet George Bell. His office was a small wooden shack, sparsely furnished with a desk, a chair, a couple of wooden benches and an impressive-

44

looking safe. It seemed dark inside after the bright sunlight, and the air was thick with cigar smoke.

Bell came to meet them as Watson made the introductions. He wore a black suit of good quality cloth, with a heavy gold chain across his old-fashioned embroidered waistcoat. A large diamond gypsy-style ring glinted on his little finger. 'Pleased to meet you, gents.' He waved his cigar towards one of the benches. 'Have a seat. Good trip, Watson?'

'So-so. Mr Bell, these two gentlemen was wanting to buy a claim. I told 'em you might be able to help.'

Bell grunted, and ran a hand over his bald head. 'Not a lot going at the moment.' He turned to a chart pinned on the wall, which showed a roughly circular shape divided into small rectangles, each of which bore a number and a name. Some names had been crossed out and new ones written in. Above the circle in crude capitals were the words 'Colesberg Kopje'. Bell tapped the chart. 'These are all the best claims,' he said, 'but there's nothing much going here. Chaps who own these aren't usually in a hurry to get rid of them.' He paused and peered short-sightedly at the chart, muttering under his breath. He stabbed at one of the rectangles with a stubby finger. 'Now I might, I just might be able to persuade old Ruddock to sell. But he'd want a hundred quid, I reckon, maybe more. Put my commission on, and it'd cost you in the region of a hundred and twenty – say, a hundred and fifty at the outside. How about that?'

Jan shook his head. 'I haven't got that much.'

'Then I can't be of help to you, gents. Sorry. Things have been going wild since you were here last, Watson. Prices have gone sky-high. You remember that claim I sold to the fellow you brought out last time. What did I charge him? Forty quid, wasn't it? He's got out already. Pulled a monkey.' He smiled. 'That's New Rush jargon – means he found a diamond weighing over fifty carats. "That's all I need," he says, and he's off back to the Cape on the next Inland Transport. You know what I paid him to get the claim back? Eighty pounds! And that was three weeks ago. And I resold it within the hour for ninety-five.'

'Come on, Mr Bell,' Watson said. 'These gents are mates of mine. You must have something.'

'How much can you afford?' Bell asked Jan.

'Thirty pounds.'

'Thirty pounds!' Bell's fat jowls shook as he laughed. 'That's a good one, that is. You won't get anything worth having for thirty pounds.'

'What about those new claims you had, Mr Bell?' Watson asked. 'The ones out on Mijnheer de Jong's farm.'

'Ah, they're no good.' He turned to another paper tacked to the wall. It showed four rectangles like those on the chart of Colesberg Kopje. 'I've only sold one, and that was to a chap who was absolutely desperate to get something. I warned him. "I've no proof there's any diamonds there," I said. But he wouldn't be put off. You see, gents, there's so much diamond-bearing ground around here, I thought it might be worth taking the chance when old de Jong offered me that small bit of land. Just enough for four claims. But I'd be cheating you if I sold you one of those.'

The door of the office burst open and a red-haired man rushed into the room. He wore threadbare moleskin trousers and a brown jersey, faded and dirty, and carried an old, shapeless hat. 'Look!' he cried. 'Look, Mr Bell! Found it this morning.' Between his horny fingers he held a small stone, which he thrust under Bell's nose. 'Just look at that! Six or seven carats.'

'Well, I'm buggered!' Bell exclaimed. He took the stone from the man and examined it carefully. 'Sorry for the vulgarity, gents, but this is the last thing I expected. This is Mr Glover. He's the chap I was telling you about – the one who bought one of the claims on de Jong's farm.' He turned to Glover. 'You found it this morning? On the claim?'

'That's right!' He put out his hand for the diamond, and then kissed the stone. 'Ain't it a beauty? A few more like that and I'll be living the life of Riley. First thing I thought was I got to show this to Mr Bell. Show him he was wrong.'

Bell was still sceptical. 'You're telling me you got this from the claim I sold you?'

'I'll show you the very spot. Come on!'

'I can't come out now. I'm talking to these gentlemen.'

'They can come too.'

Bell looked at Jan and Harry. 'What about it, gents? Want to see?'

'Why not?'

They left the office and, with the broadly smiling Glover excitedly leading the way, walked along the dusty streets of New Rush, across Market Square, and back past the wooden buildings that Jan and Harry had seen as they entered the town the previous day. As soon as the main streets were behind them, Glover turned off on to a narrow track, and a couple of hundred yards farther on stopped at a small stretch of ground from which all the shrubs and other plants had been cleared. It was divided into four sections, each about thirty foot square, marked off by posts and strings. Three of them had a rough notice planted in the earth, 'Property of G. Bell'. On the fourth claim, at one side, Glover's tent was pitched, and at the far end was a fairly deep hole. A further clearing had been made beyond the claim, and the earth excavated from the hole had been piled there, beside a strange wooden contraption which looked like two large trays, one above the other, supported on table legs. Nearby were a bucket and a couple of shovels.

Glover leaped into the hole. 'That's where it was,' he cried, pointing. 'Just there. Maybe there's another right near it.' He seized a pick and began to loosen the soil in the hole.

Jan and Harry stepped nearer to watch, as Glover broke up the clods of earth. He worked feverishly for a while, but apparently without success. When he straightened his back for a breather, Harry asked him, 'What's that thing?' He pointed to the wooden trays.

'A puddling box, of course. Never seen a puddling box before? Them two trays has mesh in them, one coarse, one fine, like sieves. You break the ground up, put it in the top tray, and wash it, see? Then you can sort through the gravel that's left. Same with the other tray.'

Bell and Watson were standing a few yards away, talking in low voices.

Harry went over to them. 'Are these other claims for sale? Can we buy one of these?'

Bell puffed at the cigar he had just lit, smiled, and put his plump hand on Harry's shoulder. 'My dear young man, no, you can't. First off, if I sold these plots at all I'd have to charge thirty-five to forty quid, just to make a small profit on them, and second, that diamond Glover found is just a fluke. I wouldn't sell you one of these claims, not seeing you're pals of Black Conrad. Too honest, that's my trouble.'

'How do you know it's a fluke? You said all the land around New Rush is full of diamonds.'

'So it is, so it is. But not here.'

'Where you find one diamond you'll always find another, Mr Bell,' said Watson. 'If I took a pick to that next door claim, I bet I'd find something.'

'I've no time for such nonsense,' Bell declared. 'I've got to get back to the office. Watson! What the hell do you think you're doing?'

Watson had already grabbed the pick from Glover, and was hacking at the ground on the neighbouring claim.

'Watson!' Bell screamed. 'For Christ's sake, stop fooling about!'

He took no notice, but continued to attack the earth, putting all his strength into the blows. In a matter of moments he had broken up a small patch of the claim to a depth of almost a foot.

'I'm going back to the office,' Bell shouted. 'If you're not back in fifteen minutes, you're sacked. You hear me, Watson?' He turned to Jan and Harry. 'Sorry, gents. There's nothing I can do for you this time, I'm afraid. I'm sorry that idiot Watson misled you.'

He began to walk away, when there was a great cry from Watson. 'I seen one!' He was scrabbling through the earth with both hands. 'No, lost it. I swear I saw one. Ah, damn it!' He spat in disgust, and then suddenly the triumph was back in his voice. 'There it is! I knew I seen it. Come on, my little darling.' He held up a tiny pebble.

Bell had turned back. 'Give it here,' he said, and when Watson had reluctantly handed it over, examined the stone carefully. 'Well, I'm buggered! He's right! It's a diamond all right. Well, I'm blowed! Maybe it's not such a bad day after all.' He put the little stone in his waistcoat pocket.

'Here! I found it,' Watson said.

'It's my land, so it's my diamond. A carat and a half, I reckon. Not enough to make me rich, but worth having, all the same.'

'Can I see it?' Jan asked. 'Hold it, I mean.'

'What's the matter? Don't believe it's a diamond? All right. Here.'

Jan rubbed his fingers over the stone. It had the right feel, the slightly soapy texture of a rough diamond. He looked at it in his palm, and it gleamed in the sunlight. He took out his loupe and examined the stone more carefully.

Bell watched him curiously. 'Know about diamonds, do you?'

'A little.' The stone appeared to be of good quality, almost without flaws, and a little larger than Bell had said – at least two full carats, he would guess.

'It's real?' Harry asked.

Jan nodded, as he handed the diamond back to Bell.

'Then maybe it's worth buying this claim.'

'No,' said Bell. 'I really can't advise you to do that.'

'He's going to keep it,' Watson said, with a malicious chuckle, 'now he's seen for himself there's diamonds in it.'

'Shut up!' Bell hissed. 'It's not that, gents, I swear it. But even if you insist on buying it, I can't sell it to you, much as I'd like to. Thirty-five quid I need, as an absolute minimum, and you said your top limit was thirty. You're sure that's your top price?'

'I could put another two pounds, I suppose,' Jan said.

'There you are, Mr Bell,' Watson put in. 'Thirty-two quid. You're not going to lose on that. *And* you've got that diamond – the one *I* found.'

'I'll have to think about it,' Bell said. 'We'd better go back to the office. I need to work out some figures.'

The four of them set off back towards the town, leaving Glover working on the claim. They had gone only a short distance when Bell said, 'Walk slowly, boys. I'll catch you up.' He hurried back to the claims.

Jan looked round and saw him talking to Glover. He took something from his pocket, handed it over, and received something in exchange. When he caught them up again, much out of breath, he was jubilant. 'Bought that diamond Glover found,' he panted. 'Gave him a good price, and I'll still make a bit on it. I'll sell it to a licensed merchant, of course – we've all got to do our best to stamp out illegal diamond buying. Well, it's my lucky day, gents – and yours.' He took Watson's arm and drew him slightly ahead. They were an ill-assorted couple, Bell short and fat beside the tall figure of Black Conrad. 'Excuse us,' he said over his shoulder to Jan and Harry. 'Bit of business to discuss.'

As they followed, Harry punched Jan lightly on the arm.

'What about that, then? He's going to sell it to us, I'm sure.'

'We've got to be careful. How do we know he owns that bit of land? If we do buy it, what proof of ownership will he give us?'

When they got back to the office, Bell excused himself. 'First things first, gents. Got to put these two little pretties where they'll be safe.' He took the two diamonds from his waistcoat pocket, wrapped them carefully in separate sheets of paper, and then, with his back to Jan and Harry, opened the safe and put the packets inside.

'Thirty-two pounds,' he said reflectively as he turned to face them again. 'Thirty-two little quidlets . . .' He appeared suddenly to make up his mind. 'All right. I'm all kinds of a fool, but I've taken a shine to you two lads, and since you're friends of Black Conrad . . . I tell you what I'll do – make it thirty-three quid, and the claim's yours.'

'Chortle!' said Harry.

'You have proof of ownership, Mr Bell?' Jan asked.

Bell looked at him and shook his head with a sad smile. 'I'm afraid I've forgotten your name, sir.'

'Shapiro.'

'Ah, yes. Well, Mr Shapiro, you have a suspicious nature, if I may say so. But you're right, you're quite right to ask. Yes, of course I have proof of ownership, and you shall see it.' He took a piece of paper from a drawer of his desk, and handed it to Jan.

It was an official-looking letter, on paper headed, 'A. Greatorex, Solicitor, New Rush, Orange Free State.' Beneath that, in neat copperplate writing were the words, 'To Whom It May Concern: This document confirms that, in consideration of payments made to me, Cornelis de Jong, farmer, by George Bell, land agent, the plot of land on my farm henceforth known as Claims Nos. 1041, 1042, 1043 and 1044 is the sole property of the said George Bell.' It was signed clearly, 'Cornelis de Jong,' and witnessed by the solicitor.

'If these claims are so full of diamonds,' Jan said, 'why haven't they been opened up before?'

'My dear boy, there are new claims everywhere. New Rush isn't the only place, you know – there's Bultfontein and Dutoitspan – there are big diggings there – and the river diggings, and hundreds of other sites as well. Now then, you want to buy? Yes or no?'

Jan hesitated once more, aware that Harry was looking at him eagerly. He took a deep breath. 'Yes,' he said.

'Right. Now a few more questions before it's a deal. I've pushed you up to thirty-three pounds, and I know you didn't want to pay that much. Does it leave you with anything at all?'

'A few pounds more. Why?'

'I'm not going to have you say I left you penniless. And there are other things you'll need. You've got a tent?'

'Yes.'

'You can pitch that on the claim, like Glover. That'll save you rent. What about picks and shovels, a sledgehammer, a couple of buckets, wood for a puddling box? You got any of those?'

Harry patted his pockets as though these pieces of equipment might be lurking within one of them. 'No,' he said. 'Not one.'

'I can let you have all you need, cheap. Say another three quid the lot. And then you'll have to buy food. And of course you'll have to register.'

'Register?'

'Every digger has to have a licence from the government. Costs you five shillings a month, and gives your claim number and so on. You'll have to go to the offices of the Diggers' Committee for that – I'll tell you where to find them – and you need two people to vouch for you. As a matter of fact, I've got some forms already made out with a couple of signatures to vouch for whatever name I put in. A couple of bob each, and well worth it. No, I tell you what – I'll throw it in for free. And the vouching doesn't mean anything, so we might as well get round it if we can, eh?' He winked at them.

'What is this Diggers' Committee?' Jan asked.

'Ah, the diggers elected them to keep law and order and run the diggings. The State – the Orange Free State, that is – supports them. Bloody nuisance, they are, if you'll pardon the language. Well, now then, you've got enough money to cover all these little extras?'

'I think so.'

'Good. Then we can draw up our agreement. Watson, you go and get pickaxes and shovels and all the rest. Make sure you give 'em good ones, mind.' Watson went out. Bell wrote busily for a few minutes, evidently copying from other papers. He passed over two sheets. 'I'll sign this one as soon as you've paid me the money and signed the second one.'

The first paper said, 'Received from Mr Shapiro the sum of £33 in payment for Claim No. 1043, being land 30ft by 30ft, the third plot along the road from New Rush to Mijnheer de Jong's farm, the same having been purchased from Mijnheer de Jong by me, George Bell, land agent.' The second bore the words, 'In purchasing Claim No. 1043 from George Bell, I acknowledge that I have done so of my own free will, knowing that the said George Bell can make no guarantee as to the diamond-bearing quality of the said claim, and I agree to absolve the said George Bell from all responsibility in this matter and promise that I will make no claim against him whatsoever for any reason.'

Bell smiled apologetically. 'That doesn't mean anything – you saw for yourself that the soil's full of diamonds – but my lawyer friend insists that I should always have a signed statement like that, just to protect myself from rogues. Not that I think you're a rogue, of course.'

Jan got out his money and counted thirty-three pounds on to the table, borrowed Bell's pen and signed the second paper. Bell signed the receipt and handed it over, and then opened the safe again and put the money inside. Returning to his desk, he said, 'And the additional three pounds, Mr Shapiro. For the equipment.'

'I haven't seen that yet,' Jan said.

'My, you are suspicious. You think I'd try to cheat you? Anyway, here's Watson.'

Black Conrad had arrived outside the office, with a collection of implements, which Jan was happy to see all appeared to be in reasonable condition. He paid over the three pounds, and with many expressions of friendship and good luck wishes, Bell and Watson shook hands with them both, and gave them directions for the office of the Diggers' Committee.

Once in the street, Harry performed one of his little dances of celebration. 'We're in business, partner,' he cried. 'When we've done this registration, I'm going to spend my last sixpence on a drink for us both. And then we'll get started on finding those four enormous, whopping great diamonds!'

5

Once they had swallowed their Cape brandies, toasting each other, Jan and Harry hurried back to their claim. They had obtained the licence from the Diggers' Committee without difficulty, though the official had raised his eyebrows when he had studied the form which Bell had given them, and said, 'Diamonds on de Jong's farm?'

'Yes,' said Harry. 'They found a couple of good ones only this morning.'

The man smiled. 'You'd be better off at Colesberg Kopje.'

'We can't afford that.'

'No,' said the man. 'I don't suppose you can.'

When they reached the claim, they were surprised to see no sign of Glover. Even his tent had gone.

They pitched their own tent, and then started straightway to dig. It was gruelling work under the fierce sun, and the soil was baked hard, so that their progress was slow. They found no diamonds, but perhaps it was too much to expect that they would strike lucky so soon. If Watson had not found that stone, one of their own picks might have turned it up, and their frustration would have turned to celebration.

Late in the afternoon, they decided to break off and to go back to the centre of New Rush. They had to buy food and replenish their water-bottles and get a drum in which they could store water. And above all they needed a meal.

They made their purchases and ate their fill, and then decided that, extravagant though it might be, this day of excitement needed to be rounded off by one more glass of spirits. They turned into the Cat and Gridiron, one of the most popular canteens in New Rush. It was a noisy, raucous place, filled thickly with tobacco smoke and the smells of the beer and liquor, the sawdust on the floor, the sweat and dirt of the customers. Jan and Harry jostled their way to the bar and ordered their drinks.

A man standing beside them turned as he heard Harry speak. 'That's an English voice, or I'm a Dutchman.'

'No, he's the Dutchman,' Harry laughed, pointing at Jan. 'He's Jan Shapiro, from Amsterdam. But you're right about me – I'm English. Harry Templeton's the name.'

'Tom Allenby.' He shook hands with them both.

'You're from the West country, Mr Allenby?' Harry asked.

'Born and bred in Plymouth.'

'Couldn't mistake that burr,' Harry went on. 'My mother comes from Devon – from up along Barnstaple.'

'Then you've got good blood in you, m'dear. New in town?'

'Yes. Arrived last night. And you, sir?'

'Oh, I've been here a good couple of months.' He eyed them, noting their dirt-stained hands and faces. 'Looks as though you've been digging already. Where's your claim?'

'On Mijnheer de Jong's farm.'

Tom Allenby opened his mouth to speak, but stopped himself and seemed about to turn away. Then he changed his mind, smiled, and said, 'Let me buy you a drink.'

Harry and Jan protested, but then accepted his generosity. 'You were going to say something just now, Mr Allenby,' Jan said.

'Was I? Oh, yes. Yes. Well, least said, soonest mended.'

'Please speak your mind.'

'Well, 'tis none of my business, but as far as I know there are no diamonds in that direction. The seam of diamondiferous ground – they call it a pipe, y'know – doesn't extend that far. Different kind of earth, y'see.'

'But there are diamonds there. One was found on our claim just before we bought it, and one on the claim next door.'

'Did you see them found?'

'The one on our claim, yes.'

Allenby hesitated again for a moment, and then said, 'Well, I wish you luck, m'dears.' He turned away.

Jan tapped him on the shoulder. 'A moment longer of your time, Mr Allenby, if you please. I think you were going to say something more, and whatever it is, I'd like to hear it.'

Allenby turned back. 'Very well, Mr Shapiro. As I say, 'tis

54

no business of mine, and I may well be wrong, but I have some doubts about your claim. How did you get it?'

'A man called George Bell sold it to us.'

Allenby grimaced. 'One of the biggest rogues in town! How did you fall in with him?'

'We were introduced by the man who drove us here from Wellington.'

'Black Conrad, no doubt. Another good-for-nothing. What did he charge you for the trip?'

'Fifteen pounds each.'

'Were there no others offering transport? Most of them charge no more than ten.'

'It was Watson who found the diamond on our claim,' Harry said. 'It was lying just a few inches under the ground.'

'A real diamond? Are you sure?'

'Yes,' Jan said. 'I've been in the diamond business. I know a rough diamond when I see one.'

'I thought it was probably a piece of glass,' Allenby said. 'They do that to fool the greenhorns – break a bottle and file one of the fragments to the shape of a diamond. If Bell used a real one, then he must be in the money.'

'What do you mean? He didn't "use" anything. I tell you Watson found the diamond in the ground. We both saw it.'

'You saw him pick something up from the ground – something that was already in his hand. They tricked you, m'dears. No doubt Bell put the stone away quickly enough and said anything found there belonged to him.'

'But the chap on the next claim found a diamond this morning.'

'Ginger hair, old clothes, name of Grover, or something like that?' Allenby smiled grimly. 'One of Bell's toadies. Gets a few bob for putting on that act, I shouldn't wonder.'

'You seem to know the whole story,' Jan said.

'I've heard it before.'

'But he did own that land,' Harry persisted. 'He showed Jan a paper saying that it was his.'

' "Tis easy enough to buy a plot like that,' Allenby replied. 'Probably cost him a couple of quid at the most.'

There was a long pause, and then Harry said, 'We'll go to the law. We can sue him for false pretences.'

Tom Allenby shook his head. 'He usually gets his victims to

sign a paper saying that he guarantees them nothing and that they have no claim on him. Isn't that right?'

Jan nodded miserably. The full extent of the disaster was now apparent to him. George Bell had sold them a pup, and where would they get the money to buy a real claim, at a hundred pounds or more? So much for proving himself to his father and bringing glory to his name.

Harry too recognised how bad this news was, but it was not his money that had been lost, and from a selfish point of view he was little worse off than he had been before, except perhaps in a hurt to his pride. But that thought lasted for a moment only – he was Jan's friend and partner, and they were both in this together and would have to fight their way out of it together, though how they were going to do it, he had no idea. 'You're saying that our claim is worthless. Totally worthless? Isn't it possible that there are diamonds there – a few?'

Tom Allenby shook his head. 'I doubt it, m'dear. You might find an odd stone that's been washed there, but it's away from the pipe. A pipe's not usually more than about five hundred feet across, and you'm nearly a mile from Colesberg Kopje.'

'Why didn't they tell us at the Diggers' Committee when we registered?' Jan asked. 'Aren't they supposed to control law and order?'

'George Bell never breaks the law – leastways, not so he can be caught. If people fall for his tricks, that's their look-out, I'm afraid. The Diggers' Committee can't be responsible.'

'Then they're not much use, are they?'

'There'd be chaos without them. For instance, 'tis they who make sure there are roads across the diggings – the main diggings, I mean. You know the claims are all thirty feet by thirty feet – well, everyone's had to give up seven and a half feet of his claim so that there are roads fifteen feet wide all across the mine. Makes sense. Otherwise we'd never be able to get the ground out. There's no system like that at Dutoitspan, and the paths there are always collapsing.'

There was a brief silence.

'Supposing I want to become a diamond merchant here?' Jan asked.

Allenby smiled. ' 'Tisn't easy. You need two people to stand surety in the sum of a hundred pounds each, and you have to be bound yourself for a hundred pounds. And the licence will cost you fifty quid.'

That was the end of another possibility. 'Thanks for the drink, Mr Allenby,' Jan said. 'And the information. Come on, Harry. We'd better go.'

'Just a minute,' Allenby said. 'You look as though you could use a little help. You got any money?'

'A few shillings.'

'I'll lend you a quid.'

Jan looked at him in amazement. 'But you don't know us.'

'I know an honest man when I see him. Go on.' He took out a worn wallet and extracted a pound note. 'Pay me back when you can. Or don't pay me back. I'm flush. Found a big one today.'

'No, thank you,' Jan said. 'We appreciate the offer, but we can't take your money.'

'Who can't?' said Harry, grasping the note. 'I'll pay you back, Mr Allenby, have no fear. The Templetons have been famous throughout history for two things – one is failing their exams, and the other is paying their debts.'

Allenby laughed. He shook hands with Jan. 'You're a fool, young feller, but I like your pride.' He turned to Harry. 'And I like a man who takes a chance when it's offered.'

They thanked him again, and left the canteen.

'I thought you told me your mother came from Scotland,' Jan said.

'She does.'

'But you told Mr Allenby she was from the West country.'

'Didn't do us any harm, did it?' Harry said.

They walked disconsolately back towards their claim and their tent. As they made their way along the crowded street, they could see and hear a great throng of shouting men. Flares illuminated a roughly square space in which two men were fighting. One was a thick-set bull of a man, as solid as a mountain, crouched in a professional boxer's stance. His opponent was much taller and broader, but it was obvious that he knew little of the art of pugilism, and though his wildly swung punches might have been damaging if they had landed, the other man dodged them with ease, and every now and then darted in to throw a punishing blow of his own.

As Jan and Harry joined the crowd, the shorter man landed a

hard jab to the heart, following with a right hook on the point of his opponent's jaw. The giant sank sprawling to the ground. Most of the spectators cheered wildly, but a few turned away in angry disappointment, and stumped off. The big man's friends carried him away, still unconscious, while the winner sat down and towelled himself.

A thin, cadaverous-faced man came into the centre of the ring. 'Who's next?' he cried, in a deep and penetrating voice. 'Five bob for anyone who can last three rounds with Ned Smith, Heavyweight Champion of Cape Province and the Orange Free State. Come on, gents. Just three rounds, see? Easiest money you'll ever make. What about you, sir? You got a fist on you.'

The man was much shorter than Ned Smith's previous opponent, but as he stripped off his coat he revealed powerful arms and shoulders. Smith eyed him contemptuously as the barker explained the rules of the contest.

The fight began, and this time Smith had a much harder job. His opponent danced and weaved surprisingly lightly. For a while, neither did much damage to the other, and the crowd began to jeer and whistle. This brought them together in a flurry of hard-hitting blows, from which the challenger emerged with a bloodied nose, while there was an angry mark on Ned Smith's cheekbone. In the second round he treated his opponent with considerable respect, using all his skill to dodge the worst blows, and stepping in now and then to jab at his face. The crowd quietened, sensing the possibility of a defeat for Smith, and then, as the fight continued in much the same way, began to shout excitedly, applauding the challenger's every punch. In the last seconds of the third round, Smith seemed to call on his reserves of strength and advanced relentlessly, his fists flailing the other man, who retreated before the onslaught, though the crowd tried to rally him by yelling their encouragement.

A great sigh of disappointment came as Smith swung a lucky blow to the temple, struck with such force that the other man staggered, slipped and crashed to the ground. Ned raised his arms in triumph, and the onlookers, despite the defeat of their favourite, cheered his skill. He looked weary, though, and after a brief whispered conversation with him, his manager announced, 'That's all, boys – all for tonight. We'll be back tomorrow, and it's five bob to anyone who lasts three rounds on his feet.'

The crowd drifted away, Jan and Harry with them. Although at first his mind had been full of Bell and Watson and their villainy, Jan had become absorbed in the fight, admiring the professional's technique, and wondering how he himself would have fared. As he and Harry walked back to their claim, his spirits had lifted. The mistake was behind them now, and they would simply have to decide on a new course of action and take it. Somehow he would make his way in South Africa. He would never go back to Amsterdam until he had made enough money to do so in style and to show his father that he was a success.

'What are we going to do?' Harry asked.

'Have a good night's sleep, and look for work in the morning. If we get jobs and save every penny, maybe we'll still be able to buy a decent claim.'

'The prices are going up all the time.'

'Then the sooner we start earning the better.'

'I know where you could get five bob tomorrow. You've only got to stand up to that chap for three rounds.'

'Apart from the fact that he's about twice as heavy as I am, he's a professional. And I haven't boxed for months.'

'You fought those thugs in Cape Town.'

'That wasn't boxing.'

'What's the matter?' Harry asked after a moment's silence. 'Afraid?'

'No.'

'Then what's stopping you? You may be out of practice, but at least you'd know what you were doing. Those characters he was fighting had never been in a ring before, if you ask me.'

'The second one had.'

'That's not the point. There's five bob to be won.'

'I'm not going to fight him, and that's that.'

'Ah well, they say the wisest men are cowards now and then.'

Jan bit back an angry retort, unwilling to quarrel. 'Come on,' he said, and they walked back to the tent and prepared for bed in silence.

Jan lay awake, wondering how he could have been such a fool as to trust Bell and Watson, remembering all that Tom

Allenby had told him, and then hearing again and again Harry's taunt of cowardice. Although he knew it had not been meant seriously and stemmed from Harry's own feelings of frustration, it rankled. He tried to recall all he had seen of Ned Smith's technique. Perhaps he could stay out of trouble for those three rounds, with the advantage of his speed and the defence that Ernie Blakestone had taught him.

He suddenly realised that everything was unnaturally quiet. He could still hear Harry breathing, but outside the tent all noises seemed to have ceased. He became aware of a slight rustling, as though a gentle breeze were sweeping along the ground, and then the sides of the tent began to stir and shake, and the breeze turned in a few moments to a wind, and he could feel it tugging at their guy ropes, and the flap at the entrance began to slap noisily at the taut canvas.

Jan was amazed that Harry had not awoken. The wind increased. It was dark, and he could see nothing, but in addition to the gale battering the tent, he was aware of dust thick in the air. It gritted in his mouth, it was on every part of him, his clothes, the ground. The wind was howling now, and he began to fear for the safety of the tent. He shook Harry awake, and they crawled out. The dust was worse here, and the force of the wind was such that they could barely stand against it.

'If we don't take the tent down, the canvas will tear and the pole will snap.'

'At the moment,' said Harry, 'I believe I could bear that with no more than a brief flicker of the eyelid. However, I suppose you're right.'

Once, with difficulty, they had taken the tent down, they had no protection against the wind, and they draped the canvas around themselves and huddled on the ground, wondering what other misfortune could possibly come their way.

'You would think,' said Harry plaintively, 'that someone would have warned us – bastards who cheat us out of our money . . . well, *your* money . . . and New Rush being cursed with the worst weather in the world. Still, there's one good thing.'

'What?'

'There aren't any flies. Perhaps they've all been blown away.'

He had scarcely finished speaking when the first brilliant flash of lightning almost blinded them. It was followed by the distant heavy roll of thunder. Another jagged lightning flash, and another, and the thunder became almost continuous and deafening. Suddenly rain was falling, great drops which drenched them to the skin in a few moments. It was impossible to find shelter from the downpour, which soaked through everything.

'At least,' said Jan, 'this will settle the dust.'

'And if any of those bloody flies weren't blown away, I reckon this'll drown 'em. Oh, by the way – quack!'

6

The next morning, when the wind had died and the clouds had gone and the sky was clear and blue, the flies were back again. The rain had turned the dust to mud, and the heat of the sun was rapidly changing mud back to dust. Everything they touched was thick with it. They put the tent up again, and tried to brush the dust off their possessions. Then they made breakfast. It tasted of dust. Every mouthful was dust-covered and their tea bore a film of dust.

When they set off into town, they felt tired and dispirited, hardly caring whether or not they found work.

They were making for the central diggings, but on the way there Jan turned off into one of the side streets.

'Where are you going?' Harry asked.

'To have a word with Mr George Bell.'

'What's the use? You won't get anything out of him.'

'I don't expect to.'

Bell was alone when they entered his office. He rose, an ingratiating smile on his lips. 'Ah, Mr Shapiro. And how are you this fine morning? Storm didn't keep you awake, I hope.'

'You cheated us,' Jan said grimly, going up to his desk.

The smile faded. 'Come now, that's a harsh word. How have I cheated you?'

'That claim's worthless, and you know it.'

Bell spread his hands. 'Oh, be reasonable, Mr Shapiro. Did I or did I not advise you against buying? If it's worthless, you have only yourself to blame. And I'd just remind you of that little piece of paper you signed, which states quite clearly that I make no guarantee of the claim's diamond-bearing quality, and that you have no legal grounds for complaint.'

'I know that.'

'Well, then. In any case, Mr Shapiro, you've decided pretty

quickly that the claim's worthless. You go on digging, and I'm sure you'll find more diamonds like those we found yesterday.'

'Which you planted there. You took us in very easily, didn't you? I know I have only my own stupidity to blame for this, but I want you to be sure, Mr Bell, that I have a long memory. I shall not forget, and one day I shall be revenged.'

'Very melodramatic,' Bell sneered. 'Let me know when, and I'll be waiting for you – with my friends. And now you can get out, the pair of you!'

'*Smeerlap!*' Jan spat the word at him.

'I don't know what that means,' Harry said, 'and I don't suppose Mr Bell does either, but I think this will make our sentiments clear.' He leaned forward, picked up the ink-pot on the desk and in one swift movement poured its contents over Bell's head. 'Just something to remember us by.'

He and Jan ran from the office, leaving Bell spluttering with rage, the ink dripping down his face on to his suit and the flamboyant flowered waistcoat.

'That was a stupid thing to do,' Jan said, as they hurried along the road. 'You've made an enemy of him.'

'He was our enemy already,' Harry panted. 'And what about you and your revenge? An eye for an eye and a tooth for a tooth, eh?'

'*Ja!*' said Jan, and there was such an expression on his face that Harry forgot the joke he had been about to make.

They slowed to a walk and headed for the mine. At the end of the main street, which led off Market Square, was a huge pile of earth, known to the diggers as 'Mount Ararat', and formed by the debris from their excavations after the material had been carefully searched for diamonds. Facing it was a row of small, single-storeyed buildings, often wholly constructed of corrugated iron. Signs above the doors proclaimed these shacks to be the premises of diamond merchants, sited so that any digger who found a stone need only walk a few yards to sell it. Jan noticed one office with a sign saying, 'Samuel Rosenberg, Diamond Dealer.' He pointed it out to Harry. 'That's Mr Meier's friend.'

'He's not much use to us now, is he?' said Harry, with unaccustomed gloom.

Just beyond Mount Ararat were the diggings. A huge pit,

several hundred feet across, was divided into squares, and the bottom of the mine was at different levels according to the depth to which the various claims had been excavated. Some of the sides of the claims were vertical, but others had been left sloping so that the diggers could climb up or down them. Roads ran across the pit, allowing access to the claims, and in some places they had become walls as the ground on either side of them had been dug away.

On almost every claim men were working, hacking out the earth and rock with their pickaxes, and loading it in wheel-barrows or on to small waggons, which they pushed or their mules hauled to the surrounds of the pit, where the ground was broken down and crumbled into fragments small enough to be washed, eventually, in puddling boxes. At this time of day, however, the activity was concentrated in the diggings themselves, for the general rule was that the mornings were spent in excavation, while the breaking up and examination of the rock, being a little less strenuous, was a task for the afternoon, when the heat was at its most intense.

Jan and Harry walked along the roads criss-crossing the mine, searching for Tom Allenby. Although it was still quite early in the morning, the heat was already almost unbearable, and the sun beat down from the cloudless sky on the miners and their native workers as they dug. Jan noticed that wher-ever a black man was working, his employer watched him continuously, no doubt to prevent any attempt to pocket a diamond. From time to time, a shout of triumph signalled the discovery of a gemstone, and there were curses too, when a fragment picked out of the rubble turned out to be a worthless pebble.

Presently they saw Tom Allenby. His was one of the deeper claims, and he was working on it alone, the muscles of his arms and back rippling as he drove his pick into the ground, tearing out great chunks of rock. He straightened his back. 'Morning, m'dears. Come to see a real claim?'

'We're looking for work,' Harry said. 'You don't know anyone who wants a couple of hands, do you? Not very experienced, but extremely willing.'

'As a matter of fact, I can do with you myself. Those blasted natives of mine haven't turned up this morning, damn their black hides. You want to do a spot of digging for me?'

'Yes, but we need to be paid for it, and we're already too much in your debt. This is a damned expensive place to live, Mr Allenby. If it hadn't been for the loan you made us we'd be on our beam ends.'

'I'm in no hurry. I'll pay you four bob each for the day. It'll be worth it to me – leave me free to cart this ground to the top.' He showed them where he wanted them to dig. 'Oh, just one thing,' he said before leaving with a wheelbarrow piled high with rock. 'Any diamonds you come across belong to me – right? I reckon I can trust you, but I've seen the most honest of men tempted when there's a diamond they can just pick up and slip in their pockets. You do anything like that, and I'll have you up in front of the Diggers' Committee before you can say "knife", and I wouldn't give much for your chances after that.'

It was harder work than it had been the day before on their own claim, or seemed so, for their muscles were stiff and their hands blistered, and the sun felt even hotter within the vast pit.

Tom Allenby was pleased enough with the amount of ground they had broken when he returned. 'Keep it up. I'm not paying for you to stand and admire the view. Keep on digging, and I'll put your pay up to five bob.'

They toiled for the rest of the day, pausing only at lunch-time, when Tom called them up to the surface, where he had built a small fire. Over it he placed a can of water and a large dixie half full of stew. 'I heat this up every day. Lasts me a week, and boiling it regular keeps it from going off. You should boil your water too. Get away, you pesky bugger!' He waved away a large fly hovering near the stew. 'That's t'other secret – never let the damn flies settle long enough to lay their eggs.'

'We'll pay for the meal, Mr Allenby,' Jan said as they ate.

'Sure you will. I just reduced your rate back to four shillings. You're doing fine, m'dears. Come back tomorrow, if you want. If those lazy black bastards turn up, I shan't be able to use you, but they've probably gone back to the bush. Not like white men, you see. Can't depend on 'em. Stupid and dishonest, all of 'em.'

Jan was not sure how much he liked these remarks, which sounded rather too similar to the things that people sometimes

65

said about Jews too. However, he had no wish to get involved in an argument with Allenby.

They told him of the encounter that morning with Bell. Tom Allenby laughed, but then looked serious, and said, 'He's a bad enemy. You'd better watch out – specially at night. He'll put his thugs on you if he gets the chance. Stay together and keep to the busy streets.' He looked at his pocket watch. 'Hey, it's time to get back to work.'

At the end of the day they received their money and wearily made their way back to the tent. Once they were out of Allenby's sight, Harry handed his four shillings to Jan.

'What's that for?'

'Our agreement. Don't you remember? A hundred per cent to you during the first year.'

'Forget it,' said Jan. 'We're partners. Share and share alike – at least until we start digging for ourselves.'

'Perish the thought. I don't think I ever want to dig another spadeful as long as I live. And I doubt if I'll be able to. I reckon that by tomorrow my muscles'll be so stiff that I'll just have to lie in the tent and starve to death.' He paused, and then said, 'Thanks about the partnership.'

'We're coming back into town tonight,' Jan told him.

'What for?'

'I'm going to stand up to Ned Smith, and earn five shillings.'

'Don't be a fool.'

'You suggested it.'

'And you've changed your tune. Because I called you a coward?'

'No.'

'I didn't mean it.'

'I know.'

'You're mad,' Harry said after a while. 'You're in no condition to face that mauler – not after what we've done today. You look, my friend, like my celebrated dying duck. Don't you feel tired?'

'Yes, but I'll be all right in an hour or so. I'll have a little sleep. Wake me if you wake up first.'

*   *   *

It was the morning sun which woke them.

When they got to the mine, they saw that Allenby's blacks were working alongside him. 'Sorry,' he called. 'Can't use you today. These good-for-nothings have come back. Try Horace Williams, or Alf Taylor – they're mates of mine.' He explained where Williams and Taylor were to be found.

Neither of them wanted to employ two young greenhorns when blacks were so much cheaper. Jan and Harry went back to Market Square to try their luck in the shops and hotels and canteens, but the story was always the same – only the most menial of work was available, and that could be filled more cheaply by black labour.

'Maybe we should go to Dutoitspan,' Harry said. 'There's another mine there.'

'How far is that?'

'A couple of miles, I think.'

'All right. We'll go there. But not till tomorrow. I'm going to get that five shillings tonight.

*   *   *

Later that evening they went to the square where Ned Smith put on his show, and discovered that since it was Saturday the reward for lasting the three rounds had been raised to ten shillings. There was never any lack of contenders, but often befuddled by drink and almost all lacking in skill, few of them gave Smith any problems. Jan watched his technique with interest. In the first round he took things very easily, dancing in and out, sizing up his opponent, seeking out his weaknesses. Some he finished off in the second round, but he usually contented himself with putting in a number of punishing blows to the body, without attempting to knock the man down. The third round was always more serious. The punches became heavier, and sooner or later a right hook, which seemed to be his favourite weapon, would end the contest. After each bout, the barker sent one of his henchmen round the crowd to collect the pennies that formed the only admission charge.

'All you'll get is a bloody nose,' Harry whispered. 'Let's go.'

'No. I'll wait a while. Let him tire himself a bit more.'

He waited nearly an hour. Smith still looked fresh, but Jan noticed that his footwork was not quite as light and that he seemed a little less eager each time to come out of his corner for the next round. When the barker again called for a volunteer, Jan shouted, '*Ja!*' and stripped off his shirt.

There was more laughter than cheering. Although his physique was excellent, Jan looked a mere stripling beside Ned Smith, and his pale skin added to his apparent fragility. Hoping to lure Smith into a false confidence, he stood awkwardly, flat-footed, and allowed his face to show concern, as though he were already regretting having come forward.

Harry was more than ever convinced that Jan was in for a hiding, and when a man sidled up to him and suggested that he might like to have a small bet on his friend, shook his head firmly. The only bet he would have taken was that he was going to have to carry Jan back to their tent that evening. The man shrugged, and moved on to others in the crowd.

Jan made little effort to withstand Smith during the first round, letting his guard drop and swinging ineffectually at his opponent. The blows that landed on his body were not hard enough to worry him, but the spectators, seeing little excitement in this one-sided contest, began to whistle and call for Smith to finish him off quickly, and the prizefighter stepped up his attack. Jan was able to read his intentions quickly enough to duck out of harm's way or to lean back to lessen the force of a blow, but at the end of the round the champion grinned as he went back to his corner. He could polish off this youngster whenever he chose to do so.

When the second round began, he found it much harder to pin Jan down. Although the young man looked clumsy, he kept moving, always retreating, making Smith follow. And whereas before he had had no guard, now he seemed able, time and time again, to cover the target Ned was aiming for.

Jan made little attempt to land blows himself. There was no point in trying to out-punch a heavier, stronger man, and his one aim was to stay on his feet long enough to earn his ten shillings. The crowd, from being against him, began to turn to his side. It was not the kind of slugging match that they preferred, but maybe this kid was actually going to last the distance.

The third round started with a heavy onslaught from Smith, and it took all Jan's skill to survive it. There was no hint of his leaden stance now, and, dancing, weaving and ducking, he began to make the champion look heavy and lumbering. A different look came into Ned's eye. They came together in a clinch, and the prizefighter whispered, 'All right, Mr Clever-Dick. You know 'ow to box, I can see that. But you just see if you can 'it me.' His intention was clearly to allow Jan to land a few punches, during which the young man's defensive guard might drop, giving Ned the chance he needed.

Jan was aware of the trap being laid for him, but could not resist the challenge. He darted in, tapping Smith on the head or chest almost at will. The crowd began to go wild. Jan decided to give them their money's worth, and to show Ned how hard he could hit. Waiting for the opportunity, he came in and landed a punch with most of his weight behind it on Smith's bruised cheekbone. The prizefighter gave a snarl of anger and pain, and rocked back. But he was heavy and experienced enough not to go down, and came forward again, determined to put this cocky young challenger in his place. Jan was beginning to tire rapidly, and the elasticity was leaving his legs. One savage punch made him stumble, and the crowd fell silent, fearing it was all over. Somehow he managed not to fall, and when Smith came in for the kill, found just enough strength to dodge once more.

He began to believe that the round would never end – surely the five minutes must be up. Some of the spectators thought so too, and began to shout and whistle derisively. The barker, holding his watch, was looking at his man anxiously. 'Time!' one of the men yelled. 'The boy's won. Give 'im 'is ten bob!' Others joined in, and reluctantly the barker called an end to the fight. The men cheered.

'You were terrific,' Harry said, as they walked slowly back to their tent. 'I thought you were a goner in the last round, but you stuck it out.'

'I shouldn't have let him get on top of me like that. I'm out of practice.'

'You know, you could make money as a fighter.'

'I can't take him on again tomorrow, if that's what you mean. They wouldn't pay me twice.'

'No, but you could do what he does. Put on a boxing

exhibition. Offer five bob – well, maybe half a crown – to anyone who can stay on his feet for three rounds against you. If you could do that well against Smith, I reckon you could make a fool out of any challenger.'

Jan considered. 'Perhaps. But he's built like an ox, and some of these diggers are as big as he is. They might not be able to put me down, but I'd never get them off their feet.'

'Go on! You rocked him once or twice.'

'We couldn't make a living that way. He doesn't get much in that hat he passes round, and he's famous. And every time someone stayed on his feet against me we'd have to pay out five shillings.'

'Half a crown. And the more practice you got the better you'd be. I could be your manager and time-keeper and take the collection. We'd just coin money.'

Jan laughed. 'And frogs could grow feathers. No, we'll find a job tomorrow.'

* * *

The following day they went, as they had earlier planned, to Dutoitspan, but again their search was in vain. Too many hopefuls coming to the diggings had squandered or lost their money and been forced to look for work, so there were always too few jobs available and too many men to fill them.

'We'll try again tomorrow,' Jan said, 'and if it's no good we'll have to go back to the Cape.'

'Ah,' said Harry. 'Don't tell me – you've found Aladdin's lamp. One rub and there's a hulking great Genie, ready to transport us back to Cape Town. "To hear is to obey, O master!" Jan, my dear old idiot, we're stuck here unless we can get money for our fares.'

'You're right. So somehow we've got to earn enough.'

'I've already told you, you could make a living at boxing.'

'It's a ridiculous idea.'

'Think of a better one.'

'Besides,' said Jan, 'we'd need ropes to make a ring, and stools for the boxers to sit on between rounds, and flares to light the place.'

'You mean you'll do it?'

'No, I won't.'

'It's worth a try, Jan. We can do without a ring – form it out of the spectators. We can find something for you to sit on, and to begin with we'll have to set up in the afternoon so we shan't need flares.'

*　　*　　*

The next morning they went into town and walked around, trying to decide where the bouts should take place. It was obviously not a good idea to try to establish themselves too close to Ned Smith's pitch, and they picked another square some distance away.

'Are you ready to start?' Harry asked.

'No,' said Jan. 'Right now I'm going back to the tent for a little nap. Then we'll come back in the late afternoon. There'll be more people about then, when they've packed up work for the day.'

When they returned to their chosen site a few hours afterwards, Harry darted to the rear of one of the canteens and came back carrying two beer crates. 'These'll do for stools,' he said. He set them out on the street, and began to shout, 'Roll up! Roll up! Presenting the great Jan Shapiro, Holland's finest exponent of the noble art of pugilism. The man who took ten shillings off Ned Smith last night, and never a mark on him. Jan Shapiro challenges any man to stand up against him for three five minute rounds. Half a crown to any man who stands on his feet for three rounds. Roll up! Roll up!'

He went on shouting, and one or two of the passers-by stopped. Harry greeted them effusively, bowing low. 'Ah, my lords, welcome to your lordships. This way, your lordships, for your lordships' seats, the best in the house.' He gave a little high-pitched scream and continued in falsetto, 'Ooh! Someone's pinched all the seats. Who could have done that? Naughty boys!' He changed to a deep Cockney. 'Rotten tea-leafs! You'll just 'ave to stand there, me lords. You'll 'ave a luvverly view.' As more men gathered, he elaborated on the performance, and before long had marshalled the spectators so that they formed a rough square about the size of a boxing ring.

'Come on,' he cried. 'Who's going to be the first to try his luck against the Doughty Dutchman? You, sir, what about you? No? Then you, sir – you look as though it would take a lot to put you on the floor.'

71

'A few pints would do it – or a bottle of scotch!' one of the man's friends laughed. 'Go on, Bert. You can buy me a couple o' beers with your winnings. Look at him – Doughty Dutchman my Aunt Fanny – he's just skin and bone. You be careful you don't hurt him.'

The man looked over at Jan and laughed. 'Reckon you're right, Cully.' He stripped off his shirt, revealing a heavily-muscled torso, and as he came towards Jan he put up his fists and shadow boxed nimbly.

'For God's sake!' Jan whispered. 'Why did you have to pick on him? He looks as though he knows a bit about boxing.'

'Well, try to look as though you're going to slaughter him – maybe it'll scare him off.'

In fact, Jan had comparatively little trouble, for though the man had clearly boxed before, he was so slow in his movements that all his blows were telegraphed. Jan's punches broke through his defences continuously, but the one problem was that he showed no signs at all of losing his balance.

After the second round, Harry whispered urgently, 'You've got to get him down, Jan. Hit him low – make him double up and get him on the chin.' But that was against all Jan's instincts, and in any case it was unlikely that the crowd would stand for foul blows. If he did as Harry suggested, the pair of them might get lynched.

He came out for the last round determined to tap away at the man's body and wait for the chance of putting in a really powerful blow. If he could get him in the right position, with his guard lowered . . . Although his punches were light, the man eventually decided to protect his chest from the onslaught. It was the opportunity Jan had been waiting for. His right arm shot out and his fist landed on his opponent's jaw with all the weight he could put behind it.

The man's head flew back, and he took a couple of staggering steps backwards, but somehow remained on his feet. The crowd was screaming in excitement, urging the big man to stick it out. But his guard was still down, and Jan came in again with another right-handed punch which landed on almost the identical spot. This time the man's legs began to buckle under him, but the two fighters were so near to the edge of the 'ring' that as he fell back he was supported by some members of the crowd.

'Clear the way!' Harry shouted. 'Let him fall!'

But the men jeered at that, and helped the challenger to keep his balance. He recovered quickly, and angry now, began to shower blows on Jan, forcing him to retreat.

Harry watched anxiously. The five minutes were almost up. He debated whether to let the round last another minute or so, but realised that Jan had little chance of flooring the big man now. 'Time!' he called, and a great cheer went up from the victor's supporters. Harry paid him his half crown, and hastily went round the crowd collecting their pennies and halfpennies. As he passed among them, he called out, 'Another bout to follow, gentlemen. And another half crown if you can stand up against the Doughty Dutchman for three ger-ruelling rounds. Only those under the age of ninety-three need apply. No ladies, no hanimiles allowed.' He suddenly thought he saw Black Conrad at the back of the crowd, and added, 'No. Nor no snakes-in-the-grass, neither.' But when he looked again, Black Conrad, if it was he, had disappeared.

Jan's next challenger was easy meat. He had little idea of protecting himself, and a succession of left and right jabs was sufficient to send him sprawling on the rough ground. This time the crowd booed, and Jan realised that he had despatched his man too quickly – they wanted to see more than a few seconds of action. He would have to do as Ned Smith had done, and wait before launching his real attack. This was not just sport, but showmanship too.

The next time he was able to control the fight more skilfully, and did not put his man down until near the end of the third round. Harry was jubilant, especially since the crowd had grown and his collections were improving.

The fourth fight would have to be the last of the afternoon. Jan was tiring, and in any case the brief twilight and the swift fall of darkness would soon be upon them. The match had just begun when a disturbance broke out at the back of the crowd. Into the circle of spectators pushed Ned Smith, followed by his barker and two other men.

'What's the bloody idea?' Smith growled. 'Oh, it's you. What the 'ell d'you think you're doing? This is my game, d'you 'ear? No one else muscles in on my business. Go on! Clear off! Or it'll be the worse for you!'

The crowd had been watching in comparative silence. Now

one of them called out, 'Leave the kid alone, Ned. He's been doing all right.'

'I won't 'urt an 'air of 'is bleeding head,' Smith shouted in apparent good humour. 'But this is a game for men, me lads, not boys. Anyway, this fight's finished, and I'm starting up in twenty minutes' time. And tonight's special. Stand up for five rounds against me, and you can win a quid – a whole quid. Come on, lads, back to Market Square.' He turned to Jan, and spoke more quietly. 'Look 'ere, lad. I'm a reasonable sort o' bloke, but there just ain't room for two prizefighters in New Rush. Besides, you need a bit more experience before you start on this kind o' game.'

'He took ten bob off you last night,' Harry said.

'Oh, 'e can box a bit, I grant you,' Smith replied, 'but 'e don't know nothing about this business.' He laughed good-naturedly. 'Anyway, I could 'ave took 'im any time I liked. Got to let someone 'ave a win sometimes, you know.'

'I'll take your challenge,' Jan said. 'I'll stand up against you for five rounds.'

'No, you won't. You're going to be a sensible fellow, and give up the idea of boxing in these parts. Like I say, I'm a reasonable bloke, and –'

'You didn't sound reasonable just now,' Harry said.

''Course not. I 'ad to put on a show for the sake of the crowd, didn't I? No, I'm not going to bash you into the ground, or anything like that. Not unless you try it on again. So now you know – right?' He turned and shouted to the spectators again. 'Come on, me lucky lads! Come and 'elp us set up. 'Oo's going to win 'isself a picture of 'Er Glorious Majesty on a golden sovereign?'

Within a few minutes the place was deserted, except for Jan and Harry. They looked at each other in despair.

'I reckon that was Black Conrad's doing,' Harry said. 'I thought I saw him at the back of the crowd, and then he disappeared. He must have gone to tell Ned Smith about us. Well, that's that idea finished.'

'Only here in New Rush. They may not have boxing shows at Bultfontein or Dutoitspan,' Jan said. 'Let's go and see tomorrow.'

'That, Professor, is a splendid idea. Meanwhile –' Harry jingled the coins in his pocket '– we picked up about three and sixpence in the collections. After paying that half crown. I reckon we can afford –'

'I know,' Jan said. 'A drink.'

7

Jan insisted on going back to their tent for a wash, and on the way they decided that as they were so near to being penniless they might as well spend most of their remaining money on a meal in town.

When they had finished eating, Harry said, 'I've got an idea. Do you remember Black Conrad talking about his girl-friend here? At the Ace of Diamonds, he said. Let's go and see what she's like.'

The Ace of Diamonds was little different from the other canteens in New Rush, except that it seemed to be more crowded. At the far end of the long room, by a small stage, a pianist was hammering out popular tunes. The tables near the stage were all occupied, and Jan and Harry realised that they would have to stand at the bar – if they could get near it. Just as they managed at last to buy their drinks, the pianist banged out a loud chord and a man appeared on the stage. 'Gentlemen!' he called. 'A little bit of hush, gentlemen! The Ace of Diamonds proudly presents Miss Kate Jessup!'

He disappeared, the pianist began to play a catchy little tune, and to the whistles and cheers of her audience, Kate Jessup bounced on to the stage. She smiled and gave a broad wink. She was not very tall, and wore her dark hair piled on her head to give her more height. Her make-up had been skilfully applied to emphasise her large dark eyes and her full red lips. From where Jan and Harry were craning to see, she was breathtakingly pretty. Her daring dress, of some red material, not only left her arms and much of her ample bosom bare, but was short enough to reveal her black-stockinged ankles and calves. Several of the men in the crowd called out ribald remarks, but she ignored them and launched straight into her song, a version of George Laybourne's great success, 'Father Says I May'.

When Johnny Clair was courting me he often used to say,
'Whatever you think of doing, love, ask father if you may.'
Whatever I might wish for, he of course could ne'er refuse,
So I made him do just what I pleased, for this was my excuse:
Father says I may, Johnny, father says I may,
Of course you can't say 'no', Johnny, if father says I may,
Father says I may, Johnny, father says I may,
So don't say 'no', for it is no go, since father says I may.

Her singing voice was harsh, but an erotic vitality spilled out of her every pore, and the audience was entranced. She was a mistress of the suggestive pause, the wink, the gesture, and the men laughed and banged their glasses on the tables, and joined in the last chorus and clapped and stamped and cheered when the song came to an end. She fanned her face with her hand, then pulled out the neckline of her dress and pretended to blow down her cleavage.

'I'll do that for you, Kate,' a man called.

'I want to cool 'em down, lover, not hot 'em up,' she said, and the laughter erupted again.

She exchanged more repartee with the audience and sang again twice, leaving the stage during the second song and making her way through the tables, skilfully eluding the groping hands. One digger who took too much of a liberty received a stinging slap for his pains, which caused much hilarity among his neighbours. Finally, she sat down at one of the tables, evidently having come to the end of her first turn of the evening.

Jan peered over the heads of the crowd. 'That's Black Conrad she's with.'

'The bastard,' Harry said. 'He doesn't deserve such luck. I wish I was in his shoes. What I couldn't do to her!'

The pianist resumed his never-ending medley of familiar songs and the Ace of Diamonds reverted from being a music hall to its normal business as a canteen. Harry fought his way to the bar and came back with more Cape brandy.

Jan took a mouthful of the liquor absent-mindedly. Although there was little physical similarity, Kate Jessup had made him think of Rebecca. If only he were settled, he thought, he could send her an address so that she could write to him.

Harry was silent too. Then he said, 'I wish we could afford to come here every night. That bastard Watson'll be going back to Cape Town sooner or later – maybe we'd stand a chance with her then. Just think what we're missing, all because of a shortage of cash.' He scratched his head. 'You know, we were doing something wrong.'

'What do you mean?'

'Ned Smith can't live the way he does just on collections. I know he gets a bigger crowd than we did, but even so . . .' He paused for a while, and then exclaimed, 'Of course! What a fool I am! *I* know where he gets the money.'

'Where?'

'When you were going to fight him, a bloke came up and asked me if I wanted to have a bet on you.'

'And did you?'

'Of course not. The Templetons are famous for never betting on losers. Wish I had, actually. But don't you see? That's how they get the money. That bloke was one of Smith's men, and when Smith knocks his challenger down, they get the bets to add to the collection.'

'But he wins almost every time. Who'd be willing to bet against him? You weren't.'

Harry thought for a moment. 'No, but I would have bet that you wouldn't go down until the second round, say. It's my guess that what they do is take bets on how long his opponents will survive. And if they can tell him how the betting's gone, then he can plan the fight and pick the moment for that right hook of his.'

'It sounds very complicated.'

'Not if you know what you're doing. If we ran a book, the money would start rolling in.'

'We don't even know if I'm going to be able to fight again.'

'No, but assuming you are. I could do it, but I've got enough on my plate already, with the barking and the collections. We need to find a partner.'

'An employee,' said Jan. 'We don't have to share the money three ways.'

'You're right. Now, where can we find the right chap?'

'What we've got to find now is the way back to our tent. I want to start early in the morning. The sooner we have another look at Dutoitspan the better.'

'I'd rather have another look at Kate Jessup,' said Harry.

'So would I. But my glass is empty, and so's yours, and we've got no money to fill them up. If we earn a bit tomorrow, we can come back.'

* * *

After a skimpy breakfast, Jan and Harry packed their tent and other belongings, ready to leave for Dutoitspan and Bultfontein. They had barely started out when they realised that everyone else appeared to be making for Market Square. They were told that the Cape Commissioners were to read a proclamation that morning concerning the status of the diamond fields, and in case it had any bearing on their future, they decided to go along and listen.

The Square was crowded, but almost the first person they saw was Tom Allenby.

'What's this meeting all about?' Harry asked.

''Tis a question of who owns this land hereabouts. The Boers in the Orange Free State say 'tis theirs, and Pretorius, the President of the Transvaal, has made a claim, and there's a Griqua chieftain called Nicolaas Waterboer who says 'tis all his anyways.'

'And is it?'

'Danged if I know.'

'Does it make any difference?'

'Might do. The Diggers' Committee has been pretty firm about not allowing blacks or coloureds to own claims or to deal in diamonds, and in keeping them off the streets at night and not letting them buy liquor. All that may go, if we get British rule. I mean, we don't exactly treat 'em as equals – well, they aren't – but we don't keep 'em under quite as much as the Boers.'

'And you think that would be bad?' Jan asked, uncertain where his sympathies lay.

'Stands to reason,' Allenby replied. 'The Diggers' Committee has brought law and order here. We stand to lose control, m'dears, and that certainly would be bad.'

When the Cape Commissioners rode into Market Square, a proclamation was read, stating that the diggings were indeed part of Griqualand West, a territory newly become British, and the whole of Market Square erupted into wild cheering –

except for those few, like Tom Allenby, who felt that this news was not to be welcomed wholeheartedly.

Harry joined in the cheers. 'You see,' he said to Jan. 'That's the way to build an empire. Just come along and say it's British, and then it is, and no one can do a damn thing about it.'

Jan laughed.

They said goodbye to Allenby and joined those of the crowd who had decided to accompany the Commissioners to Dutoitspan and Bultfontein, where the proclamation was to be read again.

The two villages were very close together, really forming one community, much smaller than New Rush, but otherwise little different, except that the mining had not been carefully controlled, so that the claims were haphazardly staked out, and the roads between them were narrow and frequently liable to collapse.

Enjoying the holiday atmosphere, Jan felt his spirits rising. He grinned.

'What's the joke?' asked Harry.

'I just feel in the mood for a fight.'

'That's good. Who with? Me?'

'No, I mean a bout.'

'Hold your horses, Jan.'

'What horses?'

Harry laughed. 'I'm not going to mime that for you. No, we've got to see whether there's any competition, and we shan't really be able to tell until it's dark. But let's take a chance and stay here anyway for a few days.'

They walked to the outskirts of the community, pitched their tent, ate some mealies, and after nightfall returned to the main street, and strolled up and down, waiting to see if any boxing bouts would be staged. Harry asked a passer-by. 'You'll have to go to New Rush for that, friend.'

'If only we had flares,' Jan said.

'I'll give you some for Christmas. Come on. Let's get some shut-eye. And in the morning you can exhibit your skills to the good citizens of Dutoitspan.'

In any of the mining towns there was much coming and going all through the day, and when Harry began his crowd-gathering routine the next morning he soon attracted a group of men.

80

Jan fought four bouts, winning them all without difficulty, though he was careful to delay the coup de grace long enough to give the spectators their money's worth.

After the last fight, Harry counted their takings. 'Four shillings and tenpence,' he announced gleefully. 'Jan, we're in business. If we could take bets too, we'd make a mint. The sooner we find a bookie the better. Let's go and have a drink and see if we can find the right sort of chap.'

'You drink too much.'

'This,' said Harry heavily, 'is not just drinking – it's business drinking.'

They went into a nearby canteen. Some of the men who had watched the bouts were there, and one of them came over and shook Jan's hand. 'My compliments. I like to see someone with a bit of style.'

'Are you a boxer yourself?'

'Used to be. Longer ago than I like to remember. Too old for it now, so you needn't think I'm going to challenge you.' He laughed. 'My name's Bob Hunter, by the way.'

'Are you a digger, Mr Hunter?'

'That's right. Got a good little claim here – well, it's not the best, but I do all right. Here, let me buy you a drink – and your friend.'

Half an hour later they were talking like old friends.

'Do you know anyone who's looking for a job?' Harry asked. 'A reliable sort of chap.'

'What sort of job?'

Harry explained.

'I know the very man,' Bob said. 'There's an old fellow who had a nasty accident, and thought he'd never be able to work his claim again, so he sold it. In fact, though he lost a leg, he's all right otherwise. But prices have gone up, and he can't afford to buy a new claim, so he's working in a hotel. Reckon he'd be glad to help you out.'

'Is he a betting man?'

'Not half! The first thing he'll say to you is, "I'll bet you a tanner you can't guess how old I am." He'll bet on anything. He's fifty-eight.'

'Is he honest?'

'He won't run off with your money, if that's what you mean.'

'What's his name?'

'Pieter Viljoen.'

Jan pricked up his ears. 'That sounds Dutch.'

'He's of Dutch descent. But I reckon he thinks of himself as an Afrikander.'

'Viljoen, you said his name was?'

'Yes, but nobody calls him that. They gave him a wooden leg, so most people just call him Pegleg. We can go and find him, if you like.'

Bob Hunter led them on a tour of the pubs and canteens of Dutoitspan until they tracked Pegleg down. He was a plump-faced man with a ruddy complexion and a thatch of grey hair. His eyes were as blue as Harry's own.

He looked at Jan and Harry. 'Bet you a tanner you can't guess my age.' He spoke with a strong accent.

'Fifty-eight,' said Harry.

Pegleg turned to Hunter. 'Rotten sod. You must have told 'em.'

'If he hadn't, I'd have said . . . let me see . . . forty-five.'

Pegleg was pleased. 'That's what most people say. I have a bet with myself on that, and I usually win.'

'You want a job, Pegleg?' asked Bob.

'Got one.'

'An extra job. You'd still be able to work at the hotel.'

Harry explained what they needed. The old man looked at him with cautious interest. 'We could pay you ten per cent of the takings,' Harry told him.

'I bet you could. Make it fifteen.'

Jan had remained silent until this point, but now he introduced himself, speaking in Dutch. The old man's eyes lit up, and he replied volubly. His Dutch sounded strange to Jan's ears, as though he were speaking a kind of dialect, but they understood each other well enough. Jan learned that Pegleg had been one of a large Cape Town family orphaned at an early age. The children had separated, and he had neither seen nor heard anything of his family for many years, except for one sister living in England with whom he corresponded from time to time. He had wandered around South Africa, scraping a living by doing any work he could find, until he came to the diamond diggings.

Ten minutes later, as Harry and Bob Hunter listened helplessly to the conversation, of which they understood nothing, Jan and Pegleg agreed that the commission would be twelve and a half per cent, rising to fifteen per cent on any sums over five pounds taken in bets in a single day.

Hunter had business to attend to, and the group broke up, Pegleg promising to meet his new employers the next morning. Jan and Harry had a meal, sitting over it for a long time, talking happily of their future. It had been dark for an hour or two when they walked back to their tent.

On the way, Harry said, 'What about going back to the Ace of Diamonds this evening? I wouldn't mind another look at that Kate Jessup.'

'No. I'm going to write to Rebecca.'

A little hesitantly Harry said, 'Do you mind if I go by myself? I'll be good. I won't spend more than sixpence. Sure you won't come?'

'No. You go if you want to. But watch out for Bell and Watson if you're on your own.'

Alone in the tent, Jan added more pages to the diary-like letter he was writing to Rebecca. He poured out his doubts and fears in a way he could never do with Harry, and then, reading through what he had written, decided that it gave a distorted picture of his feelings. He picked up his pencil, and added, 'But this sounds as if I'm depressed, and I'm not. On the contrary. I didn't come out here to be a boxer, but it's a way of making money, and one day I'll have enough to buy a claim – maybe quite soon. It will be some time after that before I can send for you, my love, for I shall not do so until I can give you a comfortable home. A hovel would be enough for me, if you were with me, but for you I want a palace. And I shall get it.'

He laid the closely-written pages with the earlier instalments – Harry was right, it was more like a book than a letter – pulled his blanket over his shoulders, blew out the candle, and settled down. He had almost forgotten what it was like to sleep in a bed, but in a few moments was fast asleep.

He awoke when Harry returned a couple of hours later.

'She was fantastic,' Harry said. 'Kate Jessup, I mean. God, she made me feel so randy! There was no sign of Black Conrad, and she didn't seem to be with anyone special, so I tried to get near, but it was no use. I gave up, and decided to come back. And then just outside the canteen there was this woman, and she came up to me, and there was no mistaking what she was after, and we went behind the canteen where it was quiet, and . . .'

'Was she a white?'

'Yes. Said she'd come out with her husband, but he'd died and left her stranded, with no money.'

'You're a fool. She's probably got all sorts of diseases.'

'I didn't . . . go all the way. She wouldn't, anyway – not for a tanner. She used her hand. A sixpenny frig, that's what it was, and worth every penny. A woman's hand is much better than your own. You'd better come with me next time and try it.'

'No, thanks,' said Jan. 'I'll wait for Rebecca.'

'Oh, you and your Rebecca!' Harry snuggled under his blanket. 'Good night, old sport. Happy wet dreams!'

*　　*　　*

Pegleg was worth every penny of his percentage. He was known and liked by most of the diggers, and proved expert at coaxing them to bet heavily, and on the rare occasions when Jan failed to knock a man off his feet, or was unable to ground him within the time on which the spectators had bet, he paid out promptly without argument.

The bouts became a part of daily life in Dutoitspan, and Jan was able to send off his letter to Rebecca, giving the local post office as his address. As the weeks went by and his savings gradually mounted, he still wondered sometimes whether he should spend the money on a ticket back to Amsterdam, admitting defeat. But he would remind himself of the bitter, contemptuous reception that he would get. He often thought of his father. His skill, his unbending honesty were admirable, but how could he be so devoid of affection, so harsh and tyrannical? Jan might not have been gifted with the qualities that his father had hoped for in his firstborn son, but did he really deserve contempt? He could not remember an occasion when his father had given him any encouragement or had attempted to understand him. There was no self-pity in these thoughts, but only anger and a burning determination to prove his father wrong.

*　　*　　*

Once he and Harry seemed assured of a steady income, Jan had decided to fight on only four nights a week. Men were still coming to the diggings by the hundred, so there were always newcomers willing to have a bout with the slim young man who looked such easy prey, but it was a punishing way of life, especially since they had been able to buy flares and could run their entertainment for the whole evening. Even if he had wanted to fight every night of the week, there were some days when he could not. The euphoria with which the news of the British annexation of Griqualand West had been greeted faded rapidly when the Commissioners refused to recognise the Diggers' Committee as an official body, and soon there were riots. Tempers then calmed for a short while, but tension continued to simmer beneath the surface, and every now and then erupted into violence. At such times it would have been madness to hold the boxing bouts.

Christmas passed and the New Year of 1872 began. The diggers celebrated, in the heat of summer, and poured their money into Pegleg's eager hands, but Jan was still a long way from being able to afford a good claim, especially as prices were rising with every day that passed. In the meantime, at least he and Harry ate regularly and well, and generally lived more comfortably than in the early days, though they still slept in their tent.

*　　*　　*

'Oh-oh,' said Harry one evening during the break between rounds in the bout that Jan was fighting. 'Here comes trouble.'

The cadaverous-faced man who was Ned Smith's barker pushed his way into the centre of the ring. 'Shapiro!' he bellowed. 'Here's a challenge for you. Not from some greenhorn for you to make a fool of, but from Ned Smith, the champion. He's back in New Rush, see? Says he told you once to get out, and since you didn't listen, he's going to show you what he meant. He challenges you to a fight to the finish.'

The crowd had fallen silent once he began to speak. Now a buzz of excitement ran through them.

'I'm not interfering with his business,' Jan said. 'He doesn't fight in Dutoitspan.'

'This is his territory, and he's not having anyone muscling in on it, see? Accept the challenge, or we break your bouts up

85

every time you start. And don't think we can't.' He beckoned, and three tough-looking men pushed through the crowd to join him.

Jan could see no way out. 'Tell him I accept his challenge,' he called.

Harry looked at him in consternation. 'It's all very well standing up to him for three rounds,' he whispered, 'but he'll kill you – I mean it – *kill* you in a fight to the finish.'

When the cheers which had greeted Jan's acceptance had died down, Ned Smith's man had more to say. 'There's one other thing.' He paused dramatically. 'If you win – I say, *if* you win – then Mr Smith will give you best and leave the field to you. But if it so happens that he hammers you into a bloody pulp, then you agree you'll never fight in New Rush or Dutoitspan or Bultfontein again, see?'

'Where?' said Jan. 'Where and when?'

'Tomorrow night in New Rush. Eight o'clock.'

'I'll be there.'

'You'd better order yourself a coffin,' laughed the man, and left with his companions.

Harry called Pegleg. 'Pay 'em all their bets. Fighting's over for tonight. We've got to talk some sense into Jan.'

They both tried to dissuade him, but Jan was adamant. 'If I back out, they'll all say I'm a coward. I'm not having that.'

'But you're going to get hurt – badly hurt. And then you'll never get a claim. You'll have to go back to the Cape. Or back home.'

'Maybe. But at least I shan't feel ashamed of myself.'

Nothing that they could say would change his mind, nor could they even persuade him to spend the following day resting. He laughed at them. 'I'm fit – I reckon I'm a lot tougher than I was the first time I fought him. And I can give him ten or maybe even fifteen years.'

'And he's about twice your weight and has twice your experience.'

'So he's going to beat me. But I'll tell you this, Harry – he's going to get a surprise, and more than he bargains for. He's going to have the hardest fight of his life.'

'It wounds me to the quick to have to say anything so soppy,' Harry told him, 'But I'm rather fond of that ugly mug of yours the way it is now. You won't look nearly so pretty when Ned's had a go at you. So don't fight longer than you need. Save your honour, if that's what you're worried about, and then give him best.'

Jan grinned.

During the morning the cadaverous-faced fellow returned. 'Need to fix the rules, see? A fight to the finish, with no time limit. Rounds will go on till one of you's knocked down or puts a knee to the ground. Then there's half a minute break. That's the way they used to run the old prizefights, see? Ever heard of Tom Sayers and John Heenan? They fought the first heavyweight championship of the world. Went on for forty-two rounds, till they was both dead on their feet, and had to call it a draw. But there won't be no draw this time. You go on fighting till one of you can't get up or gives in, see?'

Jan agreed.

8

Market Square was crowded to capacity – it seemed that almost every digger in New Rush, Dutoitspan and Bultfontein had turned out to see the fight. A great cheer went up when Jan appeared, followed by Harry and Pegleg, but it was nothing to the roar of sound that greeted Ned Smith.

'Just remember that you can get a break by going down,' Harry said. 'It doesn't count against you. If he presses you too hard, just drop to one knee.'

'Where's Pegleg gone?' Jan asked.

'Working. He reckons he'll take a lot of money tonight. As a matter of fact, he's bet me ten bob it'll be over twenty pounds – unless Smith knocks you out in the first round, that is.'

'Thanks very much,' said Jan.

The fight began. Smith advanced confidently on Jan, who retreated, dancing lightly out of reach, and for a long while, waiting for an opening, neither struck a blow. Jan was trying to remember all that Ernie Blakestone had taught him back in Amsterdam – he could hear him now with his constantly repeated warning, 'Keep yer guard up!' – and concentrating on his footwork. That had been the trouble with so many of the challengers he had met since setting himself up as a fairground boxer – many of them had had the strength to knock him to the ground, or at least to stay on their feet despite all his efforts, but he had only to wait until their feet were out of position and a comparatively gentle blow would tumble them.

After a while, the crowd became impatient at the lack of action, and started to whistle derisively. Smith closed in, and began to jab at Jan's body and head. Good though his defence was, a few of the punches landed, and hurt, and although he penetrated Ned's guard once or twice, his blows apparently caused the heavier man no discomfort. Jan's supporters from

Dutoitspan cheered his efforts, but their voices were always drowned by the roars of approval which met Smith's counter-blows.

At one point Jan glanced over at Harry, who waved an indication that he should go down and have a break. But he was not ready for that, and giving a slight shake of his head, he launched a little flurry of blows at Smith, and at last had the satisfaction of seeing him wince as his fist hammered just above his right eye. And a little blood began to seep from a cut there, sufficient to excite the spectators and to demonstrate that the fight was not going to be as one-sided as they had expected. The blow over his eye appeared to slow Ned, and for a short while it was easier for Jan to land punches. Nevertheless, he found it remarkably difficult to hit that eye again, Smith's guard always flying up in time to ward off a blow in that direction. But Jan began to think that perhaps he had a chance of winning after all, and more quickly than he had imagined possible. Over-confident, he pressed his attack, and suddenly found himself sprawling on the ground, caught by one of the oldest tricks in the book.

Smith's manager called, 'Time!' Jan got up and made his way to his corner. He allowed Harry to wipe away the sweat, but consumed with anger at himself, scarcely heard what his friend was saying. 'Just keep away from him, Jan. That round was nearly ten minutes. Your only hope is to tire him out.'

Jan was more cautious at the beginning of the second round, but he could not keep out of range all the time, and whenever Smith pinned him in a corner he simply had to stand and fight. The constant punishment of Ned's blows began to tell as the round stretched over ten minutes. He was just about to kneel to gain the thirty second breather, when Smith himself did so. That put great heart into Jan.

The pace slowed during the next few rounds, which were shorter than the first two, and ended by one or other slipping to one knee. Both of them were damaged. Jan had succeeded in hitting the cut over Smith's eye again, and it was now bleeding freely, matched by blood from Jan's nose, where one of Smith's heavier punches had landed. But these were minor compared with the bruising of ribs and chest and shoulders and cheekbones and head.

Although Smith had not again knocked Jan down since the

blow that had brought the first round to a close, by the time they got to the ninth round, and the fight had lasted for nearly fifty minutes, his superior strength was having its inevitable effect. Jan was tired, and could no longer dodge and weave. A blow to the head rocked him back on his heels, and Smith moved in for the kill. Throwing his head back, Jan minimised the force of the punch, but it was still sufficient to ground him. The crowd, scenting the end of the contest, yelled and stamped. Harry, half dragging Jan to his corner, said, 'Pack it in, Jan. He's going to kill you if it goes on.'

Pegleg had come back to Jan's corner in that break, and he agreed. 'You've done wonders,' he said. 'And so have I. You've lost your bet, Harry. Now's a good time to give in, Jan.'

But Jan got up again at the end of the brief rest period. It was surprising how that half minute and a cooling splash of water could put strength back into your legs, and determination into your heart. Within a minute he was down again, but this time it was poor footwork which caused him to fall, and at the beginning of the eleventh round, summoning all his strength, he penetrated Smith's defence once more, and timing an uppercut to perfection, caught the older man on the point of the jaw. Smith slumped, and the crowd, which had gradually become less partisan, roared their approval of the underdog.

Although Smith looked distinctly groggy as he went to the corner, there was no question of him abandoning the fight, and in the next round it was Jan who looked the worse for wear. His onslaught on Smith had taken all his power, and now he was leaden-footed, and the few blows that he landed had no force behind them. He soon fell again, and it looked as though the fight was over, for he lacked the strength to get to his corner. Harry had to come to him to wipe away the blood and sweat, and as he did so, tried again to persuade him to give up.

When Smith's man called for the start of the thirteenth round, Jan was still on the ground. Painfully he dragged himself to his feet, staggering slightly. Smith came towards him, determined to finish him off, but as he did so, slipped on a patch of blood, and though he did not fall completely, had to put his hand to the ground. At first the barker did not call the break, but the crowd shouted for it until he had to give in. The few moments of rest were very welcome, and when Jan came out again his legs did not look so rubbery, nor his punches as feeble. The round dragged on for four minutes. Then a vicious left jab to the heart from Smith, followed by quick blows to the head sent Jan to the floor again.

Some of the spectators began to call out that the fight should be stopped. 'He's fought fair and square,' one man shouted. 'There's no need to butcher him.'

'A fight to the finish, that's what it is, mate,' Smith's barker cried.

'Throw the towel in,' the man called to Harry.

'No,' croaked Jan from swollen lips. 'No, not yet.'

Harry had the towel in his hand, but Jan snatched it and threw it back among the crowd. 'The fight's not finished yet.'

Both his eyes were almost closed, the blood was pouring from his nose and lips, he was light-headed and had little control over his limbs, but his refusal to admit defeat brought a great cheer from the spectators.

Smith advanced once more. He too was tiring, but could still call upon a last reserve of strength. Jan made a desperate effort, and landed a stinging punch to Smith's damaged eye. It was as though Jan had given him a spur or a flick of the whip. Head down, guard well up, he came forward yet again. Suddenly his powerful right forearm, glistening with perspiration and blood, seemed to flash in the light of the flares. This time there was no doubt about it. Jan had been knocked unconscious by Smith's favourite hook, and there was no possibility that he would recover in time for the sixteenth round. They had been fighting for an hour and fifteen minutes.

Ned Smith raised his arms in triumph, and then himself staggered and might have fallen had he not been supported by a host of spectators rushing to congratulate him, and to chair him to one of the nearby canteens.

Jan soon came round, but had to be carried to the Cat and Gridiron, for his strength had completely drained away, and he could not have crawled the hundred yards to the bar, let alone have walked there. He was conscious of digger after digger coming to him, wanting to congratulate him and shake his hand. His courage had won him many friends, but the one thought in his mind was that he had lost, and must now leave New Rush and Dutoitspan and make the long journey back to Cape Town and perhaps even to Amsterdam.

They brought him brandy, and tried to force a little of it between his split and swollen lips. The spirit burned, and he tried to spit it out. He refused all other attempts to give him either food or drink, and after a while he fell asleep. The others did not realise it at first – his eyes were closed anyway – and it was only when he began to make a curious noise, half bubbling whistle, half snore, that it dawned on them that exhaustion had claimed him.

A doctor came and examined him as he slept. 'He'll live,' he said. 'I think he's got a broken nose, but with any luck it'll mend straight. What he needs now is a bed.'

'Where's he going to sleep?' one of the men asked Harry.

'In our tent at Dutoitspan,' Harry replied. He was a little drunk, having himself been plied with liquor ever since they came into the bar. He peered at the man who had spoken. 'Why, it's Mr Allenby.'

'That's right, m'dear.'

'I owe you a quid, don't I? I'd pay you back, only I haven't enough on me.'

'Forget it. Listen, you can't take him back to Dutoitspan. Best thing would be to get a room for the night at the Victoria.'

'Can't afford it. I've only got ten bob, and I owe that to Pegleg. Hey! Where *is* Pegleg?'

'Is he the one who was taking the collection on behalf of Shapiro?'

'Yes. Have you seen him?'

'Not since the fight.'

'Well, I'm damned,' said Harry. 'I'd never have believed it of him. He must have gone off with the money. Rotten bastard.'

'If he has,' Allenby said, 'you might as well spend the ten bob you owe him on a room at the Victoria.'

'So I might. That's a good idea.'

Allenby gently woke Jan. 'You think you can walk to the Victoria Hotel, m'dear?'

Jan shook his head.

'We'll have to carry him, lads.'

When they reached the hotel, the proprietress, Mrs Dunn,

seeing Jan's blood-spattered appearance, was at first reluctant to give them a room, but when Harry had produced his ten shillings and told her that she could keep any balance over the usual charge, her motherly instincts took over.

Despite Jan's protests, she insisted not only on helping Harry to undress him – 'Nonsense! You're not the first naked man I've seen, and I doubt if you'll be the last!' – but herself washed away the blood and sweat and gently applied an ointment, which she said was made to an old Romany recipe, to his cuts and bruises. 'They'll all heal in half the time,' she said.

Scarcely had she finished her ministrations and left the room, than there was a knock. It was Pegleg.

'Where the hell have you been?' Harry demanded.

'Looking for you two. Lock the door.'

'Why?'

'Got something to show you both. Go on, lock it. We don't want anybody coming in.' He sat on the edge of Jan's bed, reached into the inside pocket of his jacket and pulled out a thick, untidy bundle of bank notes, which he laid on the bed. From the outside pockets of the jacket and from his trouser pockets he brought handfuls of coins. He poured them on the bed and ran his fingers through them. 'Thought you'd like to see how rich we are.'

'Where did that come from?' Harry asked.

'It's what I made on the betting and the collection.'

'All that?'

'Want to bet how much there is before we count it?'

'No. I've already lost one bet with you today.'

'So you have. Ten bob.'

'I'll give it to you later. As a matter of fact, I'll make it a pound. I owe you that for having said some nasty things about you this evening. I thought you'd gone off with the money. If I'd known you'd got all this in your pockets, I'd have been even more suspicious. How did you get so much?'

Pegleg turned to Jan. 'Nobody thought you'd last as long as you did, and each time you got through another round, it meant we'd won a lot of bets. Of course, I gave up taking any after the twelfth round – didn't think you'd get up again, Jan – and started on the collection then. I told 'em all it was the end of you as a boxer and they'd better be generous, and it worked.' He ran his fingers through the money again. 'Oh, yes,' he went on, 'there's one thing I think'll make you happy – a bit of this money came from two special friends of yours.'

'Not Bell and Watson?' Harry said. 'I thought I saw Watson in the crowd – he must have got in from the Cape recently.'

'They bet right at the beginning – Bell put a pound on, and Watson chipped in half a crown. Said you'd last four rounds at the most. After they'd lost their money, they wouldn't bet again. They didn't seem very happy.'

Jan nodded. It was less painful than trying to smile or speak.

'Listen,' Pegleg said, 'I bet . . . I bet there's more than . . .'

'Shut up, Pegleg,' said Harry amicably. 'Let's just start counting.'

It came to a few shillings short of one hundred and fifty-two pounds.

'That's incredible,' Harry said.

'It doesn't surprise me,' Pegleg replied. 'It was the greatest fight New Rush has ever seen – or ever will, if you ask me.'

*　　*　　*

When he awoke the next morning, Jan could barely move, as though every part of his body had been locked into one position. Gradually, however, despite the pain it caused, he forced himself out of bed and, wrapping himself in a blanket, made his way along the corridor to the hotel's lavatory. When he returned to their room, it was all that he could do to climb back into bed. Harry was still asleep, and Jan lay there thinking about the money he had won – enough, with what they had already saved, to buy a worthwhile claim, even after Pegleg had taken his commission. It made up for all his present discomfort.

Harry was woken by a knocking on their bedroom door. Mrs Dunn had come to see how her patient was. When Jan croaked that he ached from head to toe and was almost too stiff to move, she prescribed a hot bath and further liberal applications of her ointment. A long tin bath and several cans of hot water were brought. 'Now then, Mr Shapiro – out of bed and into this nice hot bath,' ordered Mrs Dunn in the voice of a sergeant–major.

Jan looked desperately at Harry.

'I think, Mrs Dunn,' Harry said, 'my friend feels that to reveal himself to you in his birthday suit a second time might be construed as behaviour approaching the licentious.'

'What rubbish!' she said.

'Nevertheless, I think he feels quite strongly about the matter. Truly, Mrs Dunn. I'll help him. We can manage.' Harry shepherded her firmly towards the door.

'Oh, very well. After his bath, make sure he gets back into bed. He needs to stay there for the rest of the day. Tomorrow morning's early enough to think about getting up. You can both have your meals up here, if you want. I'll send up some breakfast in twenty minutes or so.'

'That's very kind.'

'Oh, he's quite a hero, your friend.' She turned towards Jan, and shouted, 'I say you're quite a hero, Mr Shapiro.'

'Just because I'm a bit bruised, she seems to think I'm deaf,' said Jan when she had gone.

'No, it's because you're a foreigner. Always talk English slowly and loudly to foreigners, and they're bound to understand – that belief is an important ingredient in the national character.'

After his bath and the anointing of his cuts and bruises with Mrs Dunn's salve, sitting up in the comfortable bed and tucking into the generous breakfast which had arrived, Jan felt much better.

'This place is like Piccadilly Circus,' Harry said, as there was another knock.

Before he could answer it, the door opened and Ned Smith came in. 'Mrs Dunn said it'd be all right if I came up,' he said. ''Ow are you feeling, me young cocky?'

'Fine,' said Jan.

'Are you? I'm not exactly a 'undred per cent myself, so mebbe "fine" is putting it on a bit. Still, I reckon you did all right for yourself, eh? Listen, I've a few questions to ask, if you don't mind. And the first is, why's that chap Bell got it in for you? No sooner did I get back in town than 'e and that thug of 'is, Watson, were round to tell me you'd set yourself up in Dutoitspan and suggesting I did something about it. Said they'd always been fans of mine and didn't like to see someone queering my pitch. Well, I'm not keen on competition, and I 'ad warned you before, so I 'ad to do something about it, didn't I? But the way they talked made me think there was more in it than met the eye.'

Jan and Harry told him the story. Smith laughed at the ink-spilling and even more when he heard that Bell and Watson had lost money betting against Jan. 'Serves 'em right,' he said.

'I haven't finished with them yet,' Jan said. 'I don't reckon the score is settled.'

'Well, mebbe you should forget it. Which brings me to the second question. You know the terms of the fight – winner to be cock of the walk in all the diamond fields, loser to clear out – back to the Cape, and preferably right out of South Africa – at least as far as public boxing is concerned. Right?'

'I'm sticking to it,' Jan replied. 'I'm giving up prizefighting. I've got enough money to buy a claim, and I'm going to dig for diamonds. That's what I came here for.'

''Old on. I got a proposition for you. A bloke like you, with real talent, 'ow'd you like to team up with me? There's plenty of money in the game. We can play it various ways. I'm thinking of going down to the Cape for a spell – always do well there. You could come with me, or stay 'ere and meet up later. We can make any kind of arrangement you like, but the idea is that for a good part of the year we can both take things a bit easier – we don't 'ave to fight every night, nor take on so many customers in one evening. See what I mean?' He turned to Harry. 'Course this includes you too. I 'ear you got quite a talent for raising a crowd, and there'd be plenty of pickings for you.' He smiled. 'Well, what do you say?'

Harry waited for Jan to respond, and then said, 'I think it's great.'

'Well, Mr Shapiro?'

At last Jan said painfully through his cracked lips. 'It's a good offer, but –'

'Think it over,' Smith interrupted. 'I need an answer by this afternoon. I'm leaving then. You'll find me at the Blue Posts.'

'I doubt if I'll get there. A pretty good boxer gave me something of a pasting last night, and I'm finding it a bit difficult to move.'

'Send a message then. It was a good fight, wasn't it? 'Ey, where d'you learn to box like that? 'Oo taught you?'

'A friend of mine in Amsterdam – Ernie Blakestone.'

'Ernie Blakestone? Well, stone the crows. 'Ow is the old sinner? Why, 'e used to teach me, back in the days 'fore 'e left England. Mind you, I was only a nipper then. Oh, well, if you 'ad old Ernie for a teacher, no wonder you lasted so well. Was it 'im 'oo taught you that one, two, feint, in with the left and step back before bringing in that uppercut from nowhere at all?'

They talked for a while of Ernie Blakestone and his craft, and went back over the previous evening's fight. Then Smith took his leave, saying that he would be waiting for their answer, and giving Jan no chance of refusing it.

Harry looked at Jan. 'Well?' There was excitement in his eyes.

'I'm not going with him, Harry. I didn't come out here to be a boxer. We can afford to buy a good claim now.'

'Yes, I knew you'd be thinking that as soon as I saw all that money. But it's a gamble, Jan. If we went with Smith we'd still be partners.'

'I remember what you said on that boat – "Shapiro and Templeton, Diamond Diggers". That's what we're going to be.'

'Yes.' The sparkle seemed to go out of him. 'Yes, I suppose you're right.'

'Go and tell Ned, Harry. Give him my thanks, and explain it to him.'

Harry hesitated. 'There's no hurry. Don't you want to think it over a bit more?'

'No. Do you?'

Harry sighed. 'No. All right, I'll go then.' But it was some minutes before he left.

When he came back an hour later he looked shame-faced. 'I don't know how to tell you this, Jan. I'm sorry.'

'What for?'

'I . . . I told Ned you didn't want to go with him, and then he said, "How about you?" And . . . well, I said I would.'

'What?'

'I said I'd go with him.' There was a long silence, and then he went on miserably, 'It's been in my mind ever since the challenge came from Ned. I thought then that there was no way you could win, and we'd have to give up the boxing and go back to the Cape. And the more I thought about that, the

97

more I liked the idea. The sooner I get out of New Rush the better. I don't care if there are diamonds falling out of every bit of ground there is. I want somewhere with a bit more civilisation, somewhere that isn't as flat as a pancake and as hot as hell, somewhere that isn't full of dust and flies, and somewhere where there are girls.'

'But you haven't said you felt like that.'

'I know. But I've felt it, all the same. Besides, I like being a barker. And I'm good at it, and I haven't been good at many things in my short inglorious life.'

'And Ned said he'd take you? Without me?'

'Yes. He wished you luck, and said he understood.'

'And what about me? What's going to happen to me now?'

'You'll buy your claim and dig for diamonds.'

'How can I, now?'

'You mean there won't be enough money for you to buy a decent claim. Well, I've worked it out. You staked me to come up here, and you've shared everything, though it's been you who earned it – well, most of it. And it was you who made that money last night. So I ought to give you the whole of my share, like we originally arranged on the boat. No,' he went on as Jan opened his mouth to speak, 'that would be the fair thing. But I need some of it, and I thought maybe it would be all right if I just took twenty pounds. Sort of my share for doing the barking. That'll give you over a hundred, and with what we've saved already, you should be able to get the kind of claim you want.'

'That's generous, Harry. But it's not just the money. You can't break up our partnership. I thought we were friends.'

'We are.'

There was another unhappy silence.

'I wish you'd stay, Harry.'

Harry shook his head. 'I shall miss you. But I'm sure this is right for me. And we'll meet again some day.' He paused. 'I'd better go and get my things from the tent. Just my clothes. I'll leave you everything else. I'll come back and say goodbye. Really you ought to be glad to see the back of me. You'll be able to find the four largest diamonds in the world all on your own.' He tried to grin, but failed, and then turned and left the room quickly.

9

In the afternoon, when Harry had come back, made his brief
embarrassed farewells and left again, Jan forced himself to
walk in the hotel room. He persevered, despite the pain, and
slowly his limbs began to lose some of the stiffness. Mrs
Dunn's ointment had reduced the puffiness of his face, and he
could just see through the slits of his eyes. Another day or two,
he told himself, and he would be as right as rain, almost fit
enough to start digging, if he could buy a claim. He would
have to be strong enough to work steadily when he found one,
since any claim left unworked for more than a few days at a
time was considered to have been abandoned, and would be
sold off.

By the evening he was feeling restless. He had asked Harry
to bring his clothes from the tent, and he dressed, went down
and deposited his money with Mrs Dunn – a man would be
foolish to walk the streets of New Rush with over a hundred
pounds on him – and despite her protests, set out for the Cat
and Gridiron, where he hoped he might run into Tom Allenby. If anyone knew if there were any claims going, Tom
would.

But then he changed his mind. Urgent though it was to find
a claim, it could wait a few more hours. What he needed now
was to relax, to laugh and joke – as he would have done with
Harry if he had still been there. He was going to miss him . . .

He realised suddenly that he had just passed the Ace of
Diamonds. He could hear what Harry might have said: 'Come
on, Jan. Let's have a drink here, and we can watch that Kate
Jessup. Cor, what I wouldn't give for a night with her.' Harry
was always talking like that about women.

Jan thought of Rebecca. If only he had been able to bring her
to the Cape and to New Rush with him . . . She would have

been the best company of all. He longed to talk to her, to touch her, just to look at her. It seemed to be so long since he had looked at a girl.

Kate Jessup was no substitute for Rebecca, but she was a girl – a girl he could look at right here in New Rush. He turned and retraced his steps.

The Ace of Diamonds was far from being the cheapest bar in New Rush, the proprietor, Wally McFarlane, having recently put up the price of a schooner of beer to sixpence and a tot of Cape brandy to fourpence halfpenny, but other bars did not have Kate Jessup, and his wife often told him that he could double the prices without complaint. He would look up sometimes and see his most recently arrived customers unable to get far beyond the door, forced to wait until one of the barmen came near enough for them to shout an order at him. As long as that went on, the cash in the till would meet all his needs.

Jan had previously been among those standing near the entrance, but this night it was different. As soon as he appeared, there was a brief moment of near silence, and then the men clapped and cheered and whistled. Wally McFarlane pushed his way through the throng towards Jan, and invited him to sit at one of the tables, unceremoniously turning its occupant out of a chair. Almost reluctantly Jan stumbled forward, and sat. He was glad to do so – the jostling of the crowd had not done his rib-cage much good. As if by magic, glasses and tankards appeared on the table in front of him. The men crowded round, asking questions, discussing the fight, congratulating him on the courage and skill he had shown. And more glasses arrived on his table.

Later, Kate Jessup made her entrance, and sang her songs and joshed the men, flitting among them, escaping just as they thought she was caught with their arms about her waist, sometimes pretending to exchange a kiss, but slipping away at the last moment. And then she came and sat next to Jan, pulling her chair close to his, and drank from one of the glasses on the table. She waved the other men away. 'Leave a girl alone, can't you? Don't you see I'm talking to this gentleman? Cut it out, or I'll give you a fourpenny one!' She turned to Jan. 'Cor, he didn't half make a mess of you, lover! Does it hurt?'

'Not much. Not now.' His voice was a little slurred.

'You can still manage a drop of booze, from the looks of it.'

'That's right.' He took a long swallow of brandy. Then he was aware, under the table, of her knee touching his, her foot rubbing along his calf, and she leaned over and whispered in his ear. He wasn't sure what she was saying. Something about 'later,' he thought, but he was too fuddled to understand.

While he was still trying to make sense of it, Wally McFarlane told Kate to sing again. He was never particularly pleased when she spent a long time with one customer, even a celebrity like Jan Shapiro – her great appeal was that she was apparently available to all. He did not care who she spent the night with – that was her own affair – but during the evening she had a job to do.

The pianist struck up a chorus of 'Father Says I May', and Kate began to sing. But Jan did not hear the end of the song, or discover what she had been whispering to him.

He awoke the next morning in his room at the Victoria Hotel. He was still fully dressed, and his head was aching as though all the discomfort he had suffered the day before had now moved up from his body and into his throbbing temples. He had no recollection of how he had got back to his room, or indeed of anything after that conversation with Kate. Gingerly he got up, and splashed water over his face. Somehow he made his way to the hotel's restaurant, and they gave him coffee, and a raw egg whipped up with a little brandy. He felt better after that – not well, but the hammering inside his skull had dulled so that it was no more than a nagging throb, and he did not feel sick with every step he took. He called for more coffee, and slowly began to revive.

When at last he felt up to it, he went in search of Tom Allenby, and found him working on his claim.

'Hallo, m'dear,' he said. ''Twas a great fight. Shame you lost.'

'I lost in one way, but I won in another.' He explained that he now had enough money to buy a claim.

'Where's Harry?' Tom asked.

'Halfway to the Cape.' Jan told him the story.

'You'll miss him, I shouldn't wonder, but maybe you're better off on your own.'

'I keep trying to convince myself of that. At least when I get a claim, I shan't have to share the diamonds. Do you know if there are any for sale?'

'There's always claims for sale. Trouble is, most of them aren't worth having, which is why they're on the market. You want a good one, you'll probably have to wait until someone finds a really big stone, and decides to get out.'

'I don't understand that. If I made a big find, I'd think there was a chance of other good ones in the same place.'

'I agree with you. But many of 'em feel like your pal – the sooner they get out of New Rush the better, especially if they've got a small fortune to take with them. I'll keep an eye open and let you know if I hear of anything. Where will I find you?'

'At my tent in Dutoitspan, or somewhere round about. Thanks, Tom.'

Jan went back to the Victoria Hotel and checked out. 'You ought to be in bed, Mr Shapiro,' Mrs Dunn clucked, and continued anxiously in the same vein as he collected his money from her safe. He deposited the cash in the bank, and walked slowly to Dutoitspan. He reached the tent about midday, feeling so tired that he lay down for a rest. When he awoke, his watch showed half past eight, and only when he went outside the tent and noticed that the sun was not where he had expected did he realise that he had slept the afternoon and night away. At least he felt better, with only slight aches and pains. He made himself breakfast, and then wondered what to do. It was so strange not to have Harry to talk to. He went in search of Bob Hunter, and asked him too to keep a look out for any worthwhile claims that might be available. Aimlessly he wandered back to his tent, thinking that he should write to Rebecca. A black whom he recognised as one of Tom Allenby's men was waiting for him. 'Boss say you come.' Jan followed him back to New Rush.

'Listen,' Tom said. 'Charlie Gisbourne pulled a monkey this morning. About seventy-five carats. Let out a whoop you could hear all the way to Cape Town. He's going to auction his claim at noon today.'

'How much do you think it'll go for?'

'Something over a hundred and eighty, I should think. Have you got that much?'

'Yes, and a bit more, if need be. Thanks for letting me know. Aren't you interested in it yourself?'

'I thought about it, but the claim's quite a way from mine. 'Twould be difficult to work the two of them. 'Sides, I couldn't really go much above a hundred and fifty.'

At noon a large crowd of diggers gathered in Market Square. Charlie Gisbourne climbed on to a beer crate. He held up his diamond for all to see. 'Here it is. It's not the only diamond I've had – it's a bloody good claim – but this is the one I was looking for, and now I've found it I'm back off to dear old England, home and beauty, and the life of a toff. So, who wants to buy my claim? I'm selling to the highest bidder.'

'Five bob!'

'You haven't got five bob anyway, Lennic,' Gisbourne said good-humouredly. 'Come on, gents all. Serious bids only.'

A short fat man in a black suit pushed himself forward. 'A hundred pounds.' It was George Bell.

'Hundred and ten,' shouted a digger.

'And twenty,' Bell responded, puffing at his cigar.

Others joined in, and the bidding soon reached a hundred and seventy pounds, by which time only one man was contesting the auction with Bell.

'Hundred and seventy-five,' Bell said.

There was a pause.

'Going at a hundred and seventy-five,' Gisbourne began.

'A hundred and seventy-seven pounds ten,' the digger said at last.

'Hundred and eighty.' Bell smiled, sure that his opponent had reached his limit.

Jan had remained silent, but now he said, 'One hundred and ninety-five.' It was the maximum he could afford.

Gisbourne looked at him with pleased surprise, and turned to Bell, who said nothing, chewing on his cigar. 'A hundred and ninety-five from Mr Shapiro,' Gisbourne said, 'Going, going –'

'Two hundred,' Bell said, and grinned at Jan.

As they walked away, Jan asked Tom, 'What did he want it for? He didn't do that just to spite me. But he's surely not going to work it himself.'

'Probably already got some greenhorn lined up with more

money than sense who'll pay him three hundred for it. Bad luck, Jan. Still, there'll be others.'

*   *   *

Jan could not remember having felt so dispirited as he did in the next few days. He had nothing to do, no wish to talk to anyone, and he spent long hours in his tent, dozing sometimes, but more often thinking back over the weeks and months since he had left home. He cursed the chance that had allowed him and Harry to fall into Watson's clutches, and vowed again that one day he would be avenged on him and Bell. He wondered whether Bell really would have bid so high for Gisbourne's claim if it had been anyone but himself against him, and then decided that he was simply imagining the man's persecution.

He wrote a long letter to Rebecca, telling her all that had happened, and doing his best to keep out any note of despondency. It made him feel better for a while, but then he began to ask himself whether he would ever be able to send for her, and that led him to think first of Harry and his constant preoccupation with women, and then of Kate Jessup. Perhaps he should go to the Ace of Diamonds again and find out what it was she had whispered to him that night. But he could summon up no enthusiasm for the idea, and told himself that it would be a betrayal of Rebecca.

Determined not to allow himself to sink into a slough of self-pity, he stirred himself one evening to go looking for Pegleg. He was serving behind the bar in the hotel where he worked.

'I wondered when you'd come and see me,' Pegleg said, with some bitterness in his voice. 'I hear Harry's gone off with Ned Smith. I said to myself, "Bet you a tanner Jan'll be round in a couple of days to see his old mate, Pegleg, and tell him what he's doing, and maybe make plans." But that's just another bet I lost.'

'Sorry,' Jan said. 'I've been a bit down. And there aren't any plans – that's the trouble.' He told him how Bell had frustrated his hopes of getting a claim quickly. 'Now I'm just waiting.'

'Why don't you go home to Amsterdam?'

'I'm damned if I'm going to do that.'

Pegleg laughed. 'That sounds more like you. Something'll turn up.'

'I wish it would hurry. What about you? I didn't expect to find you working – not with all the commission you made.'

'Gone.'

'Gone?'

'You know me – can't resist a bet. I'm all right when I'm sober, but . . . I had a few drinks to celebrate, and before I knew it I'd bet away all those winnings. You didn't seem to have anything for me, so here I am back on the job, trying to earn an honest living again.'

'I'm sorry.'

'Well, if you ever want a bookie again, don't forget your old mate.' Pegleg turned away to serve another customer.

Jan finished his drink and left the bar, even more depressed then before.

* * *

He did not understand why, but the next morning when he woke he felt different. The mood of black despair had vanished. What a fool he had been to let it take hold of him. Of course nothing good would come of lying in his tent like a sulky schoolboy. He had to get out and make things happen. He felt alive and optimistic again, ready to go out and fight Bell or Fate or anyone or anything in his way.

He hastily scribbled a few lines to complete his letter to Rebecca, took it to the post office, and then walked to New Rush and the diggings.

'Well, I'm blowed,' Tom Allenby greeted him. 'I was just going to send you a message. Paddy Mangan wants to sell his claim. He's got to go back to Ireland. Had a letter this morning telling him his father's died. Seems he's not plain Paddy Mangan, but the Honourable Patrick, and he's got to go back to be Lord Mangan, and manage the estate or summat. I asked him if he'd give you first offer of his claim. "Sure and I will that," he says. "He's a fine spalpeen of a fellow, and since I'm after selling quickly now, sure it might as well be to him." I think he talks like that because we all expect it of him, him being Irish.'

Allenby led Jan some distance along the roads criss-crossing

105

the pit to a claim which had not been very deeply dug. A slim man was sitting there, reading a letter.

'Hey, Paddy – your lordship, I mean – this is the fellow I was talking about, Jan Shapiro.'

Paddy Mangan looked up at Jan. Then his face lit up. 'Sure and I know him. Isn't he the feller who stood up against Ned Smith, to be sure.' He put the letter away, and climbed up from his claim to the road, still talking. 'A fine fight, and I'd like to shake you by the hand, sorr. Thanks to you, I won meself a few pounds that evening, so I did. There was this man going round – man with a wooden leg – and he was taking bets, saying you'd stay another round or two rounds or whatever. Now everyone else thought you'd be lucky if you lasted another minute, but he seemed to be winning his bets all the time, and I thought to meself, I'm after following his example. So I bet with another man and won meself a few quid.'

'If you'll stop talking for a minute,' Tom said. 'Jan's come to do business.'

The self-mockery in the Irishman's eyes disappeared in an instant. 'You want to buy my claim. What'll you pay me for it?'

'How much do you want?'

The Irishman chuckled. 'Tell me your top price, and I'll tell you, so I will, if it's what I have in mind.'

'A hundred and ninety-five pounds.'

The Irishman put out his hand. 'It's yours. And you needn't think because I've accepted so quickly that I'm cheating you. I wouldn't have said no to more, but I wouldn't have taken a penny less than a hundred and ninety. I've had a good few stones here, and there's plenty more. As you can see, I haven't dug very deep. I wouldn't be giving it up if I didn't have to.'

'I'm sorry about your father,' Jan said.

'The old divil only died to spite me,' Mangan laughed, but there was pain in his eyes. 'You put the money in my hands, Mr Shapiro, and the claim's yours.'

'Come to the bank with me, sir,' Jan replied, 'and we'll do it straight away.'

'Ah, it's a fine fellow you are, to be sure now,' Paddy said, reverting to his exaggerated Irish accent.

A short time afterwards, when they had been to the bank,

and then to the office to register the change of ownership of the claim, Jan had the rights to a section of ground thirty feet by twenty-two and a half feet on the west side of the great hole that was forming where Colesberg Kopje had once stood.

'You'll need help, m'dear,' Tom Allenby said.

'I was thinking of asking Pegleg to join me,' Jan said. 'But not yet. I need to find a diamond or two myself before I can pay for help.'

'I wasn't thinking of anyone like Pegleg. I meant Kaffirs. You can employ four of them without paying extra for your licence. They'll cost you twenty-five shillings a week each, or fifteen shillings if you give 'em food and water and fuel on top. 'Tis a bit cheaper that way, but of course you have the trouble of getting it all for them.'

'I'll have to wait,' Jan replied. 'Right now there's just going to be me.'

He was eager to start digging straight away, but Tom said, 'You'd better have a look first at Paddy's sorting-place, and see how much ground's there waiting to be ready for puddling. Don't suppose there'll be a lot. Paddy wasn't much of a worker.'

They went together to examine the small area at the edge of the mine where Paddy had sorted what he dug. As Tom had suggested, there was little rock there – perhaps a couple of wheelbarrow-loads.

'Plenty of room,' Allenby said. 'So you can start digging. You know you have to leave the ground here for a while, don't you?'

'Leave it?'

'Aye. When you first dig the ground out, 'tis rock-hard, but after it's been exposed to the sun and air for ten days or so, it kind of breaks down and can be crumbled and you can wash away the earth from the stones. Of course you get all sorts of worthless pebbles, but the water makes it easy to spot the diamonds. They gleam. 'Tis a wonderful sight.'

'Charlie Gisbourne didn't find his that way.'

'No. Saw it as he was digging. But that's rare. And you can't stop after every blow to see if by chance you've exposed a diamond. If one's there, it'll turn up when you puddle the ground.'

★   ★   ★

Many men might have found the next few days frustrating, waiting for the ground to crumble, but Jan was happier than he had been since first coming to New Rush. He revelled in the physical labour, and enjoyed the company of the other diggers, feeling that at last he belonged with them. In the mornings he hacked out the ground, and having spent two afternoons making himself a puddling box from the materials which Bell had sold him, occupied himself thereafter by helping Allenby with his sorting, learning the technique of washing the ground, picking out the rare tiny diamond which might be revealed, and sweeping away the worthless debris left on the sieve with the back of his hand while the other hand began to spread out more gravel to be washed and examined. In the evenings he sometimes went with Tom and some of the other diggers for a quick drink, but more often returned to his tent, had a scratch meal and then, dog-tired, went to sleep.

Before very long he had filled all the available space in his sorting area with freshly dug ground, and there was nothing for him to do in the mornings, unless he gave his help to Tom. He decided it would be a good idea to move his tent back from Dutoitspan to New Rush. It took him all day, mainly because it was so difficult to find a suitable space. The town was expanding daily, as more and more hopefuls arrived in search of a fortune. A cloud of dust seemed to hang over the whole area, not dispersing even at night, and the stench and the plague of flies intensified, and always there was the searing heat. A hell on earth, many people called it, but Jan would not have changed it for anywhere else in the world. Eventually he managed to pitch the tent a good mile away from the diggings.

At last the day came when he could begin the sorting. It was his birthday, an auspicious day, a day for celebration. There would be nothing else to mark it as special – no gifts, no congratulations – so surely he would find a diamond. In fact he could already see it in his mind – he knew exactly how big it was, just what it looked like. He could barely contain his excitement as he began to puddle the crumbling rock.

He worked at it from early morning until dusk. There was nothing – not even the tiniest fragment of a diamond, though as in all diamondiferous ground there were several small garnets. But garnets were almost worthless, and no one bothered with them. A fine birthday!

'Tomorrow,' he said to himself. 'Tomorrow.'

10

The first find took place on Jan's tenth day of sorting. He was getting near to despair. Despite knowing the rarity of diamonds and the need for patience and luck, he had really believed that his claim would quickly yield a few saleable stones, even if not a big gem like the one Charlie Gisbourne had found. And his money was getting very low.

As he puddled the ground that afternoon, he saw a flash of light. Then it had gone. Carefully he moved his hand over the gravel, and then, suddenly, there it was again. He picked the stone out and looked at it closely. Yes, it was a diamond – small, weighing perhaps a carat and a half, but still a diamond.

He stood gazing at it, turning it this way and that, and got out his loupe and examined it minutely. The quality was good. He wanted to go and show it to the other diggers, especially Tom Allenby. He wanted to drop everything and write to Rebecca to tell her about it. He would keep it for ever, he decided. No, that was sentimental. He would sell it. No, he would send it to Amsterdam, to his father. Eventually he put the stone carefully in his pocket, and went on working.

Puddling the gravel on the first layer of the double sieve, he saw again the gleam of a diamond, not once but twice, as the smaller stones dropped through the coarse mesh. He must have been dreaming. He could hardly wait to sort through the smaller gravel. Yes, there they were – both probably less than a carat, but unmistakably diamonds. He crumbled another shovelful of ground and put it on the sieve. Again! It was incredible that after so long without a single find, he should pick out four diamonds in quick succession. None of them, except the first, was of the regular octohedronal shape, like two pyramids stuck one to the other, that perfect diamonds should have. It meant that more of the stone would be wasted in the cutting and polishing process – perhaps well over half the original caratage – but few stones are ever totally free from defects.

He went on working, despite the intense heat. You could get heat-stroke, they said, when the sun was so high and the land all around was baking. Jan always took care to wear a hat, and kept his shirt on, though it was soaked in perspiration, and he had a jug of water nearby – not to drink, though he could easily have swallowed it all in one enormous draught, but to dampen a kerchief and bind it round his neck. He thought sometimes of Amsterdam – the people there had little thought of how fortunate they were never to be without water in plenty. Here it was in desperately short supply, so precious that not a single drop must be wasted. Men learned to live with thirst, and to keep their washing water until it was so filthy that it seemed to deposit more dirt on the skin than it removed. Water was needed for puddling too, and as much of it as possible was caught as it drained through the sieves, so that it could be used again and again.

Jan continued working for the rest of the afternoon, but found no more diamonds. He decided to sort one final shovel-ful, the last of the heap of ground that he had been puddling. He turned the gravel into the sieve, and sloshed the remainder of his water over it.

He could scarcely believe his eyes. It was a much larger diamond – over ten carats. He took out his loupe again. This stone too was imperfect in shape, and was not as clear as the others had been, with a major flaw at one end. But a skilled polisher would be able to cut the flaw away and still produce a large and beautiful gem. He tried to guess at its value – eighty or ninety pounds, and perhaps even more.

As he stacked his tools away, he made up his mind. He would take all the stones to Samuel Rosenberg, the diamond merchant whom Mr Meier had recommended. It was non-sense to think of keeping them, or of sending them to Amster-dam. He needed money to live on, and to save so that one day he could afford to hire help and even perhaps to buy a second claim.

The single room which comprised Samuel Rosenberg's office was dark, the shutters having been closed in the vain hope of keeping out some of the heat. When Jan's eyes adjusted to the gloom, he saw that the room was sparsely furnished, much like Bell's office. Before him was a battered desk, on which were a ledger, a pair of diamond scales, a pen and ink stand, and a chessboard. Behind the desk was a chair, and in one corner of the room stood a chest of drawers and behind it an iron safe. The wooden walls were bare, and there was no floor covering of any kind.

In the chair behind the desk sat Mr Rosenberg, contemplating the pieces on the chessboard and waiting, Jan thought, like a spider at the centre of its web. Well, if he should prove a spider, in spite of being a friend of Mr Meier, Jan would certainly be no fly. Rosenberg was thin, and looked as though, if he stood up, he would be as tall as Jan. His head was large and his face gave the impression of being a mass of bony ridges, connected by hollows of skin, as though there were no flesh. His eyes were deep-set, dark and sad. He was formally dressed in a suit of dark cloth, and wore a kippa. It was difficult to tell how old he was. His forehead was deeply lined and there was a network of tiny wrinkles around the eyes, and yet there was no grey in his hair, nor did he seem to have any of the mannerisms of an old man. He could have been anywhere between forty-five and sixty, or even older.

He did not say anything, but looked Jan up and down, and then nodded slowly several times. 'Shalom!' he said at last.

'Shalom!' Jan replied. 'I have some diamonds I want to sell. A friend of yours – Mr Meier – recommended me to come to you.'

'Isaac Meier? You know him?'

'I met him in Cape Town.'

'In Cape Town? He should have come here to see me. Yet why should he? There are no ostriches here. H'm, h'm, Isaac Meier. I have not seen him for many years, but, yes, he is a good friend. How did you meet him? Is he well?'

'I hope so.' Jan recounted the story, playing down his part in the rescue, and making it sound as though, as soon as he and Harry had appeared, the thugs had run off. He also omitted any mention of their verbal anti-semitic attack on Meier, though he was not sure why he did so.

Rosenberg listened sadly, his brow furrowed, making little sounds of concern under his breath. When Jan had finished, he said, 'Ah, my poor friend. I must write to him. And he recommended me to you?'

'Yes, as soon as he heard I was coming to New Rush. These are my first finds, Mr Rosenberg.'

Rosenberg opened the shutters to light the room. Jan brought the stones out of his pocket and laid them on the desk in front of Rosenberg, who picked them up one by one, felt them, and then examined them carefully through his loupe. He left the large stone until last, and as he looked at it gave a little sigh, and ran his fingers through his long beard. Perhaps it was disappointment, but there was no expression on his face to reveal his feelings. Then he put the five stones one by one on his scales, taking his time and checking the weights with the utmost care. The big stone tipped the scales at just a fraction under twelve carats.

Rosenberg wrote some figures on a piece of paper, muttering under his breath, and then said, 'For the lot, ninety-two pounds. For the big one on its own, eighty-five. It is flawed.'

'I know,' said Jan, 'but a skilled man can cut that flaw out.'

'He will lose fifty, sixty per cent.'

Jan laughed. 'No, Mr Rosenberg. With the flaw in that position, the most a skilled man will lose is forty-five per cent.'

The merest hint of a smile passed over Rosenberg's lips. 'You know about cutting as well as finding diamonds?'

'My father is a diamond cutter and polisher. *He* would cut that stone so that no more than forty per cent of it would be lost.'

'So. The price is still eighty-five pounds.'

'Only seven pounds for the others?'

'They are macles – irregular in shape.'

'Yes, but the quality is good.'

'What did you expect to get for them?'

'Ten.'

'Ten, I should be out of my mind. I will give you eight. My last word. Even for a friend of Isaac Meier.'

'All right,' said Jan.

'Do you want cash, or do you want to leave the money or part of it here? I will look after it, if you wish. It will be safe with me.'

'You will pay me interest?' Jan asked.

Rosenberg gave a little chuckle, and shook his head. 'A bank

I am not. I offer you a service. I do not give you anything but security, but for that I make no charge. It is for a few days only, then maybe you put the money in a bank. Or you spend it. I am not concerned.'

'I'll take thirteen pounds in cash, and leave the eighty with you.'

Rosenberg carefully made out a list of the diamonds and their prices, and then copied it. He did not hurry. He gave Jan one copy to keep, but made him sign the other as a record of his acceptance of the deal. Then he wrote out a slip of paper stating that he held eighty pounds of Jan's money. He placed each diamond in a small envelope, and, his back to Jan, put them in his safe, taking out some banknotes. He returned to the desk and counted out thirteen pounds. 'Call again,' he said. 'I give a fair price – fair to you, fair to me. And your money is safe there. Take it when you want it.'

'Thank you.'

Rosenberg did not smile, but again nodded gravely as Jan left his shop.

Well satisfied, Jan went back to his tent, wondering whether he dared yet change his way of living. He could put up with the chores of cooking his meals and washing his clothes occasionally, but it was a lonely life. He still missed Harry. Most evenings, after he had eaten, he would write a few more lines to Rebecca, and then, because there was nothing else to do and no one to talk to, would lie down to sleep. It had the advantage that he woke early in the morning and was able to make a start at the diggings before the heat of the day was at its worst. If he went to live in a cheap hotel, or even in a shack of his own in the centre of town, he would have not only additional expenses, but the temptation of the nearby canteens. It would be easy enough to fritter away all his money in a few evening's carousing. He decided that he would continue to live in his tent.

*　　*　　*

Jan ate his meal, and wrote to Rebecca to tell her of his finds, and then sat and day-dreamed for a long while, not wanting to go to bed. He should be celebrating, he thought. It was late, but on impulse he changed into his most respectable clothes – that was something else he would have to spend his money on before long – and then made his way to the Ace of Diamonds.

He had not been there since the night after his fight with Ned Smith, and he did not expect the same kind of reception. But almost as soon as he came in, Kate Jessup spotted him. She was in the middle of her last performance of the evening. She let out a shriek. 'There he is! The boxer – the bloke who stood up to Ned Smith. Where you been, lover? Come here – there's a place here for you. I been keeping it warm ever since the last time you come in.'

'Keepin' what warm, Kate?' one of the diggers called.

'Listen, sweetheart, if you mean what I think you mean, I don't have to do anything about keeping *that* warm – it stays warm all by itself. What I was referring to is a place for this gentleman to sit.' She threaded her way through the crowd to where Jan was standing, took his arm, and led him to a seat at one of the tables near the stage. 'Back in a moment, lover,' she said. 'Got to finish me act first.' She returned to the dais and sang a sentimental little ditty of love, gazing all the while at Jan.

'I reckon she's got her eye on you,' one of the men at his table said. 'Fancies you, lucky bugger. You'll be all right tonight.'

Jan grinned, and ordered another round of drinks.

As the clock over the bar approached midnight, Kate came to sit beside him. 'Thank Gawd, that's me finished for tonight.' Then she whispered in his ear. 'I'm on me own tonight. Come round the back, lover. Come and see me etchings.' She laughed, and seeing Jan's puzzlement, explained, 'A joke. It's what dirty old men say to innocent young girls. "Come and see me etchings." Only they don't mean etchings – any more than I do. Listen – wait ten minutes after I've gone, and then go out the front and round the back of the building. You'll find a door there. I'll be waiting.' She stood up and began to make her way towards the back of the room. It took her a long time, for she had to stop to chat briefly with some of the men, and to fend off the advances of others.

Jan sat for a while, then finished his drink, said goodnight to his companions and went out of the canteen. She was waiting for him at the back door. She put her finger to her lips, and pulled him inside. Tiptoeing, she led the way to a small room, the door of which she locked when they were inside. 'Have to keep quiet,' she said. 'Got me reputation to think of!' She gave a low chuckle.

A double bed stood against one wall, and in one of the corners was a washstand. A chest of drawers and an old upright chair were the only other pieces of furniture in the room, but there was a hook on the inside of the door, and several dresses and other garments were hanging on it. The bed was unmade, the washstand, in addition to the big jug and basin which stood on it, was covered in a profusion of pots and boxes containing creams and rouge and powder, and in the opposite corner of the room a heap of clothes lay on the floor. The place was neither elegant, nor feminine, as though Kate had made no attempt to impress her own personality on its squalor, but simply regarded it as a place to sleep.

A string of questions was running through Jan's mind. How were affairs of this nature conducted? Who was to make the first move? What would she think when she discovered that he had never had a woman before? Supposing he failed? When it was over, would she expect him to pay her? And, oh, dear God, what of his resolution to keep himself for Rebecca?

He began almost to wish he had not come. And yet, to hold the softness of a woman in his arms, to kiss those full, desirable lips, to experience at last the secret pleasure which no other delight could equal . . . He was aware that Kate had spoken. 'What did you say?'

She had her back to him. 'What's the matter? Dreaming, are you? I said, "Undo those hooks." Come on – don't take all night.'

Jan did as he was told, his fingers trembling slightly.

She turned and put her arms around his neck. 'You want a drink, lover? I got a bottle of brandy.'

'No.'

'No more do I.' She took his head in her hands and drew him towards her, and her mouth opened, and then he was aware only of sensation – of her lips on his, soft and warm, demanding and yielding at the same time. And her tongue darted at him, teasing and inviting.

Then she broke away, and slipped the straps of her dress from her shoulders. It fell to the ground and lay in thick folds around her feet. 'Now the laces of me corset.'

'Who does them up for you?'

'What's the matter – jealous? Who d'you think? Mrs McFar-lane of course – old bitch, she is.' She wriggled out of the corset, and flung it carelessly into a corner of the room. She gave Jan a little push, so that the backs of his knees met the edge of the bed, and he sat suddenly, giving a yelp of surprise. 'Shut up!' she said. 'You want us both thrown out? Sit there and be quiet.' She began a slow, ritual removal of the rest of her clothes, which was provocative and erotic and beautiful. It was a performance, and Kate gave to it all the instinctive artistry and the sense of theatre which made her so successful as an entertainer in the canteen.

Jan had never seen a naked woman before, and was over-whelmed by the enchanting curves, the pearly skin, the soft, pink-tipped roundness of her breasts, the mysterious darkness of her hair. More than once he tried to move towards her, but each time she restrained him with a gesture. When she was naked, she stood for a while, posing, allowing him to feast his eyes on her. Then she said, 'Now you,' and lay back on the bed as he threw off his clothes. 'M'm,' she said. 'You're a big boy.'

It did not take her long to realise that Jan was inexperienced, and gently, almost lovingly, she guided and taught him, showing him how to give her pleasure and at the same time caressing him in a way that he had never dreamed possible. 'Put your fingers here,' she said, or, 'Kiss me here,' or, 'Like that, do you?' Everything seemed to be perfect, his lean strong body complementing the richness of her flesh, and he found an instinctive ability to move with her, to vary the rhythm of their coupling, to achieve that simultaneous explosion of feeling that eventually brought them peace.

After a while they made love again, and it was even better.

As they lay together in the wide bed, Kate said suddenly, 'One thing you got to get straight, lover. I ain't no whore. I know what they says about me – I'll go with any man who offers me enough money or enough diamonds. 'Tain't true. Oh, sure, I take money or diamonds if men want to give 'em to me, but not in payment for this. I choose the men I go to bed with, and I'll go to bed with any of them for nothing – just for the pleasure of it – and that goes double for you, lover. Don't you never believe them if they say Kate puts out for money.'

'I've got money, if you want it.'

'Didn't you hear what I just said?'

'Yes. I'm not offering to pay. I'm just saying you can have money if you want it.'

'Not from you, lover, not from you. Just . . .' Her voice changed from its usual bright bantering tones, so that she sounded vulnerable, almost pathetic. 'Just don't think of me tonight and then forget me tomorrow.' She paused, and then added, 'Will you stay with me, lover? I don't mean just tonight. I mean be my feller, look after me. I need someone to look after me.'

'What about Black Conrad?'

'What about him?'

'From what he said I thought *he* was your fellow.'

'He's a bastard,' she said. 'I'm finished with him. I reckon you could see him off, lover, next time he comes to New Rush. I don't never want to see him again.'

'I'm glad.'

They lay in silence for a while, and then he was suddenly aware that she was crying. 'What's the matter?'

'Sometimes I hate this bloody life,' she said miserably. 'Singing saucy songs and winking at the boys and talking dirty with 'em.'

'They love you.'

'Love me? All they want is to poke me.' She paused. 'And I let 'em, some of 'em. I s'pose I am a whore, after all. I was a good girl once. Wouldn't believe that, would you, lover? When I first went on the halls I was that young and innocent. Soon learned.' The tears had stopped, and she gave a low laugh. 'There were lots of fellers. And some who asked me to marry them, but I turned them all down. More fool me. And then someone said I ought to come out here where the diamonds are, and I thought maybe I'd find a bloke here – get married, settle down, start a family.' She laughed again. 'Me with kids – can you imagine it?' Then she said softly, 'But it's what I want.'

Aware of Jan's embarrassed silence, her mood changed again, and she said lightly, 'Oh, don't worry, lover, I'm not asking you to marry me. What I want's a rich man, a really rich man, who'll take me away from all this and stick me in a bloody great mansion, and I'll do nothing all day but tell other people what to do. And I'll have a separate bedroom, and you can come in at night, lover.' She kissed him. 'You don't know where you are, do you, with me talking all this nonsense? But I'll see you tomorrow night. And the night after. I'll go on seeing you.' She paused again, and her last words were almost inaudible. 'Until we get tired of each other.' She snuggled down in the bed, her hand tracing patterns on Jan's chest.

At last the gentle movements stopped, and they both slept.

11

Although it was never dull, Jan's life settled into a routine. Early each day he would snatch a quick breakfast, and leaving Kate still asleep, set off for the diggings. All morning he would labour on his claim, hacking out the rock, transporting it to the area where it could dry out, and in the afternoon he would puddle the disintegrated ground. At dusk he would walk back to his tent, cook himself an evening meal, and then go to the Ace of Diamonds.

He thought often of Rebecca, but it was as though he kept her in a different compartment of his mind from that where Kate held sway. He received a couple of brief letters from Rebecca. They were disappointing, for as she had intimated, she was not a good correspondent. She was glad he was well, sorry that he had been tricked out of his money, and hoped that he would take care of himself while boxing. There were no words of affection, nor much news of his family, though the second letter, in which she said she was glad he had managed to buy a claim, described briefly a conversation that she had had with his father and Abram. Abram had asked whether she had heard from him. She had been about to reply when his father had said that the only news of Jan he wanted to hear would be the diamonds he had promised to send. Rebecca added, 'I think he is very hurt. You should write to him.'

Hurt! No doubt he wanted his elder son to crawl back home, begging for forgiveness. Well, one day he would change his tune.

Although Rebecca's letters were almost coldly formal, they touched his conscience. There was no question of love between him and Kate. He loved only Rebecca. At least he told himself that, but his relationship with Kate was developing into something beyond the mere gratification of lust. He enjoyed her vitality, the indomitable side of her nature, her humour, and her beauty, while she saw in him, perhaps, despite all that she said to the contrary, a man who might one day be her husband, a man to take her away from her tawdry life, a man to give her security and children . . . and love.

However much he kept to a regular way of life, it was Kate – and the finding of diamonds – which kept it from dullness. After that first lucky day, he had frequently picked out small diamonds, sufficient to pay for his living expenses and a little more besides. And then, as he dug deeper into the hard ground, he began to reap the rewards. The intermittent stream of stones began to increase, most of them less than a carat in weight, but all with a value. There were enough for him to send a few small packages of rough diamonds to Amsterdam. The first time he did so, he smiled to himself as he folded the paper round them, tied the parcel with string and secured the knots with sealing wax lent to him by Samuel Rosenberg. He imagined his father's surprise and delight on receiving the package. He could see him hurrying to his desk to write a letter – 'My dear Jan, Well done! The diamonds are beautiful. I look forward to receiving more from you, *and*, my beloved son, to welcoming you home whenever you are ready to come. All is forgiven. Your loving Father.' Jan laughed at the absurdity of it. That was not the way Jacob Shapiro would react.

Gradually Jan began to build up a small bank balance towards his purchase of a second claim. No digger was allowed to own more than two claims, but if you could get two, the chances of good finds increased and, especially if they were adjacent, the labour did not increase proportionately.

The regulations regarding claims were strict, but before long something more would have to be done. All the diggers were agreed about that. Many of the claims were going so deep that the roadways which had originally been planned like a grid across the mine were standing now like high walls between the diggings, and every now and then one of them would collapse, often causing serious injuries. It was very tempting as a claim slowly sank farther into the ground to dig outwards a little, especially into the seven and a half feet which you really owned, but had given up to form the road. Even if you kept rigidly to your claim and did not undermine the wall, it would sometimes still fall, simply because it was so high and unsupported.

*   *   *

'What's the matter?' Jan asked.

Kate had seemed jittery all the evening, constantly looking towards the entrance of the Ace of Diamonds, and when they were alone in their room, she had been moody and irritable. It was the first time Jan had seen her like it in the weeks that they had been together.

'If you must know, it's Black Conrad. He was due back today.'

'I thought you'd finished with him.'

'So I have, lover. But I don't know as how he's finished with me. When he finds out about you, he's going to go wild, and he'll find out as soon as he gets to New Rush.'

'Good,' said Jan. 'I'll look forward to that.'

The next day Watson made his entrance. More than a little drunk, he pushed his way through the crowd in the Ace of Diamonds and up on to the stage, where Kate was part way through her act. His huge hand flashed out and cracked against her cheek, spinning her to the ground. 'Whore!' he bellowed. 'Bitch!'

In one stride Jan was on the stage. Seizing Watson's shoulder, he wrenched him round and landed an uppercut with all his weight behind it on the point of his jaw. Black Conrad's head snapped back and he crashed down beside Kate, who was rubbing at the angry bruise on her face. Jan leaped upon him, and grasped at his throat, his thumbs pressing on his windpipe.

'Get him out of here!' screamed McFarlane.

Two of his burly barmen, who doubled as bouncers, were already on their way towards the stage. They dragged Jan away, pulled Watson to his feet and frog-marched him towards the door. He was dazed, but had not been knocked unconscious.

'Must have a jaw made of steel,' one of the customers said, and Jan nodded. His hand felt as though it were broken.

As the barmen took Black Conrad to the door, McFarlane called, 'You're barred, Watson, d'you hear? Barred from this canteen – and that's permanent!' He turned to the room at large. 'And if any of you lot see him come in and don't stop him, you'll be barred too.'

At the entrance, Watson shook off the barmen as though they had been flies. 'I'll get you for this, Shapiro!' he roared. 'See if I don't!'

Kate was too shaken to continue her act, and Mrs McFarlane bustled out and insisted on putting her to bed. 'You can have a night off,' she told Jan. 'I should think you need it anyway.'

The following evening Kate appeared as usual. Her make-up could not entirely disguise the mark of Black Conrad's hand, but she seemed to have an extra vitality, as though to prove her professionalism.

In her room that night she was very loving, praising Jan's courage, his strength, his gallantry. 'My knight,' she said. 'My knight in shining armour.'

'But I haven't got anything on, let alone armour,' Jan said, laughing.

'No more you have, lover.' She pulled him to her.

Afterwards she said softly, 'You'll have to watch out, Jan. He's a dangerous man. He'll kill you if he can.'

'I've heard that before,' Jan replied. 'Don't worry. I'll take care.'

He was confident that he could handle Watson, for all his size, in any straight fight, but a surprise attack might find him vulnerable. He was careful from then on never to walk alone through deserted streets if he knew that Watson was in town or due to arrive, and if forced to do so, moved warily, eyes and ears alert for trouble. It became a habit, even though the weeks passed without incident.

*　　*　　*

One afternoon in late March Jan took a shovelful of gravel and dumped it on the first of his sieves. Pouring water over it, he saw them immediately. Two of them, the unmistakable octohedronal shapes gleaming at him. For a moment he did not move, but just stood there, gazing at them. Slowly he picked up the larger one. He felt a tingling, as if a tiny electric shock had passed through his hand. He closed his fingers gently over the stone, and a warmth seemed to come from it, almost like that of a living organism. He opened his hand again and looked at the diamond. It was perfectly formed, like two regular-sided pyramids stuck together. Turning so that none of the diggers working nearby could see what he was looking at, he examined it more carefully. It was a good blue-white, unlike so many of the New Rush diamonds which tended to be yellowish in hue. This stone had the quality of the Dog Star, Jan thought, shining brighter than any other star in the sky with its cold blue light. He guessed the diamond must weight forty or fifty carats.

He stared at it and it seemed to glow, to be surrounded by a silvery halo. That was nonsense, of course – it was simply glinting in the sunlight – but however rationally he tried to look at it, something about the stone was extraordinary, as though it held some special meaning for him and for him alone. He shook his head to dismiss such absurd fancies – it was a magnificent find, nothing more. But he could not rid himself of the feeling that there was some strange, mystical link between the diamond and himself. This, it seemed to be saying, was what he had come to Africa for, this was his vindication, his talisman.

'What rubbish!' he said to himself. 'You are going crazy, Jan Shapiro. Go on thinking like that, and they'll put you in a strait-jacket and shut you away.'

He forced the fantasies away and picked up the second stone. Although it was very much smaller – perhaps no more than twenty carats – it was as perfect as the first one. But it did not have the same strange feel to it.

Some of the diggers would go wild with excitement when they found a really big stone, shouting and capering about, eager for everyone to be aware of their good fortune. Jan had no wish to call attention to himself in that way. He put the two stones into his pocket, and went on working, and was pleased when another diamond appeared, even though of no more than a couple of carats. But all the time he was sifting the gravel, he could feel the big gem in his pocket, or at least he believed he could, as if it were burning there.

At dusk, it was a relief to finish work. He tidied everything, as he always did at the end of the day, and then walked slowly away from the diggings. He had been intending to call on Samuel Rosenberg, but at the last moment he walked past the shop. When he got to his tent he washed and changed, and transferring the diamonds from the pocket of his working trousers to the jacket he now wore, went back into town. He was still not certain of what he intended to do. Perhaps he would go and see if Rosenberg was still open for business. He wouldn't sell him the diamonds – not yet – but he could deposit them in the safe. The shop was shut. He thought about handing them in at the Victoria Hotel for safe keeping, but again something stopped him. Patting his pocket occasionally to make sure that the gems were still there, he bought a meal in a restaurant and then went to his usual table at the Ace of Diamonds.

As soon as he saw Kate he knew that he must tell her about the diamonds. He waited impatiently for her to finish her last act, and hurried to her room.

'What's up with you, lover?' she asked, unpinning the absurd concoction of feathers and frills that she wore on her head. 'You look like the cat that swallowed the cream.'

As he put his hand into his pocket to bring out the two diamonds, he wondered for a moment whether he was making a mistake. Kate was never unwilling to take 'a little present', and if one of the diggers offered her a coin or a note, it would disappear very quickly, before the donor could change his mind. 'I got to live, ain't I?' she said once to Jan. 'I want every bit of money I can lay me hands on, lover. I'm salting it all away. One day this little girlie's going to retire.'

'What'll you do then?'

'I don't know. Maybe set meself up as a madam.'

They had both laughed at that.

But now he wondered. Would she think he was going to give her one of the stones? He dismissed the thought. Kate was not like that. 'Look,' he said, uncoiling his fingers so that the two diamonds lay on his palm.

Kate's eyes widened. 'My Gawd!' she breathed. 'They're whoppers.' She touched the stones gently, gazed at them in wonder, and then said slowly, 'Can't believe they'll turn into real diamonds.' She gave a little laugh. 'Oh, you know what I mean. They're real smashers. Where do they come from?'

'From my claim. I found them today.'

'I know that, stupid. I mean where do diamonds come from? I know they're in those what-d'ye-call'ems – pipes. But why are they there? How did they get there?'

'I'm not sure,' Jan said. 'I think it's sort of like a volcano.

The rock is heated in the depths of the earth, and then it forces its way to the surface in pipes. And the diamonds are carbon, formed into stones by the heat.'

She shook her head. 'I don't really want to know. I'd rather just look at them. Why have you brought them here?' She was well aware that his habit was to take any diamonds straight to Samuel Rosenberg – even those that he was going to send to Amsterdam.

'I wanted to show them to you.'

'What are you going to do with them?'

'I know what I ought to do. I ought to let my father have them.'

'But you don't want to.'

'No.'

'Then sell 'em, lover. Buy yourself a house, or buy me a carriage and pair.' She laughed.

'I think I'm going to sell the small one. I should get two or three hundred, and then I'm going to get a diamond dealer's licence.'

'I thought you wanted to buy another claim.'

'I do.'

'You won't have money for both. You need pots of it to be a merchant.'

'I'm going to save. I'm going to stop sending other diamonds home, and I'll save every penny until I've got enough.'

'Why don't you sell the big one – it must be worth a fortune?'

'I can't.' He gave a short embarrassed laugh. 'Don't ask me why. I just know that I have to keep it.' He picked it up and caressed it lovingly. 'Of course, it's no good like this – it's not worth half what it would be after my father cut it and polished it.'

'So why do you want to keep it?'

'I tell you, I don't know. Perhaps I'm crazy.'

'Everyone's crazy,' Kate said. 'That's what makes the world go round. Here, I'll show you something I never showed anyone before.' She opened her little reticule and took out a carefully folded linen handkerchief. She unwrapped it slowly, to reveal a silver sixpenny piece, bent at right angles in two places. 'It's a crooked sixpence. Me Mum gave it me when I was a little nipper. "You keep this," she says, "and you'll never be without money." I thought she meant it was sort of magic. And then one day I suddenly realised that, crooked or not, it's still a sixpence, so of course I shan't be without money as long as I keep it.' She wrapped the coin back in its handkerchief. 'But I have kept it. Always will. So I know how you feel.'

'It's not the same.'

'No, not really. But it brings me luck. Perhaps that's what your diamond will do for you. Let me look at it.' She took the large diamond from him and held it up towards the oil lamp to see its translucence. Then her expression changed, and she seemed to be staring into it, her eyes unblinking, as though she had been mesmerised. She looked at it for a long time, unmoving, and at last it was as though she had to wrench her gaze away from it. 'Here. Take it back. It's not meant for me.'

'What do you mean?'

'Nothing.'

'Come on, Kate. What were you looking at? Why do you say it's not meant for you?'

'It showed me things,' she said slowly, almost reluctantly. 'It showed me pictures of you. You all dressed up like a toff, riding in a smart carriage, and a woman with you. Fair-haired, pretty, done up to the nines. You with someone who was ill in hospital. You on a ship. And this diamond being . . . well, with you . . . sort of guarding you. And then I tried to see me in it, and it went all swirly and dark, and I knew I had no part in it. But it's meant for you, and . . .' She trailed off.

Jan laughed gently. 'Do you often see things like that?'

She answered seriously. 'Not often. Now and then. I'm not like them clairvoyants on the Halls – can't do it to order. Well, I'm not sure *they* can – their acts are usually fake.'

'You ought to practise it. You could make it part of your act.'

'Don't ever say anything like that again!' Her eyes flashed with anger. 'I tell you, I can't do it to order, and if I did it as part of my act – well, it would be wrong. I wish I hadn't said anything about it.'

'I'm sorry. You were going to say something else just now.'

'Oh, never mind.'

'Please. I'm sorry. I didn't mean to upset you.'

For a moment she seemed to be considering. Then she said,

'You better keep that diamond. You life's tied up with it. I reckon that's why you feel the way you do about it. Something in you knew that it belonged to you, and you to it. You keep it, Jan. Keep it always. Look after it.' She gave a laugh. 'Here, hark at me. Sound like the gypsy's warning.' The smile faded. 'You ought to give it a name.'

'A name?'

'All the big stones have names – like the Eureka.'

'It's not as big as that.'

'I think it ought to be called the Shapiro Diamond.'

12

When in the morning Jan went to Samuel Rosenberg, the larger diamond stayed in his pocket, but Rosenberg bought the smaller one for two hundred and seventy-five pounds. Although Jan had made a habit of showing him the stones he found, saying which he wanted to sell and which he was sending to Amsterdam, Rosenberg had never expressed any curiosity about his decisions. This time, however, he could not restrain himself. 'You're not sending this home to your father?' he asked. 'He would be glad to see a stone like this. Glad? He would be delirious. He could cleave it here and he would have two fine gems.'

'I'm selling it,' Jan replied.

'A lot of money.'

It was a statement, but Jan recognised that behind it was a question which Rosenberg was too polite to ask. 'Yes, a lot of money,' he said. 'It's going in the bank for a while, and then, one day, when I've saved enough, I'm going to set up in the same business as you – as a diamond merchant.'

'Oy, veh!' Rosenberg exclaimed, in mock alarm. 'Competition, is it? How shall I survive?' He smiled at this young man whom he had grown to think of almost as a son. The smile disappeared, and he looked at Jan gravely. 'It is no time to start in the business. The price of diamonds is beginning to fall, and it will go on falling. Diamonds are only worth money because they are scarce –'

'And beautiful.'

'And beautiful. But it is their scarcity which keeps the prices high. Once there is a constant supply, the market is flooded and the prices come down. There are too many people involved – the digger, the buyer like me, the wholesaler in Europe, the cutter and polisher, the retailer – and all of them have to have their share. A diamond dealer makes a living, but rich he is not.'

'I am not looking to become rich. No, that isn't true – I want to be rich, of course. But the more diamonds I can get hold of, the more I can send back to my father.'

'You are giving up being a digger?'

'No. I also want to buy another claim.'

'How can you do all that – run an office, work two claims?'

'I'll hire someone to look after the claims.'

Rosenberg shook his head, and ran his fingers through his beard. 'That's expensive, employing labour. You'll need a good man, and a good man'll cost you more than a few pennies.'

'I know. I can still make money, though. I've worked it out. I can pay for the labour out of the diamonds that are found, and send the rest to Amsterdam. The diamonds that I buy from other diggers will provide my living as well as adding to the stones I send to my father. It makes sense.'

'Already you sound like a tycoon,' Samuel said, 'a tycoon who will make no money at all for himself. So tell the truth, Jan – it is all done to make your father's fortune and your brother's?' Jan did not reply, and the old man went on, 'It is not that. It is to prove something, nu? Then be sure you are choosing the right way. Try too hard, take on too many responsibilities and maybe you'll not prove anything.'

'Do you think I'm a fool, then?'

'No. Just keep something back for yourself.'

Jan was tempted to tell him about the big diamond, the Shapiro Diamond, as Kate had called it, but Rosenberg would really have thought him mad if he had known that Jan had a gem of that value which he was determined not to sell.

'And when is all this to happen?' Rosenberg asked.

'When I've saved enough. I have to find the right claim – what I want is one next to mine – and I have to find an office available in a good position.'

'You have to get a licence too. You need two sponsors.'

'I know. When the time comes, you wouldn't be one of them, would you, Mr Rosenberg?'

'I should take the bread out of my own mouth? I'd be a fool. All right, I'll be a fool. Yes, I'll sponsor you. Who else?'

'I thought of asking Tom Allenby.'

'I doubt he's got a hundred pounds to risk. He's not been doing well lately. And it is a risk. Many diamond merchants have gone out of business in the last few months.'

'Then I'll have to think again. You don't know anyone else who might help me?'

'You want me to run the whole business for you? It's not enough for me to act as one of your sponsors?'

'Of course it is, and I'm grateful. In fact, I don't know why you should do that much.'

'Because I am meshuggah. Because, the Lord knows why, I like you. You remind me of what I was like as a boy. You should grow up as clever as I am.' He chuckled wheezily. 'And will you survive? Perhaps – if you listen to the advice I shall be fool enough to give you. That's why I'll sponsor you. But that's all. Don't expect me to do everything for you. You have your own feet – they are for standing on.'

Since he was in this rare talkative mood, Jan asked a question which had long been in his mind. 'How do you come to be here, Mr Rosenberg?'

The old man settled back in his chair. 'It's a long story. I'll tell you. When I was your age I worked for my father, a diamond merchant in London. Then he died, and it was my business, and I made a living. And I married. She was a good wife and we were happy. The only sorrow was that we could not have children. Later, we found out why. My wife, she had a growth in her womb. When she died, I could not go on. I sold the business, sold the house, sold my possessions, and decided to come to the Cape. Why? You tell me. No reason – except that it was far from London. I lived on my capital. And then they discovered diamonds here, and my money was disappearing, and I had to do something, so I came here.' He sighed. 'It is not an interesting story.'

'That's a matter of opinion,' Jan said.

The old man shrugged, and turned to his ledger. Jan recognised it as a signal that he should go. He thanked Rosenberg, and then said impulsively, 'I'll come and see you again if I can. Just to talk.'

'And perhaps a game of chess? You play chess?'

'A little. I'm not very good.'

'Good, bad, what does that matter?'

'I could come tomorrow.'

'Tomorrow is Sabbath. You want to pray with me as well as play chess?'

Jan hesitated. 'No. No. Another time. I . . . I wouldn't want to intrude.' He could not meet the old man's eyes, and knew that he was blushing. He turned abruptly and left the shop. He patted his pocket, checking that the Shapiro Diamond was still there. Much as he liked and trusted Sam Rosenberg, he was glad he had not told him about the stone. No one should know of its existence, yet. He even regretted having told Kate, and thinking of her brought back to his mind the strange visions she had described. Riding in a carriage, indeed! He had a long way to go before he was rich enough for that.

Thinking back over his conversation with Rosenberg while he worked that morning, Jan could not help laughing wryly at himself. What a young idiot he must have appeared, talking so wildly about all his plans without having stopped to think hard of the practicalities or to decide his priorities. He tried to work it out logically. With the money from the smaller of the two diamonds he now had enough to buy another claim, and probably to hire help, but it was essential that the two sites should be adjacent. Paired claims were occasionally available, not only at New Rush, but at Dutoitspan and Bultfontein too. Some men were saying that Dutoitspan was the place to be, that it would outlast the diggings at Colesberg Kopje and provide better quality stones. But if he bought a double claim it would mean giving up his present dig, and nothing would make him do that now that it had brought him the Shapiro Diamond. So he would have to wait for one of his neighbours to want to sell, and there was little prospect of them doing so, for none was of the get-rich-quick-and-get-out type.

That left the possibility of setting up as a diamond dealer. He would have to rent or buy an office, get himself a safe and a desk and diamond scales and all the rest of the paraphernalia, and he would need cash in hand for the purchase of diamonds, plus the cost of someone to manage his claim and blacks to work it. He would need a great deal more capital than he had at present. But to become a diamond merchant would give him a more comfortable way of life, and would demonstrate his success in a style that could not fail to impress his father, and above all, it would bring nearer the time when he could send for Rebecca. He could not ask her to share a tent and live as a digger's wife, but she would surely not complain, despite the heat and the flies and the smell, if her husband were a respected and well-to-do man of business. The question was whether there was any real prospect of realising such a dream. The requirements were daunting, especially when Sam Rosenberg was forecasting a glut of diamonds.

He went over it again and again. Of course the sensible answer to all his problems would be to sell the Shapiro Diamond. It was no more than a piece of carbon, a pebble. Cutting and polishing would release all its hidden beauty, and it would be far more splendid as the centrepiece of some fine necklace around the neck of a rich and handsome woman than lying in his pocket. And his father would undoubtedly pay a huge sum for it.

At the end of the morning he came to a decision. There was no question of selling the Shapiro Diamond, however absurd it was to keep it. Without the money it would bring, the only way to meet the challenge ahead of him, he told himself, was head on. He was determined to become a dealer. That would be his first priority and from then on nothing would divert him from it. For a start he would look for a second sponsor, so that once he had the money that problem would already be solved.

He talked to Kate about it. 'Who do you know who's got a hundred pounds to spare who'd sponsor me?'

She laughed. 'No one. If I did, I'd marry him.' Then she said in a different tone, 'What about me?'

'What do you mean?'

'What about me as a sponsor? I've got the money – I've got that and more. Of course,' she went on, 'I don't mean in me own name. That'd be a fine thing, wouldn't it? – you being sponsored by Kate Jessup! Shouldn't think they'd accept that. But we could find someone who'd lend his name, if I put up the money. What about McFarlane?'

'But you need that hundred pounds.'

'I'll never get what I'm saving for, so what's it matter?' she said bitterly. Then she smiled again. 'Anyway, I'm not *giving* it to you – not bloody likely. It's only a guarantee against you going bust, and I don't reckon there's much chance of that.'

'Why do you say that?'

'Oh, you're going to be rich – I saw it in that diamond of yours.'

He gripped her wrist tightly. 'Don't tell anyone about that, Kate – ever.'

She gave a little cry of pain. 'Here! What you playing at? That hurt!'

'Sorry. I just don't want anyone to know about my diamond.'

'Then what's the use of having it?'

Jan was silenced for a moment. He laughed. 'I told you I'm crazy.'

'Tell me something new.'

'Do you really mean it, Kate – about sponsoring me?'

'Yes.'

'Do you think McFarlane would agree?'

'Don't see why not. Shall I ask him?'

'Not yet. I'm not ready yet.'

'Suits me,' Kate said. 'I reckon you're not likely to leave me while I've still got a hundred quid you need.'

'I wouldn't leave you anyway.'

'Oh, yes, you would. You will. And quite right too. You'll marry your Rebecca one day. As for me, I shall become the most notorious madam on the diamond fields.'

'You could start a hotel.'

'No fun in that,' Kate laughed. 'Give me a brothel every time.'

It jarred. 'I hate to hear you saying things like that. You don't really want to run a whorehouse, do you?'

'No,' said Kate, suddenly serious. 'No. But it's where I'll end up, like as not.'

'I don't see why. Kate, if I can set myself up as a diamond dealer, you can aim at being a hotel keeper. Why not?'

'Because, ducky, you found a bloody great diamond. All I got is what I earn. I spend it, most of it, and if I try to save from now to doomsday I shan't have enough to buy meself a hotel.'

'Then how will you buy yourself a brothel?'

'I don't know. Why d'you ask me questions like that, damn you?' She began to cry. 'I'll be one of the girls in the whorehouse, that's what I'll be. Until I'm too old and ugly, and then I don't know what'll happen.' She sniffed and brushed away the tears. Then she held out her arms to him. 'Love me, Jan. Love me.'

★　　★　　★

When Jan sent the first packet of diamonds to Amsterdam at the end of March, 1872, he merely enclosed a note giving his assessment of the value of the stones and asking his father, if he agreed the price, to send him the money by the fastest route, and he continued this practice with subsequent shipments. Knowing that he could not expect to hear from Amsterdam until July at the earliest, he went back patiently to work on his claim. He made other finds, and though none even approached the two big stones in either size or quality, he was able to add to the money in his bank account.

One morning after he had mailed a small parcel to Amsterdam, Tom Allenby came to him in great excitement. 'Heard the news? Post office has been robbed.'

'When?'

'Last night. Someone broke in.'

'Did they take much?'

'The cash was all locked up in the safe, but they took all the sacks of outgoing mail. Hope you didn't have anything there.'

'I posted a package to my father yesterday afternoon.'

'You'd better go and see what's happening.'

Jan joined a crowd of anxious diggers outside the post office. Many of them sent their finds home to England or to Amsterdam, as Jan did, and the mails had always been totally secure, although no special precautions for their safety were taken. An official of the post office confirmed the robbery, took details of the various letters and packages, and assured the men that every effort would be made to track down the thief.

There was nothing to do but to go back to work. Jan's packet had been worth seventy pounds, a loss he could ill afford. He had little faith in the ability of the local police to catch the thief.

★　　★　　★

'So what is with all the plans?' Rosenberg asked. 'Here I am waiting for you to put me out of business, or at least to tell me that you own half that mine.'

'I haven't got enough money yet,' Jan said. 'I haven't had

135

any payment from Amsterdam yet, and to make matters worse I lost seventy pounds in that robbery.'

'Yes, nothing is safe any more.' He shook his head. 'But why wait? Go to your bank – get a loan.'

'On what security?'

'Your claim.'

'I could. I suppose I would if the right opportunity suddenly came. But I don't want to borrow money.'

'That is pride talking – foolish pride.' The old man smiled gently.

'Yes, I know.'

'Then that is good. The fool who knows he's a fool is half way to wisdom. It is like your need to prove yourself to your father. If you know that's what you're doing, there's hope for you.'

Jan moved his knight to a position where it threatened both Rosenberg's king and one of his rooks. 'Check.'

The old man frowned. 'H'm. A good move. Yes, there's some hope for you.'

'As a chess player?'

'That, no. I shall mate you in three moves, unless . . . There is just one move you can make which will frustrate me. See if you can see it.'

Jan found the move, and the game eventually ended in stalemate. It was the nearest Jan had ever come to defeating Sam Rosenberg.

13

In early June Ned Smith returned to New Rush. Jan went to Market Square early that evening, eager to see Harry again. But Harry was not there.

''E left me in Cape Town,' Smith told him. 'Young 'alfwit. I don't know what 'e's doing now. Told me 'e got 'isself an office job of some sort – don't ask me what it was. I was none too pleased, I can tell you that. 'E's the best barker I ever 'ad.'

'He gave you no message for me?'

'No. But then 'e didn't know I'd be coming 'ere yet. Silly young bugger. 'E used to talk about you a lot.'

'I've missed him.'

Smith nodded. ''Ow's the world treating you? Been fighting at all?'

'Not since the scrap with you. I told you then I was giving up, and I've kept my word.'

'Pity,' said Smith. 'I was 'oping you'd kept in practice. I was going to suggest you and me should put on an exhibition. Not a real old ding-dong like that big fight of course – just a show. Say a dozen five minute rounds. That way neither of us is going to get badly 'urt. I wouldn't want to see you the way you were last time, young feller.' He laughed. 'Nor me, neither. And we'd 'ave the fight in one of the canteens, where there's enough room to set up a ring, and we charge everyone ten bob to come in. If we get a 'undred and twenty there, that's an easy twenty-five quid for you. What d'you say?'

Jan smiled. 'No, my friend. I'm not sure whether I'll do it at all, but if I do, it's equal shares. Thirty pounds for you, thirty pounds for me.'

Smith punched him on the arm. 'You're a sharp one, you are. So you agree?'

'I'll think about it.' But he knew already that he would do it.

Thirty pounds was fair money for an hour and a half's boxing, and he felt sure that he was in good enough physical condition – the hard work at the claim saw to that. 'When? If I agree.'

'Saturday. That gives us time to sell the tickets.'

'I'll tell you later this evening.'

'Come back 'ere. Give me the nod, and I'll bring you into the ring and announce it.'

Jan hurried over to Dutoitspan to see if Pegleg would act as bookie for him.

'Can a fish swim?' Pegleg replied.

Jan returned to Market Square and gave Smith his agreement. The prizefighter advanced to the centre of the ring. 'Gents all! Those of you 'ere last February will remember a great fight, the toughest fight of my career, against the doughty Dutchman, Jan Shapiro. Give 'im a cheer, gents. I'm announcing an exhibition bout between myself and Mr Shapiro next Saturday evening at eight o'clock in the London 'Otel. Tickets, price ten shillings, strictly limited to one 'undred and twenty spectators, can be purchased this very evening. 'Urry, gents, or you'll be disappointed.'

When they got back to Smith's chair, Jan challenged him. 'How do you know you'll be able to book the London Hotel, and how have you got tickets already?'

'Already booked,' Smith grinned. 'I knew you'd agree.'

By the Saturday evening, all the tickets had been sold, and the London Hotel, where a makeshift ring had been set up, was packed to the doors. Before the fight Smith had a further word with Jan. 'Can't get away with play-acting, y'know. Got to give 'em their money's worth. So you're in for a pasting, lad.' He grinned and clapped Jan on the shoulder.

Within a few seconds of the start of the first round the match had become a bitter battle. Despite the extra strength in his arms, Jan found himself struggling to stay in the contest, and was very grateful that the rounds were limited in length and that there was a full minute's rest between them. He used all his skill and punched with all his strength, but it had little effect on Smith, and dance and weave though he might, Jan could not avoid all Smith's attacks, and was floored more than once. Smith had the mastery of him all through the bout, and as he sat in his corner before the last round, Jan wondered whether his opponent had held back from administering the coup de grace just for the sake of prolonging the entertainment. Still, he had survived without disgracing himself. He managed to stay out of trouble during the last round, and the fight ended with tumultuous applause for both boxers.

Later, in the bar, Smith again suggested that they should go into partnership, but Jan refused.

'Well, the offer's always open,' said Smith. 'Don't forget. 'Ope you're not going to ache too much tomorrow.'

'It's nothing that thirty pounds won't cure,' said Jan.

Smith grinned and called his manager who passed the money over.

Jan went to the Ace of Diamonds, where he had arranged to meet Pegleg. Pegleg shook his head sadly. 'Didn't do so well, did you, pal? I'm on the right side, but only just. It's a damned good job you stayed on your feet for that last round. If you hadn't, I'd 've had to pay out more than I took. My heart was right in my mouth all the way through that five minutes.' He counted out the money. 'Ten pounds and tuppence,' he announced with some disgust. 'Do me a favour, Jan – don't fight again. You nearly gave me heart failure, and it's not worth it for this measly amount.'

'Give me a fiver,' Jan said. 'Keep the rest – you deserve it.' He laughed. 'And don't worry – that's my last fight.'

'How's the digging going then? You're a lucky sod, having a claim.'

'Still hankering to be a digger?'

'I hanker for it every day, but that's just a dream. Where would I find the money? I bet claims are fetching anything up to seven or eight hundred these days – if they're any good.'

'It's just possible I shall want some help,' Jan said. He told him of his plans. 'Would you be interested in managing my claims?'

'Try me! When are you going to get this other one, then?'

'Oh, I don't know. Not for ages. Maybe it's just *my* dream.'

*   *   *

Jan was neither so stiff nor so bruised that he could not work on his claim the following morning. The digger who held the site next to his on the west side was an American named Jimmy Koster, a quiet man who kept himself to himself, with whom Jan had rarely exchanged more than a few words. This morning, however, Koster called him over. 'Say, I want to shake your hand. That was a great fight last night. He gave you a tough time, that guy, but he sure didn't have it all his own way. No, sirree.' He was standing beside the wall which had formed as he dug down at the limit of his claim. Above his head, along the roadway on top of the wall, men wheeled barrows, mules pulled carts. There was a constant cacophony of sound – picks and shovels digging into the ground, waggon wheels creaking and squealing, men's voices raised, and Koster himself shouting to make himself heard.

'Thing I liked,' he went on, 'was that time in the tenth round, I guess it was. I thought he'd nearly got you then. He'd been mauling you like a bull tossing a matador – say, did you ever visit Spain and see a bullfight? Anyway, you looked beat, buddy, you sure did. And then you put your head down, and you gave him a left and a right, and then a couple of real hard jabs with that left fist. And each time you hit him your eyes shut, and each time I –' All the while that he was describing Jan's actions, Koster had been miming them, shadow-boxing, his own eyes shutting as he thrust his fists out, oblivious to everything around him.

'Look out!' Jan cried, leaping back.

As a heavily-laden cart trundled along the road above Koster's head, part of the wall of rock cracked and fell.

Koster gave an agonised shriek as the falling rubble crushed him. Jan ran to him, followed by other nearby diggers. He was buried from the waist down, and at first they thought he was dead, for he was deathly pale and unmoving. As they tried to shift the rock which was pinning him down, he came round briefly, only to lose consciousness again. Exerting all their combined strength, they freed his legs, which were little more than a bloody pulp, with here and there fragments of bone sticking out at sickening angles. The blood was pumping out from damaged arteries. Quickly they put tourniquets on his thighs, and carried him as carefully as they could to the surface of the mine, and to the hospital at Bultfontein, fearing that by the time they got there he would be dead. It was a long way to the primitive wattle and daub huts which were all that the diggings could boast of in the way of a hospital.

They waited to hear the doctor's verdict, and eventually an orderly came to say that the American was still just alive, but the doctor was working on his injuries, and would probably not know until much later that day whether he would live or die. The diggers went back to the mine, Jan following slowly behind. It had not been his fault, but he felt an uneasy sense of responsibility. If Koster had not come over to talk to him about the exhibition fight, he would have been nowhere near the fall of rock.

That evening he went back to the hospital. A cloying, almost sickening smell pervaded the crowded ward. There were flies everywhere. It was very quiet, and it seemed to Jan as he glanced at the patients in their beds that many were dying and had resigned themselves to it, while those who were in pain groaned softly, as though they had no energy for more than that. Koster was one of them, his face grey and the sweat thick on his forehead. He seemed unable to speak, but feebly grasped Jan's hand, gazing at him intently.

'You'll soon be fit again,' Jan said, but Koster's eyes told him clearly that he saw through the lie. 'The other fellows send their regards,' Jan went on hastily. 'We'll take it in turns to work your claim so no one can say it's abandoned, and of course any diamonds we find will be yours.' He went on chatting for a while, but eventually lapsed into silence, aware only of Koster's pain-filled eyes. At last he gently withdrew his hand. 'I'll come and see you tomorrow,' he said.

On the way out he stopped for a word with the male nurse. 'They've taken off both his legs,' the man told him.

'He seems in great pain.'

'Of course. The morphine's wearing off now.'

'Will he live?'

'He may be all right, once he gets over the shock, provided he doesn't get gangrene. He probably will.'

Jan visited Koster several times in the next few days. The American had few friends, and greatly appreciated Jan's willingness to come to the hospital, which most of the diggers feared, believing that if you were ill when you went in you would never come out, and if you were healthy you would almost certainly catch something which would bring you back in as a patient. After that first day, Koster was able to talk, but their conversations were brief and halting, for he was very weak.

'Will you do something for me?' he whispered one evening.

'When I've gone, will you write to my folks back home?'

'Of course,' Jan said. 'But you'll be well again soon.'

Koster gently shook his head. 'Maybe you'll be able to send them a few dollars. I guess they'll auction my things – the picks and shovels and so on. And the claim will be worth a bit.'

'I'll buy it from you. I'll give you a fair price.'

'It could be auctioned. That way my folks'd get the top dollar.'

Jan was conscious of how ghoulish his interest might seem, but he could not let this chance slip. 'Listen. I'll go to the Diggers' Committee and ask them what they think the claim would fetch at auction. And whatever they say, I'll give you ten per cent on top.'

Koster smiled faintly. 'You want it very badly, don't you?' he said drily.

'Yes, I do.'

'All right.' He said it wearily, as though he had no strength for argument.

'But you'll be up and out of here in a day or two – you'll see.'

Again there was the slow movement of the head. Koster knew he was dying.

When Jan left the hospital he went straight to see Samuel Rosenberg. The old man listened carefully as he told his story. 'I see what is troubling you,' he said. 'People will say that you put pressure on him, and then, however fair the price you pay, they'll say you cheated him.'

'What can I do?'

'Pay over the odds. Get a lawyer to draw up a paper and get Koster to sign it. Get witnesses – as many as you can – to see him sign it and testify that he was in possession of all his faculties and that he signed willingly.'

'I've already offered to pay ten per cent over whatever price the Diggers' Committee put on the claim.'

'Make it twenty per cent.'

'That's ridiculous.'

'Of course. But if you want it so badly . . .'

'No one else would pay that much.'

'You're a Jew. You have to pay that penalty. The world is always ready to accuse us of sharp practice. It's a good claim. Its value will go up.'

Jan went to the Diggers' Committee, who considered Koster's claim to be worth seven hundred and fifty pounds. An additional twenty per cent would mean a total of nine hundred pounds. It was absurdly high, but Rosenberg was undoubtedly right in all that he had said. It was also more money than he possessed, but he swallowed his pride – 'foolish pride,' Sam Rosenberg had called it – and went to his bank and arranged an overdraft. Again following Rosenberg's advice he then found a lawyer, who drew up a simple bill of sale, and he persuaded Tom Allenby, Horace Williams and Alf Taylor to come with him to the hospital.

Koster seemed to have rallied. He was much more animated, and there was colour in his cheeks, but perhaps the redness was too angry to be healthy, and his eyes were still feverish. 'The doc says I'm fine,' he told them. 'Over the crisis. Course I shall never walk without crutches again, so my diamond digging days are over, I guess. But what's that matter? There's plenty of other things a man can do than dig diamonds.'

He was surprised and delighted by the amount that Jan was willing to pay for his claim, and readily signed the paper that Jan's solicitor had drawn up. The others signed too, under a statement testifying to the willingness of the vendor to conclude the agreement.

★　　★　　★

Jimmy Koster died that same afternoon. The news of his death spread quickly, and shocked those who knew him. They were even more shocked to learn that his claim had already been sold. Tom Allenby, aware that some of the diggers were accusing Jan of taking advantage of a dying man, advised him to keep out of the public eye for a while.

'No,' said Jan. 'They'll take that as an admission that I've done something wrong. If there's any trouble, I've got to face it. I shall go to the Ace of Diamonds as usual. Besides, I've got something to celebrate.'

'Mind if I come with you?'

'Of course not.' Jan smiled, knowing that Tom wanted to be on hand, ready to defend him if need be.

At first all seemed much as usual. Jan was well known and liked by the regulars in the canteen, and those who were perhaps inclined to believe the worst of him apparently had no desire to be the first to attack him. But part way through the evening, three strangers pushed their way to the bar, and their leader, a skinny man with a large moustache, pale eyes burning, shouted in a voice which penetrated the hubbub, 'Where is he? Is he here?'

'Who?' several men called.

'The Jew boy! The stinking Yid who cheated Jimmy Koster out of his claim while he was on his bloody death-bed! Is he here?'

Jan rose. 'I'm here.' His voice was low, dangerous-sounding, but it was barely audible over the angry murmur that spread through the canteen. The ugly sound grew, and men were shouting and arguing, rising to their feet and brandishing fists, and the whole place was on the brink of turmoil. Jan realised with incredulous dismay that the majority in the canteen were on the side of the skinny man, who was now pointing at him and yelling, 'Scum! Fucking Jew bastard!'

Everything had happened in a few moments, and equally swiftly Wally McFarlane had signalled to his bouncers, who moved in to eject the trouble-makers before violence broke out.

Jan made to follow them, but Tom pulled him back. 'Stay where you are – you'll never get through this crowd alive.' He shouted then, to make himself heard. 'Listen! Shapiro bought that claim from Jimmy Koster fair and square, and he paid well over the odds for it!' But although Allenby was much respected, not all who listened believed his words, and many others could not hear him.

McFarlane had already sent an urgent message to Kate, and she appeared now, still adjusting her dress. The men quietened a little, but never before had she had so little control of her audience. Earlier than usual in her routine, she left the stage and threaded her way through the tables, but even that did not have the usual effect. She ended the song at the bar, where McFarlane was standing. 'What the hell's the matter?' she asked him.

'They're making trouble for your friend Shapiro. You've got to get him out of here, Kate. He'll be all right if you're with him as you go through the back way. He's got to leave the building, or we'll have a riot on our hands. I'll bar the doors and make sure no one follows him. And you'd better make it clear that he isn't welcome here – or in your room – for the next week or so.'

'Now listen, Mr McFarlane – it ain't no business of yours who I choose to entertain.'

'It is when you entertain him under my roof. Look, Kate, I'm not against him. He's just got to lie low for a while. They'll soon forget about this, and if what Tom Allenby says is true they'll realise, most of 'em, that there's no truth in these stories about him.'

Jan was quite willing to leave with Kate, and she was surprised when he agreed without argument that he should stay away from her for a few days. In fact, he was scarcely aware of what she was saying, for his mind was filled with thoughts of vengeance. He ran round from the back of the building, hoping that the skinny man and his companions would be waiting for him outside the main entrance. But they were nowhere to be seen, though he prowled the neighbouring streets before walking slowly back to his tent.

He stood gazing at it, scarcely able to believe his eyes. It was in utter disorder. The guy ropes had been cut so that the tent had collapsed, and all his possessions had been overturned, scattered, damaged or broken beyond repair. In the centre of the mess was a paper on which were scrawled the words, 'Filthy Jew'. He picked it up and realised that it had been stuck to a pile of human excrement.

His anger erupted again. He looked around, wondering if the perpetrators were concealed somewhere, laughing at his fury, but the camp site was deserted and silent. He walked back into town, seeking the skinny man, and stalked the streets for hours in vain, until at last his anger had cooled a little, and he went back to his tent, and made an attempt to clear the mess and to salvage what could still be used. It was no use going to the police – they would not be interested in what they would consider a minor crime, and if they did decide to follow the matter up would undoubtedly be even less effective than in the matter of the thief who had stolen the mail.

As he thought about it more, Jan began to see that the worst part of the whole episode was not the vandalism. That had been done by a few mindless fanatics, and there had been little of real value in the tent. What hurt so deeply was the way the men in the Ace of Diamonds had reacted, men who had previously accepted him, liked him, been his friends. Just beneath the skin lay their hatred of the Jews, like the poison in a boil which would come gushing out at the merest prick of a needle.

In the morning he went to Samuel Rosenberg and told him what had happened. The old man spread his hands. 'I am not surprised. It is our lot to suffer.'

'Is that all you can say? You mean I should just accept it – a punishment for being Jewish?'

'Not a punishment – something we cannot escape from. There are few of us who do not experience something of that sort. It has been so since the beginning of time. It probably always will be so.'

'But those men in the canteen – they'd never shown any sign of feeling like that about me before.'

'Perhaps you have not drawn attention to the fact that you are Jewish.'

'I haven't hidden it.'

'No. But your friends, except for me, are Gentiles. There are how many Jews here in New Rush? A thousand? Maybe more. Many of them band together, live together, worship together, but you –'

'There's no synagogue here.'

'No, but there's a Hebrew Association. They hold services. Rabbis come from Cape Town.'

'You're accusing me –'

'I accuse you of nothing. I try to explain. Of course the Gentiles have accepted you – you are the celebrated prize-fighter, the paramour of the most desirable woman in New Rush, the Jew who does not flaunt his Jewishness, who takes no part in the life of the Jewish community here.' He held up his hand. 'I repeat, I am not accusing you. I am saying that you are accepted by the Gentiles, and I am saying too that hatred for our race is always there, and never buried deeply in them. You have met it before, I am sure.'

'Of course. Many times,' Jan said impatiently. 'You remember I told you of that attack on your friend Isaac Meier? What I did not tell you was that the scum who had set upon him were screaming abuse at him because he is a Jew.'

'I guessed that. But this is the first time that such evil has been directed personally at you, yes?'

146

Jan's anger exploded. 'And for that reason I am to suffer it? Because it hasn't happened to me before? I am to do nothing about it?'

'What can you do?'

'An eye for an eye, and a tooth for a tooth.' As he said it, he remembered Harry quoting the words to him and heard again the irony in his voice.

'To take an eye or a tooth in revenge is better than killing your enemy. That's what it means, you know. But all right, you want to take it literally? Then that is fine too, provided you can take the eye or the tooth without harm to yourself. But here? Surrounded by those who hate us, despise us, however willing they are to do business with us . . .'

His anger deserted him, and with a kind of despair, Jan asked, 'Why do they hate us, despise us?'

'They accuse us of killing their God. They envy us our talents. Above all they hate us for the guilt they feel at having persecuted us for centuries.'

It might have been his father talking. In sudden disgust he walked out of Rosenberg's office.

*   *   *

Although he searched for him, Jan never encountered the skinny man again, but a few days later Horace Williams told him that he had seen someone answering to his description boarding the Inland Transport waggon back to Cape Town. 'George Bell was talking to him,' he added.

'I might have known it!' He went to Bell's office.

'Mr Shapiro,' Bell said, with mock friendliness. 'What a pleasure to see you. It's a long time since we met, but then in a town as large as this . . .' He smiled broadly. 'I hear you've had a spot of trouble.'

'I reckon you heard about it before it happened.'

'I don't know what you mean.'

'I mean your friend – the thin bastard with the black moustache.'

'Who are you talking about? That description could fit anybody.'

'You saw him off on the Inland Transport this morning.'

Bell frowned and smoothed his chin. 'Oh, I remember the fellow. Funny eyes he had – almost colourless. He's no friend of mine. I'd never seen him before. He did talk to me – asked me some damfool question or other. But I don't know him from Adam.'

'You're lying. You set him up to accuse me of cheating Jimmy Koster, to destroy my tent and my belongings – and not just destroy them, but cover them in his own filth.'

Bell smiled, happily aware of the protection of his wide desk between himself and Jan, and of the revolver in the top drawer. 'Did he do that too? Dear me, I *am* sorry.' He slid the drawer open, just in case the gun was needed. 'Shall I tell you something, Shapiro?' he continued, still smiling broadly. 'You're right. He and his pals *were* carrying out my instructions – but of course you'll never prove it.' The smile vanished abruptly. 'I'm glad that they did such a good job. And I can't promise it won't happen again. It's only what you deserve, you and your kind.'

Jan fought to keep control of himself. 'Why do you hate us so much?'

'Jews? I don't hate Jews, Shapiro.' He paused. 'I despise 'em!'

Jan leaned over the desk, seized him by the lapels of his coat, and hauled him to his feet. He had no chance to reach his gun. The colour drained from his face and he was trembling. Jan had been going to hit him so hard that he might well have killed him, but his anger suddenly turned to utter contempt. 'It's true – I can't prove anything. But if you ever try anything else on me or on any other Jew in this place, I'll beat you to a pulp and rub your face in your own shit, whether I can prove it or not!' He threw the white-faced man back into his chair, and stalked out.

★   ★   ★

Jan thought that the law was going to catch up with Bell before he had a chance of doing so when, shortly afterwards, news came through that the police in Cape Town had, by a lucky accident, apprehended the thief who had stolen the mail from the post office. Arresting the man for some petty offence, they had discovered that he still had with him most of the diamonds he had stolen. Investigations proved that a year or so previously he had been employed by Bell, of whose complicity in the mail robbery there was a strong suggestion.

However, he was able to wriggle out of the accusations without much difficulty. 'Yes, he worked for me,' he said blandly when he was questioned, 'but I sacked him after a couple of weeks. He was cheating me – or trying to. I haven't seen him since.' As the criminal himself denied that his former employer had been involved in the robbery, there was no evidence with which to proceed against Bell, but there were many, including Jan, who were far from convinced of his innocence.

'He's got away with it again, but I'll get him one day,' Jan said to Sam Rosenberg. He had made his peace with the old man and visited him regularly again.

'You leave the Lord to get him,' Rosenberg advised drily. 'He may have plans of His own for Mr Bell.'

'I just hope He gives me a big part to play in them,' Jan said.

Further news arrived from Cape Town to the effect that most of the diamonds that had been found when the mail thief was caught had been identified and would be returned in due course to those who had posted them. All the stones that Jan had lost would be coming back to him.

'Do you think the Lord had a hand in that?' Jan asked Rosenberg. 'If so, He's a good detective, isn't He? My congratulations to Him.'

'That sounds a bit blasphemous,' Sam said, 'but He won't mind that. I'll tell Him you're pleased next time He and I have a chat.'

14

In the days and weeks that followed the vandal's attack on his property, the wound in Jan's heart slowly healed, though the experience stayed with him, a scar which would always be part of him.

His friends took pains to spread the truth of the circumstances surrounding his purchase of Jimmy Koster's claim, and the feeling against him died down. After a comparatively short while he was able to resume his old habits, going to the Ace of Diamonds and continuing his liaison with Kate.

He was delighted to have two adjacent claims and did not regret the price he had had to pay, but with interest on his overdraft, found himself financially embarrassed, and now that he had the second claim it was obvious that he would need assistance. Working even a single claim was really too much for one man, though he had managed so far, reluctant to take on the responsibility of an employer watching constantly to see that the blacks earned their keep and did not pocket any diamonds. But he could not manage two claims on his own, and he could certainly not afford to employ Pegleg. Fortunately, in the first few days of working the double claim he found several small stones, and he decided to take the risk that they would continue to appear, in which case he could perhaps chance his arm by hiring a couple of Kaffirs after all.

Before committing himself, he worked out the figures carefully. If only he could reduce the overdraft. He thought again of selling his diamond, the Shapiro Diamond, but nothing would make him do that.

Since the administrators in Cape Town had given the black man a higher social status than he had had under the Boers, it was no longer easy to find reliable native labour, but after interviewing a number of candidates, Jan at last chose two who seemed suitable. One was much older than the other, an exceptionally tall man who was perhaps in his early forties, and who claimed to have considerable experience in digging for diamonds. He said that his name was Billy. The second was no more than fifteen or sixteen, a strongly built lad, willing and sunny-natured, in contrast to Billy's sullen attitude. The boy's name was to Jan's ears unpronounceable, so he followed the custom of giving natives European nicknames, and announced that he would henceforth be known as Joey, a decision which seemed to amuse and delight the young black.

On the whole the two Kaffirs worked well – at least when under supervision. When Jan had to leave the claims he would often return to find Billy leaning on his shovel, staring blankly into the distance, or even lying asleep on the ground. Joey too would be working more slowly than usual.

A few days after he had taken them on, Jan happened to notice Billy pick something up and put it in the pocket of the shabby shorts he wore.

'What did you put in your pocket?' he called.

'Nothing, boss.'

'Show me what you've got there. Turn out your pockets.'

Sourly Billy obeyed, but if he had stolen a diamond managed somehow to conceal it.

Jan was still suspicious, and his doubts increased the following morning, when Billy failed to turn up for work.

'He sick,' Joey explained. 'He booze too much last night. Big head today.'

Billy must have bought the liquor illegally, which meant that he had paid four or five times the normal price.

'Where did he get the money?' Jan asked.

Joey shrugged.

When Billy came back to work on the third day, he appeared to be suffering still, and Jan could smell the brandy on his breath. His first impulse was to sack him there and then, but there was so much work to be done that he let him off with a warning.

A week later, he saw Billy again pick something from the rock he was digging and put it in his pocket. He said nothing, but went and spoke to some of the other diggers, telling them of his suspicions. Illegal diamond buying, or I.D.B. as it was known throughout the diggings, was in many eyes the worst crime that a man could commit. The diamonds concerned were usually stolen, those who bought them were undermining the market with the prices they paid, and however lawless they might be in other respects, most diggers felt that I.D.B. was a serious affront to the honour of the community.

Allenby and the other diggers were therefore very ready to help Jan, and it was agreed that four of them, including Jan and Tom, would follow Billy at the end of the day and see if they could catch him, and more importantly, the buyer, red-handed.

'I'll go and get Dick Brooks,' one of the men said. 'He's on the Diggers' Committee. He'll come like a shot, and then it'll be official.'

At the end of the working day, Jan and the others, joined by Dick Brooks, let Billy get a little ahead of them before following. It was easy to keep track of him because of his height, and at the same time to remain unnoticed themselves in the crowds. He led them a short way along Main Street, and then turned off, and went into one of the small wooden-walled buildings. The door shut behind him.

Certain of their quarry now, the five men gathered round the building. The sound of voices carried quite clearly.

'Big diamond,' they heard Billy say.

'Show me,' George Bell replied. Then, after a pause, 'Flawed – badly flawed.'

'No, boss. Very good diamond.'

'Where did you get it? Picked it up in the street, eh?'

'Yes, boss.'

'Took it out of your master's claim when he wasn't looking more like. All right, you black bastard. I'll give you a fiver for it. Let me see it again.' There was a pause. 'All right. Here's your fiver. And remember, I want more like this.'

At that point Dick Brooks thrust open the door of the office. 'Well, Mr Bell,' he said pleasantly. 'Caught you at last.'

Bell hastily pushed the diamond back into Billy's hand. 'Ah, glad to see you, Mr Brooks. This nigger was just trying to sell me an illegal diamond. Of course, I refused. I'm glad you're here – you can take him into custody.'

Brooks smiled. 'Save it for the judge, Bell. There are five of us who heard everything.'

'It's a put-up job!' Bell shouted. He saw Jan. 'This is your doing, Shapiro!' He turned to Brooks. 'That man's got a grudge against me. Thinks I cheated him, but it was all fair and legal.'

'Oh, I know,' said Brooks with mock sympathy. 'Isn't it sad, fellows, how an honest man like George Bell can be misunderstood?' His tone changed. 'Come on, you fat crook. I'm going to enjoy seeing you put down.'

A crowd had gathered outside. The story had quickly spread that Bell was being arrested on a charge of I.D.B., and as always in these cases, the men were in angry mood, and if Brooks had not been there would probably have torn Bell limb from limb. Brooks, Jan, Tom Allenby and the two other diggers had to form a kind of bodyguard around him and Billy as they led them off to police headquarters.

The trial, at which Jan and Brooks were the chief witnesses, took place two days later. Billy was sent to prison for five years. Bell, as the buyer and a white man, was given a sentence of ten years' hard labour. As he was taken from the dock he screamed obscenities at the judge and at Brooks, but particularly at Jan.

'He'll enjoy building the breakwater at Cape Town,' Brooks said.

'It will kill him,' Jan replied.

'Yes. Good riddance.'

In due course, Jan received back the stolen diamond. It was almost flawless, and he sold it to Samuel Rosenberg for seventy-five pounds.

*　　*　　*

'You know, I been going with you for more than three months now,' Kate said to Jan as they lay together in her bed. 'I never been with a feller as long as that before.'

He laughed. 'Maybe the others haven't been as handsome as me.'

'Oh, the conceit of it!' she replied. 'Well, Mr Handsome, it could be that you're right. Or it could be that . . .' Her hand began to travel down, over his chest and flat belly. '. . . that I like the things you do to me.' And then the hand no longer fondled him, but came back up to hold him to her. He could barely hear her as she murmured, 'And maybe it's because you treat me like a human being – not like those slobs out there who think I'm a whore.'

He looked back over the three months. Their relationship had changed, as though each had stripped away another veil. Perhaps that was what happened in marriage, he thought. Perhaps it would be like that with him and Rebecca when they were at last together. He could talk about anything to Kate. Except about Rebecca. She would occasionally mention her name, always saying, '*your* Rebecca' in an almost contemptuous tone, but he had learned that if *he* spoke of her, Kate would lash herself into a tantrum, and threaten to turn him out of her bed and her life. She was a moody person, flying into rages, sinking into maudlin troughs of self-pity, and at the next moment bubbling with laughter. Her variety fascinated him, especially since he could usually jolly her out of her anger or despair. Recently, however, she had often treated him with impatience, and then neither laughter nor tenderness would change the mood for a long time. He wondered sometimes why she stayed with him.

*   *   *

At last in late June the letter from his father came. Jan's hands trembled as he held the envelope, staring at the jagged writing. Jacob might find it difficult to forgive his son entirely, but surely there would be some word of warmth.

It was scarcely a letter – just a brief and formal note on business writing paper with a printed heading, 'J. Shapiro. Diamond Cutter & Polisher'. There was no word of praise or enquiry as to Jan's well-being, nor any family news – simply an acknowledgement of receipt of the diamonds and a statement that a bank draft was enclosed. 'I shall pay equally promptly for any further consignments that you send. Your affectionate father, J. Shapiro.'

Jan crumpled the paper in anger. 'Affectionate, indeed!' he muttered. He turned to the other letter which had arrived at the same time. It was the longest that Rebecca had sent him, full of news of places she had been, the needlework that she was completing, gossip about her friends. 'Esther Meulenstein has just left to go to America, *alone*. Papa and Mama are scandalised, and I must say I consider Esther to be rather *bold*. I could never do anything like that.' The remark was obviously meant for him, Jan thought. She would not travel to the Cape, when the time came, unless he went to Amsterdam to fetch her. 'I saw Abram again the other day,' the letter continued. 'He says your father was *very* pleased to hear from you. You really must write properly to him, Jan. Family ties are so important.' She went on in this vein for several more lines.

'If he was so pleased, why couldn't he have said so to me?' Jan said aloud.

He searched Rebecca's letter for a response to the passionate declarations of affection that he always included when he wrote to her. It ended as usual with the words 'with love, Rebecca', but otherwise there was nothing. Perhaps she felt that anything more would be too forward for a well-brought-up young lady. At least the details of her life brought her nearer to him, and he was suddenly aware of a tide of love for her washing over his heart. Instead of waiting for Kate to break off their affair, he should do it himself. 'But,' he told himself, 'Kate means nothing to me really. Just a small pleasure which bears no relationship to what I feel for Rebecca.'

*   *   *

Although the arrival of the bank draft from Amsterdam was welcome, it did not go far towards paying off Jan's overdraft, and he began to think that he would never achieve his ambition of becoming a diamond dealer. He continued to send small packages of rough stones to his father, and he received two more drafts in payment for earlier despatches, both accompanied by the same formal note. If his father had given the slightest indication of pleasure, let alone fondness, Jan would have been happy to respond. 'But,' he told himself stubbornly, 'I'm damned if I'll make the first move.'

Early in September everything changed. He and Joey, working together at the puddling, found six largish diamonds in the course of two days. They came from his original claim, the lucky claim that had produced the Shapiro Diamond. They were not of that size, but the smallest was about fifteen carats, and two of them were over twenty-five carats. He took them triumphantly to Sam Rosenberg.

'You know what this means?' he asked the old man.

'So tell me.'

'I can pay off all my debts, afford to hire a manager and extra blacks for the claims, and start up as a merchant.'

'It's a bad time.'

'Every time's a bad time.'

'True,' Rosenberg said, combing his beard with his fingers. 'You still want me to sponsor you?'

'If you're still willing.'

'I should be such a fool. A promise is a promise.'

Kate spoke to McFarlane, who agreed readily to lend his name to her sponsorship, and Jan was then able to obtain his licence without difficulty. His next need was to find an office and equipment, but first he went to Dutoitspan to see Pegleg.

'Still interested in digging, Pegleg?'

'Always.'

Jan explained the situation.

'How many blacks have you got working for you?'

'Just one. He's a good lad.'

'We'll need more than one, however good he is.'

'Yes. It'll be part of your job to hire two or three more.'

'What terms are you offering me?'

'What do you want?'

'A hundred a year.'

'A hundred pounds?'

'Listen, they tell me the English church is going to bring out an organist, and pay him a hundred a year. I'll bet you anything you like I'm worth as much as he is, and I'll produce something more than a lot of wheezy old hymn tunes.'

Jan grinned.

'And I want fifteen per cent of the value of all the diamonds found.'

'Wait a minute,' Jan protested. 'I'll agree to the hundred pounds, but fifteen per cent on top is too much. Have you been taking lessons from George Bell?'

Pegleg laughed. 'What you don't ask for you don't get,' he said. 'All right, what's your offer?'

They settled down to an enjoyable half hour of bargaining, at the end of which Jan agreed to pay him the annual salary and ten per cent of the takings after the first hundred pounds at that rate. 'So what it amounts to is that you get ten per cent of everything, with the first hundred pounds guaranteed.'

'Done,' said Pegleg. 'When do you want me to start?'

'As soon as you can.'

'Tomorrow morning, first thing.'

With Pegleg in charge of the claims, Jan went a couple of days later in search of an office. He would have preferred to be in the row of shops facing Mount Ararat, but there was nothing available, and he finally settled for a shack in reasonable condition in a side turning nearby.

Samuel Rosenberg grunted with satisfaction when Jan told him. 'Just right,' he said. 'Not too near to be real competition for me.' He smiled to indicate that it was a joke. 'It's not an ideal position, but business you will get. What flag are you going to use?'

'I haven't thought,' Jan replied. All the diamond dealers fixed a short pole outside their offices and it was the custom to run a flag up to indicate that the shop was open for business. Rosenberg's own flag was red, with a large 'R' embroidered on it in yellow.

Jan bought a second-hand safe which he had had his eye on for a long time as it sat at the back of the pawnbroker's shop, relic of a business that had failed several months previously, and went to the auction rooms and purchased an old table and a couple of chairs, promising himself that one day soon he would order a brand-new desk, with lockable drawers, to be sent up from the Cape. He cleaned the shack thoroughly before arranging his furniture. He had decided against hanging any pictures on the wall, or having a rug on the floor or curtains at the windows. Such fol-de-rols might put customers off with their ostentation. But there was one little vanity which he decided he would permit himself. He went to a carpenter and asked him to make a small box, about six inches wide and four inches tall and deep, with one glass side; the glass should be thick and strong, but crystal clear; the back of the box should be a sliding panel or door, with a lock.

When the carpenter delivered the box, grumbling about the difficulty he had had in making it, Jan screwed its base to a shelf behind his chair. He went to the haberdashery store which had opened recently for the benefit of the women of New Rush and bought a short length of black velvet, with which he made a kind of nest at the bottom of the box. One afternoon he insisted that Kate should accompany him to his office. He opened the safe and took from it the Shapiro

Diamond and put it into the glass box, settling it gently so that it showed to advantage on the black velvet.

'I'm going to have it there always,' he told her.

'Why?'

'It'll be a symbol. It'll tell them that I'm a man of substance. If I can afford to keep a rough diamond of that size and quality, then I must be well off, mustn't I? Besides . . .'

'Besides what?'

'Well, you know what you said about it. It's a sort of good luck thing to have it here.'

'I thought you didn't want anyone to know about it.'

'I've changed my mind.'

'Someone'll pinch it.' There was an irritable note in her voice, almost as though they were quarrelling.

'That box is strong, and it's screwed down. Besides, they'd have to get past me to reach it, and when I'm not here the diamond'll be back in the safe.'

'Well, I've seen the office and I've seen your precious diamond. Now can we go back?'

'I thought you wanted to see it.' She did not reply. 'What's the matter, Kate?'

'Oh, come on!' She walked out of the shack, leaving him to put the diamond away and lock up.

She was in a bad temper that night and would not allow him to make love to her.

Two evenings later, she suddenly asked him whether he yet had a flag for his office.

'No. I've had too many other things to think about.'

'Shut your eyes,' she said.

'Oh, for heaven's sake, Kate. I've got too much on my mind to play silly games.'

'Go on – shut your eyes,' she insisted.

'Oh, very well.'

There was some rustling of paper. 'All right,' Kate said. 'Open them.'

It was a small flag, perhaps two feet long and fifteen inches deep, and it had been made of three horizontal strips of material – red at the top, white in the middle and blue at the bottom.

Jan looked at it in amazement. 'It's a Dutch flag,' he said. 'Where did you get that?'

'I made it. Will it do?'

'You made it?'

'Yes. I wanted to say sorry for being rotten to you at your office the other afternoon.' When he said nothing, she went on, 'Don't you like it?'

'Of course I like it. It's the best present I've ever had.' He took her in his arms and kissed her and held her tight, and presently they fell back upon the bed, and the flag lay on the floor, temporarily forgotten.

When he hauled it up to the top of the little flag-pole the next morning, Jan hoped that it would flutter bravely in the breeze, as all new flags should. But there was no stirring of wind, and it hung limply there, as though it had been overcome by the heat and the dust and the flies. Jan did not really mind – the mere fact that it was there signified that another ambition had been achieved.

* * *

Jan did no business at all that first day, and over the next couple of weeks began to wonder whether he had been a fool to invest his money in this venture. Obviously the diggers continued to take their diamonds to the firms they had patronised before, and saw no reason to change. But gradually, as time went by, business began to pick up. It was very slow, because, as Sam Rosenberg had said, there was something of a glut of diamonds, and prices were dropping. Some diggers became reluctant to sell when they heard what merchants like Jan would offer, believing either that they were being cheated, or that before long the prices would go up again. The only consolation for Jan was that the fewer stones he bought, the less rapidly his cash reserves were depleted. He could see a time rapidly coming when he would either have to go back to the bank for a loan or wait for money to come through from Amsterdam and temporarily close his doors until it arrived.

He went to speak to Samuel Rosenberg about it, and felt like a naughty schoolboy when the old man said, 'A warning I gave you – no? A bad time, I said. And the banks have so much money out they don't want to lend more.'

'Then what can I do? I suppose you wouldn't . . .?'

'I sponsor you. I advise you. But lend you money? No, my friend. That would be bad for my business, and in the end it would be bad for your business too. This is a testing time for you, my boy. No business that hasn't been through this sort of trouble and learnt how to weather it is likely to have the strength it needs when really difficult times come.' He shook his head slowly. 'I'll give you some more advice. I don't know why I do it. I'm a fool. What do you do when you have no more money? Do you shut up shop? No, you stay open, but you don't buy. Do you say, "I cannot buy. I have no money."? No, you say, "Ah, beautiful, beautiful. But, sorry, my friend, these aren't the kind of stones my principals are looking for now. Come back next month – I'll take them then, and I'll give you the best price in New Rush." You see?'

'They won't keep their diamonds until I'm ready to buy them.'

'Of course not. But they'll remember that you said you'd pay the best price, and next month they'll come back to you.'

Jan took his advice, and weathered the bad period, and then slowly began to build up a clientele. It was not the most prosperous business in New Rush, but it made a profit, and enabled him to send larger consignments of diamonds back to Amsterdam than if he had simply been working his double claim. Always he hoped for some sign of approval from his father, but when at last a word of praise arrived, it was still in the most formal of veins. 'The quality of this batch of stones is high. Please maintain it. Your affectionate father, Jacob Shapiro.'

Some of these high quality stones came from his own claims, but there were other diggers who now came to him regularly with good diamonds, and he paid them top prices so as to retain their custom, knowing that his father was still able to buy more cheaply through him than by going to the London merchants.

A number of rogues came in to try to sell him bits of glass and other rubbish, or offering macles so badly misshapen or with such bad interior flaws that their value was only a tiny fraction of what would normally be paid for stones of that weight. And one or two had looked with greedy eyes at the Shapiro Diamond in its glass box, and asked to see it, to hold it in their hands, and Jan had smiled and shaken his head. No one was going to have the chance of stealing it.

15

Winter passed, and the sun began to get hotter, and the dust thicker, and the flies more persistent. Jan had been in New Rush for over a year, and that was hard to believe. There had been many changes. The diggings at Colesberg Kopje were biting deeper and deeper into the earth, and had now reached anything between fifty and eighty feet below the surface. And still they dug, and still they found the diamonds they sought. The roads between claims were all like tall walls now, and the kind of accident in which Jimmy Koster had lost his legs and eventually his life were becoming more and more common. The road had been repaired where the collapse which injured Koster had taken place, but Jan had given Pegleg instructions that they should exercise the utmost care whenever he or the native employees were working near it.

Although the mine continued to be worked vigorously, many people still believed that Dutoitspan might prove more valuable in the end, and the belief had brought prosperity to the village, which now boasted a broad main street and many shops with plate glass windows to line it. Several diamond dealers moved from New Rush to Dutoitspan, but some instinct seemed to tell Jan that they were wrong, and that New Rush would eventually be recognised as the more productive mine. Sam Rosenberg shared his view, and they both stayed where they were and their businesses benefitted a little because of the competitors who had left the area.

Houses in New Rush and Dutoitspan and Bultfontein grew and the tents were slowly disappearing to be replaced by more solid structures. It was not only the diggers, if they were lucky, and the diamond dealers who were getting rich, thought Jan, but the men who made corrugated iron, of which thousands of square feet were used. Stores and canteens multiplied, food and other necessities poured into the diamond fields, and there were churches and places of entertainment. More families came to the diggings, and the women demanded and got some of the trappings of civilised life. Of course, nothing could disguise the fact that New Rush was still physically little more than a shanty town. In terms of architectural elegance there was not very much to choose between canvas and corrugated iron, and the tracks that wandered haphazardly through the buildings were no less dusty or rutted for being nostalgically named Oxford Street or Piccadilly. Nevertheless, there were those who knew that the spirit of a community is created by those who live in it, whatever their surroundings, and who were prepared to lead the way, organising balls and other social events, supporting the churches, setting standards of dress and behaviour. A primitive settlement it might be, but it could be seen to have a sophisticated side. There was even talk of building a theatre soon – a proper theatre, with proper seats, rather than a bench-filled tin hut; after all, a town with ten thousand or more inhabitants deserved a theatre.

By the beginning of 1873, everyone knew that some new method of extracting the ground from the mine at New Rush would have to be found. Scarcely a roadway was left standing, and nothing could prevent their disintegration, since the rock of which they were formed was not hard enough to withstand the effects of the elements, let alone the traffic that passed over them continuously from dawn to dusk. After all, it was simply the same ground as the diggers were excavating, which could be reduced to gravel with comparative ease. And if a digger were to undermine one of the wall-like roads, even unintentionally, it would not be surprising if before long a part of that wall should collapse. Accidents multiplied every day; men and mules would be hurtled sixty or seventy feet into the diggings as a roadway crumbled beneath them; men working below would be crushed beneath great falls of rock; and others were injured as they slipped from the precarious ladders which were the only means of reaching many of the claims. When the walls disintegrated, there were quarrels over whose property the ground was, with the boundaries of the claims often in dispute.

The biggest problem, however, was that the disappearance

of the roads made it much more difficult, and in some cases virtually impossible to get the excavated ground to the surface. The solution had occurred to Jan one day when he noticed a digger directing operations from the top of one of the remaining walls while a team of blacks, hauling on a rope, hoisted huge canvas buckets full of ground dug from the claim below. At that time the problem of the disintegrating roads was not yet acute, but he could see the day coming when they would all have gone. Perhaps the best way to get the ground out then would be to pull it up by rope, but you couldn't haul a bucket from a claim in the centre of the vast pit – at least, not without some kind of rigging. If a platform or staging which would support stanchions could be built near the edge of the mine, a gantry could be erected on the claim and it would then be possible to suspend a rope between the surface and the claim and, with a system of pulleys, the ground could be brought up without too much difficulty.

He explained his idea to Tom Allenby, who was enthusiastic about it, agreeing that it would prove a practical solution to the problem.

'So will you join with me?' Jan asked.

'Join with you?'

'Yes. We can't each have staging and stanchions for ourselves – it would be very costly, and there wouldn't be room for everyone. We have to band together.'

Tom hesitated. 'I'd like to see how 'twould work in practice first.'

Jan laughed. 'I can't set up a demonstration model for you. What we need is to involve everybody. Then we can build long sections of staging to take several stanchions and we can link them so that they have greater strength. And the more diggers involved, the lower the costs for each of us.'

'What we ought to do, m'dear,' Tom said, 'is go to the Diggers' Committee. They'll call a public meeting. Of course, you may not want to do that.'

'Why not?'

'They'll take over. You won't get any credit for the idea.'

'I don't care about that. Besides, I'm no engineer, and they'll know someone who can design it all so that it works.'

'They'll have a committee of engineers and designers. Committees breed committees.'

'Then their committee can have the credit. All I want is to see it working.'

The public meeting was called in due course, and though there were many doubters, enough of the diggers agreed to go ahead with the plan for it to become viable. The staging was built, a massive frame of stanchions erected on it, ropes extended down to the claims. It was hard work hauling the ground up, and dangerous too, for sometimes a rope broke or a bucket would tip, sending its load cascading down on to claims where men were working, but accidents were commonplace in the mine, and by and large the scheme was considered a success. The doubters were soon converted and before long much of the great hole's circumference was covered in staging and hoisting gear and the hundreds of ropes descending to the claims looked like some strange spider's web, the threads so closely woven that they almost obscured the diggings from view, as though a vast net curtain had been hung over them.

As Tom had predicted, Jan's name was mentioned only briefly at the public meeting as one among many responsible for the idea. He was glad. If he had been given greater prominence there might have been some move to elect him to the Diggers' Committee, and to enjoy that one had to be addicted to formality and paperwork and procrastination and all the paraphernalia of committee work. He did not want that. But every time that he looked at the staging and saw the buckets of ground making their slow progress towards the lip of the mine he felt a small thrill of pride.

*   *   *

A letter came from Cape Town. 'Dear Old Pal, I hope the world has treated you well since last we met, as it has yours truly. No doubt you heard that I had left old bully-boy Smith. It was good fun working with him, but no way for a respectable man to earn a living, as my revered Papa would say. Ha! Ha! I got a job here in Cape Town, working in one of the Government offices, which is much more suitable employment for a person of my incomparable intelligence! I began as a junior assistant to the chap who is in charge of all the victualling arrangements for Her Majesty's troops in the Cape, Mr Ronald Tester. A real nob! You may wonder how I landed such a place, and I have to confess that my aforesaid revered parent pulled a few strings for me. Mr Tester invited me to his home and I fell for his daughter, Miss Edith Tester, like the proverbial ton of bricks. She had the good sense to be equally smitten by me, and the long and the short of it is that we are to be married next month. I wish you would come for the wedding, but I fear that by the time you receive this it will be too late and your old friend will already be revelling in marital bliss. I should have written before. Anyway, my Pater-in-law-to-be is absolutely rolling in it, and as a wedding present he's giving us a beautiful house, just outside Cape Town, *and* he's settling a large sum of money on Edith, *and* he's arranging for me to be promoted. Talk about the luck of the Templetons! The house has dozens of guest rooms, so if you come to Cape Town I insist that you come and stay with us. Food and liquor in plenty, especially liquor! Ha! Ha! Wish me happiness, old son, as I do you. Your old friend, Harry.'

Jan wrote him a brief note of congratulations, but did not respond to the invitation. He had no plans to go visiting, and fond though he had been of Harry, he had faded from his life. In any case, if he were to leave New Rush at all, it would be to return home to Amsterdam – not to stay, for he knew now, even after this comparatively short time, that he wanted to spend his life in South Africa, but long enough to marry Rebecca. But he could not see any way of leaving New Rush for the time being. He could trust Pegleg to continue working his claims, but he would have to close the diamond dealing business just as it was beginning to prosper.

* * *

Jan's financial situation had improved to such an extent that he felt he could allow himself a little extravagance, and apart from a visit to Gowies' stores to buy some new clothes, which in any case came more under the heading of necessity than of extravagance, he decided it was time to smarten up his office. Now that he was established, a small show of prosperity was unlikely to put off his customers.

The shack was set back a yard or two from its neighbour, and to make its entrance more attractive, Jan had a verandah built on. It was about four feet wide, supported in front by four iron pillars and attached at the rear to the main roof. Its sides were enclosed by a low fence of spiked wrought iron railings, which the local blacksmith made to Jan's order, and he envisaged himself sitting out on this stoep sometimes to escape the heat of the office.

He also had a new sign painted and hung on the front of the verandah. 'Johannes Shapiro,' it proclaimed. 'Licensed Diamond Dealer. Affiliated to J. Shapiro, Diamond Cutters and Polishers, Amsterdam.' All that remained was to improve the interior of the office, and he bought a large desk and new chairs, and a cabinet to hold his ledgers. He had his dealer's licence and a notice giving the address of the firm in Amsterdam framed and hung on the walls.

He spent some time arranging the furniture, placing the desk and the cabinet across the narrow room, so that it was virtually divided in two. There was only just space to squeeze between them, and while he was there it would be almost impossible for any stranger to gain access to the back part of the room where his safe stood and where the Shapiro Diamond gleamed from the glass box screwed to the low shelf behind his desk.

When he had finished, he surveyed it, and was pleased. The changes were impressive, speaking of a well-established, successful business. He wished his father could see it.

He had barely completed this project when a letter came from Abram, the first that his brother had written to him. The family concern was forging ahead, the letter said, and that was in large measure due to the quantity and quality of the diamonds that Jan was supplying. But he was writing chiefly to announce that he and his father had decided to take new premises in Sarphatistraat for their cutting and polishing works, retaining the old house on Onkelboerensteeg merely as a dwelling place. In future, Jan should send his packages to Sarphatistraat. It was almost as formal a communication as his father's regular acknowledgements of the arrival of each consignment of rough stones.

The news made him suddenly home-sick. He thought with longing of the cool clean streets of Amsterdam, the canals, the tall, comfort-filled houses. In his mind's eye he could see every room in the little house in Onkelboerensteeg, and he pictured his father, Abram, Aunt Suzanna. And Rebecca. It was funny, but he could not really see, in his memory, Rebecca's face. He would remember her eyes, or her mouth, or the shape of her nose, but he could not make them all fit together, and when he tried, the features would blur. Yet he thought of her constantly, even when he was with Kate, and continued to write to her regularly.

Perhaps he could make some arrangement for his business to be looked after while he went back to Amsterdam and brought her here to . . . to a small and tattered tent. 'The first thing I must do,' he said to himself, 'is get a house.'

Some weeks later, he found exactly the place he was looking for, a single-storeyed structure with the inevitable corrugated iron roof. The walls too were of corrugated iron, except for the front facade, which was wooden-boarded. It was far from spacious, but there was a living-room, a bedroom and a tiny kitchen. It was badly in need of repair and redecoration and would need a lot spent on it, but because of its dilapidated state was quite cheaply priced. He bought it before he could change his mind.

He persuaded Kate to come and look at it. She was not impressed. 'Rather you than me,' she said.

'It's going to be put in order and decorated.'

'H'm. Still, I suppose she'll be happy enough.'

'Who?'

'Your Rebecca. That's who you've bought it for, ain't it? Not for a whore like me.'

'You enjoy saying that, don't you?'

'It's true. And when she comes out here the pair of you will look at me with your noses in the air. Well, let me tell you this, Mr High and Mighty Shapiro – I've had enough.'

'What do you mean?'

'It's over, sonny. You can come and collect your things any time.'

'I don't understand. Rebecca won't be here for months yet.'

'And until she comes you want to go on poking me, don't you? Men! You make me sick. And who says your Rebecca ain't here already? She's here all the time. You're always thinking of her, I know you are. And I'm fed up to the teeth with it, d'you hear?' She turned and ran.

Jan hurried after her, but she pulled her arm away from his outstretched hand. 'Leave me alone, can't you?' she said, the tears streaming down her face.

Unwilling to cause a scene in the crowded street – already people were looking at them curiously – and feeling she was best left to get over this mood by herself, Jan let her go.

Kate seemed to be in her most sparkling form when she came out to entertain the customers at the Ace of Diamonds that evening, but she would not sit with Jan, and once when she passed by him and he caught her round the waist and tried to pull her on to his knee, she swiftly wriggled free and hissed under her breath, 'I've told you it's all over. I've parcelled up your things, and they're waiting for you.'

'I'm not going to take them.'

'Then they'll be thrown out. I mean it, Jan – I really mean it. And you needn't think you can come back in a few days. I'll have someone else by then.'

He waited until she had finished her last spot and had disappeared through the back of the canteen, and then followed. Outside her room was a bundle of the clothes and shaving tackle that he normally left there. He tried the handle, but the door was locked. He knocked.

'Go away,' Kate called.

'Kate! Listen to me, please. Kate!'

She made no response to his repeated pleas, and at last he went back, miserably, to his tent, trying to make himself believe that it was nothing more than a temporary rift. But the days passed with no sign from Kate. He thought it wise to avoid going to the Ace of Diamonds for a day or two, but when he eventually returned, several of the regulars were quick to tell him that she had taken a new lover, buying him drinks in sympathy, offering suggestions of where else he might find female companionship. They pointed out to him Kate's new paramour, a burly, good-looking youngster. Jan thought of going to him, challenging him, fighting him, but knew instinctively that it would not alter Kate's attitude and indeed might make her even more sympathetic towards the newcomer. Besides, he knew in his heart that he should be glad for Rebecca's sake that the affair was over.

*   *   *

Soon afterwards, the work on his house was completed and Jan furnished it and moved in. It had cost far more than he had planned and he had had to raise a small loan from the bank.

The claims were still productive, and Pegleg was going to earn well over his hundred pounds, but there were so many demands on Jan's pocket that it would be some time before he could afford the cost of a return journey to Amsterdam and Rebecca's fare back, even if he found someone to look after the business while he was away.

It was pleasant to have comfortable rooms and a certain amount of space, but he was lonely, and moreover it was a chore to keep the house in order. He had a sudden idea, and called Joey from the claims one morning and told him that henceforth he was to be his personal servant. He would clean and wash and he would learn to cook – which meant something better than mealie porridge – and he would do everything possible to make his master's life more bearable.

'You want woman?' Joey asked, grinning from ear to ear.

'No,' replied Jan sharply.

Joey was willing and learned comparatively quickly, but he was not a companion, and Jan took to spending many evenings with Samuel Rosenberg. His skills at chess were no match for Rosenberg's, but the old man seemed to enjoy playing, even when Jan, often finding it difficult to concentrate, could offer very little opposition.

'She meant so much to you?' Rosenberg asked one evening after checkmating him with ease.

'Kate, you mean? No, not really. I was fond of her. And she was so . . . alive.'

'Then it is your pride that is hurt.'

Jan could never be less than honest with the old man, who always seemed to be able to put his finger on his problems. 'Yes, perhaps. And I miss her. I suppose what I feel most of all is . . . well, puzzled. Why did she suddenly break it off?'

'You had not quarrelled?'

'No. She was a bit edgy at times, but there was nothing that led me to believe . . . What did I do? I just don't understand.'

'It is easier to count a handful of mustard seeds than to understand a woman.' Rosenberg set out the chessmen for another game. 'But my guess would be that she did not like the idea of playing second fiddle. She knew about your Rebecca, yes?'

'Yes.'

'And when you bought the house, she knew that sooner or

later your liaison would end. And when you took her to see it – that was a mistake, Jan – perhaps she felt that you were underlining the fact that it was no more than an affair, and even that it was your first move in the ending of it.'

'But I didn't want to end it. Not yet.'

'No, but she may not have seen it that way. And it helped *her* pride to break it off herself instead of waiting for you to do so.'

'Yes. I see. I hadn't thought of it like that. It's clever of you to see it.'

Rosenberg chuckled. 'A second Solomon I am. So when will you marry your Rebecca? Have you sent for her?'

'I can't. She won't come out here alone, so I have to go back to Amsterdam to fetch her.'

'Good. You will be able to see your father and patch up your quarrel with him.'

'Oh, don't you start on that, Sam. In any case, I don't see how I can leave here for . . . well, it would mean three months at least.'

'Why not? You are not short of money.'

'No. But I'd have to close my office, just when it is beginning to go really well.'

'So close it, and open it again when you come back.'

'And have to start again from scratch.'

'You might lose a little business, but a wife is worth that, nu? You would not lose much. You put a notice on your door to send your customers to me. I'll give you ten per cent on any extra business I get that way.'

'How would you know which are my clients?'

'A good point. Maybe they'll tell me.'

'And maybe you won't give them a chance to do so, you old fox.'

Rosenberg chuckled. 'Did I complain when you first set up? I must have lost pounds of business to you.' He spread his hands. 'But that is what we're here for, isn't it. To help one another – as long as we don't hurt ourselves.'

'I'll wait a while,' said Jan. 'Buying the house and the redecorations that have to be done mean I can't afford to go home yet.'

*   *   *

Towards the middle of winter, Pegleg came to see Jan in his office. He sat down in the chair in front of the desk, looking worried. 'You've heard these stories that the mine's worked out, Jan?'

'Yes, of course.'

New Rush had recently been buzzing with the report that the discovery of diamonds would soon be at an end, since in the deepest parts of the mine the nature of the rock had suddenly changed and they appeared to have come to the end of the yellowish diamondiferous ground. Some of the diggers with the deepest claims had already packed and left.

'It's happened to us,' Pegleg said.

'You mean you've reached this solid rock?'

'Yes. It's got a blueish grey colour to it, and it's much harder than anything we've come across previously. Of course, we don't go down absolutely evenly, and we've got quite a bit of the yellow ground to bring out yet, but I'll bet you a pound to nothing that within two weeks we'll be down to this blue ground right across the two claims.'

'What do you think we ought to do?'

'Sell out, I suppose. And as quick as you can.'

'The prices are ridiculous.'

'They'll be down to nothing at all before long. You'd better make your mind up quickly. The sooner I know where I stand, the happier I'll be.'

'Yes. I'll talk to some other people. I'll give you a decision tomorrow.'

When Pegleg had left, Jan shut his office, hauling down the flag, and went to Sam Rosenberg. That was always his first reaction nowadays – to talk to Rosenberg. But this time the old man could not help him. He was as worried as Jan, and was seriously thinking of leaving New Rush. Perhaps, he said, there would be a longer future at Dutoitspan, but even that was doubtful.

Jan left him and went to seek other advice. In one of the canteens he found Tom Allenby. If anyone in New Rush would keep a level head in a situation like this, and would know all the facts, it was Tom.

' 'Tis very worrying,' he admitted. 'But I wrote to a fellow back home who's a mineralogist when I first heard this was happening. Sent him some samples of the blue ground. His reply came this very morning. He says he believes the pipes that diamonds come in are columns of rock which go down a long, long way into the earth. Course I'd told him how deep the diggings already are, but he says he don't believe the diamondiferous ground would be so shallow –'

'But we're already nearly a hundred feet down,' Jan interrupted.

'I know. But he calls that shallow, and thinks the pipe is probably thousands of feet deep. As for the nature of the rock, he says the blue ground is very similar to the yellow stuff we know so well.'

'And you believe him?'

''Tis Gospel, m'dear – as far as it goes. Trouble is, he don't say definite that the blue ground is diamondiferous.'

'So what are you going to do?'

'I'm not sure. You know how little the claims are selling for now. They say the population has gone down by thousands in the last two or three weeks – people packing up and going home. So there's no one to buy, or hardly anyone. If I sell my claims now I'll get so little for them that I'd scarce be worse off in the end if I couldn't sell them at all.'

'So you're carrying on.'

'I don't know. I really don't know.'

'Maybe it's worth trying to break up this blue ground.'

'Aye. One or two diamonds have been found in it, they say, but if they're rare, 'twill be more trouble than 'tis worth to get them out.'

Jan went back to Sam Rosenberg, and told him what he had learned.

'So?' the old man asked.

'Maybe I'd be best off cutting my losses. And you?'

'I shall pray.' He chuckled at the look on Jan's face. 'You've heard of praying. We talked of it once before. In Amsterdam you went to the synagogue, you prayed, no? But since you left Holland you have not prayed.' There was no accusation in his voice – it was simply a statement of fact.

'I'm not sure that I know how to pray. Not the way you mean.'

'Praying isn't just something you do wearing a prayer shawl in the synagogue. You can also pray just by thinking about something and asking the Lord God to help. You don't have to

172

do it aloud. All you have to do is to put your trust in Him. Try
it.'

'I don't think the Lord God would waste His time on me. I
haven't spared much for Him.'

Rosenberg laughed. 'You could tell Him you're sorry.'

That night Jan delved into the bottom of his bag and
brought out his kippa and the phylactery and prayer shawl,
and put them on. But no words would come to him, and he
felt self-conscious and ridiculous. He packed the articles away
again, thinking it would be better to throw them out. But he
could not bring himself to do that.

Whether or not it had anything to do with the Lord God,
when he awoke in the morning Jan knew with absolute
certainty that he was going to stay in New Rush, at least for a
while. He told Pegleg, adding that he would guarantee him
and the black workers a month's further payment even if their
haul of diamonds should diminish to nothing.

Rosenberg was expecting him. 'You're staying, then.'

'Yes. For the time being. How did you know?'

'Did you think He would tell me to stay and you to go? He's
not crazy.'

*　　*　　*

The gloom and despondency had not been justified. The blue
ground, after it had been exposed to the sun and the wind and
the wide variations of temperature, began to decompose, and
the longer it was left, the more friable it became, and the nearer
in colour to the familiar yellow ground. And it carried within
it as many diamonds, if not more, as the ground nearer the
surface.

There was great rejoicing throughout New Rush, the price
of claims shot up to their earlier level, and mining proceeded
with new enthusiasm.

No sooner, however, had the diggings settled again than the
government announced several new legislative measures
which many felt would alter everything for good and all. The
radical nature of the changes to be made then and in the future,
including for instance the removal of all power from the
Diggers' Committee, was symbolised to the widespread dismay of most of the inhabitants by the renaming of local places.
Klipdrift, where the river diggings had been centred, was

henceforth to be known as Barkly, and Griquatown was to be called Hay, and New Rush itself was renamed Kimberley, in honour of the Secretary of State for the Colonies. It was rumoured that Lord Kimberley had insisted on these alterations because he said he was unable either to spell or to pronounce the old names.

Jan discussed the announcements with Samuel Rosenberg. The old man was uncharacteristically gloomy. 'It's the beginning of the end,' he said. 'You wait and see. Nothing will be quite the same from now on. I can feel it. New Rush just happened, and it went on thriving precisely because it was chaotic, disorganised, free. Kimberley will be different. There will be rules, logic, discipline. Oh, there'll still be fortunes to be made, there'll still be excitement, but the same it'll never be. One day the time will come for us to leave Kimberley – when it has truly become Kimberley, and New Rush is dead. We who belong to New Rush will no longer have a place here then.'

'But I thought the Lord God told us to stay.'

'Don't mock, Jan, don't mock. Yes, I believe He meant us to stay, but not perhaps for ever. Should I know what His plans for our future are?'

16

Towards the end of 1873, Jan was sitting in his office one morning, his eyes closed, thinking. The door was open, the colourful flag at the top of its pole, but no customers had come in, and he was in the middle of a letter to Rebecca. Should he commit himself firmly to the journey home the following month? There was really nothing to stop him now. He had sufficient money in the bank, and he knew that Sam Rosenberg and Pegleg between them would look after his interests in Kimberley during his absence. He took up his pen and completed the letter, telling Rebecca to prepare for their wedding in March.

As he sealed the envelope, a shadow fell in the room. He looked up and when his visitor stepped forward recognised Black Conrad. He had not been seen in the region for many months, for now that transport to and from the Cape was better organised, swifter and cheaper, there was no business for him in bringing young greenhorns to the diggings. And of course his boss, if he was still alive, was labouring on the Cape Town breakwater.

'They told me I'd find you here,' he said. He raised the shotgun he was carrying until it was pointing at Jan's chest. 'I've a few scores to settle with you.' His voice was thick, and even at a distance Jan could smell the liquor on his breath.

'If anyone's got any scores to settle, it's me,' Jan said.

'Stole my girl . . . put my boss down for a stretch . . . I'm going to blow your bloody brains out.' He laughed, swaying slightly as he stood there, but still holding the gun steady. ''Fore I do, you're going to open up that safe of yours, aren't you, matey?'

'No.' Jan stared into his eyes. His voice was calm, though he was tensed for action. 'Kill me and you'll hang.'

He saw his adversary's finger beginning to tighten on the trigger, and knew that the man was in no state to listen to reason.

'Open it!' Watson growled.

Playing for time, Jan stood up. 'Very well,' he said, and moved slowly towards the safe, which stood in the back of the room behind the cabinet where he kept his ledgers. The cabinet was quite tall, and if he could get it between himself and Watson he would be reasonably well protected from the shotgun.

But Black Conrad was not drunk enough to allow Jan out of his sight even temporarily. He stretched out his left hand, and with one powerful heave skewed the desk round so that it no longer formed a barrier to the rear part of the room. 'Go on! Open that bloody safe!'

'There are no diamonds in it,' Jan said. 'I mailed them all yesterday. And there's no money – well, maybe a couple of pounds. I pay for the diamonds I buy by cheque.' He knew there was little hope that Watson would believe the lies and leave peaceably, but it was worth trying.

Black Conrad stared at Jan suspiciously. Then he suddenly noticed the Shapiro Diamond in its glass-sided box. His black eyes lit with greed. 'All right, then,' he said. 'That'll do instead.' He reached out to take the box, but when he realised that it was fixed to the shelf, in one swift movement he brought up the butt of his shotgun and pounded it down. The glass and wood smashed.

For the first time Jan felt a moment of panic. A blow like that could have shattered his diamond into a thousand fragments. A picture flashed before his eyes of himself standing in the workshop in Onkelboerensteeg, looking in dismay at the results of his attempt to cleave a stone.

But the Shapiro Diamond was unharmed. Careless of the splinters of wood and glass, Watson snatched it out, and still menacing Jan with the gun, retreated to the door, and turned to run.

Jan flew after him. Watson, his reactions slowed by the alcohol, had paused for the briefest of moments outside Jan's office, trying to accustom himself to the dazzling sunlight. Jan launched himself at the man, and they both crashed to the ground, the shotgun skittering away from them. The surprise gave him the opportunity to grab at Watson's hand, trying to prise open the fingers which still held the stolen diamond. Black Conrad's right hand wrapped itself around his throat. He felt himself choking and was forced to release his grip on the hand holding the diamond so as to tear away the pressure from his windpipe. Watson threw him aside like a rag doll, and scrambled to his feet, but before he could make off, Jan rolled on the ground and grabbed frantically at his ankle. As Watson kicked out to free himself, he lost his balance, and fell heavily. Instinctively he put out his hands to save himself, and Jan saw a momentary gleam as the diamond shot from his grasp to land a few feet away.

He was on it before Watson could move, but just as he seized it he felt himself flying through the air, and then a sudden searing pain shot through his left leg. He lay on his back, the breath knocked from his body. Then he tried to move his leg, but his nerves screamed, and for a moment he lost consciousness.

When he opened his eyes again he saw Black Conrad struggling in the grip of four men, whose combined strength was barely enough to hold him. Other men had gathered, and while Watson was dragged away to be handed over to the police, they came over to Jan. They had seen Watson seize him and hurl him through the air towards the stoep outside his office, and as he landed one of the spiked railings had pierced right through his left calf.

Although they lifted him off the spike with care, Jan fainted again. They carried him into the office.

'Get the quack,' someone cried.

'Aye, and a pint of brandy.'

'A tot's enough.'

'No. We need it to clean him up.'

When the man came back with the brandy, they tilted the bottle so that Jan could take a long gulp, then poured the rest over the wound in his leg, from which the blood was flowing freely. Jan's head swam once more as the fiery liquor bit into his flesh.

The doctor, when he came, was complimentary. 'Best thing you could have done. With the dust and the flies, it's no wonder we get so much gangrene.'

While the doctor was treating him, Jan asked someone to

fetch Sam Rosenberg, and when the old man arrived, handed him his diamond. 'Take care of it for me, Sam. And look after the business, will you? And please post the letter on my desk.' He found it an effort to speak, the shock and the pain and the loss of blood all taking their toll.

They took him to the new Carnarvon Hospital at Dutoit-span, which offered much better facilities, including the attention of female nurses, than the rough huts where poor Jimmy Koster had died.

*　　*　　*

Jan had been in the hospital for a week when the doctor asked him if there was anyone who could look after him if he were sent home. He did not hesitate. 'Yes.'

'Then I'll discharge you, Mr Shapiro. We need the beds. The wound's healing very satisfactorily, but you must rest and you need someone to change your dressings.'

'That's no problem,' Jan answered, though he had no idea who he could call on to help him. Joey would not be capable enough, and Pegleg could not be spared from the claims, but he was determined to leave the hospital. Its facilities might be vastly better than those previously available, but there was still a smell of death about the place.

He could not walk on his injured leg, and the hospital gave him a crutch. After a little practice he could manage well enough, but by the time he had limped home, he was exhausted, and the crutch had rubbed a raw patch on the skin beneath his arm.

He sent Joey to get Pegleg, who hurried to him.

'Hello, Pegleg,' Jan said.

'Pegleg yourself! Though you're not really. I had a bet they'd take your leg off. I'm glad I lost.'

Jan grinned.

'I didn't think they'd let you out so soon.'

'Neither did I. It's on condition that there's someone to look after me. Do you know anyone who would come in?'

'Joey?'

'He's only just learning how to keep the place clean, and his cooking's appalling. And he wouldn't be able to change my dressing.'

'No. All right – bet you I can find someone.'

Jan did not respond, and Pegleg, looking at his pale face, realised just how badly help was needed. As he left he found Joey waiting outside, his eyes wide with fright, and Pegleg gave him strict instructions to let Jan sleep and to summon help at once if he became more obviously ill.

Late that afternoon there was a gentle knock on the door of Jan's house. Jan heard Joey open the door and admit someone.

'Kate! What are *you* doing here?'

'Heard you needed someone. Thought I might do as a nurse, if you're not too fussy.'

'Oh, Kate!' He leaned back, smiling. 'I'm so glad to see you. Are you going to stay?'

'I'll come round each morning. Maybe not as early as you used to get up, but early enough. And then I'll stay until the evening.'

He grinned weakly. 'What about the nights?'

She shook her head slowly. 'Naughty! That's over. Besides, you're in no state for any shenanigans like that.'

'I'm sorry we broke up, Kate. I've missed you.'

'Me too. But you wasn't any use to me, lover – not with your mind on your Rebecca all the time.'

So Sam had been right. 'Sorry,' he said. 'And thanks for coming, Kate.'

'You'll be all right at night, with your houseboy to keep an eye on you, won't you?'

During the next two weeks she tended him faithfully, but his recovery was slow. The raw patch under his arm began to suppurate, and the doctor had to be called to prescribe treatment with carbolic acid. Scabs formed, but would get rubbed off as Jan turned in his bed, and then the wounds opened again. But most troublesome was his leg. The doctor denied that it was infected. 'There'd be pus if that was the case.'

'Then why doesn't it heal?' Jan asked.

'It is healing.'

'Hardly.'

'Anything like this is a major shock to the system,' the doctor said pompously. 'However healthy you may have been before the accident, you're bound to be run down now. It would be a good idea if you could get away from here for a while. Go down to the Cape for a couple of months – get a change of air. Is there anyone there who could look after you? Not that you need much more of that. Just keep the wound clean, and Nature will do the rest.'

'I don't know anyone in the Cape,' Jan said, and then suddenly thought of Harry and his invitation to come and stay. But he could not impose himself on Harry in his present condition, not for a long visit. 'I was planning to go to Amsterdam.'

'A long sea voyage. Capital. Though I should wait a few days longer before you set off.'

'I've got to. The trial's next week. They postponed it until I could attend.'

'Trial? Oh, your assailant. Well, you should be fit enough by then. But you'll be tired when you get to Cape Town. Spend a day or two there before you take the ship.'

When Jan told Kate that the doctor seemed to think he could now manage on his own, she was obviously relieved. 'I've been a burden, I'm afraid,' he said.

'Can't let old pals down,' she replied.

'Thanks for all you've done, Kate. I'm very grateful.' He paused. 'I'm going to Amsterdam next week, after the trial.'

'To marry your Rebecca, eh? She's a lucky girl – you tell her that from me. Well, maybe not from me.' She smiled a little too brightly. 'Then I shan't see you again. Good luck, Jan. Give me love to England as you go up the Channel.'

Jan booked transport for himself and Joey to Cape Town, wrote to Harry to ask if he could stay with him for a couple of days and whether Harry would reserve a cabin for him on a boat to Amsterdam. He spent long hours with Pegleg, making sure that in his absence the working of the claims would continue without problem. And he discussed with Sam Rosenberg the handling of his business.

The Shapiro Diamond had been lying all the while in Rosenberg's safe, but Jan now asked for it back. The next time the old man came he brought a little chamois pouch from which he produced the stone. 'I've had a good look at it,' he said. 'Of course, I'd seen it often in your office, but not to examine carefully. It's a fine stone, a very fine stone.' He handed it to Jan.

As he took it, Jan imagined again that he felt a strange tingling in his fingers.

'Strange,' Rosenberg said. 'It seems to gleam more now you're holding it. Must be the light. So why do you keep it, Jan? It's worth a fortune.'

'It's sort of . . . well, a sort of talisman. I feel almost as though . . . it must sound crazy . . . as though I belong to it. No, I don't really mean that. As though it's part of me, or as though it represents me.' He laughed a little shame-facedly. 'I even call it the Shapiro Diamond.'

Rosenberg smiled. 'I used to dream of a stone I'd call the Rosenberg Diamond, but I never found it.' Then he added gently, 'Just don't let it take possession of you, Jan.'

*   *   *

Black Conrad's trial proved a farce. He denied all the charges glibly. 'I went into Shapiro's office to ask the current price of diamonds,' he said. 'I hadn't looked at the sign over the door, and I didn't even know it was Shapiro's until I got inside. Before I could ask anything, he attacked me.'

'Why should he do that?' the magistrate asked.

'He thinks he has a grudge against me about a worthless claim that George Bell sold him. I was working for Bell at that time, but the sale was nothing to do with me. Anyway, he tried to throw me out of his office. Well, naturally I fought back. As for trying to steal his diamond or threatening him, if I wanted to do that I certainly wouldn't choose the middle of the day when the streets were crowded.'

Jan's difficulty was that he could produce no witness of the threat to his life or the robbery, and though he challenged every point in Watson's evidence, it remained a case of one man's word against another's.

The magistrate had little hesitation at the end of the brief hearing. 'I do not believe a word of what you have told me, Watson, whereas Mr Shapiro's evidence has the ring of truth. In the unfortunate absence of further testimony, I can only acquit you on the charges of threatening behaviour, attempted murder and attempted robbery. However, I can and do find you guilty of creating a disturbance in the street, and since it is my opinion that at the very least you are also guilty of common assault, I shall impose the maximum sentence available to me. You will go to prison for fourteen days. And if you ever appear before me again I shall punish you with the utmost severity.'

Jan was happy enough to leave Kimberley after that.

*   *   *

Although the journey to Cape Town had become much more speedy and comfortable, with a regular coach service and overnight stops at reasonably hospitable inns, Jan found it almost unbearable. The constant jolting of the coach made his leg throb, and when at night he examined the wound it looked angry, and the flesh around it was puffy and tender. Joey did his best to look after him, but could do little beyond seeing that food and drink were brought to him.

On the morning of the last day, Jan was seriously ill, and by the time the coach reached Cape Town he was delirious, sweating and shivering as though he had malaria, brought back to reality only momentarily if someone knocked against his wounded leg. Fortunately, Harry was waiting for his arrival, with a carriage and servants, and under his direction Jan was rapidly transported to his luxurious house, a couple of miles south of Cape Town.

Dr Richard Pearson was Cape Town's most fashionable physician and surgeon, and also reputedly its best. He examined Jan carefully. On one side of his calf the healing was complete, and all that remained was a small, puckered scar, but on the other side the skin was bright red and swollen, like a gigantic boil. As Dr Pearson gently touched the area, a bead of pus appeared at the edge of the scab. Jan could not restrain a low cry of pain.

'I'm going to cut and get rid of all that poison,' Pearson said. 'It's either that or amputation. Indeed, amputation may be inevitable, but I imagine our friend would prefer me to try first to save his leg. Are you squeamish, Mr Templeton? I shall need help, but it will not be pleasant, I assure you, and if the sight of blood upsets you . . .'

'No,' said Harry. 'I think I can stand it, and if I do faint I'll try to do it where I shan't be in the way.'

Dr Pearson made ready, having decided to perform the operation on the kitchen table. He had come prepared, and had soon set out the chloroform, the carbolic acid and the various knives and other instruments he intended to use. He stripped off his coat and donned an apron. 'I think it will be best to render him unconscious where he is,' he said. 'Then we can carry him down here more easily.'

They went up stairs to the room where Jan lay, and the doctor held a cloth over his nose and mouth and dripped chloroform on to it, until his feverish movements ceased. Then they carried him down to the kitchen. Harry, whose role was to hand over the various instruments when required, had thought that he would be able to watch without qualm, but as the doctor took the scalpel and lifted the scab, and blood-streaked pus gushed out, his curiosity vanished. He managed not to faint, but turned aside, and when Pearson asked for anything handed it to him without looking.

It did not take long. Once he had cleared the area of pus, Pearson took a scalpel and cut all round and down into the wound, and then poured carbolic acid into the blood-filled cavity, explaining nonchalantly to Harry that it was the best antiseptic going, and that with luck the wound would now heal cleanly. 'As for the delirium, now that the source of the poison has been eradicated, your friend's fever should go. But his leg must be kept as still as possible. For the rest of the night and until I come again tomorrow, a couple of your servants might hold the leg to prevent any movement. They can do an hour's duty at a time.'

Joey was the first to come forward for this task. At the end of the first hour he refused to be relieved, and it was only when he had been at his vigil for over four hours that he finally obeyed Harry's order to let someone else replace him. Early in the morning he was back to tend to his master.

For nearly twenty-four hours it was doubtful whether the operation had been successful. Jan's fever increased and the sweat poured off his body, and he sometimes threshed so that Joey and the other servants had all they could do to keep his leg still. He babbled incomprehensibly. Only one word was clear in the gibberish – '. . . diamond . . . diamond . . . diamond . . .'

Joey suddenly realised. 'He want he diamond.' He went to Jan's clothes and found the Shapiro Diamond, and put it in Jan's hand.

The muttering stopped then, and Jan lay calmer, but the

fever still raged, and Dr Pearson looked at him with great concern.

'I'm afraid his life is very much in danger still,' he said.

17

A few hours after the Shapiro Diamond had been placed in his hand, Jan's fever broke, but he was still extremely weak, and Dr Pearson continued to visit him twice a day. 'It is fortunate that he has such a strong constitution,' he said. 'Many a weaker man would have succumbed already. He is not out of danger, but as long as he goes on fighting, he has a chance.'

Harry's wife, Edith, nursed him devotedly, feeding him nourishing broths, ensuring that his bed linen was fresh, and dressing the wound in his leg. Slowly Jan began to recover.

He thought Edith charming, even if remarkably plain, and Joey, who rarely left Jan's room, was devoted to her. Harry called her 'Florence Nightingale' and asked where her lamp was. He seemed to treat her more like a casual friend than as a bride of but a few months, and Jan was tempted to wonder if he had married her solely for her money and position. 'If so,' he told himself, 'she doesn't seem to regret the bargain.'

Harry made no bones about his delight in the wealth that was available to him. 'Beats a tent in New Rush,' he told Jan, 'and it's marvellous being able to afford anything I want.'

'And having a wife who adores you.'

'Edith? Yes, she's all right. Between you and me, old man, it's a bit like making love to a cold potato. I think she looks on bed as a sort of penalty she has to pay for having me around during the day. Still, you can't have everything.' He took a sip from the brandy glass that seemed to live permanently in his hand. 'I must admit I get a bit bored now and then. My work takes very little time — it's a sinecure, really, though my much-respected Papa-in-law thinks the whole future of the British Empire depends on him and me. I tried to get up some amateur theatricals, but no one else was interested. That's why

I'm so glad to have you here, Jan. You must stay a long time. I know you want to rush off to Amsterdam and your lady-love, but there's no sense in going until you're really fit.'

*　　*　　*

Christmas came. In the morning, Harry and Edith went to church, returning with Edith's mother and father and her sister, Alice, who were to join them for dinner. All morning the servants had been hurrying to and fro in busy preparation, and at four o'clock the family and Jan sat down to the feast. There was turkey and ham and a great side of beef, and a huge plum duff to follow, and pawpaws and mangoes and melons, and all the best of spirits and wines that the Cape could offer. And after the meal they played at snapdragon, snatching raisins from a dish of burning brandy. Then they moved out to sit on the stoep in the golden sunshine, with a chaise longue for Jan, and Harry kept them laughing with a string of stories, acting out the parts as always.

Alice Tester asked Jan how he and Harry first met.

'It was on the ship coming out to the Cape,' Jan said. 'And he told me I looked like a dying duck in a thunderstorm. Do you remember, Harry? I didn't know what that meant, so he acted it for me. Show them, Harry.'

Harry obliged, and they all laughed and applauded.

'And did you understand then?' Alice asked.

'Of course he didn't,' Harry replied. 'It was double Dutch to him.' He raised his glass. 'Happy days, Jan.'

Mr Tester seemed to feel that the time had come to talk seriously to Harry about their work, and Mrs Tester engaged Edith in a discussion of the latest fashions, which left Alice to talk to Jan, which she did with great enthusiasm in her high little voice, like that of a child. She was far less plain than her sister – indeed, almost pretty, with large hazel eyes and a tiny rosebud mouth, and a mass of rich chestnut hair framing her face. She asked him questions about Kimberley and the life of a diamond digger, and listened intently to his answers. Jan enjoyed the flattery of her attention, and protested that he was not in the least tired when Edith told her sister that she should cease her chatter and allow Mr Shapiro to retire to bed.

Mr and Mrs Tester seized upon this to say that it was time to go home, and the party broke up.

186

'I do hope Alice really didn't tire you,' Edith said to Jan when the others had gone.

'Indeed, no. I enjoyed her company.'

Edith smiled in satisfaction.

Jan could not yet walk without support, and Harry helped him to his room. 'Edith's matchmaking,' he said. 'She knows perfectly well that you're virtually engaged to Rebecca. Mind you, you could do worse. Alice'll have as much money as Edith, and a house like this one. And just think – you'd be my brother-in-law.' He noticed that Jan did not join in his amusement, and added hastily, 'Just joking, old man. I know you're set on marrying your Rebecca.'

But had it been said only in fun? Something had happened to Harry, Jan thought. His jokes were not so funny now.

*   *   *

Before long Jan was able to spend most of his time on the stoep, lying in the warm sunlight, enjoying the sight of the flamboyant trees and palms and the proteas and lilies and other flowers which grew in profusion in the gardens of Harry's house. He could walk a little, but he limped badly, and Dr Pearson told him that he would always be lame. 'It won't be too bad,' he said. 'You'll be able to get about, but I'm afraid you'll never win a hundred yards race.'

At first Jan was deeply depressed by the news – he had no wish to run in races, nor even to box again, but the thought of such a physical handicap was horrifying. And how would Rebecca react to the idea of a disabled husband? Then he remembered Pegleg, and had a mental vision of him scrambling about the claims with such agility that it was hard to believe he had a wooden leg. 'Anything he can do, I can do,' he told himself. 'And I'm a lot better off than he is, anyway.'

Dr Pearson recommended as much exercise as possible, provided he did not tire himself, and he walked around the grounds every day, or if it was raining, through the cool, high-ceilinged rooms of the old house, the architecture of which had all the grace of the Cape Dutch style. Different though it was from the houses he had known in his youth, Jan found in it the flavour of home. Sometimes Harry would drive him a few miles into the countryside, and as Jan's leg improved, he would take his walk there.

The days passed quickly, for Harry and Edith had a large circle of acquaintances, many of whom came to call, and Jan and Harry would often return from one of their excursions to find Edith entertaining yet another neighbour who had come principally, it seemed, in order to meet the Templetons' guest, said to be a charming, handsome, well-to-do and possibly still eligible bachelor. Of course, it was a pity he was Jewish, but still . . . Alice came often. They would hear her high piping voice as they entered the voorkamer, and Harry would say, 'Oh, Lord! There's my sister-in-law. Charming girl, but she gets on my nerves. I wish you'd marry her and take her back to Kimberley with you, Jan.' And he would lead the way into his study, and get out the brandy bottle, and suggest they should have a little snifter together until Alice had gone.

Jan had written to Rebecca to explain the delay in his journey, and now he wrote to her again. 'You will love the Cape, I know, and I have decided that although I shall maintain my business in Kimberley, I shall purchase a house somewhere near Cape Town, where the climate is more equable and where I already have many friends who will be happy to welcome you. These parts are truly delightful, with a constantly changing landscape, clothed in trees and plants of such a variety and beauty as you cannot imagine.'

* * *

After he had been with Harry and Edith for five weeks, Dr Pearson made what he said was his final visit. 'You're fit and well now,' he said, 'and I can see that the leg isn't worrying you so much. You still need to build up your strength a little, and a sea voyage should be just the thing. As far as I'm concerned, there's nothing to stop you sailing to Amsterdam straight away.'

Returning from Cape Town after booking passage on the next ship, Jan found a letter waiting for him. As soon as he recovered from the fever he had written to Sam Rosenberg to tell him of the change in his plans and that he was staying with Harry, and the old man had replied, wishing him a speedy recovery and telling him not to worry about either his claims or his business, both of which were progressing satisfactorily, and promising to let him know if any crisis should develop. But this envelope came from Amsterdam, readdressed by

Rosenberg, and must have crossed in the post with the letter he had sent Rebecca from Kimberley announcing that he was coming home. He ripped it open eagerly.

'My dear Jan, This is a very difficult letter to write, and I'm afraid will cause you much distress. For that I am extremely sorry. I am very fond of you, and always shall be, but I must tell you that Abram has done me the honour of asking me to be his wife, and I have accepted him. We are to be married in October. I hope you will wish us joy, though I know the news will come as a shock to you. Believe me, I felt great agony in making my decision, but we cannot control the dictates of our hearts, and I love Abram very deeply. Often in the past you have spoken of a desire to come home, and it would give me the greatest happiness if you were present at our wedding, and I know that both Abram and your father would welcome you with open arms. Forgive me, Jan. Your affectionate sister-to-be, Rebecca.'

Jan stared at the paper unbelievingly. He read it again, to make sure that he had not imagined it. And then a great wave of desolation overwhelmed him. How could she have betrayed him? How could she write so unfeelingly of 'distress' and 'shock'? Above all, his rage was directed against Abram – he was the real traitor. 'And it came to pass that Cain rose up against Abel and slew him.' Yes, he knew the bitterness that had entered Cain's soul. Then his anger turned against himself. If he had gone home when he first thought about it, months ago, this would never have happened. No, by then the damage had been done. But what a fool he had been! No one was to blame except himself, for believing that a fantasy was reality. Oh, God! It would have been better if Dr Pearson had let him die. Harry had guns – perhaps he should take one and end his life.

Joey came into the room. He stopped inside the door, and his face filled with concern at his master's expression. Jan was gazing unseeing into the distance. Joey came near and bent over him, and Jan suddenly unleashed his frustration and his anger and his sorrow and hit the boy with all his strength, sending him reeling into a corner of the room. His frightened eyes rolled, and blood began to pour from his mouth.

Jan came to his senses, and he went to him. 'Sorry,' he said. 'I didn't mean it. Sorry. Here.' He gave him his handkerchief, and helped the boy to his feet. 'Sorry,' he said again. He could find no other words.

'What I do, boss?' the black asked.

'Nothing. You did nothing. I didn't mean to hit you. I was – I . . . I'm sorry, Joey. And I'll make it up to you. You'd better go and clean yourself up.'

Joey stared at him with puzzled eyes, and went slowly from the room.

By lunchtime Jan was in control of himself. 'I've had a letter from Rebecca,' he said as he sat at the table with Harry and Edith. 'She's marrying my brother, Abram.'

There was a brief shocked silence.

'Oh, Jan, my dear, I'm so sorry,' Edith said.

'I shall write to her and wish her happiness,' Jan went on tonelessly. He saw Edith shoot a warning glance at Harry, and knew that she had heard the tension in his voice. 'She's invited me for the wedding. In October. I'm not going home – not now or for the wedding. Would you do something for me, Harry?'

'Of course.'

'I booked a passage to Amsterdam this morning. I'd be very obliged if you would call in at the shipping office and cancel it for me. I'd go myself, but –'

'No, don't you worry,' Harry said. 'I'll do it this afternoon. A drop of brandy, old chap? It helps, you know.'

'No, thanks.'

After a pause, Edith said gently. 'Have you thought what you're going to do, Jan?'

'I shall go back to Kimberley.'

'But not yet, old man,' Harry said. 'Dr Pearson said you must build your strength up. You must stay here with us, mustn't he, Edith?'

'I can't impose on you. You've been very kind putting up with me for so long.'

'We've enjoyed having you here,' Edith said. 'Of course you must stay. We insist.'

Jan mumbled his thanks. After another awkward silence, Edith began to chatter with forced gaiety of the dinner party she was planning. 'I thought you'd miss it, Jan, but now you'll be here, and that's splendid. I think I'll ask the Renshaws, Harry.'

'Good idea. You'll like them, Jan. Nice family – especially the daughter.'

'Harry always flirts with her quite outrageously, Jan,' Edith said, and gave a little tinkling laugh to show that she did not care. 'Then Mr and Mrs Renshaw can play whist with Mama and Papa, and there'll be Alice and the Kilbrides and Jan. Perfect.'

Jan listened as though in a trance. As soon as he could, he retired to his room and indulged his misery. First Kate and now Rebecca, he thought – perhaps there was something wrong with him. At last he fell into a restless, dream-ridden sleep.

He awoke some hours later, his head throbbing. As he opened his eyes he was aware that there was someone in the room, but the shutters were closed and in the dim light he could not make out who it was.

'Tea, boss?'

'Oh, Joey!' It was the first time he had smiled since reading the letter.

Joey tried to grin in response, despite his split lip.

*   *   *

Several days passed before the pain in Jan's heart faded to a dull ache. Harry and Edith helped by behaving ordinarily towards him, but it was chiefly Joey who restored his spirits. The fact that he bore no malice and even seemed more devoted gave Jan back a faith in himself. He had lost Rebecca, and perhaps all hope of reconciliation with his family, and he was lame, but he was young and life was for living. He began to look forward to the dinner party.

'The Kilbrides are as dull as ditchwater,' Harry told him, 'and young Edward Renshaw's a bit of a weed, but you wait till you see Helen. She's a peach, and such fun. She reminds me a bit of Kate Jessup. Do you remember her? Used to be at that place – what was it called?'

'The Ace of Diamonds. Of course I remember her. As a matter of fact, after you left New Rush I got to know her pretty well.'

Harry looked at him with interest. 'How well?'

'As well as . . . as well as you know Edith.'

Harry whistled. 'I thought that's what you meant. I'll be damned. You old dog. How did that happen?'

Jan told him the story.

'Well, I'm damned,' he repeated. 'I wouldn't mind betting she was a bit more lively than Edith in bed. And there I was thinking you were still the complete innocent. I'm not sure I should let you anywhere near Helen Renshaw now.'

He continued to enthuse about Helen to such an extent that Jan began to feel certain that he would dislike her. In any case, he wanted a rest from women for a while.

When the dinner party took place, he found her enchanting. Her dress was stunning, made of layer upon layer of taffeta, boldly striped in vertical bands of royal blue and cream. The low-cut bodice, tight-fitting to her wasp waist, emphasised the fullness of her breasts and revealed a daring hint of cleavage, and the full skirt, with its bustle and train, was gathered in swirls and decorated with a host of satin bows in matching colours. But it was not just her clothes which made her the centre of attention. She was very pretty, Jan thought, and witty in a faintly malicious way, but above all her vitality gave her a magnetism which focused all eyes on her. Her voice, in sharp contrast to Alice's childish twitterings, was low and husky. Though she said little directly to Jan, he had the feeling that she was attracted to him and that her occasional glances in his direction held more than a casual interest.

'Smitten, eh?' Harry whispered. 'Take care, Jan. Edith's right – she's a flirt, and they say she has an icicle for a heart.'

When they sat down to dinner, Jan was delighted to find that he was seated opposite her. The table-talk was lively, and Helen took a prominent part in it, seemingly able to converse on any subject, whether it was politics, literature or agriculture, yet without ever appearing forward or lacking in femininity.

At the end of the evening she came to Jan to say goodbye. 'It has been a pleasure to meet you, Mr Shapiro,' she said softly. 'I hope you will call on me. Tomorrow afternoon would, I think, be soon enough to send a suitable shock through Cape Town Society. I shall expect you at half past two.'

*   *   *

She was sitting alone in a small drawing-room. She turned her head as Jan was shown in, and smiled. 'Mr Shapiro. You remind me of the wicked Lord Byron. So dark and handsome, with that fascinating limp.'

'I don't find it fascinating, Miss Renshaw.'

'I don't suppose you do. Nevertheless, I assure you it adds to your . . . distinction. Do you mind being compared to Lord Byron?'

'I know nothing about him, I'm afraid. But if you say he is wicked, then perhaps I should protest. What form did his wickedness take?'

'They say he had an incestuous relationship with his sister, though that always seems to me less important than his ability as a poet. There, now, I've shocked you. Ladies aren't supposed to talk about incest, are they? I don't give a fig for such conventions. Now, sit down and tell me about yourself. Do you come from a large family?'

'I have no sisters, so I cannot claim to have shared Lord Byron's proclivities. I have one brother.' As the conversation continued, he studied her. She was much less flamboyantly dressed, but the pale green gown that she wore was charming, and even he could recognise its quality.

'And you and he are close?'

'I . . . I am fond of him.'

Helen laughed. 'You don't sound it. Confess now, you don't love him at all.'

'Indeed, I do.'

'I don't believe you. And you needn't be afraid that I'll think you a monster. Edward and I have little time for each other, and indeed, I often wish I were an only child. Only children have many advantages – not least the undivided love and attention of their parents. And undivided love and attention is something I enjoy. I am a very selfish person, Mr Shapiro. Selfish and self-centred.'

'I don't believe that.'

'Then neither of us believes the other,' she said, smiling. 'No wonder we get on so well together.'

She asked more about him – why he had come to the Cape, and had his quest for diamonds made him rich, and was it true that he had had an unhappy love affair. Jan found himself answering with a candour which matched her own. When he had told her about Rebecca, she said, 'Now I understand why you are less than fond of your brother. It is not for me to say, Mr Shapiro, but perhaps you are well rid of a lady who has proved herself so inconstant.'

'Thank you for saying that. Everyone else seems to wallow in pity for me.'

She smiled, and rose. 'It is time for you to inspect the house and gardens, Mr Shapiro, a tour which is obligatory for all visitors. It is one of the oldest houses in the Cape, you know.'

The house was much larger than Harry's, and the spacious, elegant rooms were richly furnished. In the drawing-room over the mantelpiece was a full-length portrait of a grim-faced man dressed in the style of the mid-century. 'My grandfather,' Helen said. 'He owned three coal mines in Yorkshire. He left an enormous fortune, in which, of course, my father had a share, thank goodness. For me luxury is a necessity.'

'Have you lived in South Africa all your life, Miss Renshaw?'

'Yes, I was born here. But I am English, of course – make no mistake about that.'

'If I may say so, you sound as though you believe it is a misfortune to be anything else.'

'Indeed, I do.' She was smiling, but he felt that there was an underlying seriousness in what she said. 'Though I assure you,' she added hastily, 'that I have nothing against the northern Europeans –'

'I am much relieved to hear it.'

'– but I am happy that you are not French or Italian or Spanish. I cannot abide the Latins. And by the way, Mr Shapiro, please spare me your irony.'

'I apologise. But I suppose you could say that I am a Levantine in origin.'

'We will not discuss that, Mr Shapiro. To me you are Dutch, and I admire the Dutch.' She laughed. 'Come, you must not take me too seriously. And to show you how much I like you, even if you aren't English' – she laughed again – 'you must call me Helen, and I shall call you Jan.'

'I am honoured.'

They went out and walked around the beautifully-tended garden, coming at length to the stables.

'Do you ride?' Helen asked.

'I'm afraid not.'

'You should. You can come here and learn. You can have Miranda. She's gentle and well trained.'

'I doubt if I'd be much good at it, with this leg.'

'Oh, don't make that an excuse,' she said, almost angrily.

They arranged that he would come for a riding lesson the next day. Then he remembered. 'But I have no riding clothes.'

'You can borrow a set of Edward's – you're about the same size.'

'Won't he mind?'

'He hardly ever rides. No seat.' Seeing Jan's baffled look, she explained, 'The way you sit on a horse. You'll do it naturally, I know. You have that look about you.'

'Who else will come with us?'

'No one. Oh, you mean a chaperone. What a comic idea!' She laughed. 'Oh, Jan, you're such fun.'

Helen was proved right, and as soon as he had mounted Miranda the following day, he sat well and seemed to know instinctively how to handle the reins, how to grip with his knees, how to rise and fall gently to the motion of the horse.

'You don't need any lessons,' Helen said. 'Let her trot.' She led the way on her bay gelding, Prospero – 'Not that he sired Miranda, poor thing.' – and they spent a happy hour in the warm autumn sunshine exploring the Renshaw's large estate.

They went out every day for a week, gradually riding farther afield. Sometimes they cantered along the coast, watching the Atlantic waves breaking over the rocky headlands or rolling gently into the sandy bays. On other days they would go inland, past orchards and ostrich farms and beautiful estates with their elegant Cape Dutch mansions.

One morning they came to a small wood. Helen dismounted. 'Come on,' she said. 'Drop the reins to the ground. Over her head. Then she won't stray.' She went on ahead. Just inside the wood was a little clearing. The ground was dry, covered in moss. She turned and held out her arms to him.

Her mouth was sweet and demanding. He was not sure afterwards how they had rid themselves of their clothes – he was only aware of the beauty of her breasts, the glorious curve of her belly, the silken skin of her thighs, and then the ecstasy that came with their joining. His lovemaking with Kate had been joy and excitement and satisfaction, but this was something more.

He rolled on to his back and lay there for a moment, gazing up at the blue sky, broken by the topmost branches of the trees beneath which they lay. Then he turned back to her, and took her in his arms again. 'I love you, Helen,' he said. 'I adore you. I have, I think, since the moment I first saw you.'

She listened contentedly, saying nothing, but when he kissed her once more, she responded with a ferocity that spurred his own. They made love again, and afterwards, lying together in the sweet haze of fulfilment, he asked her to marry him.

'Hush,' she said, and would not let him continue, saying that it was time to go back. She rode home in silence, and merely nodded when he asked, 'Tomorrow?'

Jan drove back to the Templetons' house in a daze, his mind filled with Helen. She was not very tall, and slightly built, but there was a delicious proportion to her gently curving figure – the full swell of her bosom, the narrow waist, the generous hips. She had thick hair of a pale golden colour, and Jan longed to see her let it down, to see it spread over a pillow, instead of being pinned up in an elaborate coiffure of curls and braids. Her face had an elfin quality, with a fascinating sharpness of feature – her nose was narrow, her chin pointed, her lips, though a little thin, sharply defined, and her eyes, those green eyes, could shift from laughter to soft malice and on to a mysterious remoteness, and then back again to the humour which was so much a part of her. He was enraptured too by the liveliness of her mind, and her habit of viewing everything and everyone with a gentle mockery, which, it seemed to him, held no viciousness – how could it when it embraced herself too?

On their third visit to the clearing in the wood, Jan said, 'Do you remember what I asked you the first time we came here? I'm asking you again. Marry me, Helen. Please.'

She laughed very briefly, and said, 'Oh, my dear, it's impossible. Don't you see that?'

'Why?'

'For one thing, because you're a Jew and I'm a dutiful daughter of the Church of England.'

'Do *you* mind that I'm a Jew?'

196

She gave a little gurgle of laughter. 'I told you before that I'd prefer you to be English. No, I don't mind. I think . . . I think I find your Jewishness an attraction.'

'I'm serious, Helen. Are you sure it makes no difference to you?' He was thinking of the men in the Ace of Diamonds the night that the vandals had wrecked his tent. They had been his friends until their latent anti-semitism had been aroused.

'Don't be tiresome, Jan. I've told you, I don't care.'

'Then is it that your religion means a lot to you?'

She hesitated for a moment. 'No. I suppose I believe in God, but I don't go to church.'

'And I haven't been near a synagogue for years. So what does it all matter if we love each other?'

'Oh, Jan, don't be a fool. You know perfectly well it wouldn't be acceptable to your family any more than to mine. Nor to the society we live in.'

'You don't care what people think of you, and neither do I.'

'It's not as easy as that. We couldn't cut ourselves off from everyone. It sounds fine in theory, but it's nonsense in practice.'

'But everyone here knows I'm Jewish and accepts me – I mean, at the parties we've been to, and when people visit Harry and Edith. Almost everyone, anyway. At least I think they do.' Again the spectre raised itself in his mind. What was it Sam had said? 'The hatred for the Jews is always in them, and never buried very deep.' Something like that.

'Of course,' Helen said. 'We're trained to be polite. And as long as you're Harry and Edith's guest, and do nothing to offend against the code . . .'

He tried to dismiss the ugly thoughts, and to think only of her. 'I love you.'

'And I love you.'

He took her in his arms. 'Then we must surely find a way.'

She did not reply, but kissed him again, and held his head to her, and as he caressed her, ran her hands over his body, and began to move with him, and shared the dark brilliance of their joy.

18

Edith had been very concerned at Jan's infatuation with Helen. It was so obviously on the rebound, and in any case she was not at all sure that she wanted to see Jan involved with someone as basically selfish as she believed Helen to be. She took every opportunity to throw Jan and Alice together, but Jan was not to be diverted from Helen. Edith was very relieved when the letter came from Kimberley.

Pegleg's previous letters had contained nothing of an adverse nature, except the expected grumbles about the weather. 1873 and the first weeks of 1874 had been a period of drought, with the dust and flies worse than ever. But despite the dry conditions, water had begun to appear at the diggings, and the deeper the claims went the worse the problem seemed to be. Until this most recent letter, the seepage had been little more than a nuisance, but now disaster had struck. February had brought exceptionally heavy rains, flooding the mine, and since the bottom of the pit was already water-logged, the water would not soak away. The same thing had happened at the other diggings around Kimberley, and all mining had to be abandoned until the water could be pumped out. Work on that, Pegleg reported, would commence very soon, but there was no knowing how long it would take. 'Mr Rosenberg,' he wrote, 'says it's a labour of her culies, whatever that means. I talked to him, and we have agreed to pay off the blacks. I think you should come to Kimberley as soon as possible, unless you have already left for Holland.'

Jan's first thought was of Helen. How could he tear himself away from her? But when he talked to her about it, she showed her customary common sense. Any other woman, he felt, would have fluttered helplessly and might even have felt affronted to be consulted at all on a masculine subject.

'Don't be a fool, Jan – of course you must go back. There may be nothing that you can do, but you can't leave everything to others to sort out for you.'

He decided to catch the next coach to Kimberley. Meanwhile there was something he could do which would perhaps bind her a little more closely to him. He felt for the little chamois leather bag, and took it out of his pocket. 'I want you to look after this for me,' he said, 'until I come back.' He slid the Shapiro Diamond out of the pouch.

'What is it? A diamond – a rough diamond? Indeed. I've never seen one before. It's not very . . . beautiful, is it?'

'It would be if it were cut and polished.'

'Then why don't you have that done?'

'Everyone asks that. I don't know. Perhaps I will some day. It . . . it's a sort of talisman, the way it is. I know it's stupid and illogical, but I just feel that I have to keep it this way. I call it . . .' He hesitated, afraid she would laugh at him. 'I call it the Shapiro Diamond.'

She did laugh. 'How pretentious. It makes it sound terribly important.'

He said lightly, 'It is, to me. Will you look after it for me while I'm away?'

'Of course.' She put the chamois bag into her reticule. 'I shall keep it very safe.'

*　　*　　*

At first, when he returned to Kimberley, the town did not seem any different, but gradually he realised that the hurry and bustle had gone. The streets were thronged, but with idle men, and the atmosphere was of depression. He went to his little house, which seemed very cramped after the spaciousness of Harry Templeton's splendid residence, but there was some pleasure in being once more in his own home. Everything was covered in dust, but housework could wait, and he went to the mine.

Hardly anyone was there, except for the men working on the pumps to draw out the flood water. Climbing on to the staging from which the ropes descended to the claims, Jan looked down into the vast pit that so many men had carved out of the ground. Only at night, when it seemed like a ghostly landscape, perhaps a reflection of what men would find if they ever flew to the moon itself, had he seen it so deserted. Most of the claims were covered by a sheet of water.

He went in search of Pegleg, who was delighted to see him. He explained that a firm called Walsh and Company were responsible for the pumping operations.

'What's the latest news on how long it'll take?' Jan asked.

'Months,' Pegleg replied. 'The pumps are too small, and it's so far to the top of the mine that it's a very difficult job. And the deeper a claim's been dug, the more water there is in it. We're comparatively lucky, and I reckon we'll be able to start digging again, in a limited way, earlier than some. But it's still going to be the end of winter before we can begin again.'

'What are you going to do till then?'

'As you know, I've dismissed the blacks, and as for me, well, I've decided I'll be a gentleman of leisure for the time being. Of course, I'll keep an eye on your interests. Not that much is likely to happen.'

'No. I'm not sure it was worth coming all the way back here.'

'Sorry. But I needed to talk to you, and I wanted you to see for yourself how things are. Like I say, I'm willing to keep an eye on things, and I don't expect to get my usual pay for that, but at the same time, I thought we might make a business arrangement so that I'd still be officially employed by you and could deal with things while you're away. I thought perhaps ten bob a week.'

'That's less than a black would get.'

'Yes, but you're not getting any diamonds, and I'm not working anything like full time. It'll do me.'

'All right.'

'Are you staying long?'

'No. No, I don't think so. My plans have changed. I tell you what you can do for me. How would you like to live in my house? If it's empty, it'll go to rack and ruin. Whenever I come to Kimberley, you can move out temporarily. No rent – looking after the house for me will do instead.'

'That's marvellous. Thanks. And if you let me know when you're coming, I'll have it ready for you to move in.'

'Fine. Now, I'll see you again, but I must go and talk to Mr Rosenberg.'

'Ah. He's closed his office here for the time being, and opened a new one in Dutoitspan. They had far less flooding there than we did, and they think some of the claims will be workable quite soon. You'll find him there.'

Rosenberg greeted him warmly, but went on, 'I am happy to see you looking so well, and your leg does not seem to be troubling you too much, but I had hoped not to see you at all at this time. There are too few diamonds and too many merchants – more competition I didn't want.' He chuckled at his little joke. 'If it hadn't been for the panic about the blue ground last winter, the situation would be worse than it is, but that scared away a lot of dealers as well as diggers. What am I saying? Worse? It couldn't be worse.'

'Business is bad?'

'What is bad? Non-existent? Then, yes, business is bad. They think it may pick up again before long.' He shook his head gloomily.

'Well, I shan't provide any competition,' Jan said. 'I'm going back to the Cape as soon as I can. I'm thinking of settling there.'

'So. What has made the Cape so attractive?'

Jan told him about the letter from Rebecca and his meeting with Helen Renshaw. 'I'm going to marry her.'

'She is Jewish?'

'No.'

Rosenberg sighed. 'I'm an old man,' he said. 'It is an old man's privilege to give advice. You won't take it, but I must still give it. Don't, Jan. Don't marry her. Happiness between people of such different backgrounds and upbringing is rare.' Seeing the anger rising in Jan's eyes, he added hastily, 'Well, if you won't take my advice, you won't. I shall say mazel-tov, and pray for your happiness.'

'Then the marriage can't fail,' Jan said sarcastically, and was immediately contrite. 'I'm sorry. I shouldn't have said that. But nothing will stop me marrying her.'

Although Jan was eager to return to Cape Town, he could not do so straight away. A contract had to be signed with Walsh and Company who were pumping the mine dry, and discussions entered into with government officials and the Mining Board in order to safeguard his positions. The pervading air of despondency affected him, and he wondered whether to put his house up for sale, but prices were at rock bottom, and in any case, even if he were to live in Cape Town from now on, he would still need to visit Kimberley at regular intervals, and it would be good to have his own pied-à-terre there. Besides he had offered Pegleg the use of it.

★　★　★

He arrived back from Kimberley five weeks almost to the day from leaving Cape Town. Harry had previously insisted that he should again stay with him and Edith, but Jan intended to look as soon as possible for a house of his own, even if, in view of the situation in Kimberley, a much more modest one than he had originally planned.

Joey was waiting excitedly for him at the Templetons' house. He handed Jan a note from Helen, which said that she had to see him as soon as he returned. It was too late to call on her that evening, but early the next day he presented himself at the Renshaw mansion. He was shown into the small drawing-room, and cooled his heels there for a good half hour. At last Helen came in, closing the door behind her, and turning to face him. She looked tired and pale. He stepped towards her, his arms outstretched, but she avoided his embrace, and went to sit primly on an upright chair.

'Sorry I kept you waiting,' she said. 'I had not finished dressing.'

'I apologise. Your note sounded as though it were a matter of urgency.'

'It is.' She paused, and then, gazing at him in the frank and open way that was her custom, she said, 'I am pregnant, Jan.'

'Pregnant?'

'I'm going to have a baby. Your baby.'

'I see.' He did not know what to say.

'Before you left for Kimberley,' Helen said, still in matter-of-fact tones, 'you asked me several times to marry you. If your offer still stands, then I wish to accept it.'

As the meaning of her words sank in, a great smile spread over his face. He went towards her, pulled her from her chair, and folded her in his arms, bending his head to kiss her.

She turned her face away from his lips, and pushed him back. 'The wedding will have to be as soon as possible,' she went on, 'and it will be a civil marriage. You understand what I mean by that? There will be no ceremony in a church or a synagogue.'

He nodded, bewildered by her cool manner. 'Do your parents know about . . . about the baby?'

'Yes.'

'And they've agreed to your marrying me?'

The question seemed to release the humour that she had been repressing. Her lips curled. 'It was quite amusing. Papa began predictably by acting the outraged father. I thought for a moment he was going to tell me never to darken his door again, but Mama soon put a stop to that. Then they decided I would have to have what they described as a little operation. Yes, Jan, you may well look shocked, but when, like my father, you have a great deal of money, your ability to pay for anything you require tends to overcome any moral scruples you may have. I considered it seriously, but then said I intended to have the child.'

'Had you told them it's mine?'

'Not at this stage. Don't interrupt. Well, once we had got over that little argument and they were quite persuaded that I would not agree to an abortion, the next suggestion was that I should be sent to Durban, or perhaps home to England, or maybe to Timbuctoo – anywhere far enough away from here. The baby could then be adopted. "No," I said. "I intend to have it here in Cape Town, and it will not be adopted, nor put into an orphanage." At this point my father exploded again, and it was quite a while before he calmed down and accepted the fact that I was determined to decide matters for myself. I reminded them both that I am of age.' She chuckled. 'Somewhat subdued, they then inquired politely what I did intend to do. "I shall get married," I told them. "To whom?" they asked. "To the man who is the father of my child," I replied, as enigmatically as I could. "His name?" they cried. I had not yet divulged it, so with a sense of reaching the climax of the drama, I said, "His name is Johannes Shapiro." It was rather disappointing. They had already used up their supplies of horror and indignation, and greeted my little bombshell with comparative calm. Of course, my dear Papa did make a token attempt to have an apoplectic fit. "Jewish!" he said. "And a Dutchman!" But he –'

The old scar throbbed again, and Jan interrupted her. 'Are you sure you don't mind my being Jewish?'

'Oh, for pity's sake, Jan, we've already been over that!' she said petulantly. 'Anyway, you're spoiling my story. Eventually Papa pulled himself together sufficiently to ask whether you would be able to support me and what your prospects were.' She began to laugh helplessly.

'I don't see what's funny about that,' Jan said. 'I'm far from penniless, but the way things are going in Kimberley at the moment, and with the price of diamonds dropping all over the world, I certainly shouldn't be able to provide for you as adequately as I'd like.'

'Oh, but my dear, what you don't know, though Papa knows perfectly well, is that I shall have no need of my husband's money. I have enough of my own. My grandfather left me fifty thousand pounds. It's all carefully invested and I have an income which will keep us both in the luxury we need. And you mustn't look like that – there's nothing to be ashamed of in having a wealthy wife. It doesn't diminish your manliness, of which you have already given a very satisfactory demonstration.' She smiled, and then gave a kind of sigh, as though to say that the story was finished. 'There now. What do you think of that?'

He took her in his arms, and this time she allowed him to kiss her with passionate joy. Feeling strangely humble, he dropped to his knees.

She smiled down at him, then moved away. 'Here. I have something for you.' She opened the drawer of a davenport and took out a small package wrapped in tissue paper.

When he unwrapped it, he saw a little silver box of very delicate workmanship, shaped almost like a small, thick cigar. On the lid were engraved the initials J.S.

'I had it specially made,' she said. 'It is small enough, I think, for your waistcoat pocket. Go on, open it.'

Inside was the Shapiro Diamond, lying on a bed of crimson velvet which had been moulded so that the stone fitted into the hollow. In the lid was a similar lining, shaped to fit over the diamond.

The silver box was exquisite, and seemed somehow to make the diamond even more precious. He kept it with him wherever he went, and at night it lay on the small table beside his bed. In future years, when he had suits made, he would insist on a specially deep pocket in the waistcoat, so that there was no fear of the little box slipping out, and it became a habit to check regularly with a tap of his fingers that it was still there. Helen could not have given him a more perfect gift. He saw it as a symbol of the happiness that they would find in their marriage.

$$* \qquad * \qquad *$$

Jan and Helen were married quietly two weeks later in a civil ceremony attended only by Mr and Mrs Renshaw, Edward, Harry and Edith. The Renshaws had evidently decided that, since Helen and Jan seemed to be deeply in love, and quite determined to marry, there was no point in opposing the match.

Under the circumstances, the newlyweds decided to dispense with a honeymoon. 'But people will think there's a reason for it,' Mrs Renshaw said, 'and seeing you're getting married in such a hurry, they'll put two and two together.'

'And when the baby's born prematurely, they'll make five,' Helen replied. 'Let them. I don't care what they think or say.'

After the wedding, Jan and Helen busied themselves in looking for a suitable place to live. It was essential to be near enough to Cape Town, yet at the same time, Helen wanted to put some distance between herself and her parents; and the house had to be large and well-appointed enough to indicate to the world at large that Mr and Mrs Shapiro intended to take a prominent place in local society.

Within a short time they had found just what they wanted near the coast at Klein-Koeël Bay, only some six miles from the centre of Cape Town. A spacious and charming mansion in the Cape Dutch style, built eighty years or so previously, the graciously proportioned curves of the central gable gave it an imposing dignity. Two wings projected at the rear to enclose a paved courtyard, in the centre of which was a small pool where water lilies grew, and at the back was a miniature replica of the house, used as a wine cellar. The building was in good repair, the thick walls brilliant in their whitewash, the wooden shutters shining from the frequently applied linseed oil. The rooms were light and airy, despite the dark wooden panelling.

It took little time to complete the purchase of the property, but the furnishings were a different matter, for Helen insisted that everything should be of the best, even if that meant ordering materials and such essentials as a grand piano and a Chippendale dining-room table and chairs from England. She consulted Jan over every detail, and he enjoyed having something to do after so many weeks of idleness.

The wealthy farmer who had originally built the house had named it Overyssel, after that part of Holland where his family had lived before emigrating to the Cape. Helen talked of changing the name, but Jan persuaded her not to alter it. He liked it, and he knew he was going to be happy at Overyssel.

19

In July, Jan and Helen were at last ready to leave the Renshaw's house and move into Overyssel, which event, Helen had decided, was to be celebrated with a grand dinner for as many of their friends and acquaintances as could be accommodated. 'Then we shall see,' she said.

'See what?'

'Whether we are accepted, my dear. Whether I have been forgiven for marrying a Jew, and you for being one.'

Knowing it would irritate her if he again revealed his sensitivity, Jan said, in a controlled voice, 'We've been invited to dinner with all your friends.'

'No, not with them all. We've had no invitation from the Fernalds, nor from the Brownings, nor from Sir Gordon and Lady Massingham. And there are others. I shall invite them all, and we shall see what we shall see.'

The dinner party was a huge success. The Brownings were the only ones among what Helen called 'the doubtfuls' who refused the invitation. Those who had not met him before were apparently charmed by Jan's elegant manners and handsome looks, though Helen would have been less pleased if she had heard some of the sotto-voce conversations.

'Very presentable, I agree,' said Mrs Fernald to Lady Massingham. 'But there's no disguising what he is.'

'Oh, but he's *so* good-looking, and really quite cultured.'

'Once a Jew, always a Jew,' Mrs Fernald said. 'And as for her, flaunting herself in that condition . . . In my day, no lady would dream of being seen in Society once she began to show. Shameless, I call it. What's more, she must be at least six months gone, and you know when they were married.' She pursed her lips. 'Well, one thing is certain – if she calls on me I shall not be at home.'

Mrs Fernald was in the minority, but Helen and Jan had little time to enjoy the acceptance of their social circle, for at the end of August, when Helen's pregnancy was in its seventh month, she was taken one day while Jan was out with a sudden desire to re-arrange the furniture in the sitting-room. Struggling to move a heavy chesterfield, she felt a pain so sharp that she could only fall to the floor and cry weakly for help.

Jan had still not returned home when Helen was delivered of a daughter, so tiny that Dr Pearson discovered, when he had the kitchen scales cleaned and brought to the bedroom, she weighed less than two and a half pounds. He shook his head gravely. There was little chance that so small a scrap of humanity would survive, and he told Jan as much when he returned.

'And my wife?'

'She's weak – that's only to be expected – but I think she'll be all right. I shouldn't let her know about the child yet. Let her recover first. The baby needs great care. I have sent one of your men – Joey, I think his name is – to fetch a nurse.'

Despite all efforts, Jan's daughter died that evening. Helen was inconsolable when eventually they told her. 'It's my fault, all my fault,' she kept repeating, sobbing herself into a state of exhaustion. Dr Pearson came to see her every day, and was plainly anxious about her, but the worst part for Jan was that she did not want to speak to him or even to see him. 'She is not herself,' Dr Pearson said. 'Try not to worry. She will get over it in time.'

Slowly she returned to health, and recovered her old vivacity, but her attitude towards Jan remained curiously indifferent. Not knowing where else to turn, he consulted Dr Pearson, who said that the best cure might be if Mrs Shapiro should become pregnant again. There was little hope of that, however, since she would no longer allow any intimacies, though they continued to share the same bed.

*   *   *

Letters from Pegleg and Sam Rosenberg kept Jan abreast of the situation in Kimberley. Though the pumping out of the mine continued, it would be some months before any excavating could be resumed. He had written briefly to his father to explain why he could send no further supplies of diamonds for the time being, and had informed him of his marriage, and his intention to stay in South Africa. With difficulty he had added a postscript sending good wishes to Abram and Rebecca. A brief, cool reply had reached him in due course.

The letter which came towards the end of September was from Pegleg. Since the pumping out of the diggings was all but complete, and mining would start again within days, he suggested that Jan should make an urgent visit to Kimberley. 'There's a lot of unrest among the diggers,' he added. 'Most of them have had no work and no money, so they're in an ugly mood. You may need to be here to help me protect your property.'

Jan showed the letter to Helen. 'I don't see how I can go, with you not fully recovered.'

'Who says I'm not? For God's sake, go, if you want to. I don't care. Just so long as you don't ask me to go with you.'

'I thought of leaving this afternoon.' He waited to see whether she would make any comment, but she merely sighed and continued to turn the pages of the magazine she was looking at. He left the room, packed a suitcase and walked out of the house without saying goodbye to her. Perhaps, he thought, a few weeks away from each other would do them both good.

He felt a strange excitement as he travelled back to Kimberley, and with genuine pleasure unlocked the door of his little house, poky and poverty-stricken in comparison with Overyssel, but nevertheless friendly and welcoming, and he was pleased to find that Pegleg had looked after it well. There was dust, of course, but then there always was in Kimberley, and he was used to it.

Kimberley itself had changed greatly since he had first arrived there, and especially, he thought, in the seven or eight months since his last visit. It was no longer just an encampment, but a town. The streets went at strange angles, because they followed the paths originally trodden by the early diggers, but they were now established thoroughfares, lined with new buildings. And though the flies still swarmed and the weather was often unbearable, the authorities had begun to tackle the problem of the ever-present dust by watering the streets, and sanitation was no longer so primitive. The promised theatre had been built, and sporting events took place regularly, and all in all Kimberley was beginning to consider itself a tolerably civilised place.

Boxing was still popular, but the days of the bare-knuckle challenges in fairground style was over. These days, matches took place in halls, with a proper ring and a referee, gloves were worn, and gambling on the results was forbidden, the financial rewards for the boxers coming from the entrance money. Jan went once or twice during the next few weeks, and many there recognised him and asked him to put on the gloves himself and show some of these young sportsmen what a real old-style boxer could do. He refused, pointing out that his lameness was too great a handicap.

Digging had begun again, and it seemed that the flood-waters had done no lasting damage. Pegleg and his Kaffirs were working on Jan's claims and had already found several diamonds. Sam Rosenberg had reopened his office opposite Mount Ararat, but was still keeping the branch at Dutoitspan going, with a trustworthy young man installed as its manager. 'A tycoon I am becoming,' he said, laughing.

'What about this unrest?' Jan asked. 'Pegleg seems worried.'

'So tell me, when isn't there unrest? While the mine has been closed of course there has been trouble. Now it is open again everything is back to normal – fights, murders, illegal diamond buying. Kimberley has changed, men haven't. But unrest? No.'

But perhaps Pegleg was in closer touch than Rosenberg. Sam was right in saying that there had always been unrest – it was natural in a township largely made up of adventurers, hard men motivated above all by greed – but there had been a considerable tension in the air. While the mine had been closed because of the flooding, Pegleg reported, there had been frequent outbreaks of violence and scuffles with the police. 'Nothing on a big scale,' he said, 'but pointers to the way men felt. And there've been more and more demonstrations against the Governor and his minions.'

Apparently many of the diggers had not yet come to terms with the fact that Governor Southey had effectively denuded them of power. The constitution of the Legislative Council for the diamond fields and the disbanding of the Diggers' Committee and its replacement by the Mining Board meant that control was now firmly in the hands of the government and its civil servant advisers. Many of Richard Southey's attempts to increase respect for law and order – for instance, by making any form of gambling illegal – were greatly resented by a vocal minority, but the real bugbear was his racial tolerance. How could illegal diamond buying be stamped out if natives were allowed to dig for diamonds, to own claims, to be the equals of white men? There was a great deal to be said for that argument, but some of those who sheltered behind it were in fact totally dedicated to the suppression and even the extermination of the blacks, and so were implacably opposed to Governor Southey.

However, Pegleg said, now that the mines were operative again, the unrest had died down. 'Though I bet that Black Flag business will flare up again some day.'

'What Black Flag business?'

'Oh, it's a bunch of fanatics who're talking about an armed uprising with a black flag as a symbol. As I say, they've gone to ground now, but I'll keep an eye on it and let you know if it looks like starting up again.'

Jan decided to reopen his own diamond dealing business. He was no longer much interested in the money he could make from it, and in any case the price of diamonds had fallen dramatically, but he could hear his father saying, 'Jan made a useful contribution for a while, but it didn't last. I knew it wouldn't.' The more stones he could send home the better.

Within a few days he felt he was back in the old routine. He even went to the Ace of Diamonds, but Kate was no longer there. He asked McFarlane where she was.

'Down in the Cape,' the publican replied. 'At least, that's where she said she was going.'

'Why did she leave?'

'I told her to. Time for a change. You can't keep the same people all the time. Besides, business was bad, and she was expensive – damned expensive.'

'Did she go alone?'

'What's that to you, my friend? They tell me you're a respectable married man these days.' He grinned. 'Yes, she went alone. Gave me a message for you, now I come to think of it. Said she'd look you up one day. "You be careful," I says. "You don't want to come between a man and his wife," I says. "How do you know what I want?" she comes back, quick as a flash. "Or what *he* wants." And she gives a great big wink – you know, the way she used to.'

Jan was not really sorry Kate had gone – it removed temptation. In the meantime, there was plenty to keep him busy, and some mornings, instead of opening his office, he would put on his old diggers' clothes and go down with Pegleg and enjoy the physical effort of swinging his pick into the hard blue ground and shovelling up the fragments into the bucket which would carry it to the stagings at the edge of the mine. His lameness scarcely bothered him.

He was working on the claims one morning when he suddenly became aware of shouting from a group of men standing on the surface above. 'Stop work! Get out of the mine! Get out quickly, for God's sake!' Most of the diggers thought it must be a practical joke, and took no notice, but then someone recognised the men as officials of the Mining Board which had taken over from the old Diggers' Committee. They would not be making a fuss of that sort without cause.

When Jan and the others reached the lip of the pit, one of the officials told them, 'There's a huge crack, at least thirty feet long, underneath the staging. The mine's about to collapse inwards. All work must be suspended.'

Jan tried to speak to the man, but it was impossible to interrupt him as he gave out his warning. At the offices of the Mining Board, however, Jan succeeded in obtaining a short interview with the senior engineer.

'What's causing this crack?' he asked.

'Subsidence,' the engineer replied shortly. He sighed, as if to say that he had no time to spend in idle gossip.

'Yes, I know,' Jan persisted, 'but what has caused it? I mean, has the staging and the hoisting gear anything to do with it? You see – well, I was one of the first to suggest building the staging and the stanchions, and . . .'

The engineer looked at him with more interest. 'Ah, yes. Mr Shapiro, isn't it? I don't think you need worry, Mr Shapiro. As far as we can tell the staging has nothing to do with it at all. After all, there's no sign of cracks under the staging on the north side. I suppose it is just possible that the weight of the hoisting gear has exacerbated the problem, but I doubt it very much. In my opinion, the crack is simply the result of digging a very deep hole in a rock which is of a highly unstable nature. It is not surprising that the lip of such a hole shows a tendency to crumble away.'

'It hasn't done so on the north side.'

'Quite right, Mr Shapiro. But it may. We are keeping a careful watch on it.'

'Do you think the south side really will collapse?'

'Yes, I do.'

'And that will make the whole mine fall in upon itself?'

'It's a distinct possibility.'

Jan left his office not much comforted.

Despair walked the streets of Kimberley again. Coming so soon after the flooding, this, it seemed to many, was the end. Why had it happened? A dozen different explanations were given, from carefully worked-out theories based on local geology to the suggestion that this was God's vengeance for the wickedness of Kimberley and its inhabitants. Most of the diggers wondered, like Jan, whether the staging was responsible, but there was no way of answering that question with certainty, and the authorities still denied that it had played more than the most minor part in the formation of the crack.

The mine did not collapse, but the engineers continued to make their inspections and to forbid any work on the claims. Every day groups of diggers gathered round the great pit, morosely arguing about the engineers' forecasts, questioning the authority of those who had stopped their work. When there was nothing left to say, they would stand staring at the deserted mine, cursing softly to themselves as they brushed away the inevitable flies.

Some of them, especially those who were family men, began to get very restive. This additional period of enforced unemployment meant desperate hardship and put the lives of their starving wives and children at risk. A hat was passed round among those who were better off, but even though their contributions were generous, it was no solution.

'We don't want charity,' one of the hot-heads said angrily that morning in late November. 'We want to work on our claims. We own them, for God's sake! What right have they got to stop us? Four weeks it is now. "The mine's going to collapse," they told us. Well, it hasn't in the last four weeks, and if you ask me, it won't in the next four.'

'There's nothing we can do about it, Van Zyl,' said an older man. 'The Mining Board's turned down all the applications to restart.'

'You don't have to tell me that. We ought to have the Diggers' Committee back – they understood. But these bastards –' Van Zyl spat in disgust. He was a young Afrikander who had come to Kimberley a year or so previously. Like so many others, he had not at first been able to buy a claim, and when one did become available it had taken all his money, leaving him without the reserves he had intended to keep for the sake of his young wife and infant son. The flooding and now the threatened collapse of the mine had brought his family to the brink of disaster. 'There *is* something we can do about it,' he said. 'We can go down to our claims and start mining!'

'They'd take our licences away.'

'They couldn't – not if we all went down together. Come on! Who's coming with me?'

'I will!' But apart from this response from Van Zyl's close friend, Orlepp, no one seemed willing to risk the wrath of the Mining Board.

'Come on!' Van Zyl cried again. 'It's no use unless we all go, but if we do all go, they can't touch us.'

'Oh, shut your gob!' one of the men shouted. 'You're all piss and wind.'

For a moment it looked as though Van Zyl would hurl himself at the speaker, but he turned and set off towards the staging on the north side of the mine. 'I'll show you what I am!' he called over his shoulder. 'If you won't come with me, I'll go alone.'

'I'm with you,' Orlepp cried, hurrying to join him.

Despite appeals from the more law-abiding and angry shouts from some of the officials, the two young men made their way down to the claims and began to work.

There was no noise to give a warning, no trembling of the ground. Jan was standing with Pegleg and Tom Allenby and some of the others, and like everyone else, they were all watching Van Zyl and Orlepp. Some slight movement caught Jan's eye, and he glanced over towards the staging on the south side of the pit, on which stood the tall wooden stanchions trailing their curtain of ropes down to the claims. Everything was still, and he thought he must have imagined . . . And then he saw it again . . . a few small pieces of earth and rock falling from the side of the mine just below the staging, barely visible behind the network of ropes.

Suddenly he pointed. 'Look there! My God!'

At first it was a little like the shimmering effect of a mirage. The staging, that engineering feat of which he had been so proud, seemed to waver very slightly. Then slowly and gently, like a sandcastle lapped by the groping ripples of the incoming tide, part of the reef, the outer edge of the mine, began to collapse and slip and slide away, leaving the staging to form a bridge across the gap.

'Christ!' someone exclaimed. 'The whole bloody thing's going! Get back! Get back!'

Although only a small section of rock had fallen, they all remembered that the engineers had said the whole mine would collapse inwards on itself. How far back from the edge would it be safe? As they retreated they shouted to Van Zyl and Orlepp.

For a few moments it seemed as though no more of the reef would fall, but then another huge segment trembled and slid down, and then the collapse spread and grew, as though each small stone that fell brought with it ten times its own weight in the earth which had surrounded it, and that earth in turn caused more to slip away, until it seemed that the whole of the southern side of the pit would disintegrate into a landslide of horrifying size.

They could hear it now – the tortured squeal of twisting metal and the groan and crack of timber bending and snapping under the strain as the hoisting gear and the staging broke away and fell, and then the terrifying rumbling and the crashing of thunderclap upon thunderclap as hundreds of tons of rock hurtled on to the claims below. And above it all, most of the men there swore afterwards, they heard the screams of young Van Zyl and his friend, Orlepp. They had tried to run, but had been overwhelmed before they could move more than a few feet, and now the fallen rock was their tomb. It was almost certain that they had died instantly under the avalanche, but if by some miracle they were still alive, there was no chance of digging them out from beneath the huge fall of rock.

At least it would have been a swift death for them, for

though to the horrified eyes of the spectators the cataclysm seemed to have lasted for long, long minutes, in fact it was all over in a few short moments. Now a great cloud of dust was rising, a column which drifted up into the air like smoke, as though it were from the funeral pyre of the mine. Those watching knew that they had witnessed the death not only of the two young men, but also of the great mine at Kimberley.

*　　*　　*

When the dust had settled sufficiently for them to see the devastation clearly, hope was reborn for a few of them. Although some claims were totally buried, those away from the landslide were less badly affected than they had feared. The debris would have to be cleared away, and the hoisting gear rebuilt and erected, if that were possible, farther back from the brink of the mine, but if the engineers, when they made their inspections, could declare the mine safe for the diggers, perhaps Kimberley was alive after all.

They made a collection for Mrs Van Zyl. Orlepp was unmarried.

A few days later it was announced that further falls were unlikely, that the clearance of the mine would begin straight away, and that those whose claims were relatively undamaged would be able to start mining again shortly. Pegleg was optimistic that Jan's claims would be workable within a week at the most, but Jan suspected it would take much longer, and decided to go home. He had been away from Helen for far too long.

The one problem was his shop. Business had been very slow, even before the landslide, and he recognised that it was an absurdity to open it only when he was in Kimberley. His father would have to be content with the diamonds that Pegleg produced.

Rosenberg agreed, but said surprisingly, 'You should buy more claims.'

'That's crazy.'

'So it's crazy. I just know in my bones it's the right thing to do.'

'Then why don't you buy some?'

Rosenberg grinned. 'I'm a merchant – what do I know about digging? No, if I were a young man I would buy. Today claims are cheap – tomorrow, who knows? You are allowed to own as many as ten now.'

'Most of those for sale are buried under the landslide.'

'They'll soon clear that away. I tell you I'm certain about it, Jan.'

The old man's conviction was so strong that Jan was tempted to follow his advice straight away, but he decided first to see what others thought. Tom Allenby was depressed and dubious, but he was in a minority. Most of the diggers who remained in Kimberley spoke with contempt of the chicken-hearted who were put off by small misfortunes and a temporary drop in demand.

'That pipe is deep,' one of them said. 'Mining will go on here for years, and the deeper we go, the more diamonds we'll find.'

'You can't go much farther down,' Jan objected. 'It's difficult enough already to get the ground to the surface, and the danger of floods and subsidence and the reef collapsing again will just get worse and worse.'

'You want to sell your claims?' the man said. 'I'll buy.'

Jan delayed his departure for another two weeks. He would still just manage to get home for the Christmas celebrations. By the time he left, he had sold his office, though for a trifling sum, and bought himself another eight claims. Once the debris had been cleared, Pegleg would be able to supervise work on them fairly easily, with the assistance of some suitable young Englishman or Afrikander, since they were grouped not far from Jan's original claims.

As he travelled back to the Cape, Jan felt pleased with himself. In the automatic gesture which he repeated a score of times a day, he tapped his waistcoat. As long as he had the Shapiro Diamond, nothing could go irredeemably wrong.

★　　★　　★

When he arrived back at Overyssel, Helen ran out to meet him. She kissed him passionately, regardless of the watching servants. 'Oh, I've missed you, Jan,' she cried, and added in a whisper, 'especially at night.'

Jan cursed himself for staying away so long. Perhaps absence really did make the heart grow fonder, as the English said. She led him straight to their bedroom, and they made love – the first time for months – and their shared passion seemed more intense than ever before. Into Jan's mind flashed a memory of Harry's description of Edith – 'like making love to a cold potato'. He could never have said that of Helen, but this time there was a new wanton quality in her loving, a driving sensuality she had never shown before. It made Jan wonder, as they lay in happy contentment afterwards. Was it just because he had been away? Surely she could not have learnt this new wildness from another man. If she had been unfaithful during his absence . . . He pushed the doubting thoughts away, and took her hand, and whispered, 'I love you.'

As the days passed he discovered that she had changed in many ways. Her moods were always unpredictable. She was often the gay and witty girl of old, but she had moments of deep depression too and would drift away from him, as though locked in some remote part of her mind, gazing at him with coldness in her eyes. The intensity of passion was still there when they made love, but even in the midst of it he sometimes felt that he held a stranger in his arms. He hoped that she would conceive again, but it did not happen.

Helen had resumed her social life, and filled her time with visits to and from friends, and discussions with dressmakers, and the supervision of their household. She liked to ride every day, and usually Jan accompanied her. They saw Harry and Edith only very rarely. Helen said she could not stand Harry – 'All those ghastly jokes, and he drinks far too much' – and Jan allowed himself to humour her, though he would have liked to see more of his old friend.

Sometimes he fretted at his indolent way of life. He was twenty-seven, and however little need there was for him to earn money, idleness was only for men approaching the end of their lives. He was glad he had bought the extra claims, for they meant that he was still a diamond man, with an obligation to keep in touch with developments in the trade. He wrote regularly to Rosenberg and Pegleg, and studied their replies with care, and went into Cape Town at least once every week to discuss diamond business with merchants and bankers, most of whom he had met at dinner parties and other entertainments.

He often thought of making another trip to Kimberley, but

the discomforts of the journey, the efficiency with which Rosenberg and Pegleg ran everything for him, and above all his reluctance to leave Helen, all combined to make him postpone such visits. He wanted very much to take Helen with him, to show her Kimberley and prove that it was not the primitive camp of her imaginings, and to introduce her to his friends there. But she found excuse after excuse.

True to his promise, Pegleg kept Jan informed about the unrest in Kimberley. Alfred Aylward, the editor of one of the town's newspapers, the *Diamond Field*, and the originator of the symbolic black flag, had apparently continued to try to foment trouble, principally by means of a number of inflammatory articles in his paper. The grievances were those of which Jan had heard on his previous visit, concerning Governor Southey's dictatorial rule and especially the enhanced status of the native population. 'But,' wrote Pegleg in February, 1878, 'everything's as quiet as it's ever been at the moment, and I think the whole thing's fizzled out.'

With peace in the air and the fierce heat of summer over, it seemed a good time to try again to persuade Helen to visit Kimberley, and to Jan's surprised delight she agreed. 'I know I shall hate it,' she said, 'but you won't give me any peace till I've been there.'

'It's really not as bad as you think,' he told her.

Just before they left Overyssel at the end of March, he received a letter from Abram. 'The firm is still doing well, though conditions are very difficult. You will be pleased to hear that Rebecca gave birth to a son on January 23rd. His name is Andries. He and his mother are both thriving.' The letter made no reference to Jan's marriage, and he did not show it to Helen.

*   *   *

They reached Kimberley on April 11th. Pegleg was there to greet them, looking worried. As the three of them made their way to Jan's house, it was plain that he was very bothered about something. Helen, having complained incessantly of the rigours of the journey, was only too ready to retire to bed in the little house.

As she closed the door to the bedroom, Jan turned to Pegleg. 'What's the matter with you? You've been –'

'Did you get my letter – about the meeting?'

'What meeting? No, I don't think so.'

'Damn! I hoped I'd stop you coming. There's trouble, Jan. I didn't want to say anything about it in front of Mrs Shapiro.' He drew Jan farther away from the bedroom door. 'Listen. Aylward had a meeting early in March and he called for a revolution. Then he started forming an army, and got three or four hundred men to join him. They didn't actually start a rebellion, but I wouldn't have taken any bets on what would happen. Fortunately the Governor kept calm, and it all quietened down, but it's going to explode tomorrow. I mean it, Jan – it's really going to blow up.'

'Why?'

'There's a fellow called Cowie, who's been accused of supplying arms to Aylward. He goes on trial tomorrow afternoon, and when they find him guilty, Aylward says he and his men will use their guns to prevent them carrying out whatever sentence they give him. The whole place could go up in smoke! I wish you hadn't brought Mrs Shapiro here, really I do. You'll both have to keep out of the way – stay indoors. And you'd better have this handy.' He produced a revolver and handed it to Jan.

'I don't want that.'

'Keep it. There's going to be trouble, I tell you.'

Eventually, Jan agreed to take the gun, and Pegleg left, repeating his warnings.

In the morning, Helen was appalled to find that there were no servants to wait on them and that Jan proposed to prepare their breakfast himself from supplies that Pegleg had left in the house. Grimly she repacked her bag. 'We are going to an hotel,' she said, in her clear, definite voice. 'Assuming, that is, that there is one in this godforsaken place.' She stood, trembling with anger, staring at Jan. 'This house is disgusting. It is quite filthy and it smells revoltingly of that man's tobacco. Apart from which it is so poky that it is no better than a prison cell.'

They went to the Victoria Hotel, where Mrs Dunn was delighted to see Jan again and to offer him and his wife her best bedroom. When she took them to see it, Helen looked at the room with contempt, but said nothing, her lips a thin line. After she had pecked fastidiously at a little of the breakfast that Mrs Dunn provided, she announced that she intended to pass the rest of the day in bed. 'I didn't sleep a wink last night, and I am still exhausted after that dreadful journey.'

However, back in the bedroom, she spent the morning unpacking, exclaiming about the creased state of her clothes, calling for servants to press them and to wash those that she had been wearing, sending out for cologne and hairpins and a new pair of gloves, and finding a thousand reasons to complain. After lunch, which she ordered to be sent up to their room, she at last lay down to rest.

Jan looked at her as she slept. So beautiful, so difficult.

Free from attendance on her, he decided to go and see Sam Rosenberg. He had quite forgotten Pegleg's warning about the trouble that there might be in town, and when he left the hotel was surprised to see the streets crowded as everyone flocked to gather outside the Resident Magistrate's Court and wait to hear what happened to Cowie, the man accused of supplying arms to Aylward. Although there was an atmosphere of tension in the town, Jan found it difficult to believe that there would be any outbreak of violence, and decided to stay and see what developed.

A buzz of excitement indicated at last that the trial was over, and the news spread that Cowie had been found guilty and sentenced to a fine of fifty pounds, with the alternative of three months' hard labour. He had refused to pay the fine, and as soon as this became known, a man on horseback, armed with two revolvers and a sword at his side, galloped along Main Street in the direction of the mine.

'Who was that?' Jan asked a neighbour.

The man looked at him in astonishment. 'Where've you been, mate? Alfred Aylward, of course.'

Everyone looked towards Mount Ararat. The sound of marching feet could soon be heard, as an army of some three hundred men came tramping along to the court-house, a black flag borne defiantly at their head. Nearly all were armed. From the court a small posse of policemen appeared, drawn revolvers in their hands. The marchers halted, facing them, in a moment of indecision. Then Cowie came out, surrounded by more constables, who escorted him to the gaol, a short distance away, with the army and the crowd following. Although the street was quite broad, the size of the crowd made it impossible for the army to remain in any kind of formation, and by the time they had gathered outside the gaol, rebels and spectators were closely mingled into one vast mob. From the gaol more police emerged, carrying rifles with fixed bayonets. The tension mounted. It needed only a single shot from either the rebels or the police to start open warfare.

By now, Jan was standing a little way back from the main gathering, on the wooden steps of a house, from which he had a clear view of what was happening. One other man was sharing the vantage point with him. He was, to judge by the rifle he carried, one of the rebels, but he did not seem to be in an aggressive mood. He leaned casually against the wall of the house. 'Waste of time, this is,' he drawled. But that, thought Jan, was a somewhat ambiguous comment. Did the man want to abandon the revolt, or did he want more immediate action?

The crowd roared as the Resident Magistrate made an appearance. He looked cool and unruffled. Suddenly the man beside Jan raised his rifle to his shoulder and took aim at the Magistrate – or so it appeared to Jan. As the marksman pulled the trigger, Jan's arm knocked the barrel upwards so that the bullet sped harmlessly over the roof of the gaol.

'Idiot!' said the man furiously. 'I wasn't aiming *at* anybody.' He sprang down the steps and before anyone could stop him, disappeared into the crowd.

The shot had brought a shocked silence. The Magistrate stepped forward, raised his arms, and spoke in calm tones which carried to everyone in the crowd. 'My thanks to the man who fired that shot, since it allows me to be heard. However, I would suggest that we have no more gunfire. I address myself to those of you carrying arms. Tell me, who is your leader?'

There was a pause, and then two men stepped forward. 'We are the leaders,' one of them said.

'Your names?'

'William Ling.'

'Henry Tucker.'

'Why are you causing this tumult?'

'Because we've been goaded into it,' Ling replied. 'We can't get any satisfaction any other way. Time and again we've

asked for a meeting with the Governor to discuss our grievances, but he always refuses. This time he cannot. We demand
to see him now.'

'He is presiding this afternoon at the Legislative Council,'
the Magistrate said. 'But if it will put an end to this disturbance, I will go with you myself and see if it is possible to talk to
His Excellency.'

His calm courage and reasonable attitude brought about an
extraordinary change in the situation. It was as though the
lighted fuse had suddenly gone out before it could reach the
dynamite which would blow Kimberley sky high. A great
murmur of relief swept through the crowd and the army alike,
and men began to talk again and even to joke and laugh.

The Magistrate, the leaders of the revolt, Cowie and a
strong guard of policemen moved off towards the building
where the Legislative Council sat, followed by most of the
crowd. It was almost like a gala procession.

When the principal actors emerged from the Council cham-
bers some half hour later, it was announced that Cowie's fine
had been paid and he was a free man. The people of Kimberley
cheered and dispersed to go about their business. The Black
Flag Rebellion was over.

It transpired later that Alfred Aylward had decided, with
unusually accurate foresight, that the revolt would fail, and
that as far as he was concerned, discretion was indeed the
better part of valour. Having started the army on their march
to war, he had straightway left Kimberley and fled into the
Transvaal.

No one had been aware of Jan's attempt to save the Magistrate's life. For all the rest of the crowd knew, the shot had
been fired into the air deliberately, just as the man had claimed,
in order to silence the uproar. But had he been speaking the
truth? Jan could not be sure. It had certainly looked as though
he had been aiming at the Magistrate, and if his intention had
been simply to bring an end to the hubbub, surely he would
have pointed the rifle more towards the vertical. Whatever the
answer, Jan had done no harm in his action, and it was possible
that he had not only saved the Magistrate's life but also
delivered Kimberley from the horror of a civil war. Enjoyable
as it might have been to be hailed as the Hero of Kimberley, if
anyone deserved that title it was the Magistrate himself. Jan

decided to keep his mouth shut about the incident and to forget it as soon as possible.

★   ★   ★

Helen found nothing in Kimberley to give her pleasure. The Victoria Hotel was the least comfortable she had ever stayed in; Kimberley society was vulgar and boring; the climate and the flies were intolerable; and the great mine was so deep that it gave her vertigo. Fortunately, she had been completely unaware of the Black Flag Rebellion, or that would have been yet another cause for bitter criticism. Jan's biggest disappointment was to find that she strongly disliked both Pegleg and Sam Rosenberg. The former, she said dismissively, was common; she would not put into words what she had against Rosenberg. With each day her detestation of everything in Kimberley grew, and she became almost hysterical in expressing it.

Jan's only pleasure in their stay came from confirmation of a slight improvement in the diamond trade. The claims were producing well, and Rosenberg was despatching regular shipments of stones to Amsterdam on Jan's behalf.

Helen was scathing even about that. 'I can't think why you bother,' she said. 'You don't need the money, and since you loathe your family, there's no reason why you should help them.'

They took the coach back to the Cape a week after their arrival. 'You really must sell that horrid little house,' Helen said, as they left the town behind them. 'If you have to go to Kimberley again, you can stay in the hotel. It is dreadful enough, heaven knows, but at least it is an improvement on your . . . your shack. Promise me you will send your Mr Rosencrantz instructions to sell.'

'His name is Rosenberg.'

'Rosenberg, Rosencrantz – it makes no difference.' She took out a handkerchief and blew her nose daintily. Then she examined the scrap of fine linen and made a moue of disgust. 'Oh, that abominable dust! You may be sure of one thing, my dear – that is positively the last time I shall ever visit Kimberley. What a nauseating place!'

An elderly gentleman sitting opposite her tipped his hat. 'Your pardon, ma'am, but I think you are a trifle unfair. Many of us who live there are fond of Kimberley – aye, and proud of it too.'

'Then you must be absurdly easy to please.'

The gentleman was naturally affronted, but contented himself with clamping his mouth shut and glaring at them both.

The trouble was, Jan thought, she was right. Kimberley was primitive and dull in comparison with the sophistication of Cape Town, and there was no sense either in keeping his house when he made so little use of it. But to sell it would be to tear up his roots in Kimberley for good.

The visit seemed to change the relationship between Jan and Helen once again. After their return, although they shared the same bed, they went their own ways during the day. Helen rarely consulted Jan about her plans, and showed no interest in his concerns. Yet she would often pull him towards her as he got into bed, with an urgency and a subsequent passion and, at moments, a tenderness which made him believe that she loved him still, in some strange way of her own.

$$\star \qquad \star \qquad \star$$

Early in 1876, Jan met Harry in Cape Town one morning.

'You haven't been to see us for ages,' Harry said. He had been drinking, and his speech was slightly slurred. 'I wish you would.'

'I'll talk to Helen,' Jan replied.

'Tell her Edith would specially like her to call, now she can't go out.'

'What do you mean? Is she ill?'

'I'm going to be a proud father.' He grinned. 'Of course, it's my second child – at least, I think it's only the second – but the first in wedlock.'

'Congratulations.'

'Thanks. Edith's decided for some reason that she can't appear in public until the baby's born. I said I didn't see why not and I was proud of my handiwork, if that's an appropriate word, but you know what women are – stubborn as mules. So she'd love to see Helen.'

'I'll tell her.'

Helen was not interested. 'I certainly shan't go to see her. Edith is the dullest creature in the Cape, with the possible

225

exception of that squeaking sister of hers, and you know I can't stand that soak Harry.'

*　　*　　*

A week or two later a letter arrived from Samuel Rosenberg, suggesting that Jan should visit Kimberley with some urgency to discuss important matters too complex to cover in correspondence.

Jan tried to cajole Helen into coming with him, but she just laughed, and nothing would change her mind.

'They've opened a telegraph office,' Jan told her.

'Oh, Jan, really!' she exclaimed. 'What difference does a telegraph office make to me?'

'At least I'll be able to send you a message to say when I'm coming home.'

'You realise what it'll cost?' Like many rich people, Helen could be mean over small sums. 'The paper said it would be fifteen shillings. Fifteen shillings! I ask you!'

'I thought it might please you to know when I'd be back.'

'Oh, don't be a fool, Jan. A day here or there doesn't matter.'

When he arrived in Kimberley, Jan found Rosenberg more ebullient than he had seen him for a long time. 'The price of claims is going up and up,' he said. 'You made a good buy in those other eight. Do you realise what they're worth now? Two thousand or more each. A new boom is on the way.'

'The bubble might burst. It only needs another landslide.'

'The engineers are confident there'll be no more trouble, and world-wide demand for diamonds is picking up again. All that's needed is to find better ways of getting the diamonds out. That's why I thought you should travel up. Tom Allenby came to see me the other day, suggesting a merger to make a group of some thirty claims. Pool your resources, and you'd have much more efficient mining.'

'What are the problems?'

'A good question. There are several syndicates already, and some work quite well, but others have failed because they didn't stop to ask what the problems are. I have some doubts about Allenby's scheme, but find out for yourself. Go and talk to him, talk to the others, talk to everybody.'

Jan quickly came to the conclusion that Tom Allenby's ideas

for a syndicate were impractical. 'You're asking me to put in a huge amount of capital for the equipment,' he said.

'Yes, it sounds a lot,' Tom agreed. 'But what I'm suggesting is that you and I put up the bulk of the money, and take larger shares of the profits.'

'Will the others agree to that?'

'They'll have to. None of them has enough cash for an equal share.'

Jan considered. 'Sorry, my friend. I'd like to help, but it's not going to work. We might come to an agreement about the capital, but the real difficulty is that the claims you're talking about are scattered all over the mine – that doesn't make for efficiency. You'd be better off with someone whose claims are nearer to yours.'

He went back to Rosenberg. 'Why did you make me come all the way to Kimberley? Tom Allenby's syndicate is of no interest to me. Why didn't you simply turn him down? I'd have taken your word for it?'

'And spent the rest of your life wondering whether I was right or not. You have to make that sort of decision for yourself, Jan, at least the first time. But there were other reasons why I wanted to see you. I wanted to discuss the options open to you. You've got three possible courses of action. You can sell out now, which would give you a good price – maybe twenty thousand pounds in all. Or you can wait and join the right sort of syndicate later. Or you can hold on to your claims. One day the whole mine – in fact, all the mines here in Kimberley and Dutoitspan and Bultfontein – will be in the hands of one company. It's inevitable. When that day comes, they'll need your claims too, and the longer you hold out, the better the price in the end.'

'Let's rule out the first one. I'm not going to sell yet. That leaves joining the right kind of syndicate or just holding on. If I mine independently, the deeper I go the less efficient it will be, but I'll get top prices when I do sell. Joining a syndicate might give me a lower price when, if you're right, the whole mine comes under single ownership, but in the meantime I get better profits. Is that it?'

'Yes. Not an easy choice.'

'I can't decide that now. I shall need your advice when the time comes.'

227

'Did I say I wouldn't give it? But you will have to make the final decision. In the meantime, I'll turn down any unsuitable propositions, but send for you again if something interesting comes along.'

Jan saw no reason to stay longer in Kimberley. He was able to book a seat on the next coach leaving for the Cape, and just before he left went to the new telegraph office, intending to advise Helen of his return. But there was a queue of customers, and if he had waited he might easily have missed the coach.

20

It was, Jan told himself afterwards, a classic situation – the husband omitting to advise his wife of his earlier than expected return and coming home to find her in bed with another man. Perhaps he had almost expected it, subconsciously. What he had not imagined was that the other man would be Harry.

Helen remained calm when Jan entered the bedroom, and not bothering in any way to disguise her nakedness, got out of bed, slipped on a thin dressing-gown and walked out of the room without speaking.

Harry was sitting up in the bed, holding the sheet to his chest. Jan gazed at him, at first in sheer astonishment – it took a moment for the knowledge that he had been cuckolded by his best friend to sink in. Then fury overcame him, and he stepped towards the bed, his fist clenched. Harry looked at him apprehensively. He slid out of the bed, still holding the sheet, trying to use it to cover himself. But the sheet did not give as he pulled at it, and he stumbled and half fell. 'Quack!' he whispered, without smiling. There was something so ludicrous about the sight of him that Jan's anger changed to contempt and a weary sickness.

Perhaps Harry sensed that he was no longer in physical danger, for he stood up straight, not caring that he was naked, but attempting and somehow achieving a shred of dignity. 'I'm sorry, Jan,' he said. 'I'm sorry.'

Jan tightened his fists until his nails bit into his palms. 'You bastard!' he said softly, and walked out of the room and out of the house.

Later he wept tears of anger and betrayal, and crashed his fist into a tree trunk and barely felt the pain or realised that blood was streaming from his knuckles. How long he wandered, he was not sure. He had arrived from the coach in the early afternoon. Eventually he came to his senses sufficiently to realise that it was dark and that he was on the seashore.

As he hurried back to the house, anger swept over him again. He flung the door open and marched to his room, where he washed his bloodied hand and wrapped a clean linen handkerchief around the wound. Aware of a gnawing hunger, he went into the dining-room, rang the bell, and when the servant appeared, ordered something to eat.

'What boss want?' the man asked.

'I don't know. Just something to eat.'

'What boss want?' he repeated stupidly.

'For God's sake, I don't know! Whatever there is. *Bring me something to eat!*'

Terrified, the man backed out of the room. A moment later Helen came in. 'There's no need to shout at the servants,' she said coldly.

Jan stared at her in amazement. 'Is that all you can say? You go to bed with Harry, and all you can say is there's no need to shout at the servants! Aren't you even going to say you're sorry?'

'What's the point? You wouldn't believe me. Oh, Jan, can't we be civilised about this?'

Again Jan was at a loss for words. 'I don't understand you. Civilised? My wife is unfaithful, and I'm expected to discuss it as though we're talking about the weather!'

Helen sighed in an over patient way. 'If you insist I'll go through all the business of swearing it was a moment's temptation, and I'll beg you to forgive me. But it would be false, Jan, totally false. We're adults, not children who need to be told fairy-tales. If I told you such rubbish and even if you pretended to believe me, what good would that do? We should both know it meant nothing, and it would lie there between us, and fester, and ruin everything.'

'Isn't everything ruined already?'

'No. Not if we behave in a mature way. It's happened, Jan, and I'd be lying if I said I regretted it.'

'I thought you said you couldn't stand Harry.'

'I can't. But I was lonely, and Edith won't let him near her now that she's expecting.'

'How convenient that you happened to be available.'

230

'Yes, I deserved that.'

He looked at her as she stood facing him, proud and beautiful, and suddenly knew that he loved her more deeply than ever, whatever she had done. 'Oh, Helen, Helen!' he cried in anguish. 'Is it my fault? Is it something about me?'

'No.' Was there the merest hesitation before she answered? 'I'm sorry if I've hurt you, I suppose.'

'You suppose? Is our marriage such a failure that you aren't even certain of that?'

She did not answer at once, but stared out of the window. 'I hadn't really thought of it being a failure. If it is, it's my fault, Jan. All the others, like Edith – oh, especially Edith – revel in marriage. But sometimes I feel stifled. Perhaps it would have been all right if we'd had a child.'

Jan began to feel a glimmering of understanding and almost of pity for her, and yet . . . they were married. They had a duty towards one another.

She seemed to guess what was going through his mind. 'I know I'm your wife, Jan, but that doesn't mean that you own me. Not the real *me*. Any more than I own you, or want to.' She turned back to him, and her voice was suddenly strident. 'It won't worry me if you want to have your fling. Maybe you've already got your eye on someone. How about dear little Alice? Or perhaps you fancy one of the niggers. Or a nice plump Jewess.'

He took one stride towards her and seized her neck, his fingers pressing viciously into the soft flesh. She choked, and her face began to suffuse and her eyes to start from her head. He realised what he was doing, and threw her down in disgust, and ran from the room.

He called for a horse and trap, picked up the suitcase that had not been unpacked since his return from Kimberley, and drove into Cape Town. There he found a hotel, bought a bottle of Cape brandy and drank himself into a stupor.

It took him two days to decide what to do. Some of the time he sat in the gardens at the top of Adderley Street, oblivious of his surroundings, or shut himself in his hotel room. He drank himself to sleep again the second night. He thought of finding a prostitute, of returning to Overyssel to force Helen into submission, of going back to Kimberley, of taking a passage to Amsterdam; he thought of Harry, and the thrashing he deserved, and he thought of poor silly Edith; and he thought of Helen and the need she had felt, out of her own guilt, to wound him with her vicious words. The thoughts whirled and swirled within his brain.

At the end of the two days he could not have told why he had made the decision. It certainly made little sense, and it was not even as though he were penniless and depended on her to keep body and soul together. The nearest he came to understanding why he was going back to her was when he thought that perhaps one day she might become his wife again, his alone.

Helen accepted his return calmly. 'You've come back then.'

'Yes.'

'To stay?'

'I'm not sure.'

She put her hand to her neck. 'It will be weeks before I can wear a low-cut gown again.'

★   ★   ★

A new phase of their life together began. They continued to entertain and to be entertained, but apart from that led totally separate lives, and no longer slept together. Once, when they had wined and dined particularly well, as they rode home together in their carriage, Jan put his arm around Helen's shoulders. She nestled against him, and when they reached Overyssel it seemed natural that he should come into her bedroom, and take her in his arms, and that they should undress and climb together into the large soft bed. Yet that, for him, was where it ended. Suddenly the thought of Harry came into his mind, and with it an end to desire. In the morning, neither of them spoke of the incident. Yet Jan still loved her, and hoped passionately that one day they might find each other again.

He made one other change in his way of life. Helen had never approved of Joey – 'That nigger of yours with the cheeky look' – and had insisted that he should occupy the most menial of positions among their staff, but Jan now restored him to his previous position as his personal servant. The boy, almost a man, showed his appreciation by doing his best to anticipate Jan's every wish. He was constantly in attendance, fetching and carrying, acting as valet, as coachman, and even

232

as companion. He was intelligent, and Jan decided to teach him the rudiments of reading and writing.

When Helen found out, she was incredulous. 'Reading and writing? But he's a *nigger*, Jan. You'll ruin him. You're making a friend of him, and that's – that's ridiculous. They're inferior. They're servants, for God's sake – not friends. An Englishman would never make a friend of an inferior.'

'Unless he was a Jew?' Jan suggested.

Helen laughed. 'Oh, Jan, I've just called your boy a nigger – don't try and goad me into anti-semitism too. I have too many prejudices already.'

She still had the capacity for self-mockery that he had always enjoyed in her, but Jan could not help noticing that she had not challenged his suggestion that Jews might be considered inferior. But perhaps he was being too sensitive.

Helen never mentioned the matter of Joey again, but simply ignored him as though he did not exist for her.

*   *   *

For want of anything better to do, Jan visited Kimberley twice more in 1876 and again early in 1877. The diamond trade was continuing the long slow recovery, and Jan was glad that he had not sold out the previous year. On the other hand, the problem of getting the blue ground out of the depths of the mine was increasing. The strain was beginning to tell on Pegleg, although he had taken on a young Afrikander as an assistant, and since syndication seemed to be the one satisfactory answer, Jan looked around for a suitable group to join. Perhaps he should, as Sam Rosenberg advised, have accepted one of the two offers that came to him during that visit, but neither seemed to Jan to have the right feel about them, and he returned to Cape Town, promising that the decision would finally be made during his next trip, which he planned for September of that year.

In July, a telegraph message came from Sam Rosenberg. 'Your presence urgently required. Pegleg seriously ill. Also other developments.' Jan caught the earliest coach he could, and eight days later was in Kimberley. He had telegraphed ahead, and Sam was there to meet him.

'He's dying.'

'What's the matter with him?'

'I don't know. I hadn't seen him for days, and then one of the boys brought a message to say that he had collapsed at the mine. They said he'd been coughing a lot, and sneezing. I thought it might be pneumonia, but they say it isn't. Doctors! You think they know one disease from another? No, they do not. Anyway, he's been clinging on. Keeps asking for you.'

Pegleg was barely recognisable. He had had a rather round, almost chubby face, and his eyes had looked small, deepset in the thick flesh around them. Now they were enormous, and the bones of his face seemed to be on the point of bursting through the skin. When he saw Jan his mouth moved in a grimace which Jan realised was intended to be a smile. He smiled back, and took the skeletal hand in his.

Pegleg's voice was a mere whisper. 'I'm done for, Jan,' he said. 'But I had to tell you. I've waited till you came. Sam Rosenberg said you were coming, so I waited.' He paused. 'I cheated you.'

'No,' said Jan. 'No, you never cheated me.'

'Yes, I did. I cheated you, and it's done me no good at all. And when I realised it was all up with me, I knew I had to tell you before it was too late.' He stopped, and tried to get his breath. When he spoke again it was in short gasps. 'Pull up the floorboard . . . left-hand side of the window . . . in the bedroom.'

'Of my house?'

'Yes. You'll . . .' There was a long pause. 'You'll find a box. Key's here.' He fumbled at his neck and pulled from under his nightgown a piece of string on which was tied a key. 'Send things in it . . . my sister, Margriet . . . address in box. And the . . .' Again a long pause came, as Pegleg fought for breath. He gave a shuddering sigh and was still, and Jan felt certain he had gone, but then the enormous fading eyes opened again, and he said, 'Diamond is . . . there . . . found it . . . stole it from you . . . must . . . give it back.' He drew a few convulsive breaths, and did not move again.

Carefully Jan removed the key on its string from around the dead man's neck, then called the nurse.

Sad at heart, he left the hospital and walked slowly back to Sam Rosenberg's office. His expression told everything. Rosenberg patted his arm, and the two of them sat in silence for a while.

'I've stopped the work on your claims,' the old man said at last, 'and paid off the blacks. You'll need a new manager. The young chap that Pegleg had helping him is still pretty inexperienced. In any case, you want my advice – you should sell. A big syndicate I know is interested. You'd better talk to them.'

'Yes, I will. But tomorrow, Sam, tomorrow. I don't feel like it today. Pegleg was a good friend.'

'Yes. I shall miss him too.'

When he returned to the little house, Jan went to the bedroom and tried the floorboards to the left of the window, one of which lifted easily. When he opened Pegleg's box he found a couple of bundles of letters, a notebook and a small screw of paper. He unwrapped it. The rough stone looked much like the Shapiro Diamond – he patted his pocket to make sure the little silver case was there as usual – though very much smaller, probably no more than ten carats. He wondered why Pegleg had bothered to steal it – its value was not all that great. Perhaps somehow the stone had seemed special to him, just as his own diamond had done. He smiled ruefully. Poor old Pegleg.

He looked then at the papers. The letters in one bundle were from Pegleg's sister, Margriet. The others had been written a long time ago when Pegleg was young, and he soon decided that he would not read them – they were of too intimate a nature. The notebook contained a record of the bank account which Pegleg had kept with the Standard Bank of South Africa. It contained over five hundred pounds. After his funeral expenses had been met, there would be a substantial sum still to send to Margriet. Jan looked again at the diamond, and a sudden idea came to him – he would have it made into a pendant for her, and he would tell her simply that Pegleg had asked for it to be sent to her. He would post it to his father to be cut and polished and set. That would be the first favour he had asked since leaving his home, and surely it would not be refused.

The following day Jan went with Sam Rosenberg to meet the representatives of the Amalgamated Mining Company of Kimberley, the concern which wished to buy his claims. At the end of a brief meeting, Jan had agreed to sell his ten claims and, since the syndicate was planning to market its own diamonds directly in London and Amsterdam, had secured the right to purchase at wholesale prices an annual quantity of gemstones equal to half the average weight in carats that he had sent back to Amsterdam over the past five years. His father would still have a continuing source of supply at an advantageous rate.

When he emerged from the meeting, he was a rich man. They had agreed on a total of forty thousand pounds for his claims. He was twenty-eight and he had been in Africa for less than six years, but those years seemed to stretch in his memory to encompass his whole existence, as though his childhood and youth had been merely an unimportant preparation for them. And now that chapter of his life was closed. He was no longer a digger or a claim-owner or a dealer, and his connection with Kimberley would henceforth scarcely exist.

He should have felt happy with his new wealth, but fell into a depression which was intensified the next day when Pegleg's funeral took place.

There was a great deal to do in the following days. He deposited the cheque from the Amalgamated Mining Company at the bank, arranged for his account to be transferred to Cape Town, and convinced the officials that the sums they held in Pegleg's account should be sent to his sister in England; he wrote to Margriet Viljoen to tell her that Pegleg had died and what was happening to his money; and he despatched the diamond to Amsterdam, with instructions that it should be cut and fashioned into a pendant and then delivered to Miss Viljoen; and he put his house up for sale – he would have no use for it again – and arranged for the disposal of his furniture. All could have been done in a single day, but he felt curiously lethargic, and would break off from a letter or from turning out drawers to sit day-dreaming, remembering the early days with Harry. But to think of Harry was painful, and he would move swiftly on to Kate, and the finding of the Shapiro Diamond, and to so many other memories.

On the evening when he had finally finished all his chores he went to Samuel Rosenberg's house. The old man welcomed him warmly. 'A game of chess, that is the thing to settle the mind.'

'I think my mind is settled now.'

'I did not mean you.'

'What's the matter?'

'Nothing. Let us play.'

He set out the pieces, but was obviously not concentrating, and Jan asked again, 'What's the matter, Sam?'

Rosenberg sighed deeply. 'It is the end of an era, that is all. It is always sad when a part of your life comes to a stop.'

'You mean the day of the individual digger is over?'

'That has been over a long time. No, I am being selfish – I am talking of myself. I am closing my business, Jan. All these syndicates, they are sending the diamonds away to their own agents – there is no business left for a diamond dealer here in Kimberley.'

'Then what are you going to do?'

'Sell up. I shall get nothing for my business, but perhaps someone will want the office.'

'And then?'

'Live here, I suppose, in retirement. And die very soon.'

'Why do you say that?'

'I've seen it happen so often before. I'm an old man. I have no wife, no friends here, no interests – my business has been my life. Old men die quickly when their only interest is taken from them.'

'Have you really no friends here?'

'You were the only one. I've missed you since you've been in the Cape.'

'Then come back with me now. There is plenty of room in Overyssel. You can have a room of your own, a place to read the paper or write letters or just sit if you want to be alone, a place with room for your own furniture.'

'Thank you. Thank you, but no.'

'I think I need a friend too, Sam.' Jan told him of his estrangement from Helen, and the loneliness of his own life.

'You still love her?'

'Yes. With part of me.'

'And you hope that one day she will come back to you. Then you will not want me in the way.'

'You would never be in the way. Besides, yes, I want her back as my wife, but I know, deep down in me, that it will never happen.'

'Then leave her. You are wealthy now – you could afford a grand establishment of your own.'

'While I stay with her I still have hope. But we're not talking

237

about me, Sam, we're talking about you. Come and share our house.'

'You really mean it?'

'I wouldn't ask you out of politeness.'

'Politeness, no – but pity, perhaps. I don't want to be pitied, Jan.'

Jan shook his head almost wearily. 'You know me better than that.'

'Your wife will not object?'

'Oh, for God's sake, I tell you I want you to come to Overyssel. If you don't want to come, say so, but don't keep on with the questions.'

'I just want to be sure.' He paused, his shrewd eyes fixed on Jan. 'Then thank you, and thank the good Lord for His blessing.'

They sat in silence for a while, a contentment between them.

'How old are you, Sam?' Jan asked suddenly.

'Too old. A hundred and fifty. Twenty-one. Does it matter? How old do you think? No, I'll tell you. I'm seventy-three – a few years younger than the century. Why?'

'Just curiosity. I'd have guessed you were younger.'

'I walk every day. I eat carefully. That keeps me fit.' He chuckled drily. 'And I pray to God – that's the most important thing.'

A week later they left Kimberley. Neither of them had sold their houses, demand being low when so many were uprooting themselves from the town, but the bank manager had instructions to act for them in the sale which would surely come sooner or later. As he boarded the coach in Market Square, Jan felt a sudden desire to stay where he was, despite the heat and the flies and the dust and the fact that there was nothing for him there any more. He could easily have wept, and when Sam Rosenberg arrived, laden with baggage, he clearly shared the same feelings. Unaccountably the sight of Sam's despondency raised Jan's spirits, and as the coach drove out into the flat, parched country, dotted with the occasional scrubby bush or thorn tree, he found himself thinking that though an era had ended, as Sam had said, the other side of the coin was that a new era had begun.

He grinned wryly. He was starting it with a marriage that

238

was no marriage, with forty thousand pounds in the bank that he did not really need, without any occupation to fill his time and his mind and his energies, with an old man of seventy-three as his only real friend. He had nothing to be so happy about, and yet . . .

He began to sing under his breath. 'Father says I may, Johnny, father says I may, So don't say "no" for it is no go, since father says I may.' Kate's old song. Of course, *his* father had never said, 'Yes, you may go to Africa. Yes, you may have my blessing. Yes, you are still my firstborn and you may always be certain of my love.' But he had shown him!

He smiled and tapped his waistcoat pocket where the Shapiro Diamond lay, and began to talk to Sam of Overyssel and the pleasures they would find in each other's company.

21

'It is my house,' Helen said, 'paid for with my money. You have no right to bring him here without even consulting me.'

'How could I consult you? I was in Kimberley.'

'You could have telegraphed.'

'It would have cost fifteen shillings.'

She recognised the jibe, and almost smiled. 'Touchée. But couldn't he stay in an hotel? I expect he could afford it.' Her tone was briefly more conciliatory.

'I promised he could come here.'

'Oh, for God's sake! All right, then, but only for a short while. I'm not having anyone of his sort battening on us for ever.'

'What do you mean, "anyone of his sort"?'

'You know perfectly well what I mean. I do not propose to discuss it further.' She left the room, her lips tightened in a thin, angry line.

Although Jan spent many hours with Sam and their daily game of chess became a ritual, the old man found it difficult to settle down. He was fully aware of Helen's feelings towards him, and after he had been at Overyssel for about three months, announced one day that he intended to buy himself a house in Cape Town. He had visited the city many times, often going to the synagogue, and had made a number of acquaintances there – old men, like himself retired from business, who could talk of finance and politics and of the folly of the younger generations, pretending they still had power to set the world to rights.

'Lonely?' he said. 'I should be lonely with so many friends?'

'You aren't happy here, Sam?'

'We will not talk of that. Just promise you will visit me regularly for a game of chess. That I should miss.'

Helen was pleased to be rid of him. Jan kept his word and went to see him at least twice every week. One time he took with him a set of elaborately carved ivory chess men.

'So beautiful, so beautiful,' the old man said, admiring each piece in turn. 'See how delicate they are. Only a grandmaster should play with such a set.'

'No, only you and I should play with them. They are a present, Sam. For you.'

Sam's eyes filled with tears.

*   *   *

At about the time that Sam Rosenberg moved out of Overyssel, a letter came from Amsterdam. It shocked Jan, though the news it contained was of a quite trivial nature. Jacob Shapiro himself had cleaved the diamond which Pegleg had purloined, but for reasons which they did not understand, the stone had shattered. 'Since it was a matter of some sentiment,' Abram wrote, 'we decided that the best thing to do was to substitute another diamond. Miss Viljoen will not know that it is not the one her brother wanted her to have. We chose one a little smaller – eight point eight carats. I have sent it to her, set as you requested as a pendant on a gold chain, with an appropriate letter.' Jan felt for the silver box containing the Shapiro Diamond, and vowed once more never to submit it to the cleaving blade. If it should ever be shattered . . . He could not put a name to the disasters that might befall, but the mere thought was enough to make him shudder, however much he tried to convince himself that such fears were irrational.

*   *   *

Years passed by. Jan and Helen drifted ever further apart, busying themselves with their own occupations, together only on rare formal occasions. Jan had gradually built a life for himself. He had invested the proceeds from his claims, and by playing the stock market successfully had increased his fortune. His dealings demanded regular visits to his stockbroker and other advisers in Cape Town, and when he had concluded his business for the day he would usually call on Sam Rosenberg. He also began to take an interest in politics, especially after Griqualand West was incorporated with the Cape

Colony in 1880 and the Assembly in Cape Town had the responsibility of legislating for Kimberley affairs. Although his connections with the diamond town were now only slight, his interest remained. Some of his friends tried to persuade him to stand for the Assembly, but he was reluctant to commit himself fully.

The activity which gave him most pleasure was going to a Boxing Academy in Cape Town where youngsters in their early teens came for lessons. Their coach was an Afrikander called Theodor Brand. He was a competent boxer, but was hard pressed to give sufficient attention to all his pupils, and when Jan ventured to make a few comments and suggestions, Brand soon realised that he knew what he was talking about and asked whether he would be willing to help. Jan was delighted to agree, and took classes there regularly.

*   *   *

One afternoon, walking in Cape Town, Jan saw a familiar figure coming towards him. Older, plumper, but still unmistakable in the way she carried her head and the ostentatious swing of her hips and the magnetism which drew the glance of all who passed her by, he would have known her anywhere. Oblivious of the stares of any spectators, they embraced.

'Kate! What are you doing here?'

'I live here now. Oh, Jan, it's good to see you.'

'And you. Have you been in Cape Town long?'

'Moved from Port Elizabeth a couple of weeks ago. I been thinking of looking you up.'

'I wish you had. Are you at one of the theatres, or entertaining somewhere?'

'Somewhere's right. In my own rooms, lover.' She giggled. 'I got a gentleman friend. He moved here, so I followed.'

'You haven't married?'

'No. But you remember I always said I wanted a rich husband? Well, I got the next best thing – a rich gentleman friend. Nice little place, he's bought me. And he's very understanding. I had quite a few other . . . clients in Port Elizabeth, and I shouldn't be surprised if I do all right here, once I'm known. Oh, don't look so shocked. I used to say I'd end up in a whorehouse, but I done better than that. A courtesan, that's what I am, a high-class courtesan. *Very* high–class.' She laughed, but her lower lip trembled a little and there was unhappiness in her eyes. 'And you're married.'

'Yes.'

'Pity. Tuesday afternoons are free.' She laughed again.

'But, Kate –'

'Don't say anything, lover. You wouldn't have to pay me. Not you. And you wouldn't even have to come to bed with me. Just have a cup of tea and a gossip. Oh, Jan!' Suddenly, in that disconcerting way of hers, she was crying.

'Would you like to walk a little Kate? We could go up to the Gardens.'

'Yes. Yes, that would be nice.' She dabbed at her eyes with a tiny handkerchief. 'Sorry about . . . making a spectacle of myself like this. It's just that too many old memories . . .'

'Yes, I know.'

'You still got that diamond?'

'Yes.' He remembered the strange visions she had seen. Himself riding in a carriage with a pretty fair-haired woman . . . That would be Helen. Himself by a hospital bedside . . . Jimmy Koster, perhaps, or Pegleg. On a ship . . . Was that to come? 'We've got a lot to talk about, Kate,' he said. 'Tuesday afternoons would suit me fine.'

'Randy bugger!' she said.

They did go to bed sometimes on those Tuesday afternoons. She was warm and tender, and that was something that he had missed, but he could never quite forget that she belonged to other men too, and he enjoyed even more the days when it was warm enough to walk together through the park and sit and watch the little Cape pigeons, or when in her parlour she would pour tea elegantly into the delicate china cups, and they would talk about old times.

Jan made no effort to conceal his visits, and his pony and trap were regularly to be seen outside Kate's house on Tuesday afternoons.

'Does your wife know about me?' Kate asked.

'Probably. She hasn't said anything, but I wouldn't be surprised if she does.'

'Servants gossiping.'

'Perhaps. But I expect one of her friends has told her. It makes no difference to me.'

'Why don't you get rid of her?'

'If she wanted a divorce I'd give it to her, but it's for her to make the first move.'

'For Gawd's sake, why?'

'I don't know. Some old-fashioned idea of how a gentleman should behave, I suppose.'

'Has she got a boy-friend?'

'I don't know that, either. Probably, but she's always been discreet since the time . . . Oh, let's talk about something else, Kate.'

*   *   *

One autumn morning in 1883, Jan went to call on Sam Rosenberg, and was received with evident relief by his servant, who led him to the bedroom. Sam lay in bed. One side of his mouth was pulled down, he could not move his left arm or leg, and he could not speak.

'Did you call the doctor?' Jan asked the servant, who, terrified, shook his head. 'Stay there and look after him,' Jan said, running from the house, and wondering to himself what good the servant could possibly do, and whether it was already too late.

Fortunately Dr Pearson was at home, and came at once. 'As I feared from what you said – a stroke, and a pretty massive one too.'

'Will he get over it?'

'I don't know. Sometimes they do. How old is he?'

'Seventy-nine.'

'A good age. I don't hold out a lot of hope.'

'Will you put him in hospital?'

Dr Pearson hesitated. 'There's not a lot of point. They can't do much for him, and he might be better off being looked after at home.'

'Would it harm him to take him to Overyssel? We can nurse him better there.'

'Not if he's well wrapped up and you move him carefully.'

That afternoon Sam was carried gently out from his little house into the carriage and slowly back to Overyssel.

Helen watched as he was brought into the voorkamer. She said nothing, but her eyes flashed with anger, and she hurried into her drawing-room, slamming the door.

Sam Rosenberg was installed in his old room, and a nurse

brought from Cape Town to attend him. Dr Pearson visited him regularly, but on the fifth day, when Sam's condition had worsened, his breathing coming with difficulty and a faint bubbling sound, he shook his head and whispered to Jan, 'The old man's friend.'

'What?'

'Pneumonia. They call it that. Old men get strokes and heart attacks, and lie in bed slowly getting worse, and then pneumonia comes and makes the end easy for them, so they call it the old man's friend.'

For most of the time since he had been brought to Overyssel, Sam had slept, and during his brief waking periods had made no attempt to speak. 'Quite usual,' Dr Pearson had said briskly. 'If he recovers he may regain some power of speech, but a stroke of this magnitude often makes it impossible.' Although no sounds came from his lips, Sam's eyes were eloquent in their appeal, and if he awoke while Jan was in the room he would fix a steady, and it seemed, demanding gaze on him. 'Is there something you want, Sam?' Jan would ask, and would try to think what it might be. But whatever he suggested, there was no response from the faded old eyes.

On this occasion, however, after Dr Pearson had left, the faintest of movements from Rosenberg brought Jan swiftly to his bedside. The old man's eyes seemed to be imploring him more fervently than ever, and then he realised that the lips were moving as if trying to form words. He took Sam's hand in his, and then bent his head close to the old man's face to listen. There was almost no sound, but then he made out the faintest of whispers. The words were hard to understand, distorted by the effects of the stroke, but Sam repeated the sounds again and again, apparently determined to persevere until his message had been received.

It took Jan a long time to make it out. There were three words, and they sounded like an unfinished question: 'Will my house . . .?' Suddenly he realised. 'You mean your Will is in your house?'

The old man's limp fingers exerted the faintest of pressures on Jan's hand – a confirmation, he was sure, that he had understood correctly – and then Sam's lips began to move again. This time Jan was quicker to grasp his meaning. 'Jan, my son,' he was saying.

Jan raised the thin, veined hand to his lips and kissed it gently. 'My father,' he said softly.

Sam's lips moved once more, but not to make any sound. It was simply a slight twitch on the side of his mouth that had been less damaged by the stroke. Jan believed it was a smile.

A single tear gathered in the corner of Sam's eye. As it rolled slowly down his face, Jan realised that the laboured breathing had stopped. After a while he drew the eyelids down and kissed the old man's brow. 'Dear Sam,' he whispered. 'I'm glad and honoured that you thought of me as your son.'

*   *   *

Jan had not exchanged a word with Helen since bringing Sam to Overyssel, but now he went to her drawing-room and told her that his friend was dead.

She looked at him for a moment, and then said in a strange, expressionless voice. 'Get him out of that room immediately. I shall have it fumigated.'

'He didn't have an infectious disease.'

'He was a Jew, wasn't he? A dirty, stinking Jew!'

He stood speechless, thinking that she had been overcome by madness.

'Bringing him here to my house to die – that horrible old Jew.' She seemed beside herself.

'I am a Jew too,' he said quietly.

'Do you think I don't know it? Do you think I don't rue the day I married you? How could I have been such a fool? How have I tolerated living with a Jew?'

Again he was stunned. It was incredible, worse than the time his tent had been vandalised in New Rush. That had been done by strangers, uneducated, vicious brutes. This attack was from an intelligent, sophisticated woman, his wife, who had assured him that she cared nothing for the fact that he was Jewish, who had accepted his body and his love, who had borne his child and shared his life. And all the time she had lived a lie, with this bitter, vile anti-semitism deep in her soul. She had concealed it well, though he remembered now the occasions when she had hinted . . . But she had always laughed, mocking her own prejudices, and he had never believed her to be serious. At last he found his tongue. 'If you

246

felt like that, why didn't you tell me to go? Why didn't you say this to me before?'

'And have everybody sneering at me, saying, "I told you so."? Besides, what's the use. I'm tainted now. You know what they call me? The Jewess! The dirty, stinking Jewess!' She began to cry hysterically.

It was all unbelievable. Only one thing remained plain – his marriage was over. Whether it was madness on her part or not, he could never again stay in the same house with her. He turned and left the room, calling for Joey. Together they packed all his personal possessions and clothing. The trunks filled one trap. He sent for other servants and made them carry the body of Sam Rosenberg to the carriage, and sitting beside it, and with the trap following on behind, drove to Rosenberg's house in Cape Town.

He did not sleep that night. He could not remember what he should do. Was this when he should recite the khaddish, or was that not until after the funeral? It would do no harm, he decided. He found a prayer book and a kippa and a tallit, and feeling self-conscious, put them on and recited the prayer, stumbling over the Hebrew which he had not read for so long.

In the morning he made arrangements for the funeral, and he found the Will. Rosenberg had left all his money to the synagogue, but the house in Cape Town – 'in case he needs it at any time' – he had left to Jan. 'Oh, Sam, Sam,' Jan whispered. 'You knew, didn't you?'

★　　★　　★

Jan did not see Helen again. News reached him that she had suffered a nervous breakdown, and when she recovered some months later, he received a letter from her, asking for a divorce. 'No doubt you and your actress friend can supply the evidence.' Unwilling to involve Kate, he made arrangements to be seen visiting a prostitute's rooms, and in due course the divorce went through. Cape Society was scandalised, but only the briefest report appeared in the local press – no doubt the Renshaws had paid to suppress unpleasant publicity. Some months later Helen remarried, choosing as partner a young, fair-haired Englishman whom Jan had met on one or two occasions. He had few apparent brains, but at least Helen could

247

be sure that not one drop of the Jewish blood she hated so much flowed in his veins.

It took Jan a long time to recover. When had she learned to hate him so? Had her anti-semitism been there all along, and had his attraction for her been the very fact that he was of a race she had been brought up to despise, so that marrying him was a revolt against her parents and indeed against herself? It was a long time before the questions ceased to circulate in his mind, keeping him from sleep, tormenting him, and even longer before the wound that her words and attitude had slashed into his soul began to heal.

He continued some kind of life, meeting his business friends, and going to the gymnasium to help with the young boxers. He often visited Brand in his home, enjoying the quiet evenings and the good food. He and Theodor would entertain each other with stories of boxing, and drink sufficient wine to become pleasantly fuddled. Jan was always attended on these occasions by Joey, who was allowed to pass the time with the Brands' servants, and was then able to drive his master home if he were in no fit state to do so himself.

Pleasant though those evenings were, they did not give Jan the comfort that he got from visiting Kate. Only with her could he unburden his soul. She was sanity and warmth and a kind of love. He continued to meet her every Tuesday, but now she often came to his house, the house that had been Sam Rosenberg's, where he had lived ever since leaving Overyssel.

He took to paying irregular but quite frequent visits to the synagogue. At first it meant little to him, and he was not sure why he went. A continuing tribute to Sam Rosenberg perhaps. Or perhaps it was to do with his personal experiences of anti-semitism. The attack on Meier, the vandalising of his tent by Bell's hooligans and the reactions of men he had thought his friends, the attitude of some of the Society people who had come to Overyssel, and above all Helen's betrayal – all these had taught him that there was no escape from being a Jew. Then perhaps he should accept both the responsibilities and the rewards of being Jewish . . . He continued to attend the synagogue as the months went by, slowly discovering a depth of meaning and beauty and comfort in the old familiar words and rituals.

Many times he considered returning to Holland for a long

holiday, or perhaps even for good, and once he went as far as booking himself a passage on a liner. But he did not go. He had Kate and his few other friends, and a tenuous link still with Kimberley, where the Amalgamated Mining Company still prospered. And there was the climate. Why should he change the Cape's sunshine and mild winters for the grey skies of Northern Europe?

The truth was that he felt little inclination to make any major decisions. He was aware that he was frittering his time away, but could see nothing that was worthy of greater effort. He often thought nostalgically of the early days in the Rush – the prizefighting, and the first claim, and the discovery of the Shapiro Diamond, and he wished sometimes that he could go back to it, dust and flies and all. When the gold rush to Witwatersrand began in 1887, he was tempted to join it. But what was the point? He had all the money he needed, and it would surely be no place for a lame, bitter man rapidly approaching his fortieth birthday.

Yet he could not believe that his life was over. Some day something new and exciting would happen. Each evening as he went to bed he would take the silver box from his waistcoat pocket, and before placing it on the table beside his bed, would open it and look once more at the Shapiro Diamond. Sometimes he would even talk to it. 'You know what my future holds. Tell me. Tell me.' It always seemed to him that the stone gleamed more brightly then, and once as though in a dream he thought he heard a far-off voice. 'One day . . .' it said. 'One day . . .'

*   *   *

In 1889 everything changed. That was the year when Cecil Rhodes, aided by Alfred Beit, brought together all the mines of Kimberley under the control of De Beers Consolidated Mines. Old Sam Rosenberg had prophesied it years ago, and Jan had seen the steady progress towards a total unification – first Rhodes' take-over of the old De Beers mine and then the way in which, using every means available to him, he had gradually subdued all the smaller companies, finally buying the assets of the Kimberley Central Diamond Mining Company for the unbelievable sum of five million, three hundred and thirty-eight thousand, six hundred and fifty pounds. The

Amalgamated Mining Company had been swallowed up a few months before, and Jan had travelled to Kimberley on the recently opened railway to see whether he could still protect his interests. He was told brusquely that he would have the same chance as everyone else. There would be a central diamond distributing agency, which would monitor the supplies coming out of South Africa in the light of world demand, but De Beers were not allowing any favourites. When he left Kimberley that time, he knew he would not return.

Back in Cape Town at the weekend, he looked forward eagerly to his regular Tuesday meeting with Kate. She was dressed formally, instead of in a negligee, which was how he usually found her at home. She did not come to greet him, but poured tea daintily from the tray in front of her, and handed him his cup. 'Got something to tell you,' she said. 'Better put that down.' He did so. 'Sorry, lover, but this is the last time we'll meet. I'm getting married.'

'Married? You?'

'Yes, I know it's a laugh, but a girl's got to take her chances.'

'Who to?'

'My gentleman friend – the one who pays for this house. His wife's died, so he's free.'

'Do you love him?'

'Love? What's that got to do with it? He wants to look after me.'

'I could look after you, Kate. And sometimes I think you do love me a little.'

She laughed. 'Another proposal? Get away with you, Jan. I'm not the one for you, and you know that as well as I do. No, I'm going to be Mrs Frederick Ross. Think of it – me a respectable married woman!'

She fell silent then, and Jan looked at her, seeing once again, he thought, a shadow of sadness in her eyes. Absent-mindedly he tapped the waistcoat pocket which held the Shapiro Diamond. She noticed the movement, and said indulgently, to break the spell. 'You and your old diamond.'

He took out the box and opened it. 'Do you remember looking in it, Kate, seeing pictures, seeing me in the future?' He held it out to her. 'Look at it again. See what you can see.'

'No,' she said, and she shuddered briefly. 'I wouldn't see nothing. Nothing at all.'

Her words chilled him. Slowly he put the box back in his pocket and then stood up, trying to smile. 'I'd better go. I hope you'll be very happy, Kate. You deserve it. If you ever need me . . .' He went to her, took her hands and drew her to her feet. He kissed her gently. 'Goodbye, Kate, and thank you.' He turned and took his hat and cane. He thought she was crying softly as he let himself out.

He walked home sadly, feeling bereft. That evening he came to a sudden decision. He took pen and paper, and wrote a letter which had often been in his mind, but to which, until now, he could never commit himself.

'Dear Father, I am thinking of visiting Amsterdam this year. I cannot do so, however, unless you will tell me that I shall be welcome in your home, and that even if you cannot forget all that has kept us apart for so long, you will forgive me for the grief I have caused you. I have been much at fault. Please write to me. Your son, Jan.'

He read the letter through, wondering whether it was too brief to achieve the effect he hoped for. But there was nothing else to say at this point. He tried to imagine his father's expression as he read the letter, but it was always Sam Rosenberg's face that he saw. Sam would have forgiven his son, he thought, but of his real father he was less sure.

The reply came just over five weeks later. 'My dear Jan,' his father wrote. 'Thank you for your letter which gave me great joy. Many times in the past years I have written to you, opening my heart, but always I have torn the letters up, lacking the courage – no, lacking the *humility* to send them. It is not easy for a foolish and stubborn old man to admit to his stupidity. You ask for my forgiveness, but I too have to ask whether *you* can find it in your heart to forgive *me*. All these years we have been like strangers, and it has been my folly which has kept us so. Of course, you have been a little foolish and stubborn too, but you are young, and we should not expect wisdom in the young, whereas I am old enough indeed to have learnt to overcome my pride. And even so it is you, despite your youth, who found the wisdom to break down the barrier between us. I am grateful to you, and proud of you, and ashamed of myself.

'Oh, yes, my dear boy, I am proud of you, and always have been, and yet during all these years I have pretended that I have only one son. Abram is a good boy, and he and his family are my joy. But so too are you. Of course you must come home. It will give me such pleasure to see you again, to embrace you and weep with happiness to feel that we are a family once more.

'Those letters that I wrote and tore up were much longer than this one. They told of all that we were doing and of our plans for the future, and they asked for your news in equal detail. I shall not write all that now, for soon you will be here and we shall be able to talk to each other for as long as we wish in the friendship and the love of father and son.

'I am going now to the synagogue to give thanks to God that He has given you back to me. If that sounds foolish to you, forgive an old man that folly too. Your loving father, Jacob Shapiro.'

There was a postscript: 'I shall value your advice on the future of our business, but it can wait until you are here in Amsterdam. In any case I have decided to change the name to "J. Shapiro & Sons".'

22

As the ship steamed across Table Bay, Jan looked back at Cape Town and Table Mountain, feeling a peace of spirit that he seemed not to have known for years. It was a fine afternoon. No 'tablecloth' of cloud clung to the edge of Table Mountain, and he could see clearly the churches and the Castle of Good Hope and the splendid new Clock Tower at Victoria Basin. He vowed silently that he would be back.

He watched until Cape Town was no more than a blur in the distance, and then decided, since Joey was not there to do it for him, to unpack before dressing for dinner. The black had begged to be taken to Europe, but it made more sense to leave him to look after the house, and his disappointment had been tempered by the knowledge that Jan's absence would give him an opportunity to improve on his acquaintance with a young and attractive maidservant in Theodor Brand's household.

Jan had been placed in the dining-room at a table for four. Two people were already there when he arrived for dinner – an Afrikander farmer and his wife. They did not speak English, but even when Jan addressed them in Dutch displayed no interest in conversation, sitting in silence, gazing stolidly ahead. The soup had already been served when the fourth member of their group arrived. A tall girl in her late twenties, she wore a simple but striking dress of soft green satin trimmed with mauve. Her short black hair was arranged in a mass of curls close to her head. She was pretty, Jan thought, and prettier still when she smiled, showing a perfect row of gleaming white teeth.

'Oh, my goodness,' she cried, 'I'm late again. What Momma would say, I don't know – though I guess I do. "Punctuality is the politeness of princes," she always used to tell me, and when I said I wasn't a prince or even a princess she used to get as mad as all get-out with me. Why, thank you kindly, sir,' she went on to Jan, who held her chair as she sat. 'We should all introduce ourselves, don't you think?' She looked expectantly at the Afrikander couple, who turned their eyes away in continued embarrassment.

Jan bowed. 'My name is Shapiro, Jan Shapiro.'

She held out her hand to him. 'Glad to know you, Mr Shapiro. I am Sarah Goldfarb.'

'The lady and gentlemen opposite speak no English, Miss Goldfarb. They are Cape Dutch.'

'My, how exciting!'

'I don't think it will be, since they cannot join in any conversation unless I translate. I assume you do not speak Dutch.'

'You assume correctly, Mr Shapiro. But you do?'

'Yes. I am Dutch.' He spoke to the farmer and his wife, who nodded stiffly and returned to their food.

'I guess that leaves you and me to do the talking, Mr Shapiro. You must tell me all about yourself. I just adore hearing about other people. I've been all over the world on this trip and, golly Moses, the stories I've heard!'

She chattered on. Americans were always so full of themselves, Jan thought, and shuddered inwardly at the idea of having to suffer this barrage of words at every meal throughout the voyage. She had very beautiful eyes, dark with thick curling lashes, but that was insufficient compensation. He would have a word with the Purser and get himself moved to another table.

Meanwhile, she was still talking. She came from New York. Her parents had died and she had decided to spend the whole of her small inheritance on a journey around the world, now nearing its end. She prattled on of all the places she had seen – 'I just have London to do,' she said, 'and then it's back to dear old New York. I shall land there without one red cent to my name, but it's been a wonderful, truly wonderful experience.'

'You will not see Amsterdam?'

'No, Mr Shapiro. I don't have time, or money, for that. I can't even make Paris. I sure am sorry. They say Amsterdam's a real pretty old town.'

'The most beautiful in the world.'

'Have you seen all the other cities in the world?' she asked, wide-eyed.

Jan laughed. 'No. But Amsterdam beats them all The canals, the bridges, the old buildings . . .'

'You sound as though you know it well.'

'I was born there.'

'Well, maybe I'll make it one day.'

'And what will you do when you get back to New York?'

'Find a job, I guess. And I'm going to write a book. Gee, I've got just stacks and stacks of notes.' The monologue began again.

At the end of the meal the Afrikander couple left the table.

'What you must think of me!' Miss Goldfarb said. 'Here I am chattering away and hardly giving you the chance to say a single word. I am mortified, Mr Shapiro. Do say you will pardon me, and I promise that next time we meet I shall remember my manners. "Manners make the man," Momma used to say – she was great on sayings – and I guess they make the woman too.'

'May I escort you to the ladies' sitting-room, Miss Goldfarb?'

'Why, thank you, sir. You see, I do have manners when I try.'

With relief he left her at the entrance to the ladies' sitting-room, and retired to his cabin.

The following morning he was sitting on deck enjoying the light sea breeze and thinking how luxurious this journey was in comparison with his voyage out to the Cape, when Miss Goldfarb came up to him. He rose.

'Mr Shapiro, good morning. Would you do me the honour of walking a little with me?' Before he could plead his lameness as an excuse, she went on, 'Mr Shapiro, I must apologise again for last night. I lay awake thinking about it. I promise that I am not like that at all, really. It's just that I get so nervous when I meet people for the first time, and I guess it just makes me babble on and on and on. You must have found me quite odious.'

'Oh, no.'

'Come now, Mr Shapiro, confess. Honesty is the best policy – yes, that was one of Momma's favourites. Odious?'

'No, certainly not that. A little . . . overwhelming, shall we say?'

'I'm sure I deserve worse, but I guess overwhelming will do to be getting on with. You must give me the opportunity to prove that I am not overwhelming all the time.'

'We shall be meeting at meal-times, Miss Goldfarb,' Jan said, a little stiffly.

'You make it sound like the dining-room is a penitentiary. I must have made a real bad impression.' She laughed. 'You mean you haven't changed your table?'

Jan smiled. 'I thought of it.'

'Then please don't. You might land yourself with someone even more overwhelming than me. Now please, tell me about you.'

'What about me?'

'Tell me what you have been doing in the Cape, why you went there, why you are going back to Holland. Tell me everything.'

'Even my secrets?'

'Especially your secrets.'

Whereas the previous evening she had appalled him, Jan now found her remarkably pleasant. At first, much of what she said sounded deliberately ingenuous, and he suspected her of laughing up her sleeve, but the more he talked to her the more he appreciated the simple honesty in her questions and comments. Her curiosity sprang from real interest, and when she expressed wonder and delight, the feelings were genuine. He discovered too that she was an excellent listener, knowing instinctively when any intervention from her would destroy the flow of what he was saying, and equally when a gentle prompting would elicit more of the information she found so fascinating.

He enjoyed himself enormously, and gave up all thought of asking to be moved to a different table. As the ship sailed northwards, they spent more and more time in each other's company. He learned that her mother was of English descent, but her father's parents had emigrated from Germany and had settled in New York, where her grandfather had found employment in the tailoring business, and her father had eventually joined the same firm. She had three married brothers, all older than herself and all successful, which was why her parents had left the whole of their savings to her.

'Everyone told me I ought to invest the money against a rainy day, but I told them what Momma said – "Money is like muck, not good except it be spread". And they were just scandalised that I was going to go first-class all the way and without a chaperone, but I remembered what Poppa used to tell me. He wasn't so hot on proverbs, like Momma, but he used to say that being a girl made no difference. "You're a human being first," he would say. "That gives you the right to do anything you want, just so it don't interfere with other people's rights." Well, it was my money, and it sure didn't interfere with other people's rights if I spent it. I don't regret it one little bit, and you know what, Mr Shapiro? This voyage is going to be the best part of the whole trip.' She blushed. 'After that, I guess the only thing I can do is suggest we're friends enough for first names.'

*   *   *

Jan shaved the last of the soap from his chin, and gazed at himself in the mirror. What did Sarah see when she looked at him? A strong, handsome face? That he could not judge. What else? There were several silver threads in his dark hair, and around his eyes a network of fine lines showed faintly lighter than the tanned skin surrounding them, but otherwise time and his experiences had dealt lightly with him. His nose had a slight, barely noticeable kink, the legacy of his great challenge fight with Ned Smith, but the scar on his upper lip, also caused by Smith's fists, was hidden by the moustache which spread out across his cheeks to join the thick sideburns. Was it a face that Sarah could grow to love?

Lying in bed the previous night he had recognised that he, for his part, was deeply in love with her. 'You have known her only a few days,' he told himself. 'A shipboard romance, that's all.' But his heart had no room for such reasonable thoughts, and he knew that what he felt was true and lasting.

He finished dressing, and took the silver box from the shelf beside his bunk to put it in his waistcoat pocket. On impulse he opened it and took out the Shapiro Diamond. When Kate had looked in the stone she had seen him on board a ship, but she had said nothing of Sarah. Had she not appeared in the vision, or had Kate avoided mentioning her, instinctively recognising her importance in his life? He held the stone to the light, hoping that he too might see some image of his own, but there was nothing except the ever-present glow that he knew so well. He put the diamond back in its box, and sat for a moment, clasping it tightly in his hand. Into his mind came a picture of a house. It was a little like Overyssel, but smaller and less ostentatious. The door opened and two people came out, and he recognised them as himself and Sarah. Her arm was in his and she was gazing up at him. The vision faded.

He was conscious of his racing heart and of a joyous excitement as he realised that the diamond had spoken to him, telling him that Sarah would bring him the happiness he sought, that she was his future. 'Such romantic nonsense,' he chided himself. 'You should have more sense at your age, Jan Shapiro. And don't rush in. Don't let yourself be hurt.'

In all his conversations with Sarah he had refrained from telling her about the Shapiro Diamond, but that day he showed it to her.

'It sure doesn't look like a diamond,' she said.

'That's because it hasn't been cut and polished. See how it gleams in your hand.'

'Why do you keep it like this?'

'Reasons.'

'Tell me.'

'Well, call it a superstition, if you like. I feel it would be . . . unlucky to have it cut.' He took the stone from her, caressing it with his fingers.

She seemed to sense that he had not told her everything. 'Go on, Jan.'

'You see, for years, ever since I found it, I've had the feeling that my life is bound up with it. You'll laugh at me.'

'No.'

'A friend of mine saw visions of my future in it.'

'Like a crystal ball?'

He looked for a hint of incredulity in her eyes, but saw only interest and warmth. 'Yes,' he said. 'And I believe it speaks to me too sometimes.' He laughed nervously. 'That must sound quite absurd to you.'

'No. There are more things in heaven and earth . . .' She paused. 'Wouldn't it still work if you had it cut and polished?'

'I don't know. But you remember how I told you about the diamond that shattered when I tried to cleave it in my father's workshop? Well, I'm afraid of that happening again.' After a moment, he continued, 'I know somehow that if this diamond shatters, it'll be the end of me, the end of my life.'

She looked at him steadily. 'You mean you would die?'

'It's ridiculous, isn't it? Just superstition. But I know it's true, Sarah. I know it.'

Again he searched for a sign of scepticism or of a smile which might betoken derision, but she continued to gaze at him with sympathy in her eyes. She put her hand lightly on his arm. 'I understand, I think, Jan.'

He had intended then to tell her he loved her and to ask her to marry him, but found himself talking about the diamond that Pegleg had purloined, which had shattered when his father cleaved it, and that led on to other reminiscences, and somehow the right moment did not come again that day.

* * *

The ship put in at Lisbon, and Jan and Sarah went ashore to see the sights of the city – 'Not as beautiful as Amsterdam,' Jan said – and wandered along the broad main street, lined with little gardens, and sat at pavement cafes beneath the palm trees, sipping vinho verde while Sarah made notes for her book. That evening the ship sailed down the Tagus, and after dinner they stood on deck, watching by moonlight as the river banks slipped by. It was early October, and still warm.

'Why don't you come to Amsterdam with me, instead of going to London?'

She laughed. 'I'd love to, Jan, but I must see London – for my book.'

'And despite all I've told you you're going to leave out the most beautiful city in the world? I tell you what, come to Amsterdam and then go on to London. I could come with you.'

She did not immediately take up the implication of that suggestion. 'Your family expect you to spend your vacation with them, after being away so long. Besides, what would they think of me? They'd probably consider me a scarlet woman, travelling around Europe, unchaperoned, with an attractive and eligible gentleman.'

He smiled. 'Thank you for the "attractive". They'd be delighted to know you. They'd think that you and I had formed an attachment. I hope they'd be right.'

She was silent for a while, and then said, 'Why, Mr Shapiro, that sounds uncommonly like a proposal – of sorts.' Her tone was very light.

'Supposing it were? I love you very much, Sarah.' He took her hand in his. 'Will you marry me? Please.'

She did not respond straight away. 'I can't give you an answer. Not yet. I need time to think.' She squeezed his hand. 'I'm honoured and very happy that you should think of me in that way, but I've not thought of marriage – not for many years. A girl has to get used to the idea.'

'Could you . . . could you come to care for me?'

'I already do, but . . . I guess you know what Momma always said about marrying in haste. Oh, dear Jan, don't look so sad. I promise I will give you an answer before we reach Southampton.' She leaned forward and kissed him briefly on the cheek. 'I guess I'll go to my cabin now. It's getting chilly.'

The next day the unanswered question lay between them. After a while, Sarah said, 'I know what you're thinking about, Jan – and I am too – but let's not let it spoil our fun. We have three days before we get to England.'

Later, she asked him, 'You're going back to the Cape after you've seen your family?'

'Yes. My life is there. And my diamond –' He broke off. 'I'm sure you think I'm crazy, but I know it's right for me to go back.'

'Because your diamond tells you so?'

'Yes.'

'And what will you do with your life there? Has it told you that?'

'No.' He gave a rueful laugh. 'It doesn't tell me everything. But it has told me about you.'

'Supposing I said I would marry you – just supposing, mind – and that I wanted to live in New York?'

'Then I'd live in New York too.'

'Despite what your diamond tells you?'

He hesitated for a moment before saying, 'Yes. Do you mean you will marry me?'

She put a finger on his lips. 'I said supposing. Anyway, if we do marry, I shall live where you choose to make your home. So what do you plan to do back in the Cape?'

'I'm not sure. Continue my life of idleness, probably. I have thought sometimes of going into politics.' He explained to her some of the difficulties in governing such a vast and untamed country, its outposts of civilisation scattered at huge distances, a wealthy land, with its riches of gold and diamonds, but primitive and peopled by so many races. 'The English and the Afrikanders do not see eye to eye, and there is the problem for all the white men there of controlling the native population. I can see much conflict ahead.'

'If you believe you can help, then I guess you have a duty to do so.'

'Perhaps. I need . . . Oh, I don't know. I need some spur to make me take it up.'

*   *   *

The evening before they were due to dock at Southampton, Jan suggested that they should stroll around the deck after dinner, but Sarah said she would prefer the main sitting-room. He knew that she was going to refuse him. There could be no other reason for wanting to be surrounded by other people when she gave him her answer.

When they were sitting down, she said, 'Please promise you will say nothing until I have finished. Promise?'

'I promise.'

'Good. No interruptions at all.' She had been smiling, but now she spoke seriously. 'I have thought a great deal about this, about us, every which way. I am very tempted to say, "Yes, I will marry you." It's what I want with all my heart.'

'Then –'

'Hush! Remember your promise. I want it with all my heart, but I have a mind too, and my mind tells me I'd be wrong to decide anything so important on board this ship, when I see you every day, where we live a crazy kind of unreal life. So I've decided I shall go to London and spend my four days there as scheduled. At the end of that time I shall send you a telegram. It will either say that I am coming to Amsterdam, or that I'm going back to New York. There.'

'Then I still haven't got an answer.'

'No. I'm sorry, Jan – this is the best I can do.'

'And if the telegram says you are coming to Amsterdam it'll mean that you will marry me?'

'I guess so.'

'Then I shall just have to wait and pray till it comes.'

'Yes. And now I want to ask a favour. I have to go pack my valises, and I want us to say goodbye now. Please, please don't try to see me in the morning.'

'Why not?'

'Reasons, as you once said to me.' She stood up, and held out her hand. 'Goodbye, Jan, and thanks for everything – thanks a million.'

He seized her hand, desperate to stop her leaving. 'You promise you'll send that telegram?'

'I promise. And promises are made to be kept – that's what Momma used to say.'

*   *   *

During the journey from Southampton to Rotterdam, the ship seemed desolate without Sarah. She filled Jan's heart and mind, his waking and his dreaming hours. 'It's what I want with all my heart,' she had said – surely she would not refuse him. And there was the vision that the Shapiro Diamond had brought him to cling to . . .

As they passed the Hook of Holland, he realised that he had scarcely thought of his father since he got on the boat. There would be so much to tell him – all that had happened to him since he left home and the people who had filled his life – Sam Rosenberg and Kate and Pegleg, and Harry and Helen, and now, perhaps, Sarah. The good things and the bad things. And perhaps what would please his father most would be the knowledge that, however feebly, Jan had regained something of his faith.

He had of course sent a telegram to his father before leaving Cape Town, and when the ship put in at Lisbon he had cabled again. They were at the foot of the gangway to welcome him. He recognised Rebecca at once, despite the fact that she had become matronly, but stupidly he had not expected Abram to look any older than when he left home, and at first glance took the round-shouldered man at her side for his father. But of course, Jacob would be in his late sixties by now, which was no doubt why he had not come to meet him. Or perhaps he was sheltering somewhere from the fresh wind which was blowing.

Abram came towards him, his arms open, and embraced him, and, a little embarrassed, Jan returned the hug. When it came to greeting Rebecca, he could not quite bring himself to kiss her cheek, even though she seemed to expect it.

'Welcome home, Jan,' she said. 'How are you?'

'Thank you. I'm well. And you?'

'Oh, we're fine. Did you have a good voyage?'

'Yes, very.' Continuing the stilted exchange, Jan went on, 'It's kind of you to come and meet me. It really wasn't necessary. I could have taken the train.'

'Oh, but we wanted to,' Abram said. 'Besides . . .'

'Besides what?' But Abram did not answer, and Jan asked, 'Is Father here?'

'Well, that's the other reason we wanted to come and meet you. To tell you. Father's dead, Jan.'

23

'Father dead?' Jan could hardly speak.

'A heart attack, the doctor said. It was all over very quickly.'

'When?'

'Two weeks ago.'

'It was a lovely way to go,' Rebecca said softly.

A lovely way to go! Why did people always say that? Of course, it was true – it was much better to die like that unexpectedly, swiftly, rather than with some lingering, pain-filled illness. But it always sounded to him like the remark of a stranger, to whom there was no real pain in the passing of someone dearly loved.

'I'm sorry,' Abram was saying. 'It's been a shock, but there isn't any easy way to tell something like this.'

'Two weeks ago? You didn't send a cable. It would have been waiting for me at Lisbon.'

'You wouldn't have been able to do anything. Rebecca thought it was better not to tell you at that stage. You would have been . . . well . . .'

'I thought it would have been even worse for you, Jan, cooped up on a ship, unable to do anything, thinking about . . . Father . . . and the funeral . . . and everything.'

'Yes,' he said. 'Thank you.' And he was both angered that she had kept the news from him and grateful for her under-standing. 'The funeral?' he said after a moment or two. 'You've held it? Yes, you would have. And you – we – we're in mourning, of course.'

Abram looked away. 'Well . . . yes, technically. We sat shivah, naturally, for the seven days after he was buried, but since then . . . well, life is for the living, Jan, and I'm sure Father wouldn't expect us to . . .'

'Besides,' Rebecca put in, 'we had to think of the children. It's so difficult for them to understand anything like that. It doesn't mean that we don't think of him, of course.'

'We talked about it,' Abram said, 'and I remembered how you gave up going to synagogue, and we felt sure you'd be in agreement. I don't suppose you've been inside a synagogue since you left home, have you?'

'Yes. I go occasionally.'

'Oh, do you? That's good. Of course, we still attend fairly regularly, and we observe the Sabbath and the feasts. But all within reason.'

'Yes,' said Jan. He was stunned. It seemed extraordinary that Abram, who had been so pious, should have become half-hearted in religious observances, whereas he himself had moved back towards orthodoxy. But no doubt time had altered them both.

'It was a beautiful funeral,' Rebecca said. 'A week ago last Tuesday.'

'Oh, yes,' Abram said. 'He got a fine send-off. Everyone was there, and they all said the most wonderful things about him.'

'Such a pity you couldn't be there, Jan,' Rebecca continued. 'It would have done your heart good to hear how highly he was regarded. What was it the Rabbi said, Abram? Oh, yes – "His name was synonymous with diamonds, and indeed Jacob Shapiro was like a diamond himself – pure, brilliant, a precious stone in our community." It brought tears to everyone's eyes.'

Jan touched the little silver box in his waistcoat. He wished that his father could have seen the Shapiro Diamond. Perhaps he would have understood Jan's feelings for it.

As they sat in the train on the way to Amsterdam, they chatted awkwardly, Jan enquiring after his young nephew and niece, whom he had never seen, and Abram and Rebecca explaining that there was plenty of room in the house in Onkelboerensteeg, even though Aunt Suzanna was still alive, since after the workshops had been moved, they had converted the space into a sitting-room and a dining-room and turned the rooms on the first floor into extra bedrooms. There were long silences in their conversation.

It was still light when they reached Amsterdam. Tremendous changes had taken place in the city since Jan left it eighteen years before. In 1871 construction of the magnificent railway station where they now arrived had not even begun. Abram drew Jan's attention to its every aspect, as though he himself had designed and built it. The whole of Amsterdam was proud of it, he said, as an example of all that was best in modern architecture, the blue-grey slates of the roof and turrets forming an attractive contrast to the warm red bricks of the main structure.

'The city's spreading rapidly,' Abram said. 'They're building out beyond Singelgracht now. Everything's been booming since you left. Not just our business – everything.'

When the cab drew up outside the house in Onkelboerensteeg, Aunt Suzanna was at the door, looking like a witch, bent and bowed, but still wearing her usual spotless white apron over the plain black dress. There were tears in her eyes and a gummy smile of welcome among the deep wrinkles as she looked at Jan. Dear Aunt Suzanna! He was filled with a wave of affection for her, and guilt at the realisation of how little he had thought about her during the years that he had been away. On either side of her stood ten-year-old Andries and his younger sister, Judith, slim, dark-haired, and with enormous brown eyes gazing at him in curiosity. He shook hands with them both, gravely.

The house itself was as amazing as everything else. Jan had not been prepared for the evidence of wealth which confronted him. Expensive-looking rugs lay on the floor, rich draperies hung at the windows, comfortable new furniture had replaced the battered old chairs and tables that he had grown up with, and he noticed many valuable articles – paintings, a cabinet full of delicate china, a sixteenth century carved chest, an early tapestry covering a wall. It seemed like some rich stranger's home.

Later, they sat round the handsome dining-room table, the snowy linen, the silver tableware, the bone china dishes and plates fully the equal of those that had been regularly used at Overyssel. Aunt Suzanna brought in the food, but it was Rebecca who served it, with the attitude of a Society hostess. 'More potatoes?' she asked, somehow making it sound as though potatoes were a rare and costly delicacy.

Eventually the meal was over, and Abram suggested that he

266

and Jan should carry their coffee into the drawing-room, where they would be more comfortable. He offered Jan a cigar, which he refused, and then, with great ritual, lit one for himself.

'You have told me very little about Father,' Jan said. 'Had he been ill beforehand?'

'Not at all. He was his normal self, and very active for his age. One or two coughs and colds, but nothing serious at all. Indeed, the doctor said that if his heart hadn't given out, he could have gone on for years. It was a mercy, of course, that he didn't suffer. It was all over in a matter of seconds. He gave a sort of cry – it was almost as though he were choking – and fell to the floor and by the time we got to him he was dead.' He paused. 'He was so looking forward to seeing you. Talked of nothing else, ever since he got your letter. Rebecca and I were pleased too. It's a rather difficult situation, in view of . . . well, in view of all that happened. And I'm afraid you and I never got on all that well. I used to be so jealous of you.'

'You? Jealous of me?'

Abram smiled. 'Oh, I know I was good at cleaving and polishing, and you were hopeless, but it was you that Father loved best. Didn't you realise that?'

'No,' Jan said. 'No, I didn't.'

'That's why he was so upset about your going away. "But I could never tell him," he said to me when your letter came. "I never thought he'd believe me" – that's what he said. How often we misunderstand each other, eh, Jan? Just the way we were a bit at loggerheads, you and I, when we were kids. But now – well, I hope we can let bygones be bygones, and be friends, and . . . and brothers.' He got up and came over to Jan, and solemnly shook his hand. When he sat down again, he went on, 'I suppose I ought to say something about Rebecca. It must have hurt you very much, but, well, we fell in love, and there wasn't much we could do. We've been very happy. I think she's better off with an old stick-in-the-mud like me.'

'Yes. I'm glad you're both happy.'

'I gather your own marriage wasn't . . .'

'No. I'd rather not talk about it, if you don't mind.'

'Of course. Of course. I'm sorry.' As though he were ticking off the points in his mind, Abram went on, 'Now I must tell you about Father's Will. It's in the safe at the works. I keep all important documents there. But I can give you the gist of it. Father left the house entirely to me, since it appeared to be your intention to remain in South Africa, with the proviso that if I were to sell it at any time during Aunt Suzanna's lifetime I should continue to provide somewhere for her to live in comfort. Well, I would have done that anyway, and I don't really see why he found it necessary to make a point of it. However, he did.' He puffed at his cigar. 'His money – and there's quite a sizeable amount, Jan – something in the region of half a million guilders – he's left in trust for Andries and Judith, and for any other grandchildren that may be born before Judith reaches the age of twenty-one.' Abram laughed briefly. 'I doubt very much whether Rebecca and I will add to our family, but there's still time for you, Jan. You and Helen didn't have any children, did you?'

'Our child was born prematurely, and died within a few hours of her birth.'

'Oh, yes. I'd forgotten that. I'm sorry.' He examined the ash on the end of his cigar, went to knock it off gently into an ashtray, changed his mind and took another puff. Jan watched him, amused at his brother's attempts to cover his embarrassment. 'The section on the business,' Abram continued at last, 'is the longest part of the Will. To try and summarise it, Father has left it two thirds to me, one third to you. He felt, you see . . . I'm sorry, Jan, I find this all rather difficult, but you'll see it for yourself in the Will tomorrow. He wanted, he says, to be sure that the firm would carry on in the control of the family, a condition he felt he could not secure if we were to have equal shares.'

'I don't follow that.'

'He felt that you might want to sell your share of the business. He does not in fact expressly forbid you to do so, though he does demand that if you decide to sell, you should give me first offer. But if you had had fifty per cent of the business and had sold to some outsider, then I could not have been certain of retaining full control.'

'Yes. I see that. When did he make this Will?'

'Just over a year ago. I'm pretty certain, Jan, that he would have altered it after seeing you and talking things over with you. I like to think that. But of course we just have to accept it as it stands.'

'Yes, I understand.'

'Have you any idea yet of your plans? I know you spoke in your letter to Father of this being just a visit, but things have changed now, and perhaps you're thinking of staying here for good. I needn't tell you that you'll be very welcome.'

'No,' Jan said. 'I'm going back to the Cape. I'm not sure when. That depends on . . . someone else.'

'Yes, I see. Well, of course you'll need time to think about it all, but if you do decide to sell your share of the business, I'd be very willing to buy. We could get an independent valuation.'

He was still the same old Abram, Jan thought, despite the protestations of brotherly love. Then he had a memory of himself at Jimmy Koster's bedside, persuading the American to sell his claim. Perhaps he and Abram were not so very different after all. Nothing would make him sell his share in the family business, though he was perfectly willing to leave the running of it to Abram, but he would not give an answer yet, he decided. Let the bugger sweat a little. 'Yes. Thanks,' he said. 'I'll need to think it over. And now, if you'll excuse me, I think I'll go to bed. It's been quite a tiring day.'

★   ★   ★

In the morning after breakfast, Abram made it clear that, though he would normally be at the works by this time, he was at Jan's disposal if there was anything he wanted to do.

'Father's grave,' Jan said.

They walked to the cemetery, and Jan bought some flowers and laid them on the mound of earth that had still not settled back to flatness, and stood there for some minutes, asking his father's forgiveness for the last time. When he felt at peace, he suggested to Abram that they should go to the cutting and polishing works.

The new premises in Sarphatistraat, not far from what had been the outskirts of Amsterdam at the time that Jan had first left the city, were in total contrast to the old workshop. To Jan's eyes, the four-storeyed building looked quite imposing, despite its narrowness, but perhaps that was because it had been recently decorated and its smartness made it stand out from its neighbours. Over the door, large gilt letters announced, 'J. Shapiro'.

'When he wrote, Father said he was thinking of changing the firm's name.'

'Oh? What to?'

'J. Shapiro and Sons.'

'He didn't mention it to me,' Abram said. 'And he certainly didn't do anything about it before he died. I don't think we should alter it. Everyone knows it the way it is.'

They went first to the polishing room, where six men sat at the iron wheels which were kept spinning ceaselessly at a constant speed. They were driven by steam, conveyed in great pipes from the boiler to the central spindle from which driving bands descended to the axles of the wheels. This room was only a part of the new workshops. The firm had in recent years begun to set the gems they cut and polished, and there were benches where rings and necklaces and jewellery of every kind were fashioned. Abram explained how complex a business it was. Gold and silver for the settings had to be purchased, and every gram of it had to be accounted for, the gold dust being just as valuable as the diamond dust produced in the polishing process. And the fashioning of the jewellery was a slow and costly process for which only the finest craftsmen could be employed.

They went up to the third floor and the room which was Abram's office. It was dominated by a massive iron safe – 'We had a hell of a job getting it up here,' Abram said. 'And there was some doubt about whether the floor would take the weight, but it seems to be all right.' – but there were also two large and handsome desks. 'Father and I used to share this room,' Abram explained. He opened the safe and began taking out various ledgers and papers which he put on his desk, then turned back and opened an inner section of the safe from which he took a long envelope. 'Here. Father's Will.'

But Jan had caught sight of something else within the small compartment. 'Are those polished stones?'

'Yes.'

'Can I see?'

Jan took one of the containers over to the empty desk which had been his father's, and carefully tipped the gems on to its top. There were scores of them, mostly, he reckoned, a half or

270

three quarters of a carat. He had almost forgotten how beautiful the polished stones could be. He marvelled again at those who had first discovered that the rough diamonds, the hardest substance on earth, could be cut and shaped, and then facetted so that the light striking and passing through the stone would be reflected with the utmost brilliance, releasing the inner fires of the diamond, the flashes of every hue in the spectrum. In early days, the number of facets had been limited, and the shapes into which the diamonds were cut were comparatively simple. Eventually, however, men had learnt how to produce the brilliant cut, and the marquise and the pear and oval and heart and emerald cuts, and the number of facets had increased until they had found the optimum number – fifty-six of them all ground at a precise angle, twenty-four surrounding the central table, or flat surface of the gem, and thirty-two around the pavilion, or pointed base of the stone, plus the table itself and the culet, the tiny facet at the base of the pavilion. And all important in giving the diamond its brilliance were the proportions between the height of the crown from the central girdle to the table, and that from the girdle to the point of the pavilion.

He spent some time studying the diamonds, turning them over so that they flashed and sparkled, then replaced them in the box and returned it to Abram, who put it back in the safe. Jan then read his father's Will. When he had finished, he gave it back to Abram. 'It's all very clear, and you summarised it very well. As I said, I'll have to think about what I do.'

Abram nodded. 'Jan, I hope you don't mind my asking, but I can't help noticing that you keep putting your hand on your side. I saw you doing it last night, and you were doing it all the time you were reading the Will, as though you've got a pain there. I hope you're not feeling unwell.'

Jan laughed. 'Not a pain, Abram. A nervous habit of touching something which is rather precious to me. In fact, it's the first really large diamond I found, and, if you'll pardon the conceit, I'm in the habit of calling it the Shapiro Diamond.' He told Abram the story of the diamond, but did not explain its mystical significance to him. Then he passed across the little silver box.

Abram whistled. 'Do you mind if I take it out and look at it?' He found his loupe and examined the stone with the care of an expert. 'It is beautiful,' he said at last. 'Flawless, as far as I can see, and of very good colour. It must be – what? – forty-five carats, or thereabouts.'

'Forty-four point seven.'

'It will make the most beautiful gem.'

'No.'

'A pendant, I would think. Or we could make it the central item in a collar. It would be worth a fortune.'

'No, Abram, no.' He reached out insistently for the diamond and its box, and when they were safely in his pocket again, he said, 'I'm sorry. You'll think I'm very stupid. But I've made myself a sort of vow – a vow that I shall never cut this stone.' He was aware of Abram's curious look, but was unwilling to give any other explanation. 'About the business, and my part in it,' he said.

'Yes?' Abram's voice was eager.

'Before I make a decision, I'd like to see the accounts, and learn something about the way things are run.'

'Oh, yes. Yes, of course.'

*　　*　　*

Jan spent the rest of that day and the next morning in a meticulous study of the business. Abram watched him edgily, evidently expecting criticism, but Jan was able to reassure him with a constant stream of sincere congratulations on the efficiency with which it was run. At lunchtime on the second day he announced that he had various calls to make in the city, which would occupy him for the third day too. He went to some of their competitors, to importers of rough diamonds, to jewellers, to stockbrokers, to banks, paying for advice where necessary. The survey was hurried, but he felt he had most of the information he wanted.

At one point he came to the house on the Singel with the narrow black door. Ernie Blakestone and his gymnasium had gone. 'Nine, ten years ago,' the present occupant told him. 'The old man died, you know.' Jan was sorry. He would have liked to tell the old prizefighter how valuable his tuition had been.

That evening he told Abram that he would give him his answer about his position in the family concern the following day. 'I'm expecting a telegram,' he said then. 'In fact, it has been on my mind ever since I arrived, which may explain why I have sometimes appeared a little preoccupied. If the telegram contains the message I hope for, I wonder, Rebecca, whether I can prevail upon you to accept another guest. A young lady. I thought perhaps, if you are agreeable, she could have my room, and I could move up to the attic, where Abram and I used to sleep.'

They were full of questions, but he said simply that Miss Sarah Goldfarb was a friend he had met on the boat, and left it at that.

When he went to bed, he knelt down and prayed. It was a long, rambling prayer. He spoke of his father, and of Sam Rosenberg, of Abram and Rebecca and their children, of the Brands and of Joey. At the end he came to the most important part of all. 'Oh, Lord, make glad the heart of Thy servant. Let Sarah say yes. Let her come to Amsterdam.'

24

'Arriving Amsterdam railway depot 11.15 Friday morning. Love. Sarah.'

The others at the breakfast table could see from Jan's expression that it was good news. He told them he was going to get married, and they congratulated him and bombarded him with questions, and he answered happily until he felt that they knew almost as much about Sarah as he did.

'Sarah,' said Rebecca. 'It's a good Jewish name. It is the same in English as in Dutch?'

'Yes.'

'When will you be married?'

'That depends on Sarah. As soon as possible.'

'Here in Amsterdam? Oh, how exciting!'

Jan had a sudden thought. 'No, we can't. We're still in mourning.'

'Oh, Jan! Father wouldn't mind.'

'No, but I would. I suppose the best thing would be for us to go back to the Cape and get married there. Or we could wait here until we're out of mourning. I'll have to see what Sarah thinks.'

'You're definitely going back to South Africa, then?' Abram asked.

'Yes.'

'I see. And does your marriage affect your ideas about the business?'

'No. Patience, Abram, patience. I'll tell you this evening, I promise. It's too long to go into now, and Sarphatistraat is waiting for you. Why, the whole place will grind to a halt if you're not there.'

'He's teasing you,' Rebecca said, as Abram began to expostulate. 'He's happy, so everything is a joke.'

Jan went out shopping. He did not know what to buy for Sarah. A ring, a diamond ring, of course, but that would have to wait until she was with him to choose it. So would clothes. He walked for miles, peering into tiny shops, visiting large stores and asking advice of the sales staff. He thought of a gold locket to hold his picture, of a piece of old Delft ware – Americans always loved antiques – of chocolates – but he didn't even know if she liked them – of a hundred different gifts, but nothing seemed exactly right. And then at last he saw something in the jumbled window of a second-hand shop near the Waag. It was crudely painted, and at one side the cheap plaster was crumbling, but it was unmistakably a model of Table Mountain. An absurd present, but he felt sure that she would like it and see it, as he did, as a symbol of their future life together.

The proprietor of the shop was astonished by Jan's interest, trebled the price he had been going to ask – it still cost only a few cents – and wrapped it in a piece of old newspaper. Jan decided he would give it to Sarah just like that. When he came out of the shop he felt he wanted to share his happiness. Some ragged-clothed children were playing in the street. 'Here!' he called, and scattered all the coins in his pocket in their direction. They scrambled for them and then followed him all the way back to Onkelboerensteeg.

*   *   *

After dinner he and Abram retired to the drawing-room.

'Well, let's have it,' Abram said.

'Light your cigar first. Make yourself comfortable.'

With more haste than usual, Abram lit his cigar, and looked eagerly at Jan.

'The first thing I have to tell you,' Jan said, 'is that I do not intend to sell you my share in the business. It would seem utterly wrong to me to do so.' Noticing Abram's worried frown, he went on, 'Relax, Abram. I'm not going to sell it to anyone else either. I'm part of it, and it's part of me, and I can't just cut it away. I intend to play a part in the firm. I think I can improve its profitability. But please don't look so gloomy. I want you to know that I have no desire at all to interfere in the running of the organisation here in Amsterdam. I have every confidence in you.' He sipped his coffee. 'Now, the one thing

275

that bothers me is the amount of capital lying idle in our bank account.'

'If you're thinking of expanding Sarphatistraat,' Abram said quickly, 'I've been into all that. The workshop is exactly the right size to keep our overheads down and our profits up.'

'I agree. But I want you to consider the possibility of expansion abroad.'

'Abroad? Where?'

'Two places. First of all, London. The De Beers group have recently formed something called the Diamond Syndicate, a marketing organisation which will control the sale of all diamonds coming from South Africa. Their headquarters is going to be in London. It makes sense for us to be there.'

'Doing what? Running a diamond brokerage business? Buying rough diamonds two or three times a year from this syndicate and sending them back here?'

'No. If that were all, you'd be right to suggest it would be a waste of effort and capital investment. Listen. The trade in cut and polished gems, and in jewellery, is going to increase greatly throughout the world over the next twenty, thirty years. We shall be able to dispose of all that we produce in Sarphatistraat without touching the British market, and if we're in London for rough diamonds we can get a foothold in the British market, including their Empire, by doing some polishing and making jewellery and retailing and whole-saling it there in London – in fact, by duplicating our business here.'

'H'm. You said two places. Where's the other?'

'Antwerp.'

'Antwerp! But that's ridiculous. Father would turn in his grave at the very idea. He always hated Antwerp. They're our greatest competitors – I don't mean just ours, I mean the whole of the Amsterdam diamond trade. Those cut-throats in Belgium believe Antwerp will become the cutting and polishing capital of the world, and they'll do everything they can to kill us. The last thing I want is to help them.'

'But that's exactly why we should go there. Not immediately, but in some year's time. The trade is going to decline here in Amsterdam – there's no doubt about it. If Shapiro's finds itself in difficulties, money in the bank won't save us. Even a branch in London wouldn't save us. But if we had a branch in Antwerp we should have as much insurance as we could possibly get.'

Abram puffed at his cigar. 'I must say that all these ideas of yours need a great deal of thought. I can see some sort of argument for setting up in London, but Antwerp . . .'

'They're not just *my* ideas. I've talked to dozens of people. Maybe you should do the same.'

'I was going to take you up on that point, Jan. You had no right to go discussing our affairs all over the city without even a word to me.'

Jan said nothing for a moment. Then he looked straight into Abram's angry eyes. 'I haven't been discussing our affairs. I've been talking about the diamond trade as a whole, and in the most general terms.'

'But the people you spoke to knew who you were. They'll put two and two together. Before we know where we are, there'll be rumours going round that Shapiro's is in trouble, that we're closing down. It could be very bad for business.'

'Abram, doesn't it excite you at all to think of Shapiro's established in three great centres of the diamond trade?'

Abram considered. 'Well, yes, I suppose it does. But it's not really practical, Jan. It's going to take an enormous amount of capital. We haven't got that much lying idle, as you put it.'

'No. You're right. But I have a fairly considerable fortune of my own – far more than I shall need to live on even when Sarah and I are married. I am proposing to invest a sum in the firm equal to the present unused capital that we have, in order that we can set up branches abroad. It will not affect the ownership of the business. You will still be the majority shareholder, and I shall not require an increase in my holding, nor shall I expect interest on the capital I put in – just my third share of the profits.'

Abram stared at him disbelievingly. 'That's no sort of business deal,' he said. 'You're mad.'

Jan laughed. 'No doubt. Well, what do you say?'

'I thought you were going back to South Africa.'

'I am.'

'You're coming back, then?'

'What are you talking about, Abram?'

'Well, I don't see how you can run these branches from Cape Town.'

Jan laughed again. 'Oh, that's what's been worrying you. No, Abram, I'm not going to run them. You are. At least, you'll have to hire managers for them, but the control will be in your hands. I'd hope that you'd keep me informed of what happens, but I've no wish to interfere with your management of the firm.'

'But you gave me the impression . . . Oh, I see.' For the first time he smiled. 'Oh, well, that's different. Yes, it's a pretty startling proposition, but if you really mean it, an interesting one. It's taken me by surprise of course, and I shall have to think about it. But in principle, it sounds very attractive. Let's go over it again.'

As Jan repeated his arguments, Abram began to discuss the ideas with increasing enthusiasm, and eventually promised that he would begin investigations of his own as soon as possible. 'But there's one thing I still don't understand, Jan. If you're going back to South Africa, and you're not going to be active in the firm, why are you putting all that money in? I mean, it doesn't make any business sense at all from your point of view.'

'I think,' said Jan slowly, 'I think I owe it to Father.'

* * *

Jan was waiting at the station the next morning when Sarah's train pulled in. He was clutching a bunch of hothouse roses and his newspaper parcel. He saw her as soon as she alighted, and ran towards her, enfolding her in his arms.

Eventually she broke from his kiss. 'Jan, everyone's looking.'

'I don't care.'

'Neither do I, but we can't stay here all day.'

'My darling, my darling Sarah, you've made me so happy. You do mean you'll marry me?'

'Yes, Jan, but – but there's one condition.'

'Anything.' He waited for her to speak, but she said nothing. 'What condition?'

'Wait, wait, wait, wait! Patience is a virtue, as Momma always said.'

He laughed. 'That's just about what I told Abram. Oh, I've so much to tell you.'

'Yes, and I'm longing to meet your folks. How is your father?'

'He's dead. He died before I got here.'

'Oh, my dear, I'm so sorry. Oh, Jan, how terrible for you.'

'Yes, it was a shock. I can still hardly believe it. But you'll meet the others. Rebecca and Aunt Suzanna are waiting at home to greet you, and Abram and the children will be there at lunch-time. Oh, here – I haven't even given you your flowers yet.'

'They're beautiful. Thank you. Jan, before we go to your brother's home, could we have a cup of coffee or something? Then you can tell me about your father, and I can tell you what my condition for marrying you is.'

'We'll get a cab to Onkelboerensteeg. You can tell me on the way.'

'No, Jan. You may not accept it, and then – well, I guess it would all be off. And in that case the best thing would be for me to get back on that train – it would save everybody from embarrassment.'

'It all sounds very serious.'

'It is. I know it's going to upset you. Please, Jan, some coffee, and let's be happy for a few more minutes.'

'All right. And you can open this.' He showed her the newspaper parcel.

'Another present? You're spoiling me.'

They left her luggage at the station, and found a cafe. When they were seated, Jan said, 'Now tell me what this mysterious and terrible condition is.'

'No,' said Sarah. 'First I want my present.' She unwrapped the model of Table Mountain. 'Oh, Jan! It's just darling. It's terrible, but I love it. And I know why you chose it for me. I shall keep it always. Oh, what a sentimental fool you'll think me – it's making me cry.' She brushed away the tears and leaned across the table to take his hand. 'Now tell me about your father.'

She listened with eyes full of sympathy. When he had finished, he said, 'Now, please, Sarah, tell me what this dreadful condition is.'

'I –' She took a deep breath, and he could tell that she was summoning up all her courage before she said quickly, 'I want the Shapiro Diamond, cut and polished, as a wedding gift.'

He went cold. 'You're joking.'

'No.'

'But how can you ask that? You know how much it means to me.'

'You wouldn't lose it. You'd just release all the hidden beauty inside it.'

'You know it's more than that.'

'Yes, Jan, I do. And you said yourself that you recognise your fears about the diamond shattering are no more than superstition. In any case, why should it shatter? How many diamonds has your brother cut without spoiling them?'

'But why do you want the Shapiro Diamond? Because it's so valuable? If that's what you're after, I'll buy you the largest diamond in Amsterdam.'

'That's not what I want, Jan, and I'm sure you know it. No, it's a sort of test, I guess – a test of whether your diamond is more important to you than I am.'

'Of course it isn't. You're far more important to me. Have it as it is. Here, take it now.' He took the silver box from his pocket.

'No, Jan. I'll only take it when it's cut and polished, and only then will I agree to marry you.'

He gazed unseeing out of the cafe window. The Shapiro Diamond had been with him, his talisman, for nearly half his life. It would be like cutting off a part of himself to give it up. But how could he live without Sarah? The thoughts criss-crossed his mind, until he felt like a swimmer sucked into a vicious, relentless whirlpool. He took the Shapiro Diamond out of its box once again and stared at it. He knew every plane of it, every tiny mark.

He closed his eyes. At first he didn't hear it. But then the voice inside his mind, the soundless voice that came from nowhere, grew. 'Sarah,' it said. 'Sarah. Sarah.'

It was the final decision, and it had been taken for him. He opened his eyes. Sarah was gazing at him. He looked into her eyes and saw the love in them and the understanding for his agony of spirit. He nodded, and whispered, 'All right.'

'Are you sure?' she asked.

'Yes.'

'I'm very, very happy.' Quickly, before he could change his

mind or begin to think about the diamond again, she stood up. 'Let's go meet my sister-in-law-to-be.'

★　★　★

Rebecca and Aunt Suzanna were enchanted by Sarah, who somehow managed to restrain herself from chattering too much in front of these strangers, and when Abram and the children came home for their midday meal they too took to her at once.

'When's the wedding to be then?' Abram asked.

'We haven't fixed a date yet,' Sarah replied. 'We're not going to until you've cut and polished Jan's diamond.'

A sudden silence descended, as the significance of what she had said sank in. They all knew Jan's feelings about the stone – how had this young girl persuaded, or forced, him to agree?

'You mean the one he calls the Shapiro Diamond?' Abram asked.

'Yes. He's promised to give it to me as a wedding gift – or perhaps an engagement gift would be nearer the mark.' She sensed their sudden hostility. 'I know what it sounds like. It makes me seem very mercenary, doesn't it? As though I'm only willing to marry him when he's bought me with his diamond. It's not like that at all, is it, Jan?'

'No.'

'It's just something, well . . . something private between us, that's all.' She turned to Abram. 'You'll do it, won't you?'

'If Jan really wants me to. Do you, Jan?'

Jan nodded.

'When?' Sarah asked.

'I don't know. I have to study the stone first.'

'Can we come and watch when you cleave it?'

'Watch? Yes, if you want to.'

'It won't put you off?'

'I'm like my father, Sarah. When he was cleaving a diamond you could – well, you could have let off a firework behind his back and he wouldn't have noticed, he wouldn't even have heard it. It's a gift, to be able to concentrate like that. I inherited it from him. No, you can come and watch. But I don't know when it'll be, and I won't do it a moment before I'm ready.'

He studied the diamond for five days, while Jan and Sarah explored Amsterdam. Although the cleaving of the stone was never out of Jan's mind, he was happy in Sarah's company. She teased him, comparing Amsterdam unfavourably with other places she had seen, but finally admitted that it was indeed the most beautiful city in the world.

Abram could see the grain in the Shapiro Diamond clearly, and there were no imperfections to worry about. It was a simple job, and if it had been any other stone he would have spent much less time on it.

The four of them – Jan and Sarah, Rebecca and Abram – gathered in the workshop. It was a raw winter's day, but a fire was burning in the grate. Abram warmed his hands thoroughly. Then he fixed the diamond in place. On one plane was the thin groove he had cut. He placed the cleaver precisely along the line, raised the little mallet, and gave a sharp tap.

Sarah and Rebecca turned to each other, and Abram stood transfixed, gazing in horror at the shattered stone. Jan fell senseless to the floor.

For a moment it seemed as though they were frozen, unmoving. Then Sarah ran to where Jan lay, desperately afraid. Surely there could not have been any truth in his idea – or was it that he had so persuaded himself of the superstition that it had become fact?

He was still breathing. 'Brandy! Quick!' Rebecca ran to fetch the spirits. They forced a little between Jan's lips, and he coughed and slowly the colour began to come back into his cheeks, and after a while they helped him up and took him to a chair where he could sit.

'I didn't dream it, did I?' he asked.

Abram shook his head. 'I'm sorry, Jan. I'm sure I cleaved it in the right place. There must have been some flaw inside – something I couldn't see.'

'Yes.' It was hard, very hard, to believe that the diamond had gone. It was harder still to realise that he was still alive, and in a strange way he was almost reluctant to accept that fact. He looked at the others standing round him, their eyes anxious. He stretched out his hand towards Sarah. She held it in hers, the soft, warm pressure of her fingers comforting. He felt very tired, and closed his eyes.

'It's the shock,' Rebecca said. 'It will do him good to sleep.'

When Jan opened his eyes again, the first thing that he saw was Sarah smiling at him. 'How are you?' she asked.

'All right.'

'You remember what happened?'

'The diamond? Yes.'

'But you're still alive.'

'Yes, I'm still alive.' He nodded almost ruefully. 'You were right. It was all ridiculous, that superstition of mine. But I shall miss the diamond. And I shan't be able to give it to you as an engagement gift.'

'Never mind. You're alive, Jan. Mazel-tov for that.'

'It doesn't make any difference to us, does it. I mean, you'll still marry me.'

'Yes, Jan. At least, I think so. But not yet.'

She thought for a moment that he was going to faint again, because the blood drained from his face. 'But why?' he asked, his voice a whisper. 'Why, Sarah? You promised. It isn't just because the diamond's gone?'

'Of course not.'

'Then why?' He paused, and then said softly, 'You've cheated.'

'Yes, perhaps I have. I had to cheat to get that obsession out of your mind. I had to cheat to prove to you that life isn't controlled or even influenced by some talisman. I guess I wanted to show you that you can live your life with nothing to hold you back, nothing to dangle some kind of curse over your head.'

'But that doesn't explain why you won't marry me now. I don't want to live my life without you. I love you.'

'I wish I could be sure of that.'

'What do you mean? I love you, I want to marry you – what more do you want? I was willing to have my diamond cut for you.'

'I know, and I know how much that meant, but you see, my dear, I think you're very subject to enchantment. That diamond had you in its spell, and perhaps I've bewitched you in just the same way.'

'Oh, Sarah, this is absurd – as absurd as anything I ever felt about the diamond. Are you trying to tell me that you don't really love me?'

'I love you very much.'

Jan shook his head in frustration. 'Then why won't you marry me?'

'I haven't said I won't. I only said I wouldn't marry you *yet*. I'm going back to New York, and you'll go back to the Cape. I want us to be apart for a year. If you still want me to marry you then, I'll come to South Africa on the first boat. And I promise you I'll be a good wife. If you want to go into politics I'll do everything to support you. We can build a future together, Jan. And perhaps there'll be children.'

'All that can take care of itself,' he said impatiently. 'What I don't understand is why we have to wait.'

'I want you to be sure, Jan, real sure. I want you to be sure when thousands of miles separate us. I want you to be sure when you've had time to think.'

'I'm sure now.'

It was so difficult, Sarah thought. She could not tell him that she hoped this break would give time for his obsession with the Shapiro Diamond to fade, for him to return to normality. If, when they met again, she found that he was no longer in thrall in any way to that wretched stone, she would feel that there was hope for the success of their union. But if he still thought of the diamond, wondering how, if it had not been shattered, it would have directed his life, or even if he still had that habit of tapping his waistcoat pocket, she would have to think again.

When she said nothing, Jan went on, 'If at the end of this year you say you'll marry me, what conditions will you impose then? What shall I have to do to seal the bargain? How can I be sure that you won't break your promise again? What was it your Momma said?'

'I deserve that, I guess,' she said quietly. 'You're right to be bitter. But there won't be any conditions attached next time. Just both of us feeling that we are doing the right thing.'

'Why have you got to wait a year? Why not six months?'

She considered briefly. 'All right. Six months.'

'Three months. Or just until we're out of mourning. Not even that long. Abram's right – Father wouldn't mind. A week. Tomorrow. Today.'

She laughed. 'No, Jan. Six months.'

He knew suddenly that he could trust her, that this time there would be no cheating. 'All right.' His face had been solemn, but now a hint of a smile curved his lips. 'You're the craziest girl in the world, Sarah Goldfarb, and I love you very much.'

She looked into his eyes, searching for some sign that everything would be all right, but all she could see was his adoration. Perhaps that was enough. 'I love you too,' she told him.

'And during this time, are we engaged? Or . . . just nothing.'

She gave a helpless, uncertain little laugh. 'Oh, we're something all right. I guess we're engaged.'

'Then you'll have to have a ring. What sort of stone do you want?'

She laughed properly then. 'Do I have any choice?'

HEYWOOD BOOKS

TODAY'S PAPERBACKS
– AT YESTERDAY'S PRICES!

Heywood Books is a new list of paperback books which will be published every month at remarkably low prices. It will range from glitzy, up-to-the-minute women's novels to compelling romantic thrillers and absorbing historical romance, from classic crime to nerve-chilling horror and big adventure thrillers, presenting an outstanding list of highly readable and top value popular fiction.

Look for this month's new titles:

THE BIG X	*Hank Searls*	£1.50
THE SUMMER DAY IS DONE	*Robert Tyler Stevens*	£1.75
TWIN CONNECTIONS	*Justine Valenti*	£1.75
THE SHAPIRO DIAMOND	*Michael Legat*	£1.75
A RATTLING OF OLD BONES	*Jonathan Ross*	£1.50
MIRROR IMAGE	*Lucille Fletcher*	£1.50

HEYWOOD BOOKS

FICTION

One Little Room	*Jan Webster*	£1.50
The Winnowing Winds	*Ann Marlowe*	£1.50
The Root of His Evil	*James M Cain*	£1.50
Criss-Cross	*Alan Scholefield*	£1.50
Lovenotes	*Justine Valenti*	£1.75
Perahera	*Julia Leslie*	£1.50
Alone Together	*Sherrye Henry*	£1.75
The Summer Day is Done	*Robert Tyler Stevens*	£1.75
Twin Connections	*Justine Valenti*	£1.75
Mirror Image	*Lucille Fletcher*	£1.50

SAGA

Daneclere	*Pamela Hill*	£1.75
Making Friends	*Cornelia Hale*	£1.75
Muckle Annie	*Jan Webster*	£1.75
The Windmill Years	*Vicky Martin*	£1.75
Seeds of the Sun	*Vicky Martin*	£1.75
The Shapiro Diamond	*Michael Legat*	£1.75

HISTORICAL ROMANCE

The Caretaker Wife	*Barbara Whitehead*	£1.50
Quicksilver Lady	*Barbara Whitehead*	£1.50
Ramillies	*Barbara Whitehead*	£1.50
Lady in Waiting	*Rosemary Sutcliff*	£1.75

THRILLER

KG 200	*J. D. Gilman & John Clive*	£1.75
Hammerstrike	*Walter Winward*	£1.75
The Canaris Fragments	*Walter Winward*	£1.75
Down to a Sunless Sea	*David Graham*	£1.75
The Big X	*Hank Searls*	£1.50

HORROR

The Unholy	*Michael Falconer Anderson*	£1.50
God of a Thousand Faces	*Michael Falconer Anderson*	£1.50
The Woodsmen	*Michael Falconer Anderson*	£1.50

CRIME

Here Lies Nancy Frail	*Jonathan Ross*	£1.50
A Rattling of Old Bones	*Jonathan Ross*	£1.50

NAME ....

ADDRESS ....

....

Write to Heywood Books Cash Sales, PO Box 11, Falmouth, Cornwall TR10 9EN. Please indicate order and enclose remittance to the value of the cover price plus: UK: Please allow 60p for the first book, 25p for the second book and 15p for each additional book ordered, to a maximum charge of £1.90.

B.F.P.O. & EIRE: Please allow 60p for the first book, 25p for the second book, 15p per copy for the next 7 books and thereafter 9p per book.

OVERSEAS: Please allow £1.25 for the first book, 75p for the second book and 28p per copy for each additional book.

Whilst every effort is made to keep prices low it is sometimes necessary to increase cover prices and also postage and packing rates at short notice. Heywood Books reserve the right to show new retail prices on covers which may differ from those previously advertised in the text or elsewhere.